# STALKED

"Cort!"

He jerked his head up at the tension in her voice. "Kaylie!" He grabbed the rifle and charged across the cabin, his senses on hyperalert. He sprinted into Sara's room with the rifle up, skidded to a halt just inside the door, and scanned the room.

No bad guys.

Just Kaylie kneeling on the floor in the corner, looking at something.

*She's okay*. Cort's body shuddered as a tremor of relief went through him. "Anyone else in here?"

"No. Look."

It took him almost a full minute to peel his finger off the trigger and lower the rifle. "You find something?"

She looked up at him, her eyes wide and scared, her face pale.

He swore under his breath, his fingers tightening on the gun as he strode across the room toward her. "What's wrong?"

"This." She gestured at the mess of mutilated photos on the floor in front of her. "He's hunting me."

# ICE

# STEPHANIE ROWE

LOVE SPELL  NEW YORK CITY

*For my mom, who is my best friend, my greatest support
and my anchor. Thank you for everything you have
done for me, and continue to do every day.
I love you!*

LOVE SPELL®

July 2009

Published by

Dorchester Publishing Co., Inc.
200 Madison Avenue
New York, NY 10016

Copyright © 2009 by Stephanie Rowe

ISBN 10: 0-505-52775-8
ISBN 13: 978-0-505-52775-2
E-ISBN: 978-1-4285-0701-2

The name "Love Spell" and its logo are trademarks of Dorchester
Publishing Co., Inc.

Printed in the United States of America.

10 9 8 7 6 5 4 3 2 1

Visit us on the web at www.dorchesterpub.com.

# ACKNOWLEDGMENTS

Thank you to my wonderful and brilliant editor, Leah Hultenschmidt, for believing in this book and going above and beyond in support of it. And a huge thank-you also to all the folks at Dorchester for all their hard work and their support: Tracy Heydweiller, Renee Yewdaev, Cindy Johnson, Alissa Davis, Tim DeYoung, Brooke Borneman, Tanya Reynolds, Erin Galloway, Alicia Condon, and John Prebich. I am also supremely appreciative of Lisa Jackson, JoAnn Ross, and Cheyenne McCray for taking the time out of their busy schedules to read this book and to graciously offer their words to support this book. I owe special thanks to former Alaskan bush pilot Mort B. Mason, the incredibly talented author of *The Alaska Bush Pilot Chronicles*, who patiently answered countless questions on Alaska and flying, while still maintaining his sense of humor. Thank you also to the City of Newton police department, especially Bob Hill and Ed Boudrot, for teaching me about guns and police work, and for not carting me off to jail the first time I walked up to them in the parking lot and said, "I need to know the best gun to use if I wanted to shoot someone and cause really severe injury, but not actually kill him." All the mistakes in this book are mine, and mine alone. And finally, I owe my heart to my family and friends, whom I treasure so dearly, without whose support I never would have made it through the toughest period of my life. Ariana, Vern, Mom, Bill, Ben, Sarah, Judi, Kara, Guinevere, Pete…I love you all! My future and life shine so brightly because you are a part of it.

# ICE

# CHAPTER ONE

The minute the airplane wheels bumped down, Kaylie Fletcher took one look out the airplane window at the snowy Alaskan mountains, and her stomach roiled. She couldn't see the beauty, the majestic dominance of the scenic peaks, millions of acres to be treasured and discovered....

All she saw was death.

Kaylie could still smell the tangy scent of blood. The cold thickness of a human body as the flesh turned to ice beneath her hands. The pressure of the harness tight around her shoulders as she hauled the body down the slope. Tears freezing on her cracked cheeks. Her heart numb with disbelief. Her mind reeling with anger and fury and pain. Stumbling with her broken ankle and frozen feet, alone except for a corpse...

Kaylie cringed as the anguished cry blistered through her memory, a noise so horrific, so torturous, it could be nothing but the sound of a human screaming for his life in the shadow of death's brutality—

*Stop it! Just stop it!*

Kaylie yanked her gaze off the mountains and forced herself to stare at the vanilla-colored plastic tray in the seat back in front of her. She willed herself to concentrate on the scratches on the corner. To study the faded plaid of the seat cover.

Slowly the memories faded, and the freshness of the horror receded back to where she'd kept it for so long. Kaylie groaned softly and pressed her palms to her eyes. Her hands were clammy and trembling.

She should have realized the memories might resurface. She should have been prepared.

A hand rested on her shoulder and squeezed gently. "Are you all right?"

"Fine." Kaylie managed a tight smile at the older woman sitting next to her. Her seatmate was a weathered gal with silver hair, sun-beaten skin, and callused hands. The wrinkles around the woman's eyes made it look as if she were always about to laugh. Within minutes of takeoff, she had started chatting and hadn't let up for the entire plane ride. Normally one for taking naps on planes, Kaylie had been grateful for the distraction this time.

She'd barely slept in days. Left alone, the plane ride would have been three hours of self-torture like the flashback she'd just had. She would be forever thankful that her seatmate had thirteen grandchildren she liked talking about.

"You're fine?" The woman gave a decidedly unladylike snort. "You don't look fine. You look like you just stepped in a bear trap."

Kaylie almost smiled at the analogy. Almost. "No bear traps. Just motion sickness." She wiped her damp hands on the freshly ironed slacks she'd worn in an attempt to lie to herself about where she was going. Sweat trickled down between her breasts.

"Hah." The feisty grandma picked up the faded nylon backpack she'd been using for her carry-on. "Motion sickness, my ass."

Kaylie laughed, desperate to latch onto anything that might distract her from her thoughts. "Just memories. Nothing to worry about."

Silver brows were raised at Kaylie. "Memories, eh? I've a fair share of memories myself, and none of them ever made me look the way you just did. You want to talk about it?"

Kaylie managed a smile. "Thanks, but I'm sure I'll be fine."

And she would be…as soon as she was on a plane returning to Seattle.

The woman gave Kaylie a skeptical look as the lone flight attendant hopped up and jimmied open the door, letting the glaring Alaskan sunshine into the plane. Kaylie instinctively dug her sunglasses out of her purse and slapped them on her face.

"You take care, then, hon." The woman stood and strode out of the plane without giving Kaylie a backward look, no doubt already getting excited about seeing her family.

The thought of family made Kaylie's throat tighten, and the departure of her affable flying companion was like being stripped of her last vestiges of protection. She felt raw and exposed to the hell that awaited outside the plane. "Oh, God." Kaylie dropped her head to her palms. "You can handle this," she whispered to herself. "No one else is going to die here."

*No one else is going to die here.*

Repeating the mantra in her head, Kaylie balled her hands and gazed defiantly out the door at the blue sky. She inhaled the untainted air, letting its cold purity burn her lungs—untouched nature that one could find only in remote places like northern Alaska.

Kaylie much preferred civilization. Give her the hum of cars whizzing by in the morning commute, the dry heat rising off a hot pavement in the summer, or the soft drizzle of a Seattle spring. She liked the freedom afforded by civilization: taxicabs, cell-phone reception, and a warm bedroom to snuggle in at a night. She loved stretching out on her beautiful suede sofa with a glass of wine and a soft throw blanket, basking in the nighttime view of the sparkling lights of the city, a delicious vista that was a perk of her luxurious high-rise apartment building. Not this…this…frigid expanse of openness. The alluring temptation was only a beautiful facade for the darkness that lay deep in the shadows of this territory.

Kaylie grabbed her dove gray suede handbag. The choice of purse had been a refusal to acknowledge her destination this morning. So were her turquoise pumps with the jeweled toes. The expensive silk heels couldn't be worn in rain or slush or cold weather. They were designed for indoor wear in a life of leisure. It was the type of shoe Kaylie had started wearing twenty-three days after her sixteenth birthday.

Having stalled as long as she could, Kaylie draped her pocketbook over her shoulder and made her way to the door of the plane. There was no Jetway. Just a set of steps nudged up against the door.

More of a ladder, really.

Kaylie caught the railing, pressing her lips together as she surveyed the small airport. A tiny Cessna 180 was idling nearby, its red paint mostly scraped off. She shuddered and wrenched her eyes away, searching for Sara. Somehow, her deep friendship with Sara Jenks had survived that hellacious sixteenth year. Their bond had even endured Sara's move to Alaska six years ago, a land they both knew Kaylie would never set foot in again.

Until now.

Two weeks ago, Kaylie's parents and brother had perished in a climbing accident on Mount McKinley. The entire climbing party had fallen three hundred feet into a crevasse, and the bodies had not been recovered. It had taken ten days for the news to reach Kaylie, as no one had known to notify her.

Kaylie had raged, cried, grieved, and fought to keep herself from sliding over that cliff to such a dark place she'd never get out.

Then Kaylie had received the phone call at three o'clock yesterday morning. One sentence was all the caller had spoken. One sentence that had haunted Kaylie until she and Sara had decided she had no choice but to find out the truth.

*Your mother is still alive.*

With no bodies found, it was possible her mother had survived the fall. And what about Kaylie's dad and brother, who had also been on the climb? Kaylie owed it to her family and herself to pursue the cryptic message. If she didn't see it through, that phone call would haunt her forever.

So Kaylie had made her plane reservation and headed to the land she'd tried so hard to forget.

Sara had promised to meet Kaylie and help her through it.

But as Kaylie scanned the airport again, Sara was nowhere to be seen.

No one was, really. It was late afternoon, the sun was setting, and everyone had better things to do.

Kaylie clenched the delicate strap of her bag as she began to descend the stairs, using her free hand to fish her mobile phone out of her backpack. She was two-thirds of the way down the steps and had just hit the power button on her phone when a man ducked under the nose of the Cessna. His faded jeans hugged his narrow hips. The denim encased long, muscular legs, all the way down to a pair of insulated work boots. His wide shoulders were accentuated by the thick black flight jacket that would be a lifesaver if he went down in cold weather. His collar was up, dark glasses covered his face, and his light brown hair was blowing in the flirty wind. He focused on Kaylie and his jaw hardened ever so slightly.

And Kaylie knew in that instant, with absolute certainty, that if she were going to die in Alaska, that man would be the cause.

# Chapter Two

Cort McClaine knew the minute he saw her that she was the one, despite what he'd been prepped for.

He'd been told to expect a woman in her midtwenties, with dark hair, brown eyes, and a lean build. A woman who would be ready for a trip to the backwoods of Alaska.

This woman…Yeah, her hair might pass as dark to the uninitiated, but it reminded him of the soft underbelly of a black-bear cub, catching the rays of light from the first spring sunshine.

Her eyes were hidden behind her fancy sunglasses, but she was clearly looking at Cort. Her body language was all about disapproval and resistance. Of course it was. With her wrinkle-free slacks and those delicate shoes that made her feet look…

Cort studied her feet as she resumed her exit from the plane. He hadn't seen feet like hers in a long time. They were…dainty. Nah, not dainty. Sexy. Yeah, that was it. The way he could see the curve of the top of her foot where the hem of her pants brushed over her skin…Ankles that looked too damn delicate to survive a walk across the tarmac, let alone a summer in the backwoods.

It was no surprise she was looking at him as if he were her worst nightmare.

She was his, too. A client who was in no way prepared for what he was about to deal her.

Cort dragged his gaze off her feet, scowling. For eight years, he'd stayed far away from women from the Lower 48, but damn if he couldn't keep his lower body from reacting to the sight of this female. Her pale blue sweater dipped between her breasts. Breasts he could see quite clearly, since she wasn't wearing a thick jacket and a few layers of long underwear. And her throat…Sexy, like her feet. Long, elegant…Yeah, *elegant* would apply to her neck.

He sensed her tension heighten, and he returned his attention to her face, confident she had no idea where he was looking with his dark glasses on. The tendons in her neck were taut. Her full lips were pressed in a tight line, and her left hand was clenched in a small fist around the strap of her ridiculously fancy purse.

Cort grimaced. It would be a long flight if she kept up with the attitude. But she was his job, and he'd bring her down safely, if not happy.

She turned her head away, dismissing him. The too-familiar reaction rankled him. On second thought, Cort didn't give a damn if she landed happy. He knew what she was about. His ex-wife had looked at him in exactly the same way, and he wasn't going down that road again.

If Sara hadn't begged him for this favor and if she hadn't been married to Cort's best friend, Jackson, Cort would haul ass right out of there without ever speaking a word to a woman like Kaylie Fletcher.

But Cort liked Sara, despite the fact she was from the Lower 48, and he'd never turn down a favor for Jackson. Besides, Sara had adapted just fine to Alaska and was as loyal as hell to Jackson, so Cort had to think that Sara's best friend wasn't all righteous attitude, pale blue cotton, and impracticality. He slapped on his best "client" smile and stepped forward. "Kaylie Fletcher? I'm your pilot. Cort McClaine. Welcome to Alaska."

Cort McClaine's grin was charming. Engaging. Disarming.

Kaylie knew the minute he flashed it at her that he was very, very good at his job, at least from the perspective of keeping his clients happy when the turbulence was terrifying and the ground was far closer than it should be. His smile plowed right past her defenses, reached down inside her, and made her want to smile back. Her instinct to fear him was overruled by the unexpected chills that shivered down her spine. She knew his smile wasn't personal, but it had been *so* long since anything had made her feel so warm and tingly. Kaylie had a sudden urge to snuggle against Cort and beg him to chase away that aching loneliness stalking her at every turn, because she knew he could do it....

"Ma'am?" Cort pulled his glasses down to look at her, and her breath caught at the intensity of his eyes. Sandy brown, like his wind-blown hair, they were brimming with the energy and fire of someone who craved adventure and risk.

His eyes brought back memories.

His eyes brought back nightmares.

They made her yearn to lose herself in the passion burning so brightly in their depths.

Cort's eyes terrified her.

Kaylie took a step back and folded her arms over her chest. "I thought I was meeting Sara. Or Dusty Baker. She was going to hire him to be our guide. Do you work with him?"

His smile didn't even falter as he slid his sunglasses back on, granting her a reprieve. "Sorry, ma'am, but Sara was unable to make it, and I don't know anything about Dusty being here. She arranged for me to meet you and take you out to her cabin."

Kaylie glanced at the Cessna. "In that?"

His smile hardened ever so slightly. "Safest plane around, I assure you. Do you have bags? I don't like the way the weather's shifting, and we need to move out now."

Kaylie stared at the small plane and then at the darkening sky. The sky looked dangerous, yet Cort was willing to take off in it.…A sense of foreboding took root inside Kaylie as she became aware of his casual pose, the utter confidence in his voice, and the heated masculinity emanating from him.

He was a daredevil, an arrogant male who thrived on a lifestyle that teased death as often as possible, always supremely confident that he'd come out the victor. He was handsome and compelling.…Oh, God.

She was attracted to him.

And he was just like her family—who were all dead.

He cocked his head. "You all right, ma'am?"

Kaylie clenched the strap of her handbag tighter. She had to leave. Get away. Couldn't handle it. "I—"

"Got any bags?" He was already in motion when he asked the question.

Kaylie's protest died as Cort jogged across the tarmac to the plane she'd arrived in, where a man in a navy jacket was off-loading luggage into a truck. Cort swung up onto the vehicle with the agile grace of a true athlete. He did a quick scan of the bags already unloaded, exchanged a brief word with the handler, then disappeared into the belly of the plane.

Kaylie shoved her hands into her pockets, her skin hot and tingly. She was on the edge of panic, but there was also a sense of anticipation vibrating deep inside her. Kaylie had dated plenty and had been almost engaged twice, but never had she felt such an instantaneous and compelling attraction. She wanted to feel Cort's hands on her hips, his tongue gliding along her ribs.…

Kaylie cleared her throat and wiped her hand over her brow.

There was no way she was going down that road. *No way*.

Her phone beeped as it finally caught service, indicating that she had a message. Kaylie ignored it, not wanting to deal with any work calls right now. Instead she dialed Sara, and the phone went directly into voice mail. "It's Kaylie. I'm here. Cort found me, so we'll be on our way. I wish—" Her voice broke, and she had to take a second to steel herself. "I wish you'd been able to meet me." She shut her phone resolutely, the nerves easing now that she'd heard Sara's voice, even though it was only on the recording.

All Kaylie had to do was deal with Cort long enough to get to Sara's cabin. Then she could fall apart in her friend's arms, if she needed to. Sara would understand.

Kaylie was back in control by the time Cort popped out of the plane a few minutes later. He'd found all three of her bags: two were slung over his shoulder, and he gripped the handles of the smaller one in his hand. His callused fingers looked so incongruous against the gray suede and the leather handles. He raised the satchel. "This everything?"

She nodded as he vaulted down, noticing he wasn't slowed by the weight he was carrying. Kaylie had been charged extra for overweight bags when she'd left Seattle, but apparently they weren't heavy for Cort.

He strode across the tarmac, his body lithe and lean, like a wild animal gliding through his territory. The storm clouds were getting darker and thicker in the sky behind him. The wind had picked up, and the air was heavy with the scent of moisture and ice. The weather felt ominous, like a predator lurking in the shadows.

"Let's go." Cort reached Kaylie and began to stride past her.

"Wait." She grabbed his arm, and she could feel the hard curve of his biceps even beneath his heavy jacket. Awareness jolted through her, and she jerked her hand back at his sharp look. "Maybe we should wait out the storm?"

He stopped in place and gave her a long look. Considering.

"I'll pay you for your time, though. For the waiting." Someone in his line of business no doubt scraped the bottom for cash every month. It was the nature of his work, but a man like him wouldn't care about being strapped financially. Laughing in the face of death was all the compensation he needed.

Unlike Kaylie. She'd found that a high-paying job as a senior accountant and a deluxe apartment with double-paned windows went a long way toward giving her the security she needed so badly. No, her life wasn't that exciting, and her work was hardly inspiring, but it was safe and predictable. It was the lifestyle she'd been planning since she was sixteen, and she'd achieved exactly what she wanted. Maybe her heart didn't sing for joy every morning when she woke up, but that was a fair trade-off for the fact she didn't have to worry about death every minute of her life. It was a good deal, and she was happy enough in her world—a protected, predictable existence that a man like Cort would probably say went against the laws of nature.

And he would be wrong.

Kaylie set her hands on her hips as Cort eyed her silently. Her body sizzled under his intense scrutiny, even though she couldn't see where he was looking. She *felt* his gaze on her, her skin burning from the heat of his stare.

Then he turned away, opened the door of the Cessna, and tossed her bags inside.

"Wait—"

He turned back to her and set his hands on her shoulders, tightening his grip when she tried to pull back. His touch was unyielding, but the subtle caress of his thumbs was meant to reassure. She felt herself yield to the contact.

He nodded slightly at her response. "I assure you, you'll be safe with me. I've got over ten thousand hours, and I've never lost a passenger." He rubbed her shoulders, his thumb drifting over her collarbone in a soothing gesture that eased some of her tension. "Just relax and leave it to me. You'll be with

Sara before you know it, and you'll catch some great scenery on the way. Might even see a few grizzlies."

His voice was a deep rumble of quiet confidence and arrogance. With Cort, she would be safe, and safe was all she wanted....

He smiled. "There we go. Now—"

"No." Kaylie forced herself to pull back. *Safe?* God, what was she thinking? A man like Cort would sooner die than do anything safely. For a moment, his grip tightened, keeping her close. She realized suddenly that he could toss her into his plane, and she would be powerless to stop him.

Then he released her, and she stumbled back. "It's not that I'm afraid of the plane," she explained hastily, hugging herself. "I'm not. I just can't go." Not with him. Not with the storm approaching. There were too many things wrong. Getting into the plane...just felt wrong.

And the last time something had felt this wrong, people had died.

His smile faded, and she realized he wasn't just a pilot, but a consummate expert in people. It was his job to fly anyone who needed a ride and to keep them happy. She clenched her hands, preparing to resist his attempt to woo her into the plane with his charms.

But after a moment, he shrugged, pulled her bags out of the Cessna, and dropped them at her feet, making absolutely no effort to change her mind. "I don't have time to wait, but you can stay here if you want. I'll give you five minutes to reconsider, and then I'm taking off. No need to pay me anything." He shot another assessing look at the sky off to the north, then ducked under the plane and started fiddling with the wing on the far side, completely dismissing her.

The tension immediately eased from Kaylie's body, and she knew she'd made the right choice not to fly with him. "Um, sorry for the inconvenience." She decided not to look too closely at the fact he'd let her go so easily, a capitulation that had to be against his nature. She'd take the gift and run.

He shot her a look she couldn't read behind the sunglasses. "No inconvenience, ma'am. Have a nice day."

"You too." Kaylie grabbed her bags, staggering under the weight as she arranged them on her shoulders. As she walked across the tarmac toward the hanger, she resisted the urge to turn around and look at him. Instead, she opened her phone and tried to call Sara one more time.

Voice mail again.

Kaylie frowned and hung up without leaving another message. She'd promised to call when she landed, and Sara had been expecting her. So why wasn't she answering? Kaylie thought of the unplayed voice mail on her phone and brightened. Had Sara left her a message? Maybe saying she was meeting Kaylie at the airport instead? *Please, yes.*

Kaylie punched up her voice mail to listen to the message, turning as she heard the Cessna's propeller roar to life after what had to be the shortest five minutes on record.

She watched Cort get organized and saw the large mud tires begin to roll. He wasn't wasting any time getting airborne, not even looking her way to see if she'd changed her mind.

The message began to play, and Kaylie jumped when she heard Sara's frantic voice. "Oh, my God, Kaylie! Don't come to my cabin! Do you hear me? *Don't come!* God, I didn't know! Your mom—" There was a pause. "Oh, *shit.* I think he's here. I'll call you la—"

Sara screamed, there was a gurgling sound and a crash, and then the message went dead.

# CHAPTER THREE

Cort swung the Cessna toward the runway, then swore as Kaylie ran right in front of the plane, waving her arms and shouting. He slammed on the brakes, grimacing at the protest from the Cessna, but he'd been going slowly enough to allow for the sharp stop. He threw open his door. "What the hell—?"

"Something happened to Sara!" Kaylie's face was ashen as she lunged for him and tried to pull herself into the Cessna.

Cort caught her arms as she tried to scramble into his seat. Her body was shaking violently beneath his hands, and he instinctively pulled her against him. "Kaylie. Calm down." He was used to passengers panicking on him, but something about the way she was reacting sent a chill down his spine. "What happened?"

She shook her head, her eyes hidden behind those damn sunglasses. "I don't know, but we have to go—"

"Kaylie!" He sharpened his voice, and it penetrated her panic enough to get her to stop trying to climb onto his lap. It had been a long time since he'd felt a woman with her curves crawling over his body, and he was responding in a way that made him wish he'd gotten airborne before she'd been able to stop him.

Kaylie Fletcher was a woman he couldn't afford to notice.

And if she weren't so damn terrified, he'd dump her right out of the plane and get the hell out of there.

But there was no way he could turn his back on that level of fear. Not even from her. "What happened?" he repeated.

He kept his voice calm, even with his pulse elevating in response to her apparent terror.

"This!" She punched a couple buttons on her phone and held it out to him.

He frowned as he took her phone, wondering what a woman with jeweled shoes from the Lower 48 was doing with a satellite phone with GPS. Then he heard Sara's frantic voice, and his adrenaline kicked in as he listened to the message. "Shit!"

"What happened? Can you tell?"

"No." He tossed her the phone and grabbed his headset. He made a quick call to see if any planes were near Sara and Jackson's cabin that could take a look. When Kaylie heard what he was asking, she slid off him, then ran across the tarmac to her bags.

No one was flying in or out of the area near Jackson's place, since the weather was going south fast in that vicinity. Cort realized that if he wanted to know what was going on at the cabin, he was going to have to go himself. His only chance to beat the storm was to take the shortcut through Devil's Pass, but Devil's Pass was not an option for Cort. Ever.

He'd have to take the long route, but the weather front was approaching too quickly to make that a sane choice. The control tower gave Cort a no-go on taking off in that direction. He assessed the sky again, thought about Sara's message, then told them he was going anyway.

He hopped out of the Cessna and strode across the tarmac to where Kaylie was rifling through her bags. "I'm going out there to check it out."

"I'm going with you." She pulled out a pair of microfiber pants lined with something thick.

"No. I don't like the weather. I'll go alone for a quick look."

"Three minutes ago, you were willing to fly me." She kicked off her shoes, her peach-colored toenails looking so…

endangered…on the harsh tarmac. Dammit, Kaylie didn't belong out here.

She never would.

She yanked the outdoor pants on over her cotton ones, then sat her cute little ass right down on the tarmac and tugged on a pair of thick socks.

He narrowed his eyes as he watched her transform from a piece of decoration into something hard-core. Who the hell was this woman? "The weather has changed."

Kaylie tugged a pair of thermal waterproof boots out of her bag and shoved her feet into them. Then she threw on a thick wool turtleneck over that damned cotton sweater he liked, pulled a parka out of her bag, and stood up. "So have I."

He surveyed her carefully. Her clothes were brand-new, but they were appropriate. She wore her outdoor gear with as much comfort as she'd worn her little blue shoes and her low-cut sweater. And damn if that didn't just make him get even more of a hard-on for her. Sexy and Lower 48 was one thing. Also able to carry off outdoor gear as if she were born to it?

Hot damn.

Maybe he wouldn't be so quick to send her packing. Maybe a long, slow night of Alaskan loving would go a long way toward getting her and what she represented finally cleansed from his system. Her cheeks were flushed, her sunglasses were on the ground, and she had fantastically dark eyes that were focused and determined.

And scared shitless.

He stared into those brown eyes for a long moment, unable to look away from the plea in them. Kaylie didn't turn away either, holding his gaze. Something deep in his gut reacted to the terror haunting her face and the way she clutched the parka to her chest so desperately.

"Sara's my best friend." Kaylie's voice cracked, and he sensed a commitment and loyalty he seldom ran across.

His respect for Kaylie Fletcher bounced up a couple notches, and he made his decision. He grabbed her bags off the tarmac. "Let's go."

"Oh, God, *thank you*." She touched his arm, and his awareness sparked at the contact. Her eyes widened as if she too had felt it. Then she pulled her hand back and turned away to retrieve her blue shoes.

She shoved them into her handbag and fell in beside him, jogging to keep up as he strode back to the Cessna. He didn't wait for her, almost hoping that she wouldn't follow.

She did.

No surprise. He had a feeling Kaylie Fletcher always did whatever the hell she felt like doing. And she looked damn good doing it, too.

He tossed the bags into the back, hesitating only a split second before he palmed Kaylie's waist and hoisted her up. Her hips were curvy and soft beneath his hands, reminding him of how her V-necked sweater had dipped low between her breasts. His thumb slipped beneath the bottom edge of her sweater and caught bare flesh. Hot and smooth.

Kaylie shot a startled look at him. The tension between them jacked up, and her gaze flickered to his mouth. Heat spiked straight to his groin.

She pulled out of his grasp, and he released her. She scrambled over his seat and settled on the passenger side. She tried to do the buckle, but it slipped out of her hand.

"I'll do that." Cort climbed in next to her and took over the buckles. Her hands were icy beneath his, and they were trembling violently. He cupped them, steadying them in his grasp. "It's going to be fine," he said quietly, using his best "client" voice. He caught a whiff of her tantalizing scent, and he was assaulted by a sudden urge to press his face into the curve of her long neck and inhale. Instead, he cracked a casual smile. "I'm the best there is. Just sit back and enjoy the ride."

She shot him a look of disbelief. "Enjoy it? Are you serious?"

"Hell, yeah." He realized how close she was to him. That luscious mouth of hers was only inches away, her breasts rising as she tried to catch her breath, her hands caught in his grasp. Trapped.

"Let's just go." She pulled her hands free of his, shoving her small fists into her jacket pockets. Her breath was too shallow, and she had little lines of tension around the corners of her mouth.

Cort pulled himself together and finished strapping her in, giving the harness an extra tug to make sure it was secure. The back of his hand brushed against her breast, and she stiffened.

"Accident." But he wasn't complaining, and neither was she.

He stifled a small smile, shaking his head at his reaction to her. He needed to ditch her as soon as possible. If he didn't, he'd regret it later.

Once Kaylie was snugged down, he took a moment to study her as a client and not as a woman who was making his blood boil. She was a passenger on the edge, and he needed to deal with that before getting airborne. "You okay with flying?"

She nodded, but her face was pale. "I'm worried about Sara."

Hah. There was a hell of lot more going on than Kaylie's concern for her friend. She looked as if she were going to pass out.

"Kaylie." He caught her chin and forced her to look at him, using the voice he pulled out when he had a panicking passenger on his hands. Shit, her skin was soft. He'd have bet a tank of fuel that her mouth tasted incredible.

Her gaze settled on his, and she didn't look away, searching his face desperately. He realized she had grizzly-bear eyes, dark and bottomless. Beautiful and captivating, with a heavy dose of "stay the hell away."

"If there's something I need to know before I get us at two thousand feet in bad weather, you better tell me."

She grabbed his wrist, but didn't try to pull his hand away from her face. She held tightly, as though she was afraid he'd release her. Her fingers were pale and slender around his arm, but her grip was strong enough to make him smile.

She lifted her chin, and he saw her summon her composure. "I'm not going to freak on you. Let's go."

He hesitated a moment longer. Couldn't stop himself from brushing his thumb over the corner of her mouth. So damned delicate. Flawless. No years of exposure to harsh weather for Kaylie Fletcher, no matter how comfortable she seemed in her gear. She was a groundie, for sure. Someone who lived with two feet on the ground and had storm windows keeping out the cold.

Not his kind of woman.

Not anymore.

"Cort." His name was a desperate whisper on her lips, and it struck a spot inside him that made him shudder.

He forced himself to release her. "Then let's do it." He strapped himself in and kicked the Cessna into gear, heading out toward the runway—not that he needed more than a couple hundred feet to take off with an unloaded plane and a runway that was actually paved.

"Cort?"

"Yeah?" He checked with the control tower for clearance to take off, and got the affirmative. He didn't bother to tell them he'd be circling back toward Jackson's.

"Do you think Sara—?" Her voice broke again, and she didn't finish.

He glanced over at Kaylie and saw she was hugging herself. Her feet were up on the dash, as if she were trying to curl into a protective ball. "I'm sure she's fine," he lied.

"Are you?" She turned her gaze onto him, and he saw in her a need for honesty.

He respected that need and gave her the truth. "I don't take off into weather like I think we're going to hit unless I believe someone's life is at stake and I'm the only one who can do anything about it."

Her face drained of what little color it had, and for a second he regretted being so blunt.

Then she nodded and fisted the straps of the harness, her face hardening with determination. "Okay, then."

He grinned at the ferocity on her face. Yeah, like he'd thought. The woman with rubies on her toes had some grizzly bear in her. Get too close to a grizzly, and you were dead meat. Those females would rip your damn heart out and have it for breakfast.

Cort rubbed his thumb over the scar on the back of his left hand. He'd gotten it the last time he'd let a grizzly get too close. He'd learned his lesson. From now on, Kaylie Fletcher was nothing but a client.

A favor for a friend.

Nothing more.

And it was his damned problem that he couldn't stop thinking about how good she'd feel beneath him.

The plane lurched again, and Kaylie clamped down on her seat belt. She scrunched her eyes shut even tighter, so she couldn't see the snowy whiteout blinding them or the treetops right below the wings. All the feelings of wrongness were back, and it was too late to do anything about it.

"If you look out the window to the right, you'll see Pink Creek, named after the color of the water when the salmon are running so thick that the water looks pink from the air."

Kaylie wrenched her eyes open at Cort's casual statement, then glanced out the window. She could see nothing but darkness and the swirl of snow at the edge of his wing light.

"See any grizzlies?" His voice was low and rough, but comforting. "They're usually pretty thick this time of year, going after the salmon."

She looked again and still saw darkness. "What are you talking about?"

"Tour guide. I distract my passengers when they get nervous. It's rutting season, you know. Might see some action down there, but I recommend watching from a distance. Grizzlies in rutting season are about as approachable as… well, grizzlies in rutting season." His face was barely lit by the glow from the control panel. His sunglasses had long ago hit the dash, and his jaw was shadowed in the dim light, making him look even harder and more rugged than he had out on the tarmac. Cort was all backwoods and survival, taking on Mother Nature and winning every time.

Until he finally lost, of course.

Because he would.

They all did, eventually.

"Up ahead you'll see Mount McKinley," he continued. "Snow-covered peaks year-round, but by summer, the winds get too high for climbing by anyone with half a brain or a shred of common sense."

Up ahead was whiteout backed by darkness. "It's beautiful. Such a scenic flight," she managed.

He grinned. "You climb?"

"No!" Her reaction was too quick, and she saw Cort's eyebrows raise with curiosity. She struggled to recover, not wanting him to probe further. "Do you?"

"Nah. I'm an air guy. Too much time on the ground gives me hives."

She snorted at the line that was such an echo of the one

she'd heard so many times in her life. "Maybe if you stayed on the ground longer than a fraction of a second, you'd find something there you liked."

He gave her a long inspection that was utterly male, full of raw sexuality. "Seems everything I want fits in a plane just fine."

Her nipples tightened from that one heated look, and she quickly folded her arms over her breasts. "You mean the freedom to risk your life on a daily basis?" She struggled to keep her voice even, to shift the topic from any further innuendo.

The plane bucked, and Cort turned his attention back to his instruments, but the sensual mood didn't lessen. If anything, she was even more aware of him. Of the small space they shared. Of the way he'd looked at her as if he wanted to strip off her clothes layer by layer until she was naked beneath him. She remembered his hands on her hips as he'd helped her into the plane, tossing her as though she weighed nothing. Holding on to her a fraction of a second longer than he'd needed to. She'd liked him touching her.

He was an adrenaline junkie bound for an ugly death, and yet she wanted him to touch her again. To feel his hand sliding over her hip…His touch had been more than an impersonal assist into the plane. It had been a sensual caress that had made all her nerve endings spike. That brief moment had elicited the most intense yearning to be touched. To be held. To be kissed. By this man who was so…male.

God. Was she that lonely? That desperate? That *stupid*?

"Nah," he said, interrupting her thoughts. "I'm not risking my life. I'm in control up here."

His comment irked her enough to jerk her attention back to him. "*That's* why you're risking your life! Because you don't respect the danger—"

"Hey." His voice turned to granite. "I respect it just fine. But I make damn sure that my equipment's in top shape. I know what I can do and what I can't. And I can do a hell of a lot."

"How many bush pilots die each year in Alaska?"

"None that are doing everything right." His voice was unyielding, and his arrogance was thick in his words. But it wasn't just an arrogance; it was a total and complete conviction.

Of course it was. A bush pilot couldn't do his job if he didn't believe he was better than the challenges he faced. The minute he lost confidence, he might as well hang up his wings.

She knew the drill all too well.

A man like Cort would never admit his failings, not even when his moment to die finally came. He'd proclaim his invincibility even as the Grim Reaper stood over him and took his soul.

"You're impossible," she said. Men like him didn't change.

His eyes narrowed at her hostile tone. "What's your deal?"

She grimaced. "Nothing."

"Yeah? You're in my plane giving me grief, when all I'm doing is flying you where you need to go. It's not personal, but you're making it personal. Why?"

She bit her lip and looked out the window, watching the snow fly past the light on the wing. "I'm sorry. It's not your fault."

"What's not my fault?" But his voice was softer now, a bit of curiosity mixed with concern.

"Long story." She glanced at him. "I don't really want to talk about it."

He nodded. "Got some of those, too."

They fell into silence, but this time it was a more comfortable silence. As if they'd sort of reached an understanding. She sighed and let her head fall back against the seat. The plane continued to dip and buck. The turbulence wasn't normally enough to scare her, but the sense of foreboding was getting stronger with each minute.

She stole a glance at Cort. His face was relaxed as he concentrated on flying. She might scoff at his arrogance, but since he had her life in his callused hands right now, she had no choice but to make herself believe that he was absolutely correct about how good he was.

She had to have faith in him. It was her only choice.

Twenty minutes later Cort announced, "We're almost here. I'm going fly over the cabin and check things out."

Kaylie leaned forward, straining to see the ground through the storm that raged around them. *Please be okay, Sara.*

She pressed her face to the window as Cort flew low. The ground beneath them was white, flanked by darkness. She could only guess it was a clearing filled with snow and surrounded by trees.

Cort banked the plane, and the nose came up, and she guessed that they'd flown by the cabin. "No lights."

"You were expecting lights out here?"

"Yeah. They should have a lantern out at the end of the field so I can see it to land." The nose of the plane started to drop again, and Kaylie instinctively grabbed hold of the seat.

"I'm going to have to land without it."

"Is that safe?"

He shrugged. "It'll be as safe as I can make it."

"That's not an answer!"

"Sure it is." He nodded at the windshield. "This time I'm flying by to check for anything on the field that I could hit. Moose, trees, debris. To make sure the snow's not too deep for wheels."

"Why don't you have skis?"

"Too late in the year. Not enough snow."

She glanced out at the whiteout in front of the windshield. "Not enough snow?"

"Nope."

Kaylie saw Cort lean forward, peering out the window to look for moose and branches, but she couldn't see anything.

He soon pulled the plane back up, and she assumed he'd finished the flyby. "So, what now?"

"We land."

"But how could you possibly see anything in that darkness?"

He didn't answer her, and she realized with a sinking feeling that he hadn't been able to detect anything either. "Cort?"

He banked the plane, and she knew he was coming in for the landing anyway. "Cort!"

"Today's not the day for us to die in a plane," he said. "So sit back and enjoy the ride."

"The day for us to die?" she echoed. "Don't even say that!"

There was a bump, and she lurched forward as the plane hit hard. She clutched her seat as Cort swore under his breath, making rapid adjustments with the controls as the plane skittered to the side and lurched.

Then, suddenly, all was still.

Kaylie sank back against the headrest, while Cort unbuckled himself and climbed between the seats into the back.

He emerged a scant second later carrying a rifle.

Kaylie jerked upright. "Why do you have that?"

"Never leave home without your gun in these parts." He yanked a black wool hat over his head, then climbed back in front and tossed her the pale blue stocking cap that had been in her bag.

Obviously, the man had no respect for privacy. "You went through my belongings?"

"Yeah. Saw it before you zipped up. You coming or waiting in the plane?" Cort's jaw was hard and his eyes were focused, and she realized he was far more concerned about Sara than he'd let on during the flight.

She tugged the hat down. "I'm coming."

He showed no surprise at her answer. "Stay close. Visibility's shit out there." He popped open the door and vaulted out of the plane, not waiting for her reply.

She quickly climbed down, sinking calf deep in fresh snow that was still falling hard. She tugged on her parka and zipped it up as Cort flashed a heavy-duty flashlight around them.

There was no sound but the whipping of the wind and the roar of his plane's engine, which he hadn't shut down. The cold pounded at her cheeks like miniature ice daggers, and her lungs ached. Cort turned toward the darkness and jerked his chin for her to follow. He strode off across the snow as if he knew exactly where he was going.

Kaylie ran a few steps to catch up, and she grabbed the back of his parka. It was too dark and too snowy to risk losing him, and she had a feeling if he got out of sight, she'd never find him. She shuddered, and a tinge of panic licked at her.

Cort glanced over his shoulder at her and gave her a brief smile of reassurance. Her tension eased slightly. Reassured by a man whose soul depended on his risking death many times a day? God help her.

He turned forward and they slogged through the snow. She could feel the fierce wind knifing through her waterproof pants. She hadn't bothered to spring for the heavily insulated ones, knowing it was spring in Alaska and the weather would be warming up fast.

A mistake that could easily turn fatal in weather like this.

As if sensing her thoughts, Cort reached back and tugged her closer to him. She followed his lead, pressing herself against his muscled back, using his bulk to shield most of the wind. She wrapped her arms around his waist and buried her face in his jacket as he guided them through the storm.

Tucked against Cort, the wind seemed to quiet, and she

became viscerally aware of Cort protecting her. From the wind. From the cold. From taking on Sara's mysterious call by herself.

By the time a dark shape loomed before them, she was shivering. She didn't know if it was from the cold or realizing exactly how tough Cort really was and being crushed up against him.

"That's the cabin," Cort shouted over his shoulder. "No lights on."

He strode up to the house and climbed the steps. He kept one hand anchored on Kaylie's arm where she'd wrapped it around his waist, as if to ensure she didn't lose her grip. He tried the front door without bothering to knock. It opened under his touch, and he stepped inside, his rifle ready.

He stopped so fast, Kaylie slammed into his back.

He stepped back and shoved them both outside. He backed her into the exterior wall of the cabin, pinning her behind him with his body. Rifle up, he scanned the blizzard with his light. The powerful beam reflected off the falling snow, giving them zero visibility. He swore and tightened his grip on the rifle, keeping it aimed and ready.

Kaylie dug her nails into his waist. "Cort? What's wrong?"

He shook his head once, slicing across the air in front of his mouth with his hand to indicate she should be quiet.

*Oh, God.* "What's in the cabin?" She could barely get the question out, her mouth was so dry.

"Not for you to see."

"Not for me—" She felt behind her for the door handle and shoved the door open before he could stop her. He swore and grabbed for her, but she ducked out of his grip and scooted inside.

It was pitch-black, and she moved forward to find a light.

Cort's arm snapped around her belly like a steel band, hauling her back against his body. "No."

She fought against his grip. "Turn on the light."

He hesitated, then turned the flashlight into the room.

At first, the dark splashes on the walls and the floors meant nothing to her.

And then she saw Sara on the floor.

Covered in blood.

*Shredded*.

# CHAPTER FOUR

"Sara!" Kaylie's knees gave out, and Cort caught her, anchoring him against her.

"She's dead." His voice was strained. "They both are."

"Both?" She then noticed a body next to Sara's. The heavily muscled body of a male with bright red hair and freckles. "Dear God. Jackson." His throat was slit, a pool of blood around his upper body. "No!" The cry tore from Kaylie's throat, tears burned down her cheeks, and she wrenched out Cort's grip and ran to her best friend.

Kaylie fell to her knees and tried to pull Sara's inert form onto her lap. "Sara! I'm here. Oh, God. I'm here now. It's okay. I'll get you help." The floor creaked under Cort's weight, and his boots appeared beside her knee. "Bandages, Cort. We need bandages to stop the bleeding!"

"Kaylie." He crouched beside her, his voice rough. "Look at her. You can't save her."

He let the beam settle on Sara, and Kaylie finally saw the death on her friend's face. Sara was gone, truly gone. "Oh, God, Sara." Sobs wracked Kaylie body, and she fell into Cort as he scooped her up in his arms. Loneliness crushed her, made it impossible to breathe. "Cort—"

"I know, babe. I know." He held Kaylie tight as he crossed the floor and took them outside again.

Cort struggled to keep his composure as Kaylie clung to him, her sobs of grief ripping at him. He concentrated on the feel of her body against his, trying to fight down his own memories of the last time he'd seen that much blood. He pressed his face into her hair, finding refuge in her scent and her warmth, whispering soothing comfort to her that he knew would mean absolutely nothing. Words would never change what had just happened.

"We can't leave them," she moaned against his neck.

"I need to call it in." Cort lifted his head and searched their surroundings, his rifle ready. His internal radar registered no one, but he didn't believe it. He quickly began to slog through the snow back toward the plane, and he continued to scan the blizzard for any sign of the son of a bitch who'd killed Cort's best friend and his wife. Sara's blood had started to dry, but Jackson's had been fresh. Jackson, an ex–Navy SEAL and one of the toughest bastards Cort knew, had been taken down mercilessly.

Easily.

With one stroke.

Blood that fresh meant that unless the killer had come in by plane, he was still nearby.

And deadly.

But Cort couldn't see shit, and he had Kaylie in his arms, limiting his mobility. His spine tingled with awareness at the sensation of being watched, and he hustled through the snow, eager to get Kaylie stashed in the plane so he could hunt the bastard down.

Something brushed against his back and he whirled, rifle and flashlight up.

Nothing but blinding snow.

He did a slow 360, straining to see into the snow.

"Cort?"

He realized Kaylie's sobs had stopped, and her body had gone rigid against him. "Yeah?"

"He's still here?"

"Think so."

"Stalking us?" Her voice was a mere whisper.

"Maybe." He began to move slowly toward the plane, while she clung to him, barely breathing.

There was a flash of darkness in the snow right beside him. Cort fired, the shot a deafening explosion in the snowy woods. Kaylie startled against him. Then neither of them moved, both waiting for an indication he'd hit something.

But there was nothing.

A few more steps, and they were at the plane. Kaylie started to scramble off him, and he set her down in the snow. "Stay here." He vaulted up into the plane, doing a quick search of the baggage area, but no one was in there. "Okay."

She was already in her seat by the time he made it back up front a split second later. "You stay here. I'm going to go after—"

"What?" She grabbed his arm before he made it out of the plane. "You can't go out there! You can't see him coming! Did you *see* what he did to Jackson?"

"I saw." Fuck, he'd seen it. The blood flashed in his mind again, and he had to close his eyes for a second to wipe the scene out of his mind. Goddamn memories. "If I don't go now, he'll be gone by the time anyone can get back here." Cort checked the ammunition in his rifle. "If I don't come back, I want you to—"

"What? Fly out of here?" Kaylie tightened her grip on him. "Damn you, Cort. Don't get yourself killed!"

Cort opened his mouth to tell her he wasn't going to get killed, and then he saw streaks of Sara's blood on Kaylie's face and jacket. Jesus. The bastard could come in the plane after Kaylie while Cort was stumbling around blind as hell in the blizzard.

Shit.

He had to get Kaylie out of there.

"Buckle up. We're leaving." He yanked his door shut and fired up the propeller. He threw on his headset and taxied the plane around as fast he dared. His skin was crawling, and he knew with absolute certainty that their departure was being watched.

He ground his jaw against the urge to stop the plane and go after the bastard. Kaylie was his responsibility, because Jackson had taken her under his protection on Sara's behalf. Cort could practically hear Jackson yelling at him to take care of the girl first. An ornery bastard even in death.

Shit. Jackson was *dead*.

Grief welled hard and fast, but Cort shut it off ruthlessly. Instead, he forced himself to focus on the plane. The weather was for shit, and he had no business taking off, but there was no way he was staying on the ground with Kaylie.

He turned at the end of the field and caught a flash of movement at the edge of his lights.

"Did you see that? I saw him." Kaylie jumped back in her seat.

"Saw him." Cort gritted his teeth as he launched the plane, knowing he had only one chance to get them the hell out of there. If he had to abort and circle around again, someone would be waiting for them.

Kaylie gripped the seat tightly as the plane bounced over the rough ground. They weren't quite going fast enough to take off, but the end of field was rapidly approaching…Then they caught air. They both heaved a sigh of relief as the plane lifted off, and he called Max at the control tower to report their findings.

His buddy took the news grimly. He told Cort that no one would be able to get in there until the storm settled, which it looked like might happen by morning, but that he'd call the authorities immediately.

Cort nodded and signed off, grinding his jaw at the realization that the bastard would be long gone by morning. If Cort had followed his instincts and left Kaylie behind originally, he might have had the guy at gunpoint already.…

He glared at Kaylie, and his irritation vanished instantly when he saw how destroyed she was. She was hunched over, her arms wrapped around her stomach, and she was moaning softly. He swore under his breath, wishing he had words to comfort her, but knowing he didn't.

"Kaylie—"

Then there was a loud crack, and the plane lurched and started fighting him. He checked the gauges, trying to figure out what had just gone wrong.

And then he saw blood on his dash.

Kaylie followed his glance and made a small noise of distress. "He was in here."

"Sure was."

She whipped around to inspect into the back of the plane, and he barely resisted the urge to do the same.

"I checked back there," he said. "He's not in here."

Kaylie turned on Cort's flashlight and shone it back there anyway. "Why would he get in the plane and then get out?"

Cort had a grim realization. "He wanted to know who was flying this plane."

Kaylie jerked her gaze to him. "*Why?*"

"So he could know who to go after if we saw too much."

"Oh, God." Her face went white. "You think he'll come after us?"

Cort was still trying to concentrate on keeping the plane above the tops of the trees. Something was seriously off with the Cessna, and he didn't know what. "Me. He'd have no way of tracking you." Cort glanced over at Kaylie and saw her shoot him a look that said she wasn't buying it. He didn't either.

If the killer wanted to find her, he would.

The plane lurched again, and Cort realized the killer wouldn't even be a factor if he didn't get the plane on the ground soon.

"Cort?"

He gave her a calm smile. "Just a little turbulence," he lied easily. "But I'm not risking going all the way back to the airport."

He could see her pulse hammering in her throat, and her voice was shaky. "Where are we going to land, then? On a field or something?"

He banked the plane, well aware that the stress was going to snap her composure unless he did something to bring her back. A panicking passenger was the last thing he needed, and he wasn't in the mood to crack an elbow to her head and knock her out, as he'd done to the last drunk hunter who'd gone berserk in his cockpit.

"I'm taking you to my place." Knowing she needed a distraction, he glanced over at her and let his gaze sweep blatantly over her chest. "I gotta warn you, though. I only have one bed."

Her eyes widened. "Are you insane? How can you possibly be thinking of sex right now?"

He shrugged lightly, fighting hard to keep the plane level. "I'm just saying."

From the look she gave him, he knew he'd succeeded in distracting her.

She wasn't thinking about blood right now. But the shock would hit later. It always did.

And he'd told the truth. He did have only one bed.


By the time Cort taxied his plane into his heated hangar, he was seriously worried about Kaylie. She hadn't moved or spoken in over an hour.

He shut the plane off and turned to her. "Hey," he whispered, touching her shoulder. "You with me?"

Kaylie shook her head and pulled his emergency blanket tighter around her.

He unhooked her harness, frowning when he felt how much she was shaking. "We're here. Safe."

She finally opened her eyes and looked at him, her expression blank with numb shock. "Sara—"

"Sara would want you to take care of yourself." He thumbed a strand of hair off her cheek and tucked it behind her ear.

"But—"

"Inside. You need food." He tugged her out of the seat and lowered her to the ground. Three planes were inside the pristine hanger, but the plane favored by Cort's business partner wasn't in residence, which meant Luke was out on a run somewhere.

The office would be closed down at this hour, as it usually was. The gal they hired for bookings and billing only worked a few hours a week, leaving the operation pretty much in Cort's and Luke's hands, the way they both liked it.

The way it had been when Cort's parents had run it.

Cort tucked the blanket more securely around Kaylie's shoulders. Her hands were ice cold, her eyes were haunted, and blood was still smeared over her hands and face. He retrieved her bags from the back and slung them over his shoulders.

Once he was loaded up, he set his hand on her back to guide her past the planes toward the door at the back. He tried to think of something to get her mind off the images he knew were haunting her. "I have to warn you, my housecleaner hasn't come in lately, so the place is a mess."

She blinked at him. "You have a housecleaner?"

"Yeah. She comes about once every six years. Or longer. Can't really remember." He opened the door. "Ready?"

She took one look out at the driving snow and pulled herself together. She tugged her hood up and shoved her hands into her pockets. "I hate this kind of weather," she muttered.

Cort wrapped his arm around her shoulder, tucking her against him as they stepped outside. He nodded with satisfaction when she burrowed into his side. "It'll clear up by morning. Just a late spring storm." Despite the whiteout, Cort unerringly guided her the short distance to the house he'd inherited after his parents had burned up in the crash in Devil's Pass seventeen years ago, almost to the day.

Cort followed Kaylie inside as she stumbled over the entryway. He kicked the door shut, then strode across the uneven wood floor and dropped her bags in his room. "You can stay in here. Bathroom has hot water. High luxury for these parts."

But when he turned back, Kaylie hadn't followed. She was standing in the middle of the common room, staring at the only picture on his wall: Mount McKinley in a light fog at dawn, as seen from two thousand feet.

"Sara painted that," she said quietly. "She never shows her paintings to anyone."

Cort walked over to Kaylie and stood beside her while he studied the picture. He hadn't noticed it in a long time. "Yeah, I made Sara sell it to me." He wasn't into art, but when he'd seen it at Jackson's two years ago, he'd had to have it.

Cort remembered now why he'd needed it so badly. In this picture, Sara had painted freedom and joy. The feeling of absolute bliss and complete abandonment of responsibility had been so vivid for Cort—exactly what he'd been trying to attain for so long. Sara had caught it in this picture in a way he'd never been able to in real life.

Kaylie looked at Cort, her forehead furrowed faintly. "You couldn't have forced her to sell it to you. She must have wanted you to have it."

"Yeah, to get me out of her hair."

"No." Kaylie cocked her head, studying him as if seeing him for the first time. "She must have really liked you."

"Yeah, I guess." Cort shifted uncomfortably and gestured toward his bedroom, not sure it was the best thing, for Kaylie to be focusing on Sara right now. "Your stuff's in there." He brushed his hand over her cheek. "You might want to wash up."

"Really?" Kaylie touched the crusted blood, and she sighed with weariness. "A shower would be great."

Cort stepped aside as she walked into his room, aware that she was too quiet. Shock would hit soon. He caught her arm and forced her to look at him. The moment he had her attention, he softened his touch and ran his hand up and down her arm. "Take a hot shower and clean up. Put on something warm and then come out and eat. I'll defrost some chili."

She looked down at his fingers touching her, and a tremor ran through her body. Then she pulled away, her face still haggard and pale. "Are you always this bossy?"

He grinned. "Actually, this is me being considerate. Ask my business partner, Luke, about me ordering him around."

Kaylie rolled her eyes and walked past him into the bedroom. "Thanks, but I'll pass."

Cort leaned on the doorjamb and folded his arms over his chest. He refused to move when she tried to close the door on him.

She rested her cheek on the edge of the door and stared at him. "What now?"

He brushed the tip of his finger over the dark circles beneath her eyes, and she closed her eyes for a moment, as if drinking in his touch. He knew the feeling. The craving to haul her against him and lose himself in her was killing him. But he forced himself to drop his hand. "You okay? Want me to stay?"

"No, I'm fine." She managed a trembly smile that made his gut churn for its sheer courage. Her cheekbones were high, her skin flawless, and there was a strength in Kaylie Fletcher that drew him to her. Strong, sexy as hell, and with an attitude.

His type of woman...

Shit.

It didn't matter that she was all wrong for him. She wasn't getting out from under his skin until he had her.

"I just need a minute," she said, interrupting the dangerous path of his thoughts. "Of privacy."

"Yell if you need anything." He pulled back and let her shut the door. Now was not the time. But instead of walking away, he leaned his head against the door, listening.

For a moment, there was no sound, and then he heard the floor creak as she walked across the room. He heard the sound of her zipper and knew she was doing what he'd instructed her to do. Kaylie was okay for now.

With a groan, Cort levered himself off the door and walked into his kitchen. He stood in the doorway for a minute. The reality of what had happened to Jackson was finally hitting him, now that Kaylie wasn't front and center to distract him. He closed his eyes and balled his fists, fighting against the swell of grief. The memories. The feeling of loss so great it ripped at his gut and flayed him raw. Not again. Not fucking again.

He didn't move for almost ten minutes, using every shred of discipline he'd learned from years of flying. It took far too long, but he finally pulled his shit back together.

Under control again, Cort grabbed his hunting knife from above the woodstove and walked over to his front door.

For a moment, he simply stared at the two names carved above the frame.

PEGGY MCCLAINE

HUFF MCCLAINE

Cort had been fourteen when he'd carved their names. Too short to reach, he'd stood on a stool, carving for hours until his shaking hands had gotten it done.

His throat tightened, and for a second the letters blurred. In the seventeen years since, plenty of people he'd known had died. But his parents were the only two names above that door.

Except for one more. Carved eight years ago. Small letters in the corner.

SIMON

Barely visible, unless Cort looked for it—which he never did. But he knew it was there. Every minute of every day, he was aware of the name of his son carved in that wood.

*Fuck.*

Cort lifted the knife and slammed it into the pine. A wood chip splintered off and hit his hand.

His vision blurred again, and he began to carve Jackson's name.

# Chapter Five

Mason Fletcher was going to lose his leg.

He'd been in this kind of pain before, and he knew it wasn't good.

Especially when he was so fucking cold his hands were numb and his insides felt like they were going to shake themselves to pieces.

He was still lying on dirt, just as he had been the last time he was conscious. Cold, hard dirt. Grinding into his face.

But this time, his mind was alert, not the blurred fog he'd been in the last several times he was conscious.

Willing strength into his body, Mason rolled onto his back. The bones in his shoulder slid around, eliciting a groan he couldn't suppress. Broken. Definitely.

The place was pitch-black. He couldn't see a damn thing.

Last time he'd woken up, he had a vague memory of a sliver of light visible beneath an ill-fitting slab of wood pulling door duty. Now it was dark. May in northern Alaska meant about eighteen hours of functional daylight, so the darkness didn't tell Mason much, besides that he was seriously screwed.

Which he'd already figured out.

What he hadn't figured out was where the hell he was, and how he'd gotten there.

He thought for a minute, trying to determine the most recent clear memory he had: A header down the side of a mountain…The shouts of his dad…The screams of his mother and his girlfriend, Kristina.

His parents. *Too old to climb*, he'd told them jokingly before this trip. Joking, but also half serious. Knowing he'd never be able to stop them from doing it, but too aware of the number of hard years they'd subjected themselves to. In their fifties, they weren't too old to climb. But they were too young to die.

Mason had gone on this climb with them not for himself, but to be their anchor, just in case.

And he'd brought Kristina. After dating for six months, Mason had finally been ready for her to meet his parents. He'd told her he'd keep her safe, even though she wasn't an experienced climber.

And he'd failed.

*Kristina.*

*Fuck.*

Mason's head began to throb, but he kept replaying that fall in his head. What the hell had happened to everyone else? The last thing Mason remembered was the anchor rope snapping. He recalled catapulting down the side of a snowy crevasse and shielding his head as he bounced off rocks. Hearing the screams of the climbing party. He didn't remember landing. Had no memory of what had happened to the rest of the crew.

How the hell had he gone from the side of a mountain to sprawled on the floor in some ramshackle hut? And where was everyone else?

*Shit.*

He had to get out before they came back.

Mason had been in this kind of position before, stranded on a mountain. Hurt. He knew how to conserve his strength, saving it up so he could do the impossible: whatever it took to survive.

So he lay there. Willing his broken body to respond. Concentrating on nothing but the image of standing. He visualized walking to the door. Opening the damn thing and getting the hell out.

Eventually, his muscles began to tingle, and he felt them kick in, responding to his orders.

Mason took a deep breath, then rolled onto his stomach again, gritting his teeth against the pain. Sweat broke out on his brow. At least one broken rib. Jesus, he'd forgotten how much they hurt.

On the count of three.

One. He palmed his hands on the ground beneath his shoulders.

Two. Toes anchored in the dirt.

Three. He shoved himself to his knees, a roar of agony filling the air.

Triumph singing through his veins, Mason dropped his head, fighting against the dizziness as he prepared for the final assault. One more second and he'd be on his feet, and—

The door slammed open, and a bright light blinded him.

Mason swore and ducked his head, closing his eyes to save his vision. "Turn off the light," he ordered.

"You're alive." It was a male voice Mason didn't recognize.

Not that it meant anything.

This guy could have been sent to represent the others. The flashlight didn't budge from Mason's face, rendering him essentially blind. "Where's everyone else in my party?"

The light wavered, and Mason heard footsteps nearing. He tensed, skin prickling on the back of his neck. His muscles bunched, and he kept his head averted from the light, waiting for his chance....

A boot slammed into his side, and Mason bellowed with agony. He dropped to the ground as his hand went to his side, trying to protect his broken rib.

"I like you better in the dirt."

Fighting to stay conscious, Mason stiffened when the man crouched beside him. There was a familiar cadence to the man's voice. Not from Seattle…Mason had encountered him more recently. Someone from Alaska…

*Shit*. Had he been tracked ever since arriving?

Mason remembered his captor's voice mixed with the screams of his climbing team. This man had been there when they'd fallen. "Did you kill them?"

"Why do you care?" The man sounded pissed. "You fucking blew it. I had it set up perfectly. But you broke protocol." He shined the light directly into Mason's eyes. "You fucked it up, and the wrong people died."

Kristina. His mother. His father. The others, seven strangers, in the climbing party. "Who died?" A deep, dark fury unlike anything he'd ever felt boiled in his veins. "You son of a b—"

"Shut up." The man slammed him in the chest, and Mason gasped for breath as he collapsed again.

"Who are you?" Mason wheezed. "Who are you working with?"

The man glanced up, a thin smile on his face, as he held up Mason's driver's license. "Same last name as Alice. Husband?"

"Alice?" Mason realized his captor must have gone through his wallet. "Alice is my mother, and if you hurt her—"

"Mother?" The man studied the license again, then stiffened. "Jesus, it was you. You're the reason."

"Reason for what?" Mason flexed his muscles, testing them while he tried to draw information from his jailer. Anything that would help him figure out who he was up against while he assessed what his body would be able to do.

"You son of a bitch. It wasn't him. It was *you*." The stranger's voice turned lethal, deadly, and Mason knew the man was going to kill him.

There was no other outlet for that kind of deranged fury.
*Bring it on.*

But the man didn't make a move toward him. Instead, he seemed fixated on something else in the wallet.

The man turned a photo toward Mason. "Tell me everything about this woman. She looks exactly like Alice." His voice had gone dangerously soft. Obsessive. On the edge.

Violent aggression, Mason could take. This creepy lust was something else entirely.

Mason squinted at the picture of his sister, who did indeed look like their mother had when she was in her twenties. Even with thirty years between them, they still looked very similar. And Mason didn't like the way this crazed bastard was looking at his sister's picture. "Underwear model," he said. "Cut it out of a magazine."

The man's fist snapped out, cracking him in the ribs again. Mason's breath came tighter, and he gasped for air, the pain too intense now. Had his lung just been punctured? Holy fuck.

Holding his side, Mason saw his captor was reading the back of the photo now, and Mason remembered Kaylie had written him a note on the back, along with her address and phone number. They barely kept in touch, but Mason carried that picture as a reminder of his sister, and of his resolution that someday he would find time to reconnect with her.

The man raised his eyes to Mason's, something dark flickering in them. "Kaylie." He traced his finger over the photo. "She's coming for me."

Adrenaline surged at the thought of Kaylie at the hands of this psychopath. "She'd never set foot in this state."

"No?" The monster smiled. "I already called her. She's coming for her mother. No girl can stay away when her mama needs her. And will she come for you as well? Her brother? Is that what you are? You're my bait, in case I need it."

Sweet Jesus. Kaylie at the hands of this madman? "No!"

Mason lunged at the bastard, knocked him over, and sent him sprawling to the ground. The man slammed his flashlight into Mason's shoulder, and then his broken ribs. Mason fell, unable to move.

Panting with the agony, Mason could do nothing but lay there as his captor turned on the light and grabbed something from the corner. Metal. Heavy. Chained to the wall.

Shackles.

Struggling to stay conscious, Mason was unable to fight as the son of a bitch grabbed his injured leg. The shackle snapped shut on his ankle with enough force to bring him off the ground, grabbing for his leg.

*Motherfucker.*

The metal was digging in, pressing against the damaged tissue.

His captor stood just out of Mason's reach. "Kaylie's already in Alaska, and she's going to be mine."

"No. Whatever your problem is with me, leave her out of it." Mason clenched his jaw against the pain as he struggled to sit up. "It's you and me."

"No. It's not complete until she is here. Once I know I don't need you anymore, it'll be payback time."

"Goddamn you!" Mason lurched to his feet and the psychopath yanked on the chain.

The shackle ground into Mason's leg and he screamed, falling back down, grabbing for his leg. "You son of a bitch."

His captor held up the photo of Kaylie and pressed his lips to it. "I have work to do. Try not to die. If your sister proves difficult, I might have need of you to provide leverage." He rubbed his hands together. "She is mine."

"She's not yours!"

But he was gone, leaving Mason alone in the darkness.

With a shackled leg and a sister who was about to deliver herself into the hands of a sick bastard.

* * *

Kaylie's hands were shaking as she rifled through her bag, searching for her yoga pants. They were the low-slung black ones with a light pink stripe down the side. The cuffs were frayed from too many trips to the grocery store late at night for comfort food, and they were her go-to clothes when she couldn't cope.

But she couldn't find them.

"Dammit!" Kaylie grabbed her other suitcase and dug through it, but they weren't there. "Stupid pants! I can't—" A sob caught at her throat and she pressed her palms to her eyes, trying to stifle the swell of grief. "Sara…"

Her voice was a raw moan of pain, and she sank to the thick shag carpet. She bent over as waves of pain, of loneliness, of utter loss shackled her. For her parents, her brother—her family—and now Sara.

Dear God, she was all alone.

"Dammit, Kaylie! Get up!" she chided herself. She wrenched herself to her feet. "I can do this." She grabbed a pair of jeans and a silk blouse off the top of her bag and turned toward the bathroom. One step at a time. A shower would make her feel better.

She walked into the tiny bathroom, barely noticing the heavy wood door as she stepped inside and flicked the light switch. Two bare light bulbs flared over her head, showing a rustic bathroom with an ancient footed tub and a raw wood vanity with a battered porcelain sink. A tiny round window was on her right. It was small enough to keep out the worst of the cold, but big enough to let in some light and breeze in the summer.

In Alaska, for sure. God, what was she doing here?

Kaylie tossed the clean clothes on the sink and unzipped her jacket, dropping it on the floor. She tugged all her layers off, including the light blue sweater that had felt so safe this morning when she'd put it on. She stared grimly at her black lace bra, so utterly feminine, exactly the kind of bra that her mother had always thought frivolous and completely impractical. Which it was. Which is why that was the only style Kaylie ever wore.

She should never have come. She didn't belong here. Couldn't handle this. Kaylie gripped the edge of the sink. Her hands dug into the wood as she fought against the urge to curl into a ball and cry.

After a minute, she lifted her head and looked at herself in the mirror. Her eyes were wide and scared. There were dark circles under her eyes. Her hair was tangled and flattened from her wool hat. There was dirt caked on her cheeks.

Kaylie rubbed her hand over her chin, and the streaks of mud didn't come off.

She tried again, then realized she had smudges all over her neck. She turned on the water and wet her hands…and saw her hands were covered as well.

Stunned, Kaylie stared as the water ran over her hands, turning pink as it swirled in the basin.

Not dirt.

Sara's blood.

"Oh, God." Kaylie grabbed a bar of soap and began to scrub her hands. But the blood was dried, stuck to her skin. "Get off!" She rubbed frantically, but the blackened crust wouldn't come off. Her lungs constricted, and she couldn't breathe. "I can't—"

The door slammed open, and Cort stood behind her, wearing a T-shirt and jeans.

The tears burst free at the sight of Cort, and Kaylie held up her hands to him. "I can't get it off!"

"I got it." Cort took her hands and held them under the water, his grip warm and strong. "Take a deep breath, Kaylie. It's okay."

"It's not. It won't be." She leaned her head against his shoulder, closing her eyes as he washed her hands roughly and efficiently. His muscles flexed beneath her cheek, his skin hot through his shirt. Warm. Alive. "Sara's dead," she whispered. "My parents. My brother. They're all gone. The blood—" Sobs broke free again, and she couldn't stop the trembling.

"I know. I know, babe." He pulled her hands out from under the water and grabbed a washcloth. He turned toward her and began to wash her face and neck.

His eyes were troubled, his mouth grim. But his hands were gentle where he touched her, one hand holding her face still while he scrubbed. His gaze flicked toward hers, and he held contact for a moment, making her want to fall into those brown depths and forget everything. To simply disappear into the energy that was him. "You have to let them go," he said. "There's nothing you can do to bring them ba—"

"No." A deep ache pounded at Kaylie's chest, and her legs felt as if they were too weak to support her. "I can't. Did you see Sara? And Jackson? His throat—" She bent over, clutching her stomach. "I—"

Cort's arms were suddenly around her, warm and strong, pulling her against his solid body. Kaylie fell into him, the sobs coming hard, the memories...

"I know." Cort's whisper was soft, his hand in her hair, crushing her against him. "It sucks. Goddamn, it sucks."

Kaylie heard his grief in the raw tone of his voice, realized his body was shaking as well, and she looked up. There was a rim of red around his eyes, shadows in the hollows of his whiskered cheeks. "You know," she whispered, knowing with absolute certainty that he did. He understood the grief consuming her.

"Yeah." He cupped her face, staring down at her, his grip so tight with desperation that mirrored her own. She could feel his heart beating against her nearly bare breasts, the rise of his chest as he breathed, the heat of his body warming the deathly chill from hers.

And suddenly, for the first time in forever, she didn't feel quite as alone.

In her suffering, she had company. Someone who knew. Who understood. Who shared her pain. It had been so long since she hadn't felt consumed by the loneliness, but with Cort holding her…there was a flicker of light in that hell trying to take her. "Cort—"

He cleared his throat. "I gotta go check on the chili." He dropped his hands from her face and stood up to go, pulling away from her.

Without his touch, the air felt cold and the anguish returned full force. Kaylie caught his arm. "Don't go—" She stopped, not sure what to say, what to ask for. All she knew was that she didn't want him to leave, and she didn't want him to stop holding her. Just for a minute.

Cort turned back to her, and something ticked in his cheek.

For a moment, they simply stared at each other. She raised her arms. "Hold me," she whispered. "Please."

He hesitated for a second, and then his hand snaked out and he shackled her wrist. He yanked once, and she tumbled into him. Their bodies smacked hard as he caught her around the waist, his hands hot on her bare back.

She threw her arms around his neck and sagged into him. He wrapped his arms around her, holding her tightly against him. With only her bra and his T-shirt between them, the heat of his body was like a furnace, numbing her pain. His name slipped out in a whisper, and she pressed her cheek against his chest. She focused on his masculine scent. She took solace in the feel of another human's touch, in the safety of being held in arms powerful enough to ward off the grief trying to overtake her.

His hand tunneled in her hair, and he buried his face in the curve of her neck.

"Cort…" She started to lift her head to look at him, to see if he was crying, but he tightened his grip on her head, forcing her face back to his chest, refusing to allow her to look at him.

Keeping her out.

Isolating her.

She realized he wasn't a partner in her grief. She was alone, still alone, always alone.

All the anguish came cascading back. Raw loneliness surged again, and she shoved away from him as sobs tore at her throat. She couldn't deal with being held by him when the sense of intimacy was nothing but an illusion. "Leave me alone."

Kaylie whirled away from him, keeping her head ducked. She didn't want to look at him. She needed space to find her equilibrium again and rebuild her foundation.

"Damn it, Kaylie." Cort grabbed her arm and spun her back toward him.

She held up her hands to block him, her vision blurred by the tears streaming down her face. "Don't—"

His arms snapped around her and he hauled her against him, even as she fought his grip. "No! Leave me alone!"

His mouth descended on hers.

Not a gentle kiss.

A kiss of desperation and grief and need. Of the need to control *something*. Of raw human passion for life, for death, for the touch of another human being.

And it broke her.

Kaylie's lips were like a breath of life in the black abyss trying to consume him.

Cort growled as her arms circled his neck and her mouth parted for him. She leaned into his chest, her kiss mirroring the desperation driving him.

As if she needed the touch of a human being as badly as he did.

Her spine was a seductive curve, down to those fancy slacks that screamed indoor parties with champagne and candlelight. But she was fire and passion, her skin soft as the fur on a newborn husky pup.

*Jesus.*

Cort deepened the kiss, thrusting his tongue into the moist heat of her mouth. His erection went into overdrive when she kissed him back just as fiercely, tangling her tongue around his with a need grinding down to the very marrow of his bones.

He wrapped his hands about the lush curves of her bottom and lifted her against him. She locked her legs around his waist, kissing him frantically, as if afraid he'd let her go before she'd gotten all she needed.

No chance in hell of that.

Not breaking the kiss, he shoved them through the doorway into the bedroom. He raked his hands over her back, her shoulders, her ass. He needed to touch more, to lose himself in the depths of her kiss, in the sensation of her body entwined with his.

Cort tossed her bags aside, then dumped her on his bed, collapsing onto her as the mattress groaned in protest. He braced himself over her, kissing her until their teeth hit, until he felt like he was going to drown in the kiss. She grabbed his hair and tugged him closer, kissing him even more fiercely.

There was an urgency in her kiss, a passion that shanghaied him with the force of her life energy.

So different from Jackson, who was dead.

*Dead.*

Suddenly Cort was back to that moment seventeen years ago. Climbing out of the wreckage, trying to pull his mother free of the flames, his panic when the fire grew. Cort could still see his dad's eyes glazed in death, as if disgusted by Cort's inability to get his mother free. So much blood, her screams—

*Goddammit!* Cort tore his mouth from Kaylie's and dropped his head to her breast, cupping the soft flesh as he sucked her nipple into his mouth, desperate to escape the memories.

Kaylie gasped and arched into his kiss, pulling at his T-shirt.

Cort reared back and ripped the fabric out of his way. His gaze fixated on Kaylie's tearstained face as she quickly unbuttoned her fly. Her eyes didn't leave his as she kicked off her pants. He unfastened his jeans, ditching them across the room.

And then he was back on top of Kaylie, unable to suppress a groan as her soft skin slid against his. Jesus. It had been so long, and she was so alive....

He kissed her so fiercely, so deeply, and it still wasn't enough to wipe the screams of his parents from his mind. It didn't spare him the memory of Jackson's body sprawled on the ground, Jackson's hand across Sara's as if he'd been trying to protect her even in death.

Kaylie anchored her legs around Cort's hips, and he reached between them. A low sound reverberated in his chest when he found her drenched. He whispered her name, and then plunged deep into her.

A small noise of surprise came from Kaylie, and then she lifted her hips for him. She twisted her hands in the comforter and threw her head back, delivering herself over to his mercy.

Cort thrust again. She was so tight around him, so hot, so pulsing with life. His muscles quivered, and he bent his head to her throat. He breathed deeply, inhaling her scent. She smelled like spring and sweat—fragile and female, but so hot, as if her soul were burning through her skin.

Cort drove deep again, and again, until his body was screaming for release, until all he could think of was Kaylie, of her body, of the way her fingernails were digging into his shoulders, fighting to keep him close. Cort kept driving her to the edge and bringing her back, not willing to let the moment end.

He wanted to be here forever, deep inside her body, his body shaking with need for her, only for her. He wanted to stay in this place where nothing mattered except them, except sex, except the heat roaring through his veins.

"Cort."

Kaylie's throaty plea was the most seductive sound Cort had heard in his life, and it snapped the last threads of his control. He threw her legs over his shoulders and slammed himself to her very core.

Kaylie shouted his name as her body convulsed beneath him. The orgasm hit him so hard, his muscles ripped out of his control. He was suddenly thrusting again and again, and she was writhing beneath him, tears streaming down her cheeks as she clung to him, hanging on until the final tremors shook him to his soul.

# CHAPTER SIX

Kaylie awoke to a heavy weight across her chest.

She opened her eyes and saw an unfinished wooden ceiling: rough-hewn beams crossing above the bed in an architectural style she hadn't seen since she was sixteen, the last time she'd set foot in the mountains—

And then Kaylie remembered.

Alaska.

The call about her mother.

Sara.

*Cort.*

Her cheeks flaming, Kaylie turned her head to see Cort passed out next to her. It was his arm pinning her to the bed. They were both on top of the covers, still naked. His muscles were bunched even in sleep, a tattoo of a bald eagle in flight on his upper right arm. His face was hard, a muscle twitching in his cheek as if he was having a bad dream.

Unable to resist touching him, Kaylie traced his face with her fingertips, and his tic stopped. Whiskers covered his jaw, and there was a small scar on his hairline, just above his right temple. She recalled the amazing sensation of being in his arms, of his enormous strength coupled with his gentleness. Cort was everything she didn't want, but at the same time… he was sexy and strong and he made her feel safe.

Cort muttered something in his sleep and rolled away from her, exposing his back.

Kaylie recoiled at the sight. The skin across his shoulders

was twisted and shiny from a horrific burn. There was a long white scar across his lower back and around his side, as if he'd nearly been sliced in half a long time ago.

It was the body of a man who lived dangerously. Who thumbed his nose at death and kept right on challenging it at every turn.

Dear God, what had she done?

Kaylie scrambled off the bed, grabbed her small duffel and raced into the bathroom. She shut the door and leaned against it, as if she could keep him out.

She caught sight of herself in the same mirror that had undone her earlier. Her cheeks were flushed, her hair tousled, whisker burn on her face. The appearance of a well-loved woman. She looked sensual and seductive. Alive.

Even now, she could taste his kiss. She could feel the roughness of his hands on her skin, and the weight of his body as he'd trapped her beneath him. Heat began to throb between her legs, her body sore in a thoroughly satisfying and dangerous way.

She groaned and closed her eyes. Sex with a stranger was bad enough. Unprotected sex was beyond stupid. And to have it with a man like Cort McClaine…Dear God. What had she been thinking?

He would destroy her.

She simply didn't have enough left in her soul to survive Cort McClaine.

"Are you insane?" The question was snapped at Cort as his front door slammed open less than an hour after he'd climbed out of the bed he'd just shared with Kaylie, letting a blast of frigid air into his cabin.

Cort glanced over his shoulder at Luke Webber, his business partner. Even the pilot's dark sunglasses didn't hide the annoyance on Luke's face. Nothing like a cranky bush pilot to take Cort's mind off the woman showering in his bathroom. "Am I insane? Yeah, probably."

He sure as hell felt like he was losing his mind, listening to Kaylie shower. Picturing her naked.

Like last night.

Cort got hard the minute he let his mind go back to that moment, and he jabbed his fork into the hash he was cooking. What the hell had he been thinking? Women like Kaylie were so far off-limits for him, he didn't even bother to think of them as females, let alone take them to bed.

For eight years, Cort had been too smart to go down that road again, and in one night, he'd fallen off the damn wagon.

And he wanted to march right in there and do it again.

Which definitely made the answer, yeah, he was insane. Not that it was anyone else's business.

Bottom line, Cort was done with Kaylie.

No more sex.

No more carting her around in his plane.

He was pawning her off on someone else, and that was it.

"What's your problem?" Luke kicked the door shut in a show of physical aggression he rarely exhibited.

"My problem?" Cort raised his brows at the uncharacteristic hostility in Luke's voice. Luke was the stable one of the partnership. "What are you talking about?"

"What I'm *talking* about is the fact that if you kill a client, our business is shot to hell." Luke stamped the snow off his boots with enough force to drive a stake into frozen ground. "Taking off into a storm like that with a *client?*"

Cort took a slow slug of the sludge he called coffee, realizing that Luke must already have heard the details about his trip to Jackson's cabin yesterday from Max. "It was an emergency."

"Fuck that." Luke tossed his jacket over the couch and

strode across the floor, helping himself to a battered mug and the coffeepot. "Even you should have known better than to take off in those conditions."

"Don't recall asking for your postmortem. The situation was complicated." Cort leaned against the counter and folded his arms over his chest as the shower shut off. It was about damned time. How much water did that woman need running over her body anyway?

Luke took a gulp of the coffee and made a face. "You're the only one in this godforsaken state who still drinks crap like this. Try a Starbucks, for God's sake. You might like it, and it's easy as hell to get off the Internet, even up here."

"And take the first step toward becoming civilized? Not my style." Assuming Luke was there to poach food, Cort cracked five more eggs into the hash of sausage and egg, mixing it up on his range top.

Luke grabbed a kitchen chair and lounged back in it, elbow on the table. He was wearing a thick black sweater, jeans, and his insulated boots. Something about that damn sweater made him look like the Lower 48 scientist he used to be, instead of the bush pilot he'd turned into. Even after eight years as an Alaskan, Luke Webber would always fit in with the geeks he flew all over the state to research some plant or migratory pattern.

"What's going on with you?" Luke asked.

Cort grabbed a jug of orange juice out of the fridge and sloshed juice into two beer mugs, handing one to Luke. "What's riding your ass now? Did I leave crumbs in the Cub?" Luke cherished the tiny Super Cub, the first plane he had soloed in.

Luke ignored the drink. "You trying to go down like your parents?"

Cort shot a sharp look at his partner as he set the OJ on the table. "What are you talking about?"

"You've always been crazier than most bush pilots, but you know your limits. You're insane, but you're so damned smart about it that you're safer than anyone else in the sky."

Cort dumped most of the egg and sausage concoction onto two plates. "I know what I'm doing."

Luke shook his head. "You're crossing that line. Going up yesterday based on some cryptic phone message? And taking a client with you? Even you wouldn't have done that six months ago." Luke leaned forward. "Everyone knows you go a little off around the anniversary of your parents' death, but this time, it's different. You want to kill yourself, that's your business. But it's not acceptable to take me down with you. I didn't liquidate my retirement to fund this operation just to have you destroy it."

Cort dropped down into the seat next to Luke, tossing the two plates on the table. "Your investment is safe." He was well aware that Luke's infusion of funds eight years ago had kept his business from going into the sewer. Luke had needed a new start, and ten years of having Cort fly him around Alaska for scientific expeditions had convinced the Lower 48 scientist who wanted to learn to be a pilot that Alaska was where he needed to be. Cort had been scraping the bottom due to legal fees and a seriously fucked-up personal life, and it had been a perfect solution for them both at the time. And ever since.

Luke was the cash and the business sense. Cort was the one with the experience and the contacts. The partnership worked, and worked well.

Cort considered Luke a good friend. He was smart and levelheaded, and a hell of a pilot. But he was a pain in the ass, the way he thought that he could stick his nose into Cort's personal life whenever he felt like it. Luke had never quite figured out personal boundaries. Probably a scientist thing.

"What's your obsession with getting yourself killed?" Luke asked.

"I have no intention of dying." Cort shoved a forkful of hash into his mouth, annoyed by Luke's calling him out. So he liked to push the edge. The only time Cort felt alive lately was when Death was sitting on his shoulder, thinking he was finally going to get a chance at him. Flying was in Cort's blood, but it hadn't been enough on its own lately. It took more and more to make him remember he was alive. To feel.

Except last night. With Kaylie. Cort's body was still burning from that encounter.

"No interest in dying?" Luke scoffed. "You could have fooled me."

"A two-year-old could fool you."

Luke snorted, then leveled a hard look at him. "Do me a favor."

"Depends on the favor." But they both knew Cort would. In Alaska, you took care of your own, and Luke definitely qualified. Besides, a favor owed was a boon that could save a man's life in the future. "What is it?"

Luke leaned forward. "Avoid killing any clients, at least for the next few weeks until we get delivery of the new plane, okay?"

Cort took a bite of the hash. "I'll do my best."

Luke surveyed him. "You need anything, you let me know."

Cort finally met Luke's gaze. "I'm okay."

Luke studied him a minute longer, then nodded.

Point made. Discussion closed.

The problem of Cort's restlessness was not. That issue was still dogging him, and the only reprieve Cort had gotten was currently getting dressed in his bedroom. Hell. Maybe he shouldn't kick Kaylie out. Maybe he should keep her around and use her to take the edge off.

"Sorry about Jackson," Luke finally said. "He was a good man."

"Thanks." Steeling himself against emotion, Cort briefed Luke on what had happened.

By the time he finished, their plates were empty, and Luke was looking grim. "Think it was a grizzly attack?"

"Hell, no. Since when do grizzlies slice a throat?"

Luke leaned back in his chair. "Who'd go after Jackson? And kill Sara? The girl couldn't have made a single enemy in her whole life. She was as sweet as—"

The door to Cort's room opened, and both men swung toward the entrance as Kaylie walked in. Her hair was damp, curling over her shoulders. Her jeans showed every curve of her body, and a shiny black shirt dipped low, showing acres of glistening skin. Diamonds glittered in her ears, and a red stone on a gold chain hung between her breasts.

The woman was dressed for a cocktail on a candlelit balcony, not for a hash breakfast in a rustic cabin on the edge of an airfield.

Kaylie was all female, and Cort knew exactly what she was hiding beneath those I-don't-belong-here clothes.

Cort swallowed, blood shooting for his groin like a mule deer with a cougar on its tail. Every cell in his body came alive with a hello-Mary wake-up shout, and he couldn't stop his slow smile as he recalled sinking deep inside her last night. "Morning."

Her gaze flicked to his, then slid away almost instantly. "Hi," she muttered.

He narrowed his eyes at her obvious withdrawal from him. She was clearly broadcasting she was not "available." And that message transformed her from a one-night refuge into a challenge he couldn't resist.

He had to get her back into his bed.

Luke's jaw dropped as his gaze shot back and forth between them. *"Hell."*

He shot a questioning look at Cort, but Cort ignored his friend.

Instead, he kept his gaze relentlessly on the woman trying to diss him. "Sleep okay?"

Her cheeks flushed. "Yes, fine."

Cort gestured to Luke. "This is my business partner, Luke Webber. Luke, this is Kaylie Fletcher. The client from yesterday."

Kaylie focused on Luke, making an obvious effort not to look at Cort. But he knew she was as aware of his presence as he was of hers. The appealing rosy hue across her chest and the rapid pulse in her throat was a dead giveaway.

"Nice to meet you, Luke," she said.

Luke inclined his head. "Sorry about Sara. Always liked her. A real sweetheart."

Kaylie's smile began to tremble. "Yes, she is. Was."

"Made some extra for you," Cort interrupted, gesturing toward the stove to give Kaylie a break, when he saw her eyes begin to glisten. "If you like eggs and sausage, it's all yours." He started to shove his chair back. "Take a seat."

"Thanks. I'll help myself." Still not looking at him, Kaylie walked past the men, and Cort caught a whiff of the same flowery scent he'd inhaled last night. It sent the lower half of his body into high alert, straining at his jeans.

Luke raised his eyebrows at Cort as Kaylie served herself, and Cort shrugged. "She crashed here. Storm."

"Storm?" Luke echoed, letting his skepticism show.

"Yes, the storm." Kaylie sat down at the other end of the table, her plate fully loaded. "Trust me, Cort's not my type, so there's nothing to gossip about." She glanced at Cort, and her cheeks reddened before she ducked her head and began eating.

An awkward silence fell, broken only by the roar of an approaching vehicle. "I'll check that out. Probably the state troopers, to head out to Jackson's place." Luke was on his feet and out the door, coat in his hand before the first echoes had faded.

The door shut behind him, leaving Cort and Kaylie alone.

Silence, except for the scraping of her fork on the plate. Cort clasped his hands behind his head and leaned back in his chair, content to watch her for a moment. The movement of her throat when she swallowed, the way she licked a crumb off her lip, the slope of her collarbone...

She set her fork down and looked at him. "Stop it."

He raised his brows. "Stop what?"

"Last night was a mistake."

"Yep. It was." Amen to that. Getting tangled up with a woman like Kaylie was more stupid than getting between a mountain lion and his prey.

Kaylie hesitated. "Then why are you looking at me like you want to do it again?"

"Because I do."

"No." She folded her arms over her chest, but the pulse in her neck was beating faster. "Absolutely not. It can't happen."

"Okay." He shrugged and took a swig of his coffee.

She hesitated. "Okay? Just like that?"

"Sure."

Her eyebrows knitted together. "You're not even listening to me, are you?"

Cort leaned forward suddenly, startling Kaylie into jumping back in her chair. "Listen, Kaylie. Last night was a mistake, yeah. I wasn't going down that road with you, but I did." He trailed his finger over the back of her hand, not surprised when she jerked it away. "You got under my skin, and that's not going to change. You have two choices." He gestured at the door. "You can sashay that pretty little ass of yours out the door and go back to Seattle, and we'll never see each other again."

She swallowed. "I'm not—"

"Or you stay with me and end up in my bed again. It's the way it is."

Her eyes flashed with fury and she leaned forward, into his space. "I'm not going home until I have answers about Sara and—"

"I'll find the answers." He didn't keep the lethal coldness out of his voice, and her eyes widened. "Jackson was my friend, and I take care of my own. His death *will* be addressed, as will Sara's. You don't need to stay in Alaska for that."

"I do." Her anger had subsided, replaced with a grim determination. "It isn't just Sara. My family has gone missing on Mount McKinley, and if there's any chance they're alive, I have to stay to find them. They're all I've got left, and I'm not leaving until I have answers about all of them."

He frowned. The locals now called McKinley by one of its original names, Denali, but the unforgiving nature of the mountain hadn't changed. "Your family's missing? Is that why you're here?"

She looked surprised. "Sara didn't tell you?"

"She wouldn't tell us a damn thing about you. Said it was your business."

"Oh." Kaylie's face softened. "Sara was like that."

"How long has your family been missing?"

"About ten days."

Shit. He hated this part of his life. "Listen, Kaylie, the weather's been shit up there for the last couple weeks." He softened his voice, though well aware that how he delivered the news wouldn't soften the blow. He knew it, because he'd had to give this speech too many times when a worried friend or family member had shown up to hire him for a fruitless mission. "If your family has been missing for a week on the mountain, the odds are high that it'll be a search for bodies, not living people."

"Stop." Kaylie held up a hand to silence him. "I know the facts, but there might be a chance this time. I have to know."

Her defiant tone made him pause. "What chance?"

Kaylie scooped up the last bite of hash. "I got a call two days ago. The man said my mom was still alive."

Cort waited, but she didn't add anything. So he asked, "What else did he say? Who was he?"

She swallowed her food and shrugged. "That was all. Just, 'Your mother is still alive,' and then he hung up."

Oh, hell. She was hanging her hopes on some random crank call? Son of a bitch. Cort was going to lay out the bastard who'd called her, if he ever found out who it was. "Listen to me, Kaylie. If it had been a legitimate call, he would have identified himself, given you contact info or something. Not just a random one-liner and a hang up."

"I know." Kaylie sighed, some of the light fading from her eyes. "I know it's probably just a prank. But I have to find out. Don't you get it? How could I not? Otherwise I'd always wonder if I could have saved her."

"Kaylie." Cort leaned forward, took her hand before she could pull it away, and tightened his grip when she tried to free herself. "It's a sick joke. Don't let some bastard set you up."

She yanked her hand out of his. "I have to do this. I owe my family that much."

He swore. "I—"

"Don't worry, I'm not going to burden you with my problems. Sara had already hired a guide named Dusty Baker, so I'll find him and he can fly me around."

"Dusty Baker?" That made no sense. "He has no business flying you around Denali. He's not a mountain flier. You sure that's who Sara hired?"

"Of course I am." Challenge flashed in Kaylie's eyes. "I suppose you'd be better?"

"Yeah, I would, but I'm not an expert on Denali either." Cort rubbed his jaw, aggravated that Sara would have hired Dusty, no doubt taking pity on the ancient guide who needed the job. But Old Tom was the resident legend on Denali, the logical choice. Jackson would have known that, which meant that Sara hadn't bothered to consult her husband...a thought which made Cort shake his head. He'd always liked Sara, but her heart had always been too soft for the bush.

"Well, I'm not hiring you to fly me, so it doesn't matter."

Cort's attention snapped back to Kaylie at her comment. "You shouldn't ride with Dusty. He's not sharp enough anymore."

Kaylie snorted. "You just want me to stay with you so you can get me into bed again. Well, forget it. I'm not—"

"Hey." Cort cupped her neck and pulled her close, his thumb stroking over her bare skin as she caught her breath. "I don't need to lie about other pilots to get you back into my bed." Kaylie tried to pull back, but he didn't release her, closing the distance between them until he was in her space. God, she smelled phenomenal, and he could recall with vivid clarity how her mouth felt against his. "You came here under Jackson's protection, which means you're now under mine. If I say someone's not safe for you to fly with, then you're not going with him. End of story."

"Let go of me." There was a desperation in her voice, a vulnerability in those beautiful eyes, but the way she was leaning toward him belied her request.

"No."

"Please." She grabbed at his hand and tried to pry his hand off. "I can't...Just let me go!"

Her near panic hit him, and he instantly released her.

She recoiled back in her chair, her hand clenched in a small fist over her heart. "Don't *ever* touch me again."

He was surprised by the vehemence in her voice, but equally intrigued by the way her gaze was fixated on his mouth. Slowly, he raised his palms in surrender.

"Really?" She looked startled by his capitulation.

"For now."

She closed her eyes, and when she opened them, there was a raw vulnerability on her face. "You can't tell me who to fly with, and I'm going to hire Dusty. Today." She ignored his growl. "But I'm going with you this morning, back to Sara and Jackson's cabin, with the state troopers."

He was already shaking his head. "No reason for you to go back there and see that."

"She was my best friend, Cort. I have to go."

He swore under his breath at the look on her face. He knew nothing could keep him from going out there on Jackson's behalf and realized Kaylie felt the same way. Shit. He had to honor that kind of commitment. "Fine. Be outside in five minutes or we're leaving without you."

The smile she flashed him would have melted most men.

Fortunately, he was not one of those men.

Not anymore.

Yeah, he might want Kaylie naked and writhing under him, but it was only sex. It was for the high he'd gotten from being buried inside her last night. She was the only relief he'd gotten in a hell of a long time, and he wanted more of it.

But it was only physical. Nothing else, no matter how much torment was buried in the depths of those luscious brown eyes of hers.

Kaylie jumped up and hurried toward the bedroom door. She paused on the threshold, turning back to look at him. "Don't touch me again. I can't deal with you, in addition to everything else. Promise?"

He knew how bad she was hurting. Not his style to make things worse. "Yeah—" He stopped himself, realizing she deserved the truth. He shrugged. "No. Can't promise that."

"Cort—"

"In fact, I can pretty much promise the opposite." He stood and grabbed his coat off the back of his chair. "Your choice. Take it or leave it. If you're coming with us, be outside in five minutes." He yanked his jacket on. "But if you call Dusty for a ride, I'll come after you and haul you out of that plane so fast you won't know what hit you."

Then he turned and walked out.

He didn't bother to turn around to see her reaction. The slam of his bedroom door told him all he needed to know.

As he vaulted down the steps, he couldn't suppress the feeling of anticipation at the thought of Kaylie Fletcher sticking around for a little while.

Then he saw the two state troopers talking with Luke, and Cort's anticipation vanished, replaced with the grim reality of his best friend's murder.

# CHAPTER SEVEN

Despite her rush, by the time Kaylie was dressed in mountain gear and heading outdoors, propellers were already spinning. Today's plane was a slightly bigger version of the one she and Cort had flown in yesterday. She could see the silhouettes of two men in the backseat, and Cort was already positioned behind the controls. Luke was leaning against the pilot's door, chatting with Cort. The way Luke looked at Kaylie when she walked out told her exactly what they'd been talking about.

Cort leaned forward to peer around Luke at her, and her body tightened at his intense inspection. Damn him for making her unable to forget last night! "Don't stare at me like that," she snapped as she walked up.

Luke's brows went up, and a broad grin broke out over his face. "I think I like you, Kaylie."

She couldn't help responding to his genuine smile, and some of her nervousness eased. "Thanks."

Cort leaned back in his seat and held out a hand to her. "Come on. The Staties are on a deadline."

Heat suffused Kaylie's body. "You want me to climb over you?"

He jerked his head at the passenger seat. "Only one door in this baby. Come on."

Kaylie caught a glimpse of two troopers in the plane behind Cort, and swallowed her orders for him to get out first. He was already buckled down in his harness, and forcing him to get out would have made a scene. She couldn't let him get to her. "Fine." She planted a foot on the frame of the plane and set her hand in Cort's.

His grip was solid and warm, and he hauled her expertly into the plane, sweeping her across him so efficiently, she realized he'd done it thousands of times before. She barely had a second to realize she was in his lap before she was deposited gracefully in her seat. Not a single inappropriate touch.

But the way Cort raised his eyebrows at her told her he knew she'd been expecting him to grope her.

How embarrassing. Climbing over the pilot was probably standard operating procedure, and Cort knew she'd had her mind in the gutter.

Oy. Cort hadn't needed to touch her to get her hormones into a frenzy. His earlier promise to get her in his bed again was working her over just fine.

Kaylie busied herself with her harness, using the seat belt as an excuse to avoid eye contact with Cort while he finished giving Luke instructions about handling the clients who had been on Cort's schedule for the morning.

Once Cort was finished, Luke banged his fist against the plane and stepped back. "Yeah, so, keep in touch. I'll be done with today's flights by early evening. Let me know if you need anything." He paused. "You sure you want to take this flight? We can trade—"

Kaylie jerked her head up at the concern evident Luke's voice. He didn't trust Cort to fly?

"No chance." Cort pulled the door shut on his partner, and Kaylie's stomach tightened at Luke's reluctance to step away. What did he know that she didn't?

"Um…Cort?"

"All buckled in?"

"Yes, but Luke—"

He shot her a hard look. "Don't worry about Luke."

"I'm not. I'm worried about *me*." She leaned toward Cort,

too tense to keep the agitation out of her voice. "I know you think you're invulnerable, but I'm not, and I am *not* into taking stupid risks. If you shouldn't be flying, don't you *dare* put this plane in the air!"

Cort's fingers white-knuckled around the control stick and he slowly turned his head toward her. His eyes were blazing, and he looked furious. "Please excuse the outburst, gentlemen," he said with a calm belied by the tendons that had gone rigid in his neck. "Ms. Fletcher is from the Lower 48 and not exactly in her comfort zone. Overreaction is common in outsiders like her. No need to worry."

She bristled at his dismissal of her concerns. "How dare you—"

He slapped his hand over her mouth and leaned toward her, his eyes steely. "Ms. Fletcher, taking you along on this trip is a courtesy out of respect for your friend. The invitation could and would be revoked if the pilot, in his extremely competent assessment, were to decide you are too unstable to fly and could present a risk to the other passengers or the pilot himself."

Anger fueled by a lifetime of being belittled by people willing to risk their lives for stupid things exploded inside Kaylie, and she ripped his hand off his mouth. "Don't—"

Cort's eyes narrowed, and she realized he was absolutely committed to following through on his threat. He'd leave Kaylie behind and deprive her of the chance to see Sara, just because she questioned his competence.

*Bastard.* "Just because I'm not stupid enough to get a high out of risking my neck doesn't mean my opinions aren't valid."

Cort opened his door. "You getting off?"

Kaylie snapped her lips shut and folded her arms over her chest, shooting him a venomous look. He knew damn well she couldn't walk away.

"You done, then?"

She pressed her lips together. "Yes, I'm finished. Fly." *And try not to kill us.*

Anger ripped across his face and she realized he'd caught her unspoken sentiment. He waited an extra second, then yanked his door shut. "Then we go."

She turned her head away from him and caught sight of Luke watching them from the edge of the snowy runway. He was frowning, his mouth in a grim line.

There was sudden warmth against her neck, and she whirled to find Cort leaning over her shoulder. His lips brushed against her ear. "Never, ever, question my competence in front of other passengers again," he whispered, his unyielding voice barely audible over the roar of the plane. "And never, ever, pass judgment about what's going on with me. You will always be wrong." He yanked roughly at her harness, clearly using it as an excuse to get close enough to threaten her without the two law enforcement officials realizing what he was doing.

Cort was so near she could smell the musky scent from last night. The scent that defined him. Her body tightened instantly, and she glared at him, angry that he could still bring out that reaction in her when he was such a bastard, such an embodiment of the hell she'd endured with her family for her entire life. "You're an ass," she hissed.

"But I'm a hell of a pilot." He yanked the buckle one more time, then released her.

The loss of his presence as he returned to his side of the plane was like a sudden drain of vitality from the air around her, leaving behind an empty void. A void that should have been peaceful, but felt more like a small death unto itself.

God, she was screwed.

The flight back to Sara and Jackson's place was a torturous hour and a half for Kaylie. Ninety minutes of tension, while Cort and two state troopers talked about Sara and Jackson, then moved on to local gossip. The entire time, Cort made sure she was excluded from the conversation.

His hostility was palpable, and she caught more than a couple curious looks from the state troopers, but Cort didn't give them a chance to ask any questions. His only acknowledgment of her existence was a curt introduction to Trooper Bill Mann and his partner, Trooper Rich Parker. Trooper Mann looked like he was in his fifties, with a weathered face and a salt-and-pepper beard, and sharp eyes. She sensed he was assessing every inch of her, and she knew from the way his gaze settled on her manicured nails and her diamond and ruby pendant that she had fallen short. All he gave her was a curt nod, and then he ignored her.

And she saw from the look that Bill and Cort exchanged that Cort felt the same way. It made Kaylie realize that his dismissal of her concerns about his flying because of the way she was dressed and where she was from hadn't been solely for the benefit of his other passengers. He actually believed it.

Their attitude grated on her, and a part of her itched to tell them that her baby booties had been crampons and she'd gotten her first case of frostbite when she was six months old, just to get that dismissive look off their faces, but she bit her tongue.

She knew she should be glad they saw her as nothing but a glass-slipper girl who refused to get dirty. Kaylie had worked hard to leave frostbite and crampons behind, and it was a testament to the woman she'd become that three hard-core Alaskans couldn't see it in her at all, despite her boots and parka.

Except that outdoor toughness *was* still a part of her. Even if she chose not to live that life, she hated being judged incapable of it. Yes, she was a dry cleaner's best customer now, but she was also more than that…even though she didn't want to be. But she wanted credit for it.

God, she didn't even know anymore who she was.

What Kaylie did know was that Cort's dismissal of her took all the glow out of the memories of the prior evening's lovemaking. There had been times last night when Cort had looked at her with respect, but it was gone now. Faded in the light of the morning and the grim postorgasm reality.

At least the other trooper, Rich Parker, didn't seem to be bothered by her jewelry. He was closer to her age, his face young and his eyes a little too squinty, as if he'd been fighting Alaska snow glare for too long without sunglasses, or as if he'd spent too long peering through peepholes into girls' bathrooms as a kid. Rich wasn't looking at her as if she were an intruder from the land of the civilized. He was looking at her as if he wanted to get her alone behind the gas station for ten minutes.

Which maybe wasn't much of an improvement over Cort's valuation of her.

By the time they landed, Kaylie was so happy to be out of the plane, she nearly landed directly on top of Cort when she leaped out, not realizing that he hadn't moved away from the door yet.

Cort turned and caught her just before she hit him, his hands firm on her waist. His eyes met hers, and her stomach jumped—

Then he set her down and turned away without a word.

Kaylie pressed her lips together, quelling the urge to protest. What did she care if he ignored her? It made it so much easier not to worry that one night of great sex would compel her to go down a road that would destroy her.

"This way." Cort led them across the clearing. Bill scanned the area carefully, and his partner imitated him. It was clear that Trooper Bill Mann was the leader and his partner was just the young follower.

She hurried to catch up to Bill. "Excuse me, Trooper Mann?"

His eyes were hidden behind his mirrored sunglasses. "What?" His tone wasn't friendly, and she stiffened.

"My family's climbing party went missing on Mount McKinley…uh, Denali…a few weeks ago, and I was wondering if you would be able to help me find out what happened and—"

"Sorry. Not my case." He turned away. "Hey, Cort! Don't get your civilian boots in my crime scene! Stay out of the cabin!" Still yelling orders, Bill broke into an easy jog, leaving her behind, his partner on his heels like a well-trained dog.

Seriously? What a jerk. "Thanks for your help," she called. "I really appreciate it."

Neither man responded, and they strode quickly toward the side of the clearing where Cort had paused on the steps to wait for them.

The steps of Sara and Jackson's house.

Kaylie caught sight of the small log cabin nestled on the edge of the woods, with an incredible view of a wooded valley below. And beyond that rose Mount McKinley, glistening white as if it were an angel, not a demon dressed in a white coat. Was her family dead somewhere on that mountain, or were they hanging on, struggling to survive until someone found them?

But if someone knew Kaylie's mother was alive…didn't that mean someone *had* found them?

It made no sense.

The only thing that made sense was what Cort said. That it had been a prank call.

Kaylie pressed her lips together against the sudden feeling of falling, of losing a battle she'd hadn't even known she was fighting.

"No." She forced herself to stare at the mountain. To really see it. The rocks, the ridges, the cliffs. She would not give up. There was a reason she'd gotten that call, a reason she had to come here. To reconnect with her family or bring their bodies home and make peace with her demons. She was staying until she had the answer.

The minute she and Cort returned to his house, she was calling Dusty Baker and hiring him to take her up to the mountain, no matter what Cort had to say about it.

Then she realized she didn't even know where her family had been dropped off. The mountain was too big. She had to find out where to start. But how?

"Kaylie? You coming?"

At the sound of Cort's voice, she jerked her attention off the mountain and hurried after the men.

Bill was just stomping up the steps when she reached them. "No prints in the snow," Trooper Mann noted, gesturing at the pristine snow around them. "Bad timing, with the storm. The time to find him would have been last night, before the snow came in and wiped out his trail."

Cort shot a cranky look at Kaylie, and she remembered how he'd wanted to go out after the killer and she'd kept him from doing so. A mistake, or a decision that had saved their lives? She shivered, taking a careful look at the woods surrounding them. He could be hidden there even now, watching them.

The men mounted the stairs, and Cort caught Kaylie's arm as Trooper Mann opened the door. "Wait out here."

"But—"

Cort's grip tightened, something in his eyes making goose bumps pop up on her skin. It was a haunted look, an expression she'd seen too many times on the people she'd grown up around. People who'd seen things they wished they hadn't.

"You walk into that scene in the daylight, and you'll never forget it. Trust me, you don't want to do that to yourself."

The two Staties disappeared into the house, and Kaylie lifted her chin. "Why do you care?"

"Because Jackson was my friend," Cort said quietly. "He wouldn't let you walk in there."

Her throat tightened at the pain in Cort's eyes, and also at his concern for her well-being, despite the tension between them. Despite the fact his friend had been killed last night, he was trying to protect her from the horrors of what was inside that cabin. "Thank you," she said, meaning it. "I appreciate your concern, but I owe it to Sara—"

"No, you don't. Nothing will change for her if you go in there." Cort squeezed her arm. "Just don't do it."

"Hey!" Trooper Mann's voice echoed out of the cabin "You sure this is the right place? There's nothing in here."

Kaylie and Cort exchanged startled glances, then, as one, they turned and sprinted into the cabin.

Cort couldn't believe it.

Jackson and Sara's cabin was immaculate.

No bodies. Not a single drop of blood. No sign of a struggle. Even the pillows were in place on the couch.

Two coffee cups were sitting on the counter, and dirty pots were in the sink, as if Jackson and Sara had just run out the door after breakfast.

"Oh, my God." Kaylie grabbed the waistband of Cort's jeans, her fingers digging into his side. "What happened?"

Trooper Mann walked in from the back bedroom "Jackson's favorite hunting gun is gone. Seems to me they just went off for a hunt."

Cort shook his head, still stunned by the state of the cabin. "No, they were there." He gestured to the floor. "Dead. I—"

"You sure you didn't get the cabins mixed up?" Trooper Mann asked.

"Dammit, Bill. I've been out here a thousand times. I wouldn't make a mistake like that." Cort squatted and shoved the carpet back off the floor, but the wood was clean. Not so much as a speck of dust on it, let alone bloodstains. What the hell?

Rich nudged aside the rug with his toe, but there was nothing underneath except clean wood floor.

"Then you must have been mistaken about what you saw," Trooper Mann said. "There's nothing here to see."

Cort stood up, running his hands over the wall where he'd seen the worst bloodstains. Nothing. *Nothing*. The wood was clean. "I swear—"

"There's no way to clean up that kind of mess." Trooper Mann said. "Not this fast. No one's been here since at least two this morning, given the lack of footprints."

"You didn't check out back," Cort snapped. "Check the back."

Trooper Mann narrowed his eyes, but nodded at Rich. "See if you can find any legitimate footprints outside. I don't want to hear about deer prints or moose tracks."

"Yes, sir." Rich snapped to attention and headed outside with purpose in his step.

Trooper Mann faced down Cort. "Listen, son, I know you get a little twisted around the anniversary of your parents' death, but seeing two murders…" He shook his head. "Best if you don't let that get around. Won't be good for business."

Cort's shoulders tightened at the accusation. "Dammit, Bill, I'm not crazy."

"Cort's not imagining things," Kaylie interrupted. "I saw it too. I had blood on my hands. I—"

"And you, little lady…" The trooper eyed her, and something about the way he was looking at her irritated Cort. "I don't know what little game you're playing, trying to get Cort's attention by lying for him, but we don't like outsiders coming in here and messing with us. Cort's a fine man, and he doesn't need you screwing around with him. I suggest you walk away right now."

"What?" Kaylie's eyes flashed in a show of fire Cort hadn't expected to see from her. He almost caught himself grinning at the way she was standing up to the grizzled Alaskan who had shut down many drunken brawls simply by walking into the room.

"I'm not lying for him!" Kaylie snapped at the trooper Cort had known for nearly thirty years. "Why would I? All I care about is Sara! Don't you even want to bring in experts to do some forensic something in there? I'm sure they could find evidence that—"

"Now you think you know how to do my job?" Trooper Mann's gaze hardened.

"No, but—"

Cort set his hand on Kaylie's arm, and she hesitated, looking at him. "Bill." Cort kept his voice calm, when inside he wanted to react exactly as Kaylie had. But he knew Trooper Mann too well. Accusations would only piss him off, and they couldn't afford that. "I know what I saw. Can you risk not believing me?"

The older man hesitated. "You know I respect you, but there's not a damn sign of anything in this place. If there was anything, even a set of footprints, I'd be all over it. But I can't bring out a posse when there's not a single shred of evidence, and the only witnesses are a guy everyone knows is about to fall off the edge and some woman trying to get into his pants."

Bill didn't hide his disgust for Kaylie, and she bristled. "I'm not lying, and I'm not trying to get into his—"

Cort's grip tightened on Kaylie. She snapped her mouth shut, as if understanding that pissing off the local cops would do nothing to help their cause. Angered by Bill's treatment of Kaylie, Cort had to fight to keep control of his own temper. "Bill—"

The door slammed open. "Nothing out there," Rich said, coming back inside and stomping snow off his boots. "Not a single footprint. Even from an animal. Given the amount of snow that's fallen, it looks like the place has been untouched since at least two this morning."

"Then it was swept clean." Shit. It had to have been. Someone had been there! "No way has that snow been untouched all night. There are animals all over the place out here."

"You don't think I can read snow?" Rich's upper lip wrinkled in annoyance. "Take a look yourself."

"Damned straight." Cort headed toward the door, then stopped when Trooper Mann clapped him on the shoulder.

"I'll make a deal with you, son. You find something to convince me, and I'll be all over it. In the meantime, I'll put out a call for anyone who sees Jackson and Sara to call it in. Once we hear from them, it'll all be settled."

"They're dead, and the bastard who killed them is running around laughing his ass off at us right now. You won't hear from them."

"Put yourself in my shoes, son." Bill gestured at the pristine cabin. "What choice do I have?"

"You could choose to have faith in me," Cort ground out. "If not for me, for my dad. He was your friend for over fifty years, for God's sake. You'd trust his word. Trust mine."

Bill gave him a long look. "Not with your history, son. My bosses would fire me in an hour if I launched a manhunt in this situation, and I'm too close to retirement to risk it." The older man hesitated. "I'm sorry, but I recommend you take some downtime. Get a grip on things. This is bad shit you're heading toward." He glanced at Kaylie, then leaned close to Cort, lowering his voice. "I'll be honest, son. Your dad started to crack before he crashed that plane, and I hate to see the same thing happen to you."

Cort's gut went cold. "What are you talking about? My dad was fine—"

"He wasn't, and then he killed himself and your mother."

The trooper shrugged. "Watch yourself. I'd hate to be picking my way through your remains." Bill looked at Kaylie. "And hooking up with a woman from the Lower 48 is going to put you over the edge. Be smart, son. Take some time and don't take on her problems."

Then he snapped his fingers at Rich and they walked out.

"What a bastard!"

Cort's irritation dissipated instantly at Kaylie's unladylike outburst. "Don't worry. We've got the whole flight home to convince them."

She scowled at him. "Change his mind? How?"

Cort opened the door and gestured for her to go first. "Trooper Mann's got a weak stomach when he's not the one flying the plane, and there might be some bad turbulence on the way home." He caught a whiff of her delicate, flowery scent as she moved past him, and his groin tightened. Damn. After all she'd done to piss him off, he still wanted her.

Kaylie glanced up at the utterly still trees and the bright sunlight. "Turbulence? In this perfect weather?"

Cort hesitated, wondering if he should have come clean about his intentions with her. People from the Lower 48 sometimes had different ethics than those necessary to survive in Alaska. "Yeah," he said a little cautiously. "Bad turbulence can still happen on a sunny day."

Her mouth tightened in disapproval. "You're going to do some risky flying to get him to agree to help us?"

"Yeah. I'll be under control, but Bill won't know it."

Kaylie set her hands on her hips. "You are a piece of work."

"Hey." Cort spun toward her. "Jackson is dead, and the cops don't believe me. If screwing around in the air will get them to pursue Jackson's murderer, then I'll do it all day long. You have a problem with that, you stay on the ground."

She pressed her lips together and worked her jaw. "I can't stand your attitude."

"And I'm loving yours," he snarled. "You in or not?"

Kaylie sighed, then surprised him with a nod. "For Sara, yes, because I don't have any other ideas. But I don't approve."

"Can't imagine you approve of much in this state." But Cort had to admit, he was impressed with her willingness to go along with it. Surprised. His ex-wife sure as hell wouldn't have, no matter what was at stake. Much as he might have disliked what Kaylie represented, anyone willing to go against everything they believed in for the sake of someone they cared about went up a few notches in his book.

"If you think it'll help," Kaylie said slowly, "I could scream a little bit and act like we're going to crash."

Shit. Could she be more of a contradiction? He grinned. "Hell, yeah. That'll bring Bill to his knees. You have a good scream?"

They both stared at each other, clearly remembering her vocalizations last night when they were having sex. Yeah, she had a good scream. The tension jacked up tenfold, and his gaze dropped to her mouth. She was less than a foot way. All he had to was take one step and—

"You guys coming or what?" Bill's shout broke the spell, and Kaylie's cheeks turned red.

"He'll buy it." Her voice was businesslike and a little stiff. She slipped her sunglasses over those doe brown eyes of hers and began to head toward the plane.

"Excellent." Cort studied her as he followed her down the snowy steps and across the clearing. Even in her jeans and parka, there was a seductiveness to her walk. She was all female, pure sensuality. And she was willing to cross some ethical lines, same as he was.

Luke was always riding him to play by the rules. And his ex-wife? Shit. Cort still bore the marks from her trying to destroy who he was. Hadn't had a partner in crime since his dad had died.

There was no doubt Kaylie disapproved of him, but she was still willing to step up and shake things up when it suited her. No matter what she claimed, Kaylie Fletcher was turning out to be more than jeweled shoes and diamond earrings.

Damned if Cort didn't find that incredibly hot.

# CHAPTER EIGHT

Kaylie grinned to herself as she slapped mayonnaise on the bread she'd found in Cort's cabinet. She was whipping up sandwiches while Cort waited outside for Bill to stop vomiting in the woods behind the hangar.

Her initial hesitation with his fake turbulence plan had dissipated when Trooper Mann had pulled her aside and told her that Cort was a good friend of his and he was going to look out for him. The older trooper had then ordered her to stay the hell away from Cort and not drag him down into her problems.

So when Cort had hit that first pocket of "turbulence," Kaylie had let out a good gasp of horror with only a small amount of discomfort with what she was doing and a large amount of true nervousness about Cort's strategy. But she'd watched Cort carefully the whole time. He'd been relaxed, handling the plane as if it were an extension of his own body. He'd exuded such complete competence that she'd been caught in his web of quiet assurance.

He'd been in control the whole time, and she'd known it in her core. That peace of mind had allowed her to relax. The third time Cort had dropped altitude and let loose with a stream of swear words that she'd never heard before, she'd almost started laughing. He'd been truly hilarious, a gifted actor, creating fear in his passengers just as easily as he dissipated it with his calm assurance.

She'd almost betrayed their secret when Cort had dropped the plane about a hundred feet in a split second. Trooper

Mann had let out a moan, she'd screamed, and then Cort had winked at her.

That utterly playful wink had done her in. She'd burst out laughing before she could stop herself, and Cort had had to cover for her by shouting warnings back to the officers to drown out her sputters.

She couldn't remember the last time she'd laughed, *truly* laughed, with anyone, but the moment had been so…right? Cathartic? After so much stress, after feeling so consumed by grief and loss, after feeling so powerless…For the first time in ages, Kaylie had taken control of a situation she hated. She'd stood up for herself against someone who'd belittled her, and she'd had fun doing it. Having Cort at her back had given her a strength she hadn't felt in a long time. And she hadn't been afraid at all. It had been fun, and for once, she'd done something a little risky and not been scared, or worried about dying. She'd been happy, caught up in the moment in a way she hadn't been in so long. Rainy commutes and spreadsheets had never made her feel as alive as she had in that moment with Cort.

His irreverence and confidence had been contagious.

Kaylie's smile faded as she realized how easy it would be to get sucked into Cort's devil-may-care attitude. To forget that what he did every day was so dangerous. He was exactly like her family, and it had taken complete withdrawal from them for Kaylie to survive. Even the state trooper had said Cort was cracking, pushing the edge even beyond what was acceptable for a bush pilot.

For a man like Cort, Kaylie would never be enough. Risk would be his best friend, adrenaline would be his first choice for a lover, and death would take him early. If she fell for a man like Cort, her soul would slowly shrivel up and die. Moments like today were just the start. The next one would be more dangerous, and then the next one would push it further, and it would continue to escalate until someone she cared about died. She had to remember who she was and who she had to be, in order to survive.

The front door of the cabin flew open, and Kaylie looked up as Cort walked inside. "So? Did it work?" she asked. "Are they going to search for Jackson and Sara's killer?"

"No." Cort's jaw was tight, his shoulders rigid, and there was anger vibrating off his body.

"No? Are you serious?" She set down the sandwich she'd been making as he strode past her into his bedroom and slammed the door.

A loud thud sounded from the bedroom, and then another.

Kaylie abandoned the lunch and hurried over to his room, tapping lightly before opening it. "Cort…"

He was in the corner, hammering at a punching bag strung up by a thick cord, a stream of curses accentuating each hit. His shoulders were ripped, his biceps straining at his shirt sleeves, the tendons in his neck flexing. Raw male power and fury unleashed. Cort McClaine didn't hold back.

No social mores restrained him from doing what he felt like doing. As she watched him thrash the punching bag, she envied his ability to just *be* who he was and not care about the ramifications.

He caught the bag and leaned his head against it, breathing heavily. He turned his head and looked at her, his eyes dark and turbulent. "I'm going back to search the place, and I'm not leaving until I find enough proof to force them to launch a manhunt."

Kaylie nodded, not surprised. A man like Cort would have no other response than to take over. "I'm going with you."

He scowled. "I'm going alone."

She folded her arms over her chest. "Do we really need to have this discussion again?"

He ground his jaw, and she felt him gearing up for an argument.

"I know Sara so well," Kaylie pointed out. "I'll be able to know what's out of place or missing. I'll cut the time in half, and that means the cops can start tracking him twice as fast."

"What about your family? On the mountain? Clock's ticking."

She shifted uncomfortably. "While you were out, I left a message for Dusty. When he calls, I'll have him pick me up at Jackson and Sara's."

Cort slammed his fist into the bag again, then caught it and leaned against it. "You are *not* flying Denali with him."

Kaylie lifted her chin. "Don't you dare try to keep me from finding my family."

"I'm trying to keep you *alive*."

His words startled her into silence, and Kaylie realized he meant it. Whatever the rest of his agenda was, Cort meant to keep her safe. No one ever tried to keep her safe. Everyone in her family had wanted her to take more risks and endanger her. It didn't make sense that a man of Cort's reckless lifestyle would care about keeping her safe... but God, it was the most amazing feeling to look at the hard expression in his eyes and realize he meant it.

It didn't matter that it was because of Jackson, and not because Cort cared about her.

It was still a gift, a first for her, and Kaylie realized right then that was what she wanted. A partner who wanted to keep her safe. And Cort had shown her that. It was a gift, and she didn't want to let it go. "Okay," she whispered.

He raised his brows. "Okay, what?"

She spoke more loudly. "I won't fly with Dusty. If you'll help me find someone else. Who you trust."

Cort hesitated, as if he wasn't sure how to take her unexpected acquiescence. "Yeah, okay. I'll find someone."

"Soon?"

"Yes, soon." He muttered something under his breath and knocked his forehead lightly against the bag before shoving away from it. "We leave as soon as I fix the Cessna. Pack enough to stay for a couple days. We're not coming home until we have answers."

She was already shaking her head. "I don't have a couple days. My family—"

"We'll leave from there to go after your family."

Her breath caught. "You're going to help me with them? *You're* going to fly me?"

He shot her a hooded look, his eyes searing with intensity. "I don't know yet. But for now, you're staying with me. Day *and* night."

His extra emphasis made anticipation tingle down her spine. "No sex."

Cort slung a towel around his neck and walked up to her, leaning down until his mouth was almost on hers. She stared at him, unable to force herself to back away.

He brushed a thumb over her throat. "No promises."

Then he turned and walked into the bathroom, shutting the door behind him.

Kaylie stared at the heavy wooden door, her body hot, her skin jangling at his touch and his words.

The only safe place for her was away from him.

He was simply too tempting, on so many levels. More time with Cort, and she didn't know if she'd be strong enough to resist him. But he would break her, both her heart and her soul, robbing her of the fragile existence she had created for herself. He'd strip her of everything, and this time she wouldn't recover.

Kaylie looked at the door, knew all she had to do was walk out. Call Dusty again. Leave Sara's death to Cort. It would be smart. Safe.

But no one in this godforsaken state had a personal motivation to help her the way he did. In this tight-knit community, where she was so clearly the outsider, could she really find the kind of help she needed on her own? Or was Cort's personal stake in it the only thing strong enough to get her what she needed?

She thought of Trooper Mann's reaction to her and knew she couldn't risk putting her family's well-being in the hands of a stranger.

Her family and Sara were more important than whether she managed to keep her heart intact.

Kaylie had no choice.

She was staying with Cort.

The rain was pounding on the roof.

Fuck, he was thirsty.

Mason opened his eyes, trying to ignore the throbbing in his left leg. The excruciating burn told him infection was setting in.

His captor had been back several times to drop off food and kick him in the ribs a few times. Hadn't answered any questions about Kaylie or why he was after either of them.

None of it made sense. If Mason's old boss had tracked him here, he would have shown up by now, or at least have had Mason killed. Toying with Mason wasn't part of JC's business model. Maybe it was one of JC's enemies trying to use Mason for leverage? Too bad for them that JC wouldn't do shit to bail him out. A year too late for that strategy.

Not that it really mattered right now. He had no doubt that he'd be dead as soon as his captor had no use for him.

Mason's only choice was to get the hell out of there before that happened—and before Kaylie was pulled into this mess.

It was still dark in the shed, but he could see a sliver of light under the door.

Light.

Exactly what he'd been waiting for. It was time to get that door open and see what the hell his options were.

Gritting his teeth so hard his jaw ached, Mason tossed off the rancid deer skins he'd found in the corner, all that had kept him from freezing to death.

Then he sat up.

He paused to press a hand to his side. Sweat broke out on his brow at the pain. It was getting more difficult to breathe.

His left arm almost useless from the busted shoulder, Mason used his right hand to position his left hand on the shackle. He wrapped his fingers around the steel base so he could drag it as he moved the leg, trying to take the pressure off his damaged bone. He swore at the agony, but it was doable. Holding on to the shackle took enough pressure off his leg to allow him to move.

He began to inch across the floor, using his right arm and leg to support his whole body, dragging himself and the shackle along in the dirt.

Inch by inch.

Slow progress.

Felt like hours.

Probably was.

But Mason finally reached the door. He turned the knob experimentally, expecting it to be locked, but it turned easily under his grip.

Hanging on to the door, his body shaking with exhaustion, he stared out at the woods, carefully inspecting his surroundings, taking note of every relevant detail.

Thick woods. A small cabin barely visible through the trees, probably belonging to the bastard who'd chained him up.

Nothing else.

In the middle of fucking nowhere.

Not even a stick within reach.

Swearing, he pulled himself farther along, reaching the end of the chain before he'd gotten his lower body out the door. He grabbed the chain and yanked it again, as he'd done a thousand times since his captor had left.

And like the last thousand times, it didn't give.

No sign it was even weakening.

With a groan, Mason let himself collapse, rolling onto his back, staring up at the gray sky. Rain poured down on him, cascading off the roof in a stream that was hitting right beside him.

He rolled onto his good shoulder and held out his hand, letting water fill it and sucking it greedily into his parched mouth.

Again.

And again.

All the while, he scanned his surroundings, looking for something he could use to get away. Refusing to give up. There had to be something—

Then he saw it.

It was about fifty yards away, almost hidden in the shadows of the trees. But he could see clearly enough to know instantly what it was.

A bare arm. A booted foot. Sprawled on the ground. "Hey!" Mason yelled, his voice echoing in the woods. "Can you hear me?"

But there was no response, and as Mason looked more closely, he could see flies buzzing around the person. Whoever was over there was dead. Dear God, was that his family? He forced himself to look more closely to see if he could identify someone he loved. But it was impossible to tell from the one arm and the sprawled leg peeking out from the shadows of the forest. He could tell that the boot was smaller than that of his captor, so it wasn't that bastard. Was it someone else his assailant had killed?

If so, the man hadn't even bothered to hide the body. It was just sitting there in the woods as a snack for the wild animals, for anyone to see.

Which clearly meant that the son of a bitch was dead certain that absolutely *no one* would be coming this way.

No one except Kaylie.

A cold rain was driving hard by the time Cort and Kaylie arrived at Jackson and Sara's cabin. It had taken Cort longer than he'd expected to repair the plane. After that, he'd had to make a run to deliver supplies to a group of climbers he'd dropped off three days ago, and check on two other groups while he was up there, to make sure everyone was still alive.

Luke had taken his other scheduled runs, but no one had been available for these. Skipping the flights would have risked the survival of three sets of climbers who'd trusted their lives to him, so Cort absolutely had to go.

Surprisingly, Kaylie had understood. In fact, when Cort had told her, she'd gotten a weird look on her face, as if she'd been surprised by his values or something. As if she wanted him to be a hero, or some shit like that.

Checking on his climbers had made Cort think of Kaylie's family on Denali. How had they disappeared? And who had flown them up there? The pilot was usually the one who knew the most about the climbers' intentions for the trip. Cort had called his buddy Max to check the situation on Kaylie's family, to see if he'd heard anything.

No word back yet, and the flight to the cabin had been awkward and silent. Cort had been unable to stop thinking about Jackson and Sara, his mind going down roads he didn't want it visiting, and the only thing that cleared his head was thinking about Kaylie.

About kissing her. Feeling her body beneath him. The silkiness of her skin.

Cort was taking her tonight.

He had to get back to that place that she'd taken him, or he was going to snap. He could feel himself on the edge. His blood was restless, his mind agitated and distracted, and his senses dulled—any of which was the kiss of death for a bush pilot. Cort needed to be calm and focused, and the only time he'd found that spot had been in Kaylie's arms last night.

But from the way she had her arms folded over her chest, he knew it wasn't going to be a cakewalk to convince her.

By the time he brought the plane down, it was nearly dark, which meant that searching outside the cabin for clues as to how the killer had gotten in and out to clean the place was off-limits till morning.

Which meant they were spending the night there.

Cort glanced over at Kaylie as he killed the engine. She was wearing heavy rain gear and was waterproofed all the way up to her long, dark lashes, but she still had diamonds in her ears and her coat was open at the throat, revealing that gold necklace.

Where had she gotten it? It looked like the kind of necklace a man would give to his woman.

Cort hadn't even been thinking about other men last night, but now...a dark sensation began to close down around him.

Kaylie glanced at him as she unbuckled her seat belt, and she paused, a wary look on her face. "What's wrong?"

"Nothing." Shit. The last thing he needed was to start thinking of her and other guys. She was sex, she was the anchor keeping him from going batshit crazy, but that was all she was. Even if she'd been with a thousand guys, it didn't matter. Yeah...right. "I'm going inside. Meet you in there." He was down on the slushy ground and away from plane before she responded.

Even as he slogged his way through the sloppy snow, Cort felt like an ass for ditching her in the plane like that. It was against his nature to leave clients to fend for themselves—but she was no longer a client.

She was…Hell, he wasn't sure what she was.

And it wasn't like anything was going to happen to her in the fifty feet she had to walk to the cabin.

Cort shoved open the door to the cabin and stepped inside. Shit. He couldn't leave her out there alone. He was going to go back for her.

A shadow moved on his right, and before he could react, someone burst out of the darkness at him. He hit hard, got flesh, and then something cracked him in the head. He had a split second to think of Kaylie alone in the plane, and he was out.

A powerful flashlight clutched in her hand, Kaylie had made it only a few yards from the plane with her bags when she heard the roar of a snowmobile starting up. It emerged from behind the cabin, headlights illuminating the rain-sodden snow.

The vehicle turned toward her, then stopped.

Engine idling.

Lights blinding her. As if the driver was sitting there, watching her.

The hair on the back of Kaylie's neck prickled. She shielded her eyes against the bright light, trying to see what the driver was doing. "Cort? Is that you?"

No response. Just the ominous rumbling of the engine. The vehicle facing her, waiting. For her to move? Planning his attack?

She peeked over her shoulder, but the plane was too far away for her to make it there before she was overtaken by a snowmobile.

The cabin was still dark. Where was Cort? There was no way he wouldn't have heard the snowmobile....

Jackson's slit throat leapt to her mind, and her throat clogged with fear. "Cort!"

The engine revved and the snowmobile leapt into action, shooting right at her.

She dove to the side as it swerved to miss her at the last second, and then it was gone into the woods, the roar of the engine taking longer to fade than the glow of the headlights.

Then the sound of the engine grew louder, and she saw the headlights weaving around trees as the machine made its way toward her again. She scrambled to her feet and raced toward the cabin, running faster as the snowmobile closed in.

Kaylie leapt onto the steps, yelping as her pursuer whizzed past the porch. Something touched her back and she ducked, lunging toward the open door of the dark building.

She leapt inside the door and tripped. She tumbled to the floor and hit a bookshelf. Pottery crashed to the floor and pain shot up her side. Gasping, she rolled onto her side, struggling to get back on her feet. The sound of the snowmobile grew distant. Preparing for another assault? Or leaving for good?

"Cort? Are you in here?"

No response.

Where *was* he?

Kaylie shoved herself to her knees and felt along the floor for her flashlight. A shard of something sharp pierced her palm, and she winced. Her head bumped into a table, and she felt her way to its surface. She found a lamp and turned it on, squinting as the cabin was suddenly flooded with light.

There was a moan from behind her, and she spun around to see Cort sprawled on the floor, blood streaming down his face. "Cort!" She was behind him in a second, her hands going to his neck.

*Dear God, his throat hasn't been slit.*

But as she saw the ax on the ground next to him and realized the blood was cascading from a wound on his head, she realized his assailant could easily have dispatched him, just as he'd done to Jackson.

But, thank God, he hadn't killed Cort. Instead, he'd left him alive.

Kaylie stared at his ashen face and couldn't stop wondering: Why had the killer chosen to leave Cort alive?

Consciousness hit Cort with a flash of light and mind-numbing agony in his head. *Kaylie.* He snapped his eyes open and saw her leaning over him.

Adrenaline rushed through him and he grabbed Kaylie and yanked her down to the ground. He rolled her beneath him, using his body to shield her. He tucked her head under his shoulder, and only then did he pause to scan the room for his assailant.

Empty.

No one was there.

"Cort! You're crushing me." Kaylie squirmed beneath him, but Cort didn't loosen his grip.

"Quiet," he snapped.

She went still, and he was able to hear the sound of the snowmobile in the distance, growing fainter.

Shit.

The bastard was getting away.

Cort tried to lunge to his feet, and dizziness hit him. He stumbled and went back down on top of Kaylie. With a curse, he dropped his head, fighting the ringing in his brain. He had to get up. Go after the bastard. Now.

"Cort?" Her hands were on his face, soft and warm, frantically fluttering over his skin. "Are you okay?"

He pried his eyes open and lifted his head so he could look at her. Vision was blurry, and he couldn't focus. Couldn't see her well enough to determine if she was all right. "Are you hurt? Did he touch you?"

"Me? You're the one covered in blood! I thought you were dead, and—" Her voice cracked and she broke off. Her fingers were warm and tentative on his skin, making him viscerally aware of her body beneath him. And the panic in her voice at the thought of him being dead?

Made him even harder. He caught her hand, pressed his mouth to her palm.

She stared up at him, a flush rising in her cheeks. "You're thinking of sex *now*?"

"I'm a guy, so, yeah." Not that he was going to do anything about it. Yet. He'd noticed that the sound of the snowmobile's engine was still distant, but it hadn't continued to fade. The bastard was sitting out there in the woods…doing what?

Planning to come back, Cort hoped. He would be ready.

"Let's go." He shifted Kaylie off him, then sat up. The room tilted abruptly, and he lost his balance. He pressed his hand to the side of his head and felt the thickness of the blood. Son of a bitch.

He grabbed the table and pulled himself to his knees, swaying dangerously.

Kaylie caught his arm. "No, just lie there. We need to get you medical attention."

"No." Cort pulled out of her grasp and lost his balance again. "Gun. Jackson's room. Get it. Might come back."

Her eyes widened. "Might come—"

The roar of an approaching snowmobile made her head snap up, and she stared at the open door. Cort swore and shoved her off him. "Get the door!"

She jumped up and ran over to it, slammed it shut and threw the bar across it. Cort shoved himself to his knees. Light illuminated the cabin as headlights filled the living room window. "Turn the lamp off." He grabbed the door frame and hauled himself up as Kaylie raced to follow his commands.

The snowmobile lights faded as the vehicle circled around the cabin. The roar of the engine was crushing in the night. Light flashed through the kitchen window, and Cort realized the crazy bastard was circling them. Winding the noose around their necks?

No chance of that. The son of a bitch was a dead man.

While Kaylie hit the lights, Cort staggered toward the bedroom, the roar of the snowmobile whizzing around the cabin making his head spin. Couldn't tell which way was straight. Too much noise…

Kaylie caught up to him and slipped herself under his shoulder. She wrapped an arm around his waist, silently offering herself as support. His arm snaked around her and he let himself lean on her as he struggled toward the bedroom.

The room was pitch-black, but Cort had crashed there plenty of times during Jackson's bachelor days. He went unerringly across the room to the gun rack above the bed, and he caught a shadowed glimpse of his options as the snowmobile lit up the room again.

The flash of light sent a wave of dizziness through him, and he leaned against the gun rack for balance. "Bullets are in the closet," he shouted above the roar of the engine. "Get me the ones in the white box."

The engine was louder now, and Cort knew the circles were getting tighter, that the crazy bastard was closing it on them. Toying with them. A power trip, to scare the shit out of them until he decided to hand them their fate, as he'd done with Jackson and Sara.

Fuck that.

Cort was ready.

Kaylie ran to the closet and tugged open the door as he pulled a rifle down from the wall. "There's a metal footlocker in the back right corner," he yelled.

"Got it!"

Cort moved to the window and wedged his shoulder against the wall for stability, then peered through the glass.

The engine was so loud, Cort knew the bastard had to be circling within ten feet of the house now. There was no room to get any closer. He suspected it was the last lap and the bastard was going to play his hand, whatever it was.

Kaylie came up beside Cort still smelling of roses. Roses? Here? Now? Insane. But damn, he liked it. Grounded him.

She handed him a box. "This what you wanted?"

"Perfect." He quickly loaded the rifle, then yanked her down to the floor as the headlights lit up the room again.

She crouched beside him, and he could feel her pulse hammering beneath his grip. "What's he doing?"

"Playing with us." Cort checked the rifle. "Stay low. I'm ending this now." He wiped the back of his hand across his face to clear off the blood, then stood and jacked open the window.

He pushed the barrel of the gun out the window, lined up his sights, and waited for the snowmobile to come back into view. But his vision blurred, and he realized that the muzzle of the gun had dipped. With a curse, he rubbed his hand over his eyes.

*Come on, McClaine. Focus, for hell's sake.*

The engine grew louder, and Cort leaned his head against the wall. Too damn heavy to hold up.

"Cort? Are you okay?"

"Yeah." He shook his head and summoned his focus. Headlights lit up the snow, and he slid his finger over the trigger.

Waited.

The snowmobile came into sight, the light flashed in Cort's eyes, and the world began to tip again. He felt his equilibrium going, and he tightened his grip on the gun. Waited until the light was right in front of him, and fired.

The snowmobile slowed, and Cort fired again. Couldn't even tell where he was aiming, just aimed for that white light that was making his head protest so badly. Shot twice more, and then the snowmobile kicked into high gear, turned, and sped away from the cabin, heading deep into the woods.

Getting away.

# CHAPTER NINE

Kaylie was shocked by Cort's appearance when he finally turned on the light.

His shirt was covered with blood and his face was deathly pale. It was exactly the same state as her dad on that awful day when she was twelve. His rope had given out and he'd fallen more than twenty-five feet to a rock bed below. She still remembered her absolute terror when she'd finally reached him and seen her daddy stretched out on those rocks, covered in blood, his face ashen—that moment of absolute terror until he'd moved his hand and she'd realized he was still alive.

Cort swayed as he turned, and she caught him. The feel of his heavily muscled body against hers immediately wiped out thoughts of her father. Cort wasn't her dad. He was raw, untamed testosterone, and he was far from dead.

He leaned into her, and she staggered under his weight, helping him down to the bed. He landed on her arm, trapping her against him as he eased back. Her face was up against his shoulder, the heat from his body searing her before she managed to get her arm free, leaping to her feet as soon as she could.

"I have to go after him." He tried to shove himself back to his feet, but she didn't move out of his way, blocking him.

"No chance. You can barely walk. Stay here in case he comes back."

Apparently realizing she was right, Cort punched the pillows and sank down into them, one hand pressed to the side of his head. She could see from his pinched expression that he was in extreme pain. He had to be, for him to not to argue with her. "I can't believe I missed him."

She ripped the case off one of the pillows and pressed it to his head, trying to stem the flow of blood. "You need a doctor." She threw her leg over his waist, sitting on his stomach so she could apply pressure to his head. His erection pressed hard against her, and she pretended not to notice, embarrassed that her body was tingling in response when he was lying there with an ax wound. "We'll have to call someone to come pick you up."

He leaned his head back and closed his eyes, his hands going to her hips, thumbs doing slow circles on her sides. "It's just a headache."

"A headache?"

"Yeah. I heard sex is a great remedy for headaches." His eyes slitted open. "You want to take care of this bell ringer for me?"

*Yes.* She swallowed. "I don't think sex would work for gaping head wounds."

"Want to try?"

"No."

"Heartless wench."

She couldn't help smiling. "Sorry if the sight of a man covered in blood isn't an automatic turn-on for me."

"I don't turn you on?" He opened his eyes, lifting his eyebrows skeptically. "Well, damn, you sure fake a good orgasm. I never would have guessed you weren't really getting off when I had you under me, and your heels were digging into my ass while I buried myself deep inside—"

She smacked her hand over his mouth. "Stop it."

He grinned, his whiskers prickling against the palm of her hand. "I turn you on. Admit it."

"How can you possibly be thinking about this right now?"

"Because your tight little ass is parked right on my lap, and every time you move, you're grinding it harder against me."

"Oh." Her cheeks flamed and she scrambled off him. Let him tend to his own damn wound.

His eyes were still glistening with amusement. "If you're not going to help me ditch the headache, can you at least hand over that fancy phone of yours so I can call our friendly law-enforcement officials?"

"Of course." She dropped her hand to check her pockets, and then remembered. "I dropped all my stuff outside when he came after me with the snowmobile."

*"He came after you?"* His eyes turned hard, all amusement gone, replaced by steel. "Tell me what happened. Now."

The simmering intensity of Cort's reaction as she told him was an incredible sensation. She could see his anger building, his fury that someone had tried to hurt her, his absolute determination that no one would come near her again. It was...heady. Exhilarating. Amazing.

She finished, and he closed his eyes. The muscles in his neck were so tense, she had no illusions he was asleep. "Cort?"

"I'm thinking."

"Can you think out loud?"

"Not yet. My thoughts aren't fit for female ears."

She rolled her eyes. Yes, he was still Cort. "Why don't I go get my phone—"

His hand shot out and clamped around her wrist. "You're not setting foot outside this cabin without me. For all I know, he ditched the snowmobile a half mile away and he's hiking back to catch us unaware."

"Oh." Kaylie swallowed and looked at the still-open window. "So maybe we should leave?"

"No." Cort levered himself to a sitting position, far steadier than he had been a few minutes before. "I want him to come. Easiest way to catch him. We're staying."

"Fantastic idea." Yeah, it did make sense, but seeing the blood still leaking from Cort's head made it a little difficult to drum up excitement for the idea. Kaylie shivered, realizing the window was still open from when he had been shooting out of it.

She walked over to the window and slammed it shut. No locks. Of course. Who needed locks in rural Alaska? She shaded her eyes and peered out through the glass, but it was too dark to see anything. Though it wasn't too dark for someone to see inside easily. Oy. She rubbed her arms and faced Cort.

"So, what do we do now?"

"Same plan as before. Search the place. Just make it fast and be alert to any sounds." He swung his feet to the floor. "I'm going to go clean up. Find some aspirin." He sat up and took off his bloody parka. The T-shirt beneath was stained with blood around the neck and down the front. "You know how to fire a gun?"

She shook her head, unable to tear her gaze away as he ripped off his shirt, revealing a well-toned body and a ripped stomach. He was lean and fit, a body that was strong because of his lifestyle, not because he spent a couple hours a day in a gym and from taking over-the-counter supplements.

There were several scars on his chest, and the dried blood on his neck seemed to fit him perfectly. With the rifle in his hand and his jeans slung low around his waist, he was wild and untamed all the way down to his core.

And he had an erection straining at the front of his jeans.

Heat flamed her cheeks, and she jerked her gaze to his.

"Bed's comfortable." His voice was low. Heavy with suggestion.

She glared at him, her clothes suddenly itchy against her skin. "Sex would be a mistake."

He shrugged. "Mistakes happen." He strode into the bathroom, wobbling only the slightest bit. "Start searching, and keep alert. If you get out of my sight, I'll be coming after you. So don't expect privacy from me. Not here. Not now."

He turned on the shower and went for the waistband of his jeans.

She hesitated, heat pooling between her legs as she watched him unzip his pants. "Do you need help?"

He paused, jeans halfway down his hips, raising his eyebrows at her. "Getting my pants off, or with the shower?"

"With your head."

His eyebrows went up higher, and she flushed. "With the ax wound that nearly crushed your skull. You need help cleaning it or stitching it or anything?"

He turned his head and peered at himself in the mirror, inspecting the damage. "Been hit worse. I'm fine."

Then he dropped his pants.

Kaylie felt like she was standing on the tracks in front of an oncoming train, but she still couldn't make herself turn away as Cort bared all. She'd never really gotten a good look when they'd made love the other night, but now…God, he was huge. Hard. Ready. The hair on his belly was dark and curly, diving right down to the thick patch surrounding his—

"Going to write a report on it?"

She jerked her gaze away, horrified to find him watching her, an amused smile on his face. "Don't you have any sense of modesty?"

"Nope." He strode deliberately across the floor toward her.

Her heart began to race, and her nipples tightened. Some faint voice in her head was screaming at her to run, to hide, but she couldn't take a step. All she could do was watch him approach.

He reached her, stopping only when his body was mere inches from hers. One deep breath would put her breasts against his naked chest, one twitch would put his penis against her belly.

He bent forward, his breath teasing over her lips. His hands hovered over her hips. Not touching anywhere, but so close everywhere. "Shower's built for two."

"No," she whispered. "I can't."

He raised his eyebrows. "I can attest that you actually can. Quite well, in fact."

"Stop!" She slammed her hand into his chest, and he didn't move. Didn't even flinch. "I can't."

"Why not?"

"Because—" She cut herself off. How did she admit to this man that sex with him would be more than just sex to her? Already, she was finding herself getting sucked into his powerful persona. Becoming intimate with him at this stage…It would be like seeing an avalanche crashing down the mountain and racing right into its path on purpose.

Stupid beyond belief.

Suicidal.

"Because…?" He still looked amused, not at all concerned about her rejection.

Probably because he could see her nipples puckered through her shirt and knew that she was too close to giving up the fight and letting her hands drift over that washboard stomach—

God! What was she thinking? With Sara dead, her family missing, a madman on a snowmobile after her? Had she lost her mind? Was she too weak to keep herself from being sucked into Cort's reckless embrace of life regardless of the consequences or costs?

She pulled back, tried to find her way back to the person

she wanted to be. "Because we're standing here in the bedroom of our best friends, who were just murdered. It's horrible to even be thinking about sex right now."

"Hey!" He grabbed her upper arms and yanked her close, scowling down at her. "I know Jackson's dead. I fucking know that. I feel it in every single cell of my body every second of the damn day."

"Cort—" She tried to pull away, but his fingers dug into her arms so hard she knew they would leave marks.

"But *I'm* not dead. I'm fucking *alive*." His eyes glittered with anger, with pain so deep and so entrenched, she felt her own heart break. "I'll find the bastard who killed him and Sara, and I'll take him down, but I owe it to Jackson and to everyone else I care about who died too early to keep on living the life they didn't get a chance to live. It's an insult to all of them if I don't." He shook her once—not hard, but his biceps were flexed tight, trembling with the effort of maintaining rigid control. "So never, *ever*, even suggest to me that my refusal to die along with him is immoral or insensitive or any of that crap. Do you understand?"

Wordlessly, she nodded, having no response to the intensity of his response, to the brutal grief he'd shown her.

He released her sharply, then turned and walked back into the bathroom without even a backward look.

She didn't move until after he was in the shower, its steam rising into the air, still stunned by his words. By his truth. After a long minute, she walked into the bathroom and tapped her knuckles lightly against the glass.

The door opened, and she raised her gaze to Cort's. Water was streaming down his face, matting his dark hair to his forehead. "What?" he snapped.

"I'm sorry. I didn't understand. I—I judged you, and I was wrong. I'm sorry."

He studied her for a minute, as if trying to decide whether she meant it. Then he gave a curt nod. "Thanks."

Cort started to close it, and she caught the door. "My parents are adrenaline junkies, like you."

"I don't ca—"

"When I was eleven, we were on a climb. On the final day of the ascent, I broke my leg. My parents had never summited that peak, and it was the last day to try to make it."

He stopped trying to close the door, his light brown eyes on hers.

"They didn't want to miss their chance, so they handed me off to a party on their way down. I still remember staring at them in shock when they took off, hurrying to make up the time my injury had lost them." What an awful feeling that had been, watching them leave her behind with her leg throbbing and five strangers standing around her. "The people took me back down to our base camp and then continued on their way. I waited alone in that tent with a broken leg for seventeen hours before my parents came back."

His eyebrows shot up. "You were only *eleven?*"

Kaylie nodded, not wanting to revisit that time. "For my parents, getting their fix was more important than anything else, including a scared, injured girl. I judged you wrongly, assuming that you wanting sex meant that you were like my parents, that you were more concerned about your next high than the people in your life."

He said nothing, but his attention was fixed on her.

"So, yeah, I just wanted to tell you that. To explain why I reacted the way I did and to apologize for assuming you had the same values as my parents." She managed a small smile, unsettled by the intense way he was watching her. "So, yeah, I'll go search Sara's stuff. Just wanted you to know. I had no right to judge you about Jackson."

Not waiting for a reply, she ducked out of the bathroom, but she felt his eyes on her back as she hurried out of the bedroom to the family room.

Her parents had been ruthless in their pursuit of their next adrenaline high, and she'd thought that was what Cort was doing. She'd thought that was what *she* was doing by thinking about him and sex in this situation.

But there had been naked, raw anguish in Cort's eyes, in the rigid lines of his body. She'd felt the intensity of his words, the depth of his beliefs. And it had made sense. In a land where there was too much death, so much wildness, and not enough sun...you survived or you died.

Cort was a survivor.

How could she blame him for that?

If she was honest with herself, she wanted to live, too. Not just breathe, but to wake up in the morning and feel life rushing through her body like sunshine. She hadn't found that on the mountains with her family, and she hadn't found that in Seattle. But she'd been content in the Pacific Northwest, able to embrace her careful life. Being with Cort was changing things. Making her want more. But there was no way to have it all, and she had to remember that.

This life, this wasn't what she wanted. Seattle was safe and secure, and that was worth everything to her.

Kaylie let out a breath as she turned the light on in the family room again, illuminating the floor where the bodies had been. With the dishes on the sink and Sara's paintings all over the walls, the silence was eerie. Sara should be here. Laughing. God, Sara had had the most contagious laugh.

All it used to take was the sound of it to make Kaylie start laughing as well. That was half the reason Kaylie had been excited to see Sara. She missed laughing.

And now...she felt that it would be wrong to laugh again.

But after Cort's speech, she just didn't know anymore. All the rules and beliefs she'd lived her life by...Cort was stripping them away, leaving her with what? Nothing?

Kaylie didn't want to be like her family. Or like Cort. But Cort was different from her family. And also the same.

God, she didn't know anything anymore. Kaylie shook her head as she headed toward a closed door on the other side of the living room, figuring that it was Sara's sewing room. All she wanted was a nice, quiet, safe life, and here she was: in Alaska, surrounded by death, chased by a murderer, and wildly attracted to a man who was the antithesis of everything she needed in a man and in her life.

Yeah, she was managing her life exactly how she wanted it. What a talent she was.

Rolling her eyes at herself, Kaylie lifted the wrought-iron latch of the sewing room door and entered the room.

What she saw brought tears to her eyes.

On a mannequin in the middle of the space was an iridescent turquoise-aquamarine dress. The one she and Sara had designed while stuck at base camp when they were fourteen. They'd both been so miserable, they'd decided to design the most impractical dress they could imagine, one that was the antithesis of the boots, jeans, thermal underwear, and parkas that made up their wardrobes.

Sara had pocketed the design and said she'd make it someday.

And she had.

Kaylie's throat clogged as she walked into the sewing room and approached the mannequin. She brushed her fingers over the fabric, so thin that it almost disintegrated under her touch. The material had been sliced into microthin strips, and she waved her hand through them, watching them float across her skin. Gossamer thin and fragile, the strands tickled her hand, spreading apart to reveal her palm beneath it. If she were wearing the dress, even the slightest breath or movement would have exposed all her skin for the world to see.

It was what an angel would wear.

It was the most beautiful thing Kaylie had ever seen, and it was exactly as she'd imagined it.

The dress had begun as a teenage vision drawn in the glow of a flashlight, with the wind whipping around. Sara had made it into reality, even down to the blown-glass beads around the neck. Blown-glass beads on a dress. Was there anything more impractical than that?

Kaylie realized suddenly that the mannequin was the same height as she was. Sara was six inches shorter.

Sara had made the dress for Kaylie.

After more than a decade, she'd finally made it.

And died before she could give it to her.

Tears stung Kaylie's eyes and she fisted a bunch of the material. "I love you, Sara. I always will." She lifted the skirt and let it sparkle in the light. Tears blurred her vision. "I don't know whether to laugh with you and wear this dress, or to curl up in the corner and cry until I can't move anymore."

There was no answer in the empty room.

Her only company was a dress that was the manifestation of Kaylie's teenage dreams. Despite all her efforts, her life wasn't like that dress, even before she'd come to Alaska. The gown was light, delicate, free, drifting in the slightest wind. Carefree in a way she never would be.

The dress wasn't her.

Or she hadn't become the dress.

Either way, it wasn't a fit. It was a dream that had failed.

Kaylie turned away, dropping her hand from the dress, to inspect the room. It was filled with bolts of incredibly beautiful material. A rack of five in-progress dresses hung in the corner. Kaylie knew each dress sold for more than five thousand dollars.

Sara's passion and her joy.

Left unfinished.

A loud bang sounded against the side of the cabin, and

Kaylie jumped, spinning toward the wall. She waited, heart racing like crazy, but no other sound followed.

It could have been nothing.

Or it could have been a murderer.

She glanced at the large picture window. She could see nothing but blackness outside. There was no shade to lower. Someone could be outside. Watching. And she would never know it.

There was a clank again, and then the shower shut off. Was that the sound she'd heard? Water going through the pipes? She didn't know. "Cort?"

"Yeah." His deep voice rang out in the small cabin, and some of her tension eased.

"You hear anything?"

Silence. "No, but I'll go outside and look around in a second."

Kaylie bit her lip and debated going back into the bedroom until he could accompany her into Sara's office, and then she felt ashamed of her fear. Her entire life had been rooted in fear, and where had it gotten her? She hadn't become a match for that dress, and everyone she cared about had died anyway. The least she could do for Sara was find the courage to search her sewing room.

Kaylie squared her shoulders and walked farther into the room, forcing herself to concentrate on inspecting the area, glancing only occasionally at the window to make sure no one was peering in.

This was Sara's room, and Kaylie would know if something wasn't right. This room was her job.

Expensive bolts of material were piled in an order only Sara ever understood. Three sewing machines were lined up on a table by the window. The antique apothecary's cabinet she used to hold all the different trimmings was on the south wall, carefully polished and well loved.

An empty frame was lying on its side on the top of the

apothecary's cabinet. It was the frame Kaylie had given Sara when Sara had moved to Alaska. It had contained a photo of the two of them from their last dinner together before Sara had moved.

But there was no photo in it anymore, and its back was removed, as if someone had yanked out the picture and tossed the frame aside. Frowning, Kaylie picked it up, a prickle of unease rippling through her.

Why would anyone want a picture of Sara?

Or had Sara simply put the photo into one of her albums instead? This room was Sara's sanctuary, so her photo albums had to be here.

Kaylie paced the length of the room, scanning for the albums, and when she found them, she almost wished she hadn't.

They were in the corner by the closet. On the floor. Pictures everywhere, as if someone had been in the middle of going through them and had been interrupted. Sara was obsessive about order in her sewing room. Never would she have left pictures behind in that kind of disarray.

Her skin getting colder, Kaylie eased over to the mess and crouched next to the pile of photos, her neck prickling with the certainty that the man Cort had disturbed was the one who'd been going through them. She began flipping pictures over to see if she could determine what was missing.

Pictures were cut up, remnants left behind. So many pictures of Sara, the other half cut off.

Kaylie picked up a photo, remembering the day it had been taken at the beach. She'd been in the picture, too, but her image had been cut off, leaving behind only Sara.

She selected another photo. Christmas eight years ago, when they'd dressed as elves for a party. Again, her picture was gone and only Sara's remained.

Kaylie looked down and realized that photos of Sara were

strewn across the floor, all of them once pictures of Sara and Kaylie. And Kaylie had been cut out.

But there weren't any pictures of Kaylie to be seen.

Not a single one.

It wasn't the pictures of Sara he'd been after.

He'd been looking for Kaylie.

# CHAPTER TEN

Cort leaned heavily on the bathroom counter, scowling at his bandaged head.

Shit, he was lucky.

The ax had glanced off the side of his head instead of scoring a clean hit. A solid blow could have taken his head right off. But why hadn't the bastard stayed to finish the job, as he'd done with Jackson?

Cort would be sure to ask him before he made the monster pay for Jackson's and Sara's deaths.

For now, the wound was under control. Cort had used the butterfly bandages Jackson kept in the fully stocked medical kit in the bathroom. It had taken him ten minutes to find the damned thing, but every backwoods Alaskan with half a brain knew how to patch himself up, and he'd finally found it behind a stack of pink towels in Sara's half of the cabinet.

Cort probed the bandage, which was already stained with blood. He figured it would bleed for several hours. It had been a hell of a blow…and he hadn't even seen it coming. How could he not have sensed the man lying in wait?

But he knew why. He'd been so distracted by Kaylie, he'd totally missed any clues that the bastard had been in the cabin. Jesus. What if he'd had Kaylie with him? What if she'd been the one to take the ax to the head?

Cort gripped the counter, his muscles going rigid at the thought of that bastard getting his hands on Kaylie. He recalled his absolute terror for her when he'd gone down from that blow and realized she was still outside. Alone. Vulnerable.

*Jesus.*

"Cort!"

He jerked his head up at the tension in her voice. "Kaylie!" He grabbed the rifle and charged across the cabin, his senses on hyperalert. He sprinted into Sara's room with the rifle up, skidded to a halt just inside the door, and scanned the room.

No bad guys.

Just Kaylie kneeling on the floor in the corner, looking at something.

*She's okay.* Cort's body shuddered as a tremor of relief went through him. "Anyone else in here?"

"No. Look."

It took him almost a full minute to peel his finger off the trigger and lower the rifle. Shit. She'd scared the hell out of him. He didn't want to think too much into that. "You find something?"

She looked up at him, and his adrenaline kicked right back on. Her eyes were wide and scared, her face pale.

He swore under his breath, his fingers tightening on the gun as he strode across the room toward her. "What's wrong?"

"This." She gestured at the mess of photos on the floor in front of her. "He's hunting me."

He crouched beside her and set his hand on her back. Needing to touch her. To feel the heat of her skin, to know she was really okay.

Kaylie leaned into him, and he wrapped his arm around her waist. He pulled her to him and twisted his hand in her hair. His tension eased, as it always seemed to when he was touching her. Kaylie calmed his demons. Somehow, some-way, she was his relief. He squeezed her shoulders once.

"You're okay. I've got you covered." The fragile smile she gave him twisted his gut, and he forced himself to drop his arm. "What's going on?"

She handed him a picture. "This is a photo of Sara and me together, but my face has been cut out. Same with this one, and this one, and this one." She kept piling photos in his hand. "He took the pictures of me, not the ones of Sara."

"Jesus." Cort stared at the photos, a dark anger exploding inside him. The bastard had targeted *Kaylie*? Sara's shredded body flashed across Cort's mind, and he instinctively looked around the room, taking a couple steps to the right to position himself between Kaylie and the window.

"You think he's after me because I was at the cabin with Sara and Jackson…when we found them?" Her face was pale, worried. "Is that why?"

Cort swore and ran his hand through his hair, trying to pull his shit together. To focus. To be logical. "How do you know Sara didn't cut the photos up? Like, to make you a collage or something?"

"Because a collage would have had both of us. Not just me. Plus, she'd have used scrapbooking scissors with scallops or something." Her voice was certain, expressing absolute conviction, and his blood ran cold as she stood up and grabbed an eight-by-ten frame. "This picture's missing, too. It was of me and Sara."

Cort rose to his feet, fighting off the urge to toss Kaylie over his shoulder, throw her in his plane, and get her the hell out of there. Instead, he called upon years of flying experience to keep his head and stay focused so he could assess the facts. "Listen, we don't have any way of knowing what's going on with these photos. Let's search the rest of the place and see if we can find the photos of you. It makes no sense that'd he would take twenty pictures of you. One, yeah, if he wanted to be able to find you. But twenty?" Cort shook his head. "There has to be something else going on."

Kaylie still looked worried, and he was unable to keep himself from squeezing her shoulder. "We'll figure it out, Kaylie. I'm ready for him now. Jackson was caught unprepared, and so was I. No longer." He held up the rifle. "According to everyone who knows me, I'm a badass on the edge, apparently. Nothing to fear."

She cocked her head at him, a small frown puckering between her eyebrows. "Is it true? That stuff Trooper Mann was saying? That you're...trying to get yourself killed?"

Cort's amusement faded. "He didn't say that."

"It's what he meant." She fixed her gaze on him as he wandered around the room, searching for the pictures. "I know people like that. It's...a bad way to live."

"Don't judge me based on anyone else." After that little story she'd shared in the bathroom, he had a suspicion the people she was referring to were her family. He got it, yeah, but it still pissed him off to be deemed a suicidal jackass. Trooper Mann calling him on it was one thing, but with Kaylie, it annoyed him more. Felt more personal. Like she'd shoved a hot poker right into his kidney and was grinding it deep.

Just as his ex-wife had done. Repeatedly.

Yeah, maybe Kaylie had a better reason to judge him than Valerie had, but it didn't change the fact both women were cut from the same mold.

He shoved a stack of glittery material out of the way so he could see into the corner. "You think it's acceptable to cross the street only when you have the light? Is that your deal?"

"What's wrong with being safe?"

"It's not about being safe." He paused, noting that a pile of fabric in the corner was messed up and wrinkled. He knew that material cost more than his truck, and that Sara had protected it like a mama bear protected her babies. He knew it firsthand because he'd once made the mistake of sitting on a pile of it while waiting for Jackson to get back from a hunt.

"Living in fear is like going through life as a dead person."

"You don't have to risk your life to feel alive!"

He edged the material aside. "You don't even know what it's like to feel alive, do you? You've never truly felt your heart explode and your brain hum with such energy you feel like you'll never sleep again, have you?"

"I…" Kaylie stopped her protest and fell silent. "I don't need that," she finally said quietly. "That high is overrated."

There was a catch in her voice that made him look over at her. "You so sure about that?"

She lifted her chin. "I am." Her voice was stronger now, more certain. Had he imagined her hesitation?

"As you say." He resumed his search and moved aside the last pile of wrinkled material. What he saw made his entire body go rigid. "Oh, shit."

Kaylie went still behind him. "What did you find?"

"The missing picture." Cort closed his fist around the rifle, his fury rising so hard and fast he felt as if his entire body were on fire. He stared at the soiled photo of Kaylie.

It was covered in semen. A raw, in-your-face statement by the bastard that he could leave his DNA behind and they still wouldn't catch him.

Cort swore again, and knew he was stuck with Kaylie now.

Until that psychotic pervert was caught, she wasn't leaving his sight. Cort wasn't leaving her alone to be caught by this fucker.

No matter how badly it burned him.

Kaylie squeezed up beside Cort, leaning around his arm to peer over the stack of materials at the photo. It had been torn, and Sara's half was gone. But Kaylie's photo was there and it was covered in—

Her stomach turned. "He masturbated on my picture?"

Cort's hand went to her lower back. "Looks like it."

Bile rose in the back of Kaylie's throat and she closed her eyes. "Oh, God. I—"

"Hey." Cort took her shoulders and turned her toward him, away from the photo. "Listen to me."

She opened her eyes, staring into Cort's hard face as her hands instinctively went to his wrists, holding tight. "What?" Her voice was scratchy, terrified. Dear God. What kind of man was this? And why had he targeted her?

"I'm not going to let him get to you." His fingers were digging in now, and it felt good. "I *will* keep you safe, and we'll find this bastard before he hurts anyone else."

Kaylie nodded numbly, grasping desperately at the fierceness in Cort's expression. He looked wild and angry, a predator who would hunt and destroy at will. She wasn't alone out here. For the first time in a very long time, she wasn't alone. "Okay. Yeah, okay."

He squeezed her shoulders, then his hands slid down her arms, his grip softening. "You all right?"

"Yeah." She realized how weak her voice sounded, so she cleared her throat and tried again. "Thanks. For being here. For me."

Cort nodded, then dropped his hands. "Don't touch the photo. I'm calling Trooper Mann. He needs to see that." He leaned over to look at it again, then released a low whistle. "Would you recognize Sara's jewelry? Because if that's not hers, then it looks like our friend left behind something else we can use to track him."

Kaylie moved up beside him, her shoulder brushing against his arm as she peered again at the display. His arm settled around her shoulder in an instinctive gesture, and she didn't pull away. Instead, she leaned against him. Her gaze strayed toward the photo again.

"Don't look at the picture." Cort's voice was firm, but gentle. "The ring's on the windowsill behind it, as if he took it off before he got started."

Concentrating on the reassuring warmth of his touch, Kaylie followed his directions and saw a simple metal ring on the windowsill. "No, that's not Sara's—" Her breath caught. "Oh, my God. It looks like—" No. She had to be wrong. There was no way. Her hand shaking, she reached for it.

Cort caught her wrist. "No, don't touch it. We've already screwed up enough by touching all the photos."

"I need to see it." Her throat was scratchy, her mouth dry. "I have to. I think…" She looked around, found a scrap of white silk, and carefully picked up the ring. She turned it so she could read the inside of the band.

ALICE & KIX. THIN AIR FOREVER.

Her hand started to close around it, and Cort slipped it out of her grasp. "What is it?"

"My mother's wedding ring." Kaylie stared at it as Cort set it back. "She broke her ring finger twelve years ago, and she can't get it off anymore. She always wears it. *Always*."

Cort said nothing, but she saw from the look in his eyes what he was thinking. That her mom wasn't wearing it now, so someone got it off…."That call you got about your mom still being alive. Was it a man?"

Kaylie nodded, realization dawning as she recalled Sara's message. "Sara said something about my mom on that message she left me. About a man and my mom, and—Oh, God." She stared at Cort. "This wasn't ever about Jackson and Sara, was it? It's about my family. My mom. And Sara got caught in the middle." She felt sick. Sara and Jackson had died because of her family?

Cort caught her arm and she looked up at him. His face was grim. "It may have started being about your mother, but now it appears that it's about *you*."

\* \* \*

Kaylie sat up in Jackson and Sara's bed. She hugged her knees to her chest and continued to stare at the picture windows that took up two entire sides of the bedroom. She was sure the view was incredible during the day.

At night, they were invitations for a madman to spy on her.

Or line up his gun and take a shot.

Cort had cut off the search as soon as they'd left a message for Trooper Mann about the photo. They were both exhausted, and it was past midnight. Cort was right, of course, and she knew he'd called it a day because of her strain, not his. She was too drained to focus, to cope with what they'd learned, but she'd been completely unable to sleep.

The man had killed Jackson and Sara. Attacked Cort with an ax. Masturbated on a picture of her. Done God knows what to her mother. And he was out there, somewhere, and he knew they were in the cabin. What was he waiting for? When would he be back? And what would he do to Kaylie when he returned?

An ax, like Cort?

A knife, like Sara and Jackson?

Or would he play out his sexual fantasies on her?

"Okay. That's it." There was no way she could sleep.

Kaylie kicked back the covers and padded across the bare wood floor, slipping through the open door to the living room. It was so dark she couldn't see more than a shadowy outline of the furniture.

There was no sound.

Not even Cort's breathing.

Was he still here? Had her stalker slipped inside and taken him out silently?

A hand touched the back of her neck, and she screamed, whirling around as she lunged out of his reach.

"Hey! It's me."

The familiar cadence of Cort's deep voice penetrated her panic, and she spun toward him. "You!" She slammed her fist into his chest. "Don't scare me like that!"

Cort caught her fist in his hand and squeezed lightly, immobilizing her with hardly any effort. Making her too aware of how vulnerable she was. "Tonight's not the night to sneak around in here," he said, his voice rough, as she heard the thud of him setting down something heavy. "You need something, you speak up. Tell me you're coming. Got it?"

"Yes. Sorry." Kaylie bristled at his annoyed tone, but it also reassured her. No one would be catching Cort unaware tonight, and that was such a solid feeling. She hugged herself as she strained to see his face, but it was too dark. All she could detect was the outline of his shoulders towering over her. "I just…um…You mind if I camp out on the chair out here while you sleep?"

There was silence for a minute, long enough that she started to shift uncomfortably.

"Why?" His voice had gone deep and husky, and her body kicked into hyperawareness of how near he was, of their total isolation in the woods.

They could do anything they wanted out here.

No one would know.

It was so far away from reality.

"Kaylie. Why do you want to sleep out here?" His voice had gone deep, sensuous, his thumb tracing seductive circles on her fist, still imprisoned in his hand.

"Because…" She swallowed, trying not to remember that his sexual interest wasn't about *her*. It was simply sex. A testosterone-overloaded wild male who was alone with a woman he'd pounded into bliss twenty-four hours ago. What male wouldn't be thinking about it? But in the morning, she would still be who she was, and he would still be who he was, and there would be no common ground.

But her heart would be tangled up in his a little bit more.

"I want to stay in here because the windows are too big in there. I'll just sit in the chair. I won't bother you or anything."

"If we're going to be sleeping together, we might as well be comfortable." He turned and walked into the bedroom. She heard the creak of bed springs and the sound of him tossing back the covers.

"We aren't sleeping together," she called out.

He didn't answer.

Kaylie bit her lip. "I'm not having sex with you."

He still didn't answer.

"Are you listening?"

"Nope."

To her surprise, a smile burst out of her at his unapologetic reply. So arrogant. So entirely committed to who he was. She doubted he'd ever apologized for anything in his life, whereas she spent her life feeling guilty about abandoning her family, struggling with who she was, trying to silence the demons stalking her every time she closed her eyes or saw a mountain in the distance.

She slowly walked into the bedroom, barely able to make out the lump in the bed. Her whole life, she'd hated all the adrenaline junkies who had been a part of her world. She'd despised them and dismissed them. Even after all these years, she couldn't understand them, and she resented how easy it was for them to hurt her.

But Cort…He was more than that. Sure, he would break her heart and he would die young, but there was more depth to him that that. It wasn't enough to change him from being her worst nightmare, but enough to make her wish, a tiny little bit, that she could be like him. Be sucked into his world. To relive again and again that joyous fun they'd had in the plane when he was flying like a madman to scare Trooper Mann, when the wind was whipping past the plane and she was playing just the tiniest bit outside the rules.

To simply live her life and not care. Not worry. Just *be*.

Cort made her realize, just a little bit, the appeal of living life that way, because Cort, more than anyone she knew, was *alive*.

And when they'd made love, Cort had made her feel alive, too. Despite the grief, her fear, her years of knowing how to be alone, he'd helped her connect to another human and brought her soul to life. For that brief moment, she hadn't been afraid, she hadn't been fighting memories and fears, she'd simply been in the moment. And an amazing moment it had been.

Did Cort feel like that all the time? Because if he did…For the first time, she understood the allure of that lifestyle.

Climbing mountains had never given her that high, but sex with him and being sucked into the vortex of energy that emanated from him…That had definitely taken her to new levels of exhilaration.

And it was too addicting.

Kaylie couldn't afford to go down that path again. But as she readied herself to climb into bed with him, she wished she could forget about real life just for one more night in his arms.

Grabbing the corner of the quilt, Kaylie slipped beneath the covers. Her foot brushed his bare leg, and awareness shot up her calf. If she were like Cort, she would jump him right now and not care about the ramifications. She'd be able to have sex tonight and walk away in the morning without a thought, other than to wonder where her next adrenaline high was coming from.

Because Kaylie wanted Cort to make love to her so much, if there was any way to let go of her fears, she would climb right on top of him and start kissing. To feel his arms around her, his mouth hot on hers, the sweat on his chest as he pounded her into oblivion…

Her nipples tightened, and she felt her cheeks burn. She

was suddenly grateful for the darkness that made it impossible for him to see her face as she tugged the covers up.

Cort shifted, and his arm went around her, pulling her up close.

She stiffened. She wasn't Cort. Unlike him, she would break. "Let go of me," she whispered.

"No." He nuzzled her hair, and tingles went down her spine. "You smell so damn good."

His lips trailed over her neck and she closed her eyes, fisting the sheets as she fought not to throw her arms around his neck and pull him close. Why was he such a temptation? Why did she want him so badly? Was she the one with a death wish, not him?

Because getting involved with him would surely kill her.

His hand slid beneath the hem of her silk camisole and spanned her belly, and her resistance began to slip away. His touch was warm. Gentle. Caressing. Touching her the way she'd yearned to be touched.

In the darkness, he could be anyone.

Cort kissed her throat.

In the darkness, he could be a banker.

His lips brushed over her eyelid.

In the darkness, he could be an accountant.

He bent his head and caught her mouth in the softest kiss she'd ever experienced. His lips were slow and precise, his tongue a delicate tease as it slipped between her lips, eliciting the most delicious spirals of desire curling through her body.

It wasn't the kiss of an adrenaline junkie out for a night of hot sex. It was the kiss of a lover, a man who was prepared to spend the next six hours worshipping her body in a slow, delicious, passionate night of loving.

His hand slipped around to her bottom and caressed her through her silk boxers. His hand moving in tantalizing circles across her rear, he dropped his head, his tongue teasing over her chest, moving lower toward the edge of her lace camisole. Her pulse began to pound, and she tipped her head back, anticipation building in her as his hand moved to the back of her thigh, cupping her leg, his fingers so close to the part of her body screaming for him—

He stopped abruptly.

She opened her eyes, felt his gaze on her. Burning her up. "Cort?"

He lifted her ruby necklace, and she realized he'd encountered it when he was kissing her chest.

"This has to come off." He touched her earrings. "And these."

She frowned. "Why?"

"Because I don't like them." His voice was hard.

"But I do." She couldn't remove them. The jewelry was the essence of who she had worked so hard to become. The jewelry, the silk lingerie—she didn't want to be anyone else. She *couldn't* be someone else. Couldn't even open that door. "They stay on."

Cort stared at her for another second, then fisted her hair and kissed her again.

But this time it wasn't gentle. It wasn't tender. It was a domination, a kiss meant to strip her of all thought, all sanity, a kiss that took control and allowed no room for anything but what he wanted.

Kaylie fought it—she did. She struggled not to respond to him, but it was impossible. She needed that intensity, that passion, that fire. It reached into her core and grabbed her in a way that she couldn't resist. She clung to him, kissing him back, unable to stop. Her body was on fire, her nipples aching, heat spiking in her belly….

He moved over her, his body pressing her to the bed, his hips between her thighs. He was heavy, he was hot, he was utterly dominating, not giving her a chance to stop, to think, to breathe…and she didn't want to.

She didn't want her brain to wake up and stop her.

She just wanted to lose herself in this moment, in him, in who he was.

He swore and rolled off her to the other side of the bed.

Cold air hit her. Cold air and a feeling of complete loss. "What's wrong?"

"Take off the earrings."

She propped herself up to look at him, her body screaming for his, for more. For him to touch her, to kiss her, to—"What is your problem with my earrings?"

"They're diamonds."

"So?"

"So, they don't belong out here."

She stared at him, realizing what he was saying. "You want me to take them off so you don't have to think about who you're making love to? So you can pretend I'm something else? Someone else?"

He didn't answer.

Kaylie flopped back, staring at the ceiling as a horrible ache settled in her chest. Yes, it was the same thought she'd had while he was kissing her, but it had been a fleeting thought. She'd known the entire time that she was kissing Cort, and it was Cort she wanted.

But *he* couldn't kiss *her* unless she became someone else? It was something her parents would have said. Diamonds, all of her life choices, made her worthless in their eyes. "You're brutal," she whispered. "You don't deserve me."

There was silence, her words heavy in the air.

"I don't deserve you?" He repeated her words slowly, disgust building with each phrase. "You're too good for me? With your fancy clothes and jewelry? I'm not worthy?" The sarcasm dripped from his voice, the sneer of disdain. "Yeah, trust me, I've heard that before."

She winced. "I didn't mean it like that."

"Fuck that." He punched the pillow and shifted away from

her. "Fancy jewelry and a couple degrees don't matter out here. Out here, it's about your soul, and trust me, you're the one who doesn't measure up."

Kaylie closed her eyes as the decades-old hardness settled around her heart again. She hadn't even realized her shield had begun to fall until she felt the old protections rebuilding, creating a hollowness in her chest, as if her heart were encased in a hard shell. But instead of making her feel safe, she felt empty, alone. Dead.

At least he couldn't hurt her anymore.

No one could.

But Kaylie couldn't let his words be the last ones between them. "I like my jewelry," she said. "But I don't think I'm better than you. Just…" She trailed off, not sure how to say it without sounding exactly like the person he'd accused her of being.

Yes, he didn't deserve her.

Not because she was better than he was.

But because she needed someone who loved the person she wanted to be. Not someone who wanted to pretend that person didn't exist. "I won't be dismissed," she whispered.

Of course, he didn't answer.

But she heard his breathing catch, and she knew he was still awake and that he'd heard every word.

# CHAPTER ELEVEN

*I won't be dismissed.*

Kaylie's words burned in Cort's brain as he paused on his way out of the bedroom the next morning, rifle in hand. She was sprawled on her back, one delicate arm flung above her head on the pillow, her fingers curled ever so slightly, just enough for him to see her glossy nails. He doubted she had a single callus on her body, a scar anywhere.

She was flawless, an unsoiled beauty who could never survive Alaska. Who wouldn't want to, even if she could. How had she wound up with a family that had gone missing on Denali? Probably rookies, out for a joyride, totally clueless as to what the mountain would do to them. Rich people who thought they could buy their way into finding passion in life again.

He'd seen it plenty of times, flown those fools right up into the mountains, then come back two days later to cart home people with frostbite, broken legs, and an oath to go back to their comfortable little worlds and never return.

But then he thought of her story about when she was eleven. Getting ditched on the mountain with a broken leg. It didn't fit her. Summiting at that age? It must have been some small hill that Alaskans would consider nothing more than a hump in the earth.

Cort's gaze wandered over the lushness of her brown hair. He knew how it smelled. He could still remember how soft it was. There was nothing hard about Kaylie. Nothing at all.

And being up close with her…He'd liked it too damn much.

She made him forget about everything else. With Kaylie beneath him, he was in the moment. He simply was.

The blankets were around her waist, and she was wearing some pale pink shiny top with the thinnest damn straps he'd ever seen. Lace teased him, and he could make out the dark pink of her nipples beneath the fabric.

His cock hardened.

She shifted slightly, and the diamond in her left ear blinked as the sun caught it. It was a big diamond. He wasn't any expert, but he knew money when he saw it, and Kaylie had money.

*You don't deserve me.*

Her comment came back to him, and his grip tightened around his rifle. How many times had Valerie said that to him? And then she'd made him pay. Kaylie's comment last night had been cut from the same cloth.

Scowling, he turned and walked outside, leaving her behind.

*I won't be dismissed.*

Her whispered comment reverberated in his mind as he opened the front door. One thing he knew: Valerie never in her life would have come out to this cabin to search for her friend's murderer. She'd have hired the best, but she never would have gotten her own hands dirty.

Kaylie had courage, depth of character. Yeah, she wore diamonds. And she disdained everything about him, exactly as Valerie had.

He stepped out onto the porch and yanked the door shut behind him.

Not that it mattered what Kaylie was like. He knew enough. He'd made the mistake once before of trying to make a woman like Kaylie into more than she was, and he still paid the price.

So had his baby.

A black anger closed in on him at the memory, and Cort stomped down the steps and into a frigid downpour. He embraced the icy rain. He let it drive into his skin and wipe away the memories he hated. But he couldn't stop thinking about Kaylie and how good it had felt last night when he'd rolled over on top of her. He had no willpower when it came to her body.

He slogged into the soggy snow. Another day of rain and the snow would be gone, along with any chance of following the snowmobile tracks.

Already, it would be almost impossible. Too many spots where the snow was already melted to the ground.

Cort should have stayed that first night to find the bastard. Should have fought him in the snow right then. But Kaylie's big brown eyes and her vulnerability...She'd turned him soft in a split second.

And now the cost was Jackson's killer on the loose, and the monster was stalking Kaylie.

Less than a day, and she was already cutting off Cort's balls.

Best thing to do was to shut her out of his mind. Quit thinking of her as a woman or a person. The sex? Yeah, it was great, and that was as far as it went.

The rest? Leave it behind.

He stalked through the slush, getting more annoyed by the minute as he looked at all those snowmobile tracks crisscrossing each other. The bastard had been toying with them last night. Amusing himself.

A game.

Why hadn't he killed Cort right away? He hadn't hesitated to kill Jackson.

Cort worked his way around the cabin, checking for anything out of place while he thought about the situation. Had he caught the intruder unaware? Was that why the bastard hadn't stayed to kill him? He'd been lying in wait for Jackson, but was not ready for Cort? Or had he had something else in mind?

Something having to do with Kaylie. And her family. Her mother.

Cort ground his jaw as he reached the bedroom window, shaded his eyes to check on Kaylie.

She was still sleeping, still looking like an angel.

He narrowed his eyes as he studied her. There was something about Kaylie and her family. Something that had gotten Jackson and Sara killed.

Pulling back from the window, he looked down at the ground, at the snow bank below the window from all the snow that had fallen off the slanted metal roof.

The snow was packed with footprints.

The bastard had been back.

Watching Kaylie.

Wanting her? Wanting the ring?

Cort squatted and studied the prints. Boots. Bigger than his. A large man. Kaylie would have no chance against him. Slowly, he rose to his feet, acknowledging the truth.

The bastard wasn't going to walk away from Kaylie. Plus, she was the answer to Jackson's death. She and her family.

Yeah, Kaylie was a temptation Cort couldn't afford.

Yeah, if he stayed near her much longer, he was going to bed her again, and there'd be no going back.

Yeah, he'd be better off packing her on the next plane back to wherever she was from.

Didn't matter.

He needed her.

Rising, he fisted his rifle and surveyed the woods. The snowmobile tracks were already fading in the rain. Tracks too broken for him to track from the air. Tracks that would be gone before he could hike them out.

Kaylie was his only clue.

And she was in danger, and there wasn't a damn soul Cort would trust to keep her safe. Not when he didn't know who was after her.

Dammit.

There was no other option.

He was keeping her.

A shadow passed in front of Kaylie's eyes, jerking her into consciousness. She opened them and saw the outline of a man outside the window…and then realized it was Cort.

"Oy." She flopped back down, hand over her hammering heart.

He was standing with his back to her, rifle in one hand, facing the woods, as if listening for something. A chill prickled down her skin. Had her stalker come back?

She swung out of bed and padded to the smaller side window. Cort turned sharply as she cranked it open. "Cort? Is everything okay?"

"He came back." He pointed to the ground. "He was out here a good part of the night, I think. I didn't hear him. He's good."

A shiver that had nothing to do with the cold air wracked her body, and she pressed her face to the screen to look down.

Footprints everywhere.

Big ones.

"Oh, wow." Suddenly, the awkwardness between them last night didn't matter. She was just so grateful Cort had been in that bed with her. What if he hadn't been? What would have happened? "Can you follow the tracks?"

"Already tried. Too melted." He walked over to the window and draped one arm over the frame, leaning toward her. Rain dotted the shoulder of his jacket and matted down his hair. The bandage on his head was stark against his hair, a dark spot in the middle indicating that it was still bleeding.

Seeing that bandage was a reminder that, despite his strength and his aura of indestructibility, he was human. He could be hurt. He wasn't immune from the risks of his lifestyle.

She had to remember that. Had to stay focused on that fact.

His gaze went to her chest. "Nice outfit."

She looked down, her cheeks heating when she realized she hadn't remembered to cover up when she'd gotten out of the bed. Her nipples were dark and puckered with cold, the sheer material doing nothing for modesty.

Then she got annoyed at herself for being embarrassed. For letting him make her feel self-conscious. The earrings, the sleep attire...She set her hands on her hips and smiled. "Thank you." He'd already made love to her. What was the point in hiding from him?

He stared at her, and then the corner of his mouth quirked up, as if surprised by her reaction. "No. Thank *you*."

Heat suffused her again, and this time it wasn't embarrassment. "My pleasure."

They stared at each other for a long moment. Then she intentionally touched her earring, making sure the back was still secure. He watched her do it, a muscle ticking in his cheek.

She dropped her hand and smiled, trying to pretend it didn't bother her how he felt about who she really was. "So? What now?"

"No secrets."

"No secrets? What are you talking about?"

He leaned closer, making her forget the screen was still between them. His presence was so powerful, so strong, that she could practically feel the heat emanating off him. He was a man who would dominate any room he stepped into, no matter who was in it. "From what I can tell, my best friend and his wife died because of your mother. Because of your family."

Her throat tightened at his words. Was she really respon-sible for Sara's dying? God, if it was about her, and her mother...

His face softened. "That doesn't mean it's your fault," he said quietly. "It's not the same thing."

"You don't believe that. And I don't either."

Cort's hand went to the screen, his fingers digging, as if he wanted to grab her. "I *do* mean that. It's not your fault." His voice was hard. Unyielding. "But you're our best lead to fig-ure out what's going on. You're going to need to tell me ev-erything about your family. I need answers."

Kaylie wanted to run from the intensity of his gaze and the hard set to his jaw. From Alaska. From the dangers of this place. From the world she'd tried so hard to deny for so long. From the way she wanted to lean into that screen and press her face against it so she could get as close to him as possible. "What about Trooper Mann? Won't he help now?"

Cort gave a small snort of disgust. "Oh, I'm going to track Bill down and tell him, but you want to trust him to see it through the right way? You have that much faith in him?"

Kaylie bit her lip. She thought of the how Trooper Mann had dismissed her concerns about her family. The way he'd accused Cort of being crazy. How he'd thought she was lying for Cort so he would sleep with her. Thought of the discon-certing way his partner, Rich, had looked at her, as if he was picturing her naked.

No, she didn't trust the state troopers to see it through.

Cort was personally invested in this because of Jackson. Kaylie had been a part of Cort's grief that first night, and she knew he wouldn't walk away from this situation. But could she withstand being close to him? What if he tried to kiss her again? Would she succumb as she had the last two times? How long would it take for her heart to get involved?

For him to destroy her.

She didn't understand why, but she couldn't deny that he

affected her in a way no one else had. Even in the light of day, with the rain dripping on him and footsteps of a stalker in the snow outside her window, she wanted him.

Badly.

"Do you trust the Staties to keep you safe when that bastard comes back for you?" Cort asked. There was a dark turbulence in his eyes that made her stomach tighten. A fierceness. A protectiveness. "Because he's coming back," he said. "You know he is. And I'll be waiting. You with me, or not?"

*He's coming back.*

Kaylie knew Cort was right, and she didn't want to be alone when the murderer returned.

There were more than half a million people in Alaska Kaylie could ask for help.

But Cort was the one she wanted. He was the one she trusted. Anyone could have killed Jackson and Sara. Trooper Mann, his partner, anyone she approached. But she knew, she knew down to the marrow of her bones, that Cort was innocent.

So, it had to be Cort.

She set her hands on her hips, knowing she was dooming herself even as the words came out of her mouth. "Okay. I'm in."

# CHAPTER TWELVE

By nighttime, they were in Twin Forks, a town forty-five minutes from Cort's hangar. He hadn't been able to track down Trooper Mann or his partner anywhere, so when she and Cort finished searching the rest of Jackson and Sara's cabin, he'd decided to take control.

Now it was almost nine o'clock, the rain hadn't let up, and they were hunting a state trooper.

According to Cort, the Shed was the place to go, both for a state trooper who wouldn't return calls and to find the bush pilot who had flown her family up to the mountain.

Cort had been disappointed with the details about her family. No smoking gun suggesting why someone would be after her mother or herself. Kaylie hadn't seen her parents in five years. Her brother e-mailed her periodically, but he hadn't revealed some dark secret that would explain what was going on. She didn't even know what part of the mountain they'd been on or what peak they'd been trying to climb.

He was surprised to learn the members of her family were legitimate climbers. He asked a few questions about why she didn't climb now, but she hadn't wanted to go into it with him. He hadn't pried, and it had left him with no answers.

They'd both realized they had to find the pilot who'd flown them in. They needed a place to start.

And so, there they were. Walking into Twin Forks's local tavern, a small wooden building with dim lighting and a huge stone fireplace taking up the center of the room. From what Cort said, it was the main watering hole for bush pilots.

Even with the flickering glow from the flames and the dusky sunlight outside, the bar was dark. Crowded. Packed with people who looked as if they could handle the worst Mother Nature offered and not even spill a drop of their beer.

It wasn't their clothes or weathered faces that made them seem so tough, though most were in jeans and boots. Not a diamond earring to be seen.

It wasn't the weathered faces that gave some of the patrons a roughened, lined expression. And it wasn't the casual way they all chatted with one another, as if they'd known each other for thirty years and had no secrets left to hide.

It was the low energy humming from them, a fire, a realness much like what she'd felt off Cort the first moment she'd met him.

Heads turned as they entered, and Kaylie felt fifty sets of eyes dissect her, judge her, and then dismiss her.

She didn't belong here.

She stopped, but Cort put his hand on her lower back and forced her to keep walking. He moved closer to her, his body brushing hers. "They don't bite," he said under his breath, low enough for only her to hear.

"Am I that obvious?"

"I can feel the muscles in your back clenching." His hand slipped around her waist, and he tucked her under his arm.

Her body tightened at his nearness and she tried to pull away, hating her body's reaction to him.

He kept her anchored ruthlessly to his side. "I know you think I'm not good enough for you," he muttered. "But I'm pretty sure your stalker is a local, and I want it to get back to him that you're under my protection. I want him to realize that he's going through me to get to you. So get over your issues with me and try to look like you can't wait to get into my pants."

Her lower body quivered at his words, but he wasn't looking at her. He didn't even seem to have noticed what he'd said. Was he no longer interested in seducing her? Had last night cured him? If so…that was good. Really. It was. "You think he'll hear about us here?"

"If he's not here already. He knows I fly. He'll come here eventually."

Kaylie looked around the bar that seemed far more threatening than it had when she first walked in. People watching her out of the corner of their eyes, some staring with blatant curiosity. Did one of them have Sara's and Jackson's blood on his hands? Was one of them the person who'd taken her photo and—

She stopped fighting Cort's grip and wedged herself against his side, taking comfort in the hard strength of his body, in the way she fit beside him.

He gave a grunt of satisfaction. "I see Rich in back, getting drunk. Probably means Bill is around here somewhere, as I thought." Cort nodded at almost everyone they passed, but he didn't stop to talk to anyone. Instead, he steered them ruthlessly toward the rear of the bar.

Kaylie tensed even more when she caught sight of Rich in the back. He was leaning against a wall, a pool cue in his hand, and his eyes were on her.

Watching her.

Without any pretense that he wasn't.

Cort's arm stiffened around her waist and he stopped. "I think," he said quietly, "I need to have a private conversation with Rich."

Kaylie glanced nervously around the bar. "After that little speech, you're going to leave me alone in here?"

Cort steered her toward an empty table up against the

wall. "Once the room realizes you're with me, no one is going to let you be dragged out of here." He pulled out a chair. "Sit."

She eased into the chair, and Cort set one hand on the back of the chair and one palm on the table, leaning over her. "These are my rules," he said. "You stay in that chair, and you don't get up for any reason. Don't go to the bathroom, don't go out to the truck, not even if there's a fire. I'll be right out back, and I will return for you. Do you understand?"

He was so intense, so close, that Kaylie had to lean back to look at him. His face was hard, determined, nothing like the carefree man she'd seen on several occasions. This guy was a warrior.

This man would keep her safe.

He leaned closer. "Don't pull away," he said quietly. "This is my insurance to make sure no one in this room touches you while I'm gone. To make sure everyone here understands exactly what the situation is."

"What—?"

He kissed her. Not a gentle kiss. A deep invasion that stated to everyone in that room that he was her lover and that he wanted them all to know it. His tongue was wet and demanding, his lips fierce, and she couldn't stop her hand from going to the back of his head as she kissed him back.

She wasn't kissing him because of their audience. She was kissing him because she wanted his mouth on hers. She craved the taste of him, the feel of his hair beneath her hand, the heat of his body against hers.

Maybe it was because she was terrified of everything she was facing, and he was all she had.

Maybe it was because he was her worst nightmare and she was too stupid to know better.

Or maybe it was something else.

Something she didn't dare acknowledge.

His hand went to the back of her neck, and he locked her

against him, immobilizing her as he deepened the kiss. She knew the moment it switched for Cort from a stage kiss to raw wanting. His hand tightened on her, and the kiss took on a desperation and intensity that made tingles race down her spine. Her belly clenched, and her whole body cried out for him.

Cort wrenched his mouth from hers, staring down at her, still gripping the back of her neck. "Hell."

Heat suffused her body. "You don't even like me."

He gave her a grim smile. "And you think I'm not good enough for you. It's a helluva match, isn't it?"

"It's not a match. It's stupidity."

His thumb rubbed over the back of her neck, sending chills over her entire body. "Yeah, well, I'm a bush pilot. Pushing the edge is what I do best." Then he turned and was gone, melting through the crowd and heading straight for Trooper Parker.

Who was still watching her, and now he looked angry.

Pissed.

As if Kaylie was his girl and she'd cheated on him.

Cort reached him, had a word, then the two of them walked out the back door.

Leaving her alone in the bar—

"Here you go."

Kaylie jumped at the interruption, turning to find a young woman in jeans and a green apron setting a beer in front of her. Kaylie frowned when she saw the label. It was her mother's favorite beer. She looked up and caught the waitress's arm as the girl began to walk away. "I didn't order this."

The waitress smiled. "No worries. It's been taken care of. Welcome to Twin Forks."

Kaylie's fingers curled into the waitress's arm. "Who took care of it? Who ordered it?" It was a common enough brand. It could be a fluke. Or it could be a statement that *he* was there and wanted her to know it.

Her smile fading as she pulled out of Kaylie's panicked grasp, the waitress shrugged. "I don't know. Some folks like to stay anonymous out here. There was a note on the bar with a five."

Her voice said to back off and accept it, but Kaylie couldn't. "Do you still have the note? Can I see it?"

The waitress frowned. "I tossed it. There's no name. Trust me, I can read."

"No, it's not that." Kaylie hesitated, embarrassed that the waitress would think that about her. Did everyone in this state assume she was elitist snob just because of the way she dressed? "I just... There's been a creep following me back home, and I'm worried he's tracked me here."

"Oh." The waitress nodded. "Been there before. Well, that's different. I'll see if I can find it."

Kaylie managed a smile and released her. "Thank you so much."

"No problem." The waitress seemed to relax a bit now that Kaylie wasn't trying to arm wrestle her to floor. "My name's Annie, if you need anything." Her voice took on a curious tone, and an interested light came into her eyes. "Is Cort coming back? Want to order for him? Food? Drinks? How long you two staying?"

Kaylie glanced past Annie and saw several people at the bar watching them, and she knew Annie would be reporting back. "Sure, bring whatever Cort usually drinks and a couple burgers. And I'll have some water."

"Sure thing..." Annie raised her brows, waiting for Kaylie to fill in.

"Kaylie."

"Kaylie." Annie repeated, a smug look in her eyes, no doubt for being the first one to get Kaylie's name. "You staying out at Cort's place? How long you in town? You from California or something?"

Kaylie looked at the beer sitting in front of her and made

the decision to offer herself up. Lay it out there for anyone to hear. Anyone looking for her. It was the only way. She met Annie's eyes. "I'm staying at Cort's house, yes. I'm not sure how long I'll be there. Until I'm ready to go."

"Until *you're* ready to go?"

"Yes."

Annie looked like she wanted to ask more, but the bartender, a grizzled man who could have been anywhere from fifty to eighty, bellowed her name. Annie wrinkled her nose. "I'll be back with the rest of the drinks and some food. Nice to meet you."

"You too." Kaylie watched Annie go, then carefully surveyed the rest of the bar to see if anyone seemed unduly interested in her.

Then she sighed.

*Everyone* seemed unduly interested in her.

She dropped her gaze to the only brand of beer her mother had ever drunk, and felt a sudden chill.

The choice of beer wasn't a coincidence. She knew it in her gut.

It was all Cort could do to keep from slamming Richie into the back wall of the building once they stepped outside. "What the hell was that about?"

Richie turned to look at him, his jaw extended in hostility. "What's your problem?"

"The way you were looking at Kaylie." Cort narrowed his eyes. "Got blood on your hands, Richie?"

Richie blinked "Blood? What blood?"

Cort leaned forward. "You were looking at Kaylie like you wanted to throw her in the trunk of your car and cart her off to your shack and violate her ten ways till Sunday." He couldn't keep the snarl out of his voice. He couldn't stop the anger from making his fists clench. Richie was a well-known womanizer, and Cort had picked more than a couple drunk female tourists out of Richie's clutches as he'd been carting them out the back door of a bar to his truck.

It hadn't made them friends, and it was a damn small community for enemies. Cort had assumed Richie's uselessness at the cabin had been because of their past and the fact that he was Trooper Mann's lapdog.

Now he wasn't sure.

Richie's eyes widened, and he held up his hands. "Hey, man, back off. Kaylie's a beautiful woman, and every guy in there was thinking the same thing. Why are you riding my ass? Just because she's your tail doesn't mean I can't look at her. Since when are you jealous?"

Cort saw the flicker of fear in the trooper's eyes, and he became aware of his aggressive stance, of the fire simmering beneath his skin. Carefully, he rocked back on his heels, giving Rich some space. Shit. Since when did he walk around with a hard-on for a fight? He got all the fight he needed from bad weather and his planes.

"I'm trying to find a murderer," Cort replied, not quite able to keep the sharpness out of his voice. "It makes me testy."

Richie eyed him skeptically. "That wasn't about Jackson."

"You know nothing about Jackson." But even as he tried to deflect Richie, Cort hesitated. Was he overreacting? Was Kaylie screwing with his focus? Or was his gut feeling about Richie right? He'd never liked the guy, and the way Richie had looked at Kaylie...

Hell. Richie was right. He was jealous.

Or maybe his gut was telling him something about Richie that he needed to listen to. "Where's Bill? I've been trying to raise both of you all day, and I'm getting nothing back."

"Bill's in Anchorage for the weekend. What's doing?" Richie cocked his head, an interested gleam in his eyes. "You find something?"

Cort fingered the bagged photo in his jacket pocket. Trust him or not? If Richie sat on it, they would lose time. But if

Richie didn't act on the evidence, then Cort would know he wasn't clean.

He pulled the bag out and explained what was in it, watching Richie's face carefully.

"No shit? That's good stuff." Richie took the bag. "Never dealt with a pervert before."

"And a murderer," Cort reminded him drily.

"Yeah, maybe." Richie tucked the photo in his pocket. "See, the thing is, this doesn't mean anything, other than that some guy jacked off on it. Could've been Jackson, before his wife got home and—"

Cort's hand was around the trooper's throat before the man could finish. "Don't speak badly of Jackson. Do you understand?"

Richie was undaunted. "Hell, it could have been you. The way you reacted when I was checking Kaylie out—"

Cort shoved Richie up against the wall. "What is your fucking problem, Richie? Why are you trying to piss me off?"

Richie narrowed his eyes, and his hand went to his gun. "My problem is you. Back off."

"I am your problem," Cort agreed, not budging. "But I could go away real nice if you'd take that bag back to your office and send it off to people who can check that stuff out. You'd be amazed at how pleasant I could be if you started taking Jackson's and Sara's murders seriously."

The trooper didn't back down. "Already said I'd take care of the baggie. Doesn't mean there's a killer, though, and you know that."

Cort's jaw began to ache, and he loosened his grip on the younger man. He hated to admit it, but Richie was right. Completely right. Semen on a photo didn't prove a murder to someone who didn't believe Jackson and Sara had been killed.

Richie was correct by the letter of the law, but not right by the law of the land. Not by Cort's gut.

Richie and Bill were men with badges who were afraid to step up and do their job. Afraid to piss people off.

Cort didn't suffer from the same affliction. "Did you see the diamonds in Kaylie's ears?"

Richie grinned. "Oh, yeah. I sure did."

"She's got people with money back home who will be riding your ass right to hell if something happens to her out here. And who do you think's going to fry when they find out the state troopers knew someone was stalking her and didn't take it seriously?" Cort had a suspicion that there wasn't actually a single person back home who would send out the posse if Kaylie disappeared, and he didn't like that idea at all.

He didn't want to be her posse.

But she needed one, and he needed to find out who killed Jackson and Sara.

He bent down so his face was in Richie's space. "Kaylie is *mine*, so I will be leading the charge. You heard the stories about my dad?"

Richie nodded once, his face slightly paler than it had been before. Everyone in the state knew about Huff McClaine and how protective he'd been of his wife. If Huff hadn't been the number-one search-and-rescue flier for the state, saving more lives than all the other bush pilots put together, the cops would have put in him jail by the time he was twenty-five. As it was, they let him skate and covered up the trail of destruction he'd left behind.

Cort had inherited his dad's love of flying and the thrill of going against the odds and pulling people out of the jaws of death, but he'd never understood the jealousy that had driven his dad, the way he'd reacted if his woman was threatened.

Until now. Until Kaylie. Until Cort had seen that photo. "What Huff did won't measure up to what I'll do if Kaylie gets killed. And I'm going to start with you." He managed a thin smile. "I'm already cranky about Jackson and Sara. You don't want to push me."

Richie shrugged off Cort's grip, and Cort let him. "Don't threaten me, McClaine."

"I'd never threaten an officer of the law." He turned and walked away, leaving Richie out in the rain.

Cort knew he hadn't handled him well. Hadn't clarified whether Richie was just a pain in the ass, an incompetent newbie, or an actual suspect. Hadn't done anything to convince Rich that Jackson and Sara had been murdered.

But he'd gotten some good information.

He now knew for absolute certain that he and Kaylie were on their own.

# CHAPTER THIRTEEN

Kaylie was being watched.

The back of her neck tingling, she glanced toward the door Cort had disappeared through, but he still hadn't returned.

She scanned the room to see if she could determine who was making her skin crawl. A man with a shaggy gray beard at the end of the bar was watching her. Dirty, wrinkled hands wrapped around a beer. Cheeks ruddy from too much exposure. Eyes dark and hooded. Shoulders hunched.

He looked down at his beer when their gazes met.

The front door opened and the movement caught her attention. A burly man with a tan flak jacket eased outside. He was checking Kaylie out as well.

A man with a black ball cap pulled low raised his beer at her as her gaze passed over him. He was drinking a Rolling Rock, like the one on Kaylie's table.

And so was the man next to him.

Fingering the point of a dart, an older guy in the corner kept glancing in her direction, his eyes sliding away before she could make eye contact. A Rolling Rock was sitting on the table near him.

It could be *anyone*.

It was time to find Cort.

Kaylie pushed back her chair to stand up, then paused when a shadow fell across the table. She looked up as a beautiful woman with dark hair and brilliant blue eyes sat down across from her. "Well, hey there, new girl."

Kaylie was stunned by the vitality of the woman. Her cheeks were flushed from the cold, her eyes were vibrant, and her full breasts were obvious even beneath her heavy sweater. This was a woman who didn't need diamond earrings and sexy lingerie to feel like a siren.

Fingering her necklace, Kaylie managed a smile. "I was just leaving."

"Glad I got you before you left." The woman patted the table. "Sit. We need to talk."

Kaylie glanced around the bar again and saw that almost everyone was watching them now, not bothering to pretend they weren't. It gave Kaylie the creeps, but on the plus side, with a roomful of witnesses, the odds of her being abducted by a psycho without anyone noticing were small.

Probably safest to stay right where she was. The center of curious attention.

Cautiously, Kaylie eased back into her chair. "Um, hello." Her gaze flicked around the room. Cort still wasn't back, and the bearded man at the bar was gone.

The woman smiled, a genuine expression of friendship that made her eyes light up. So friendly, so open. Kaylie realized this woman was as natural as the land she lived in. A friend who would be loyal forever.

She reminded her of Sara.

"I'm Charity Sims."

Kaylie couldn't resist the warmth of Charity's voice, or the way she leaned forward, as if she really wanted to talk. It was so welcome after the cold reception Kaylie had received at the bar and after the uncertainty of her relationship with Cort, who was the only one she had on her team. "I'm Kaylie Fletcher."

The bearded man from the bar was now in the corner, near the man with the darts. They were talking quietly, shooting occasional glances in Kaylie's direction.

Charity cocked a perfectly sculpted brow. "You don't know who I am, do you?"

"Should I?"

"No, I guess not." Charity gestured for a drink from Annie. "A couple of the house specials. Kaylie and I are going to be a while." She returned to gaze to Kaylie. "You aren't Cort's type."

Kaylie stiffened. "How do you know?"

"Because I've known him a long time. He taught me to fly."

Another bush pilot? This woman was far too female to play in the world of bush pilots…wasn't she? "So, you know Cort from flying." That was nice. Kaylie was so thrilled to meet a beautiful woman who shared Cort's passion.

"Yep. We've put in a lot of hours together. You mind?" Charity pointed to Kaylie's beer.

Kaylie pushed it toward her. "Not at all. Please take it."

Charity took a long sip, then set it down. "Plus Cort and I dated for two years. So, yeah, I know his type. And you're not it."

Oh, wow. *This* was Cort's type? Beautiful, a daredevil, a woman so comfortable in her own skin Kaylie envied her. No wonder Cort didn't like Kaylie. She was as far from Charity Sims as it was possible to get. Charity made her feel like some made-up porcelain doll.

Restlessly, Kaylie shifted her feet under the table, wondering how long she had to stay to be polite.

Charity's smile faded, and she paused, as if searching for words. Finally, she clasped her hands on the tabletop and spoke. "What I'm trying to say is that if you want to keep Cort, you're going to need a little help from a woman who knows what it will take."

Kaylie's gaze jerked back to Charity in surprise. "Keep him? I don't want to keep him."

"No? Well, that's probably a good thing." Charity took another sip of beer.

Kaylie waited for further clarification.

Charity just drank the beer, but the twinkle in her eye said she clearly intended to drive Kaylie insane until she caved.

Argh. "Okay, fine, so I'll bite," Kaylie finally said, throwing up her hands. "Why is it a good thing I don't want to keep him?"

Charity grinned. "He's hot, isn't he? A woman's fantasy in bed?"

"We haven't—"

"Of course you have. I know Cort. That kiss was something else. He never laid one like that on me."

Curiosity definitely aroused now, Kaylie propped her chin up in her hand. "Really? He didn't?"

Charity's smile widened. "Tell me again you don't want to keep him. I'm not sure I heard that right."

There was something so warm about Charity that Kaylie couldn't resist. She needed someone to talk to, and she had no one.

Not anymore.

But Charity was here...and Charity reminded her of Sara so much in the way she chatted up a stranger and was so quick to smile. Maybe Charity was nothing more than a jealous ex with an agenda, and she was definitely a stranger, but she was someone who knew Cort and was willing to talk, so Kaylie would take it.

"So?" Charity pressed.

"So, Cort would break me."

"Oh." Charity's smile dropped off. "Yeah, he might." Her blue gaze settled on Kaylie's earrings. "Yeah, I guess he really might."

Kaylie touched her diamonds. "What is *with* my earrings around here?"

Charity chewed her lip for a second. "Listen, Kaylie, I love Cort. But I don't love him as a woman loves a man, and he doesn't love me that way. We were fillers for each other because neither of us had anything better. He's broken inside, and I'm not the one to fix him. But he was good to me when I needed it, and I owe him." Charity gave Kaylie a considering look. "If you're going to mess him up more, that's not okay with me."

"I'm not—"

"But if you're going to save him, and I just think you might be able to, then I'll help." Charity smiled. "He's complicated."

"He's an adrenaline junkie."

Charity raised her brows. "And that's a problem." She let out a low whistle and leaned back in her chair. "You're going to destroy him forever, or you're going to be the greatest gift he's ever had. How much do you love him?"

"I don't love him at all."

Charity gave her a penetrating gaze. "Could you?"

Kaylie stared at her. "God, I hope not."

A friendly grin broke out over Charity's face. "That's a yes if I've ever heard one." She nodded. "I think you're okay, Kaylie Fletcher. If you want Cort, I'm not going to stand in your way."

Kaylie should have bristled at Charity's assumption she had any say over what happened between her and Cort, but she couldn't resent the woman's genuine concern for him. Charity cared, and Kaylie appreciated that so much. Sara had been that kind of loyal friend, and it was one of the attributes Kaylie had treasured about her.

Sara's gift to Cort of one of her paintings proved that she was as fond of him as Charity was. Kaylie realized suddenly that if Sara had noticed the electricity between her and Cort, she probably would have sat her down and said the same things that Charity was saying.

Tears swelled suddenly in Kaylie's eyes, and she ducked her head to hide them. God, she missed Sara. How could Kaylie possibly resent Charity, when she was so much like the friend she had lost?

She brushed the back of her hand over her eyes to clear them, then inclined her head in acknowledgment of Charity's endorsement of her relationship with Cort. "Thank you for your support."

Charity nodded, studying her watery eyes, but she didn't ask.

Kaylie wasn't sure whether she wished Charity would pry or not. With a sigh, Kaylie took a sip of the house special, a fruity wine she'd never had before. After a moment, she had regrouped enough to focus on the one person in her life she cared about who was actually still alive. "Why is Cort broken?"

"Ah…" Charity swished the wine around in her glass and reclined in her seat, putting distance between them. "That has to come from him. He'll tell you when he's ready. But be forgiving if he seems like an ass sometimes." She cocked her head and gave Kaylie a thoughtful look. "That is, if you want to love him. If you don't, then chalk him up as a bastard and don't look back."

"He's not a bastard." The words were out of Kaylie's mouth before she could stop them.

Her instinctive response brought a broad smile to Charity's face. "No, he's not. But not too many people realize it. You must be special if you can see that about him."

Kaylie had to look down at her drink to hide the pleased expression on her face. She didn't want to save Cort. She just wanted to survive him long enough to find Sara's murderer and save her family.

She jerked her gaze back to Charity's. "You said you're a bush pilot, right?"

Charity's face took on a guarded expression. "Used to be. Not anymore. Why?"

"Oh." Kaylie sighed. "My parents and my brother were part of a climbing party that was declared officially missing—"

"Oh, I'm so sorry about your family." Charity patted Kaylie's hand, a spontaneous gesture that felt truly sympathetic, not just an act. "I know how awful it is to have someone you love just disappear."

Something in her expression told Kaylie that Charity was speaking from experience, and she felt a twinge of camaraderie with this beautiful woman who was so close to Cort. "Did you ever—?"

At Charity's sharp look, Kaylie broke off in the middle of her inquiry. She'd been about to ask Charity if she'd ever found whoever it was she'd lost, but her expression made it apparent that it was a private topic.

Even though a part of Kaylie wanted to comfort this woman who had reached out to her, she also respected pain that was too private to share. So, instead of pursuing the topic, Kaylie switched back to her own problems. "Cort and I are trying to find the pilot who flew my family. I don't suppose it was you?"

Charity's face was tight. "I haven't been in the air for almost a year."

Kaylie cocked her head at the tension in Charity's voice, and knew something had happened to take away her wings. Was that why she and Cort had split up? Because he wasn't interested in a woman who didn't fly? Or was it something worse? Kaylie felt sudden empathy for this woman who had quit a high-risk life, just as she had. Something had happened to Charity. And it had been bad.

"Charity—"

"Hello, ladies. Is this seat taken?"

"Luke!" Charity's her eyes lit up, the weightiness vanishing from her eyes as she pulled out a chair. "Come join us!"

*Luke.* Kaylie jerked her gaze to the man who'd just reached their table.

Cort's business partner was wearing jeans and an untucked navy shirt. Dark hair shagged over his collar, and he clearly hadn't shaved for a few days. His clothes were all bush pilot, but there was a refinement to him that made Kaylie think that, in his blood, he wasn't all Alaska.

"Evening, Charity." Luke nodded at them both. "Kaylie." He swung his leg over the chair at the head of the table, not taking his eyes off Kaylie as he sat down. "Hair's dry this time, I see." His voice wasn't particularly friendly, but it wasn't exactly mean, either. Curious, definitely. Thoughtful. Assessing.

Kaylie felt her cheeks heat up, saw Charity glance curiously between them. But before Charity could ask any questions, Luke leaned toward Kaylie, his expression serious.

She tensed, waiting for criticism, the warning—whatever Luke was going to lay on her.

"I think," he said, "that you just may save Cort's life."

And then he smiled. A real smile.

And Kaylie relaxed.

Another friendly overture

Two in one day. First Charity, then Luke.

Alaska didn't just deliver death.

It granted the possibility of friends.

And Kaylie needed friends.

Cort eased in the back door of the Shed, keeping to the shadows as he carefully inspected the bar. The first place his attention went was to the table where he'd left Kaylie. He stiffened when he saw Luke and Charity sitting with her.

Shit. Those two knew far too much about him and weren't afraid to talk about it.

"Hey, Cort."

Cort stifled a grimace as he looked down at Annie Stockton. Barely in her twenties, she was a shameless flirt with every guy who came into the bar. She was so sweet and innocent, it made Cort uncomfortable when she came on to him. He still remembered when she was twelve, and he couldn't shake that image out of his mind. "Hi, Annie."

"So, is Kaylie your new girlfriend?"

Cort studied her, something clicking in his mind. "Someone ask you to ask me that, or are you just curious?"

Her cheeks flushed. "Both. People here are too scared to ask you. But I'm not. I don't know why everyone's so scared of you."

He smiled at her innocence. "You should be."

She snorted. "Why? Because you might frown me to death? Whatever." Annie leaned closer, and he had to avert his eyes from her chest. "So, tell me. Girlfriend?"

"Who asked you to ask me?"

She rolled her eyes and began ticking names off on her fingers. "Jake, the Maxtor twins, Jillian, Rob, Maria..."

Cort studied the bar, picking out the names of the people as she listed them, mentally cataloging them. If Jackson's killer was local, the odds were high that Cort knew him.

Cort couldn't think of anyone off the top of his head who'd go around slicing Jackson's throat, but he'd had plenty of surprises with people over the years, and he knew not to underestimate anyone.

But of the names she listed, none struck him.

"Who else has been here tonight?"

Annie's eyes widened. "You want me to list everyone?"

"A twenty if you can."

"Oh... This is for that stalker of Kaylie's, right? I'm on it." Annie started rattling off names almost faster that Cort could keep track. But by the time she finished, he had one on his list that was interesting: Dusty Baker, a local guide known to be one of the very best in the business for the last forty years. The one Sara had hired to take Kaylie over Denali to search for her family.

Annie finished her list, and Cort slapped a twenty in her hand. "Is Dusty still here?"

"Nope. He slipped out while you were in back with Richie. Said he had a flight."

"Keep an ongoing list, okay? Let me know if anyone new comes in."

Annie stuffed the bill in her front pocket. "You got it." She frowned and pulled a crumpled napkin out of her pocket. "Oh, and here's the note Kaylie wanted. Can you give it to her?"

Cort looked down at the balled-up paper Annie was holding out to him. "What's this?"

"Someone bought her a beer. Left a note and a five on the bar. I told her I'd get it for her." Annie leaned closer. "So? New girlfriend or what?"

Cort took the note. "She's under my protection."

"What kind of answer is that?" Annie set her hands on her hips. "What does that mean?"

"Whatever you want it to mean." He left Annie pouting and headed over to the table, not happy to see that Luke and Charity were in heavy discussion with Kaylie. They were all grinning, as if they'd been trading secrets they all thought were hilarious.

Shit. Kaylie had a beautiful smile. He hadn't seen it much.

Cort got closer, realizing he didn't like how close Luke was to Kaylie. How much did Kaylie know about Cort's past now? Luke was sure to distort it. And Charity was too damn irrepressible. Scowling as he approached them, he unfolded the note and looked down at it.

In rough block letters was written *Rolling Rock in a bottle for the new girl.*

Rolling Rock in a bottle?

Cort reached the table, and no one looked up.

Kaylie was staring at Luke intently, her brown eyes fixed on him as if she couldn't tear her gaze away. She nodded once, twirling her hair around the end of her finger. She looked relaxed and focused, and Cort had a sudden urge to grab her and kiss her.

Just so Luke knew whom she belonged to.

Shit. Cort was in trouble.

Transit to: PATERSON
Transit reason:
LIBRARY
Author: Saunders,
Kate, 1960- author.
Title: The secrets of
wishtide : a Laetitia
Rodd mystery
Item ID:
30204003650555
Transit date:
8/25/2021,9:42
Current time:
08/25/2021,9:42

# Chapter Fourteen

Kaylie looked up suddenly, as if she'd felt Cort's presence. Relief flickered in her eyes, and she gave him a warm smile. "You're back." There was genuine warmth in her voice, and she lifted her hand toward him, gesturing for him to sit.

And with that, all the tension left Cort's body. "Yeah. I am."

He took the seat next to her, aware that Luke and Charity had fallen silent and were watching him.

Cort ignored them. He leaned toward Kaylie, close enough that he caught a whiff of her flowery scent. He braced his hand on the table in front of her and used his shoulder to cut out Luke and Charity. Then he bent his head and kissed Kaylie.

Slow. Precise. Just so everyone would see.

Her mouth was warm and wet, her breath tangy with the scent of wine. It was heady and exhilarating, and she didn't hesitate to kiss him back, making hot desire shoot straight to his groin.

He forced himself to break the kiss before he leaned her back in her chair and took her right there. "You okay?" He kept his voice low, a question for her ears only.

Kaylie nodded, scooting her chair a little closer to his. "Someone sent me a drink."

He handed her the note. "Annie told me."

She scanned it quickly, her face paling. "It was Rolling Rock on purpose, then."

Glancing at the half-drunk wine in front of Kaylie and the Rolling Rock in Charity's hand, he frowned. "You don't like it?"

Her brown eyes were worried when she looked at him. "It's the only beer my mom drinks. Rolling Rock out of a bottle. My dad used to get so annoyed when she packed glass bottles up a mountain, but she insisted. Ever since her first trip to Alaska—"

Cort held up his hand. "Her *first* trip? When was that?"

"A long time ago. Before I was born. She came for a climb and spent six months here."

"How often does she come back here?"

Kaylie shook her head. "She came back once more, the next summer. That's where she met my dad. They'd never been back before this year."

Cort narrowed his eyes. "Why not?"

"Why not?" She frowned. "I don't know. Why would they?"

"Because this place gets in your blood," Luke said. "That's why."

Cort rolled his eyes and swung his head. Luke and Charity were leaning forward, clearly straining to hear the conversation. "Don't you guys have somewhere to go?"

"No." They answered in unison, and Kaylie giggled.

Startled by the sound of Kaylie laughing, he glanced at her. Sure enough, there was a twinkle in her eye as she grinned at Charity. Wasn't much of a twinkle, and her face still looked strained, but damn, that smile. Gorgeous. "You should smile more."

She looked at him and her smile faded. "So should you."

"The only time he's smiling is when he's hanging on to life by one fingernail," Luke said. "Psychotic bastard."

Cort didn't miss the look between Charity and Kaylie. What the hell was that about?

Not that it mattered. They needed to focus. Cort draped his arm over the back of Kaylie's chair and resumed the conversation they'd been having before Luke had interrupted. "You know who your mom talked to or climbed with when she came before?"

Kaylie frowned. "Of course not. Why would I know?"

"Why'd they come back this time?"

"Thirty-year anniversary of when they met," she said.

"Why not every year?" Cort said. "Why wait thirty years?"

"My mom said she hated Alaska. Didn't want to come back. The only time my dad came here was when she wasn't with him."

Luke leaned back in his chair, hooking his arm over the back of it. "Something happened when she was here before."

Kaylie frowned. "Why do you say that? Maybe she just didn't like Alaska. It's possible, you know."

"Denali is a climber's dream. You don't hate it. You climb, and the mountains bring you to life," Luke said. "Outsiders who come…once the land gets in their blood, they can't leave. It's impossible."

Cort looked over at his friend. Yeah, Luke knew. All too well, he knew the price that could be demanded of those falling in love with Alaska.

Kaylie was frowning. "So, you think something happened when my mom came before?"

"Something that came back to bite her when she returned, yeah." Cort rubbed his jaw. "But how the hell does it relate to you? Or Jackson? Or Sara?"

"It's easy," Charity said. "You all are so blind."

Cort eyed Charity. "You going to fill us in on your brilliance?"

"Of course." Charity glanced at Luke, then focused on Cort and Kaylie. "A woman comes to Alaska for a short trip, but winds up staying six months? And then she comes back the next year for another extended stay? That has 'I met a hot guy' all over it."

Kaylie shook her head. "My mom never said—"

"Then, on the second trip, she meets a new guy, jumps ship and never returns to paradise? And now you've got a wedding ring and a guy who knows what your mom drinks?" Charity shrugged. "Your mom was a player, Kaylie, and the guy she met thirty years ago never forgot her. She came back, and things got stirred up."

Luke snorted, and Cort rolled his eyes. "No guy's going to have a hard-on for a woman he hasn't seen in thirty years."

"A girl thing to say," Luke agreed. "Women pine. Men have sex with other women to forget. It's how it works."

Charity folded her arms across her chest. "It's Alaska. Ratio of a thousand men to every woman. The men out here have nothing else to do *besides* fantasize about the women they've bedded." She grinned. "Right, Kaylie?"

Kaylie glanced at Cort, her cheeks red.

Charity leaned forward. "Tell me, Cort. If Kaylie left today and you didn't see her for thirty years, would you forget about her, or would you think of her every time you saw the sun reflecting off the snow like diamonds?"

There was silence at the table, three sets of eyes fixed on him. Charity sparkling with mischief, Luke looking somber, as if he was thinking of the one woman Cort really couldn't get out of his nightmares, and Kaylie, looking just the faintest bit curious.

"Snow is just snow," he muttered. "A place to land."

Kaylie looked away as Charity sighed with disgust. "You're such a guy." Charity turned her attention to Kaylie. "Do you know anything about your mom's trip out here before? Or this time? Did she ever mention a guy besides your dad?"

"Oh, come on," Cort interrupted. "Trying to re-create something that might or might not have happened thirty years ago is a waste of time." He pulled his arm off Kaylie's

chair, getting annoyed by all the talk of endless love and obsession. "We have to start somewhere, and the best place is
with someone who talked to Kaylie's mother on this trip,
who can tell us something about who she was with, who paid
attention to her, who she was talking to. And that's going to
be the pilot who flew her party. Anyone hear of her team going lost?"

"On Denali?" Luke studied Kaylie.

Cort set his hand on the back of Kaylie's chair as she got a
hopeful look on her face. He didn't like Kaylie looking at
Luke as if he were her savior. "Yes," Cort answered for her.

"Six in the party?" Luke asked.

Kaylie shrugged, biting her lip. "Actually, I don't know
who was in the party, other than my family—my parents and
my brother. I don't know."

Cort slid his hand down to the back of her neck and
stroked his fingers over the skin. Her muscles were tight, and
Cort knew it was difficult for her to admit she had no idea
about the details of her family's excursion. As the only one
left home, she should have been their base, knowing when to
call them in as missing.

And yet Kaylie knew nothing. It spoke volumes about the
relationship she had with her family.

Luke snapped his fingers. "I heard about this. Pilot couldn't
find them when he went to check on them two weeks after
dropping them off. Three-day search turned up nothing.
Search officially called off last week."

Cort snapped a sharp look at him, annoyed that Luke
could deliver for Kaylie where he hadn't been able to. "You
heard about this? Why didn't I?"

Luke glanced at Kaylie, then back to Cort. "You haven't
been around lately."

"I've been here."

"No." Luke tapped the side of his head. "You haven't been
present. First time you've been in town for months. You're

always in the air, taking every search and rescue we get. How many times have you slept in your bed lately?"

"Nothing's changed."

"Think about it. That's all I'm saying."

"You know…" Charity started in on him. "Luke's right. I haven't seen you in here in months. Everything okay?"

Cort became aware of Kaylie watching him. "Are we looking for Jackson's killer or playing psychiatrist? Who flew that party, Luke? You remember?"

"Thinking…" Luke nodded. "Yeah, I remember. Tom Gracien."

"Old Tom?" Cort rubbed his jaw. "He's been flying for more than thirty years. He might know something." And Old Tom was one of the few guys in the state who'd be straight up with Cort. Old Tom was one of the few who hadn't judged Cort after the mess eight years ago.

Kaylie touched Cort's arm. "Isn't Tom the one you said Sara should have hired to fly me?"

Cort nodded, giving her a thoughtful look. "Yeah, you're right." The wiry pilot was more than capable of taking down Jackson, and on some levels, Old Tom was crazy enough to do just that. But Cort didn't see it being the case. Just didn't make sense.

Annie set a burger in front of Cort and one in front of Kaylie. "Old Tom's in Devil's Canyon tonight. Heard him talking last night."

Luke's and Charity's attention swiveled to Cort at the mention of Devil's Canyon. The only way to Devil's Canyon was through Devil's Pass, and they both knew Cort didn't fly Devil's Pass.

Ever.

Not even for this.

Kaylie surveyed the three serious faces. "What's wrong with Devil's Canyon?" When no one answered, Kaylie turned to Cort, lines of strain reappearing around her mouth. "What aren't you telling me?"

He cupped her shoulder and squeezed it. "Nothing that affects you. Something that happened a long time ago."

She gave him a doubtful look. "Well, can we fly up there right now? I don't want to wait any longer."

Cort ground his jaw, but Luke immediately spoke up. "I'm heading that way anyway. I can stop in."

Shit. Cort felt like an ass. Luke offering to fly up there for him? Like Cort was so pansy assed he couldn't fly himself. "No—"

Annie leaned forward. "Why do you guys want Old Tom?"

Cort leveled a steady glare at Annie. "Eavesdropping again?"

"Of course. It's the only interesting way to learn anything." She grinned. "Like, because I'm listening to your conversation, I can save you the trip of going up there. Old Tom will be back around midnight. He usually comes in here when he lands. So just kick back and eat dinner, and he might be in."

*No trip through Devil's Pass tonight.*

The tension eased from Cort's shoulders, and he looked at his watch. "That gives us a half hour to kill. If he's not here by twelve thirty, we'll head out to his place and wake him up."

He picked up his burger as Annie directed her attention to Kaylie. "So, Cort won't spill. Are you his girlfriend or what?"

Kaylie's cheeks flushed. "Um, yes." Her gaze slithered toward Cort. "Yes, I am."

Cort couldn't stop his satisfaction at her statement. Sure, it was because they were trying to goad a psychopath into action, but it still felt good. He grinned and stroked his hand down her arm, leaning close against her so her shoulder was pressing into his chest. "Hey, gorgeous. What do you say we raise the stakes and see if we can tempt our friend into taking a little action?"

Her eyes widened. "What are you talking about?"

He took her hand and pressed his lips against the back of it, thoroughly enjoying the flush that stained her cheeks. "Let's dance."

She swallowed. "Here?" Her voice was husky, sensual, making blood rush to his cock.

He grinned. "Hell, yeah." Before she had a chance to reply, he bent his head and trailed his mouth over the side of her neck. Just to let her know exactly what kind of dancing he had in mind.

"Dance?" Kaylie's entire body became warm when she looked past Cort at the jukebox in the corner. Dim lights, a small space, two couples dancing.

Slow music.

Oh…

"Oh, yeah." Cort's hand closed around hers, and he pulled her to her feet.

"I don't know if—"

Cort didn't give her a chance to finish. He simply headed across the bar toward the dance floor, towing her along. He wasn't looking at her, his gaze sharp as he noticed everyone around him.

Kaylie knew he wasn't asking her to dance because he wanted to, but because it was part of his plan. But she also couldn't fail to notice his thumb tracing small circles on her palm, an intimate gesture that no one would see.

It was just for her.

The kisses, the anticipation of the dance…It was almost enough to make her forget why they were there.

Almost.

She glanced at the corner where the bearded man had been. He was gone, but the guy with the darts was still there, a Rolling Rock by his elbow.

The man nodded at her, and she shivered. "Cort."

Reaching the floor, Cort pulled her into his arms, one hand tight against her lower back, the other enfolding her hand in his, tucking it against his chest. "What?"

"That man by the dart board. Do you know him?"

Cort's shoulder tensed beneath her hand. Deliberately, he spun Kaylie around so he was facing the corner. He bent his head to trace his mouth over her neck. "Yeah, I know him. Rolling Rock, huh?"

Shivers crept down her spine as his mouth feathered over her skin. "Who is he?"

"Titus Marr. Been around forever. Sort of a drifter. He's helped me out sometimes. Loner mostly. Never seen him in here before." Cort's voice was thoughtful, quiet, but his body was positively vibrating with energy. "You recognize him? From any old pictures of your mom?"

He turned Kaylie again so she could see Titus. The man was watching them through narrowed eyes, and she tensed as Cort's hand slid over her bottom. "Don't think about me," he whispered into her ear. "Just concentrate on Titus."

She swallowed hard, but her body was already responding to his touch, to the feel of his hard body against hers. His hand was unyielding, pressing her against him, into the solid mass of muscle. "I don't recognize him," she whispered, her blood pulsing thickly in her belly.

"Anyone else?"

"There was a man…" She hesitated, searching for the bearded man. "He had a beard. He was talking with Titus earlier. He was watching me."

Slowly, Cort turned them, teeth grazing the side of her neck. "Scan the bar. Tell me if he's still here."

He bit lightly, and she jumped.

A low chuckle reverberated in Cort's chest. "You liked that?"

"Stop distracting me," she whispered, still searching the bar. The shadows were heavy, and she couldn't see the people in the corners very well. Was one of them the bearded man? The skin prickled on the back of her neck, and she felt a threat.

"I'm not distracting you. I'm distracting everyone else from noticing how hard you're looking around the bar." He squeezed her butt, and yanked her tighter against him, pressing her pelvis right against his. "Trust me, they aren't paying attention to where you're looking right now. They're waiting to see how long it takes for my hand to actually go in your pants."

His erection was hard against her belly, and she sucked in her breath, her body becoming hyperaware of everywhere they touched. Of his scent. Of the way she fit against the shield he was creating with his body. Unable to stop herself, she allowed herself to melt against him, her chest tightening when he accepted her surrender, folding her against him.

"You see him?" His lips went to her ear, and he lightly nibbled her earlobe.

"No," she whispered. God, it felt good to feel the heat from his body.

"Are you even looking?"

She jerked back to the present and forced herself to look. That's when she saw him. The man with the beard. In the back corner, his gaze on them intently. And he looked angry.

Cort tightened his grip, as if he'd felt her tension. "Where is he?"

She told him, and he turned her again so he was facing the corner.

"Who is—?"

He kissed her before she could finish the question. It wasn't tender. It wasn't shallow, just for show. It was instant heat, a kiss of possession, a statement of ownership and domination.

And she loved it. She'd never been kissed like that before, and her body responded instantly. He was strength, he was passion, he was so utterly male. So arrogant, as if he was staking a claim on her that he knew she wouldn't protest. But he was more than that. He brought her spirit to life in a way she hadn't known she was capable of feeling. Yes, that scared her, but it was also the most amazing sensation she'd ever experienced.

Because of Cort, the thought of going back to her life in Seattle didn't sound as appealing as it used to. And at the same time, a part of her wanted to rush back there and let it consume her, draining her of what Cort was doing to her....

God, she didn't even know what she wanted anymore. All she knew was that she wasn't ready to walk away from him yet.

He released her hand, tunneling his fingers through her hair as he anchored her against him, plundering her mouth with a kiss so demanding she felt the heat melting through her body. She wrapped her hands around his neck and pulled him down toward her, wanting more, needing more. He made her feel safe, protected.

He made her feel beautiful and perfect. The way he kissed her, as if he couldn't go another second without tasting her— it was heady and exhilarating.

Cort broke the kiss, nuzzling his way down the side of her neck, hands roaming her back. "He's gone," he whispered.

She blinked. "Who?"

He laughed softly, nipping at her neck. "The guy with the beard."

"Oh." Embarrassed at the way she'd lost herself in the kiss, especially since it was clear Cort had been watching everyone during the interlude, she pulled back slightly.

Cort's eyes were dark as he tunneled his hand in her hair. "The guy with the beard was Etsy Smith. He's harmless."

"Harmless? He didn't feel harmless."

"He got in a fight with a grizzly a few decades ago, and he's never been quite right since." His gaze went to her mouth. "He's not capable of what this guy has done. It's not Etsy."

She felt like stomping her foot in frustration. "Sara's murderer has to be here. The beer he sent—"

"I know." Cort's expression was grim. "I was hoping to piss him off with that kiss, but I didn't see anyone react."

She stiffened at the reminder that Cort hadn't kissed her because he wanted to. That it had all been for show. She'd been utterly unable to keep herself from responding, but he'd kept his head the whole time. "Let me go." Pushing at his chest, she shoved him away from her. "I don't—"

His fingers tightened in her hair, anchoring him against her. His eyes were blazing. "Oh, no, sweetheart. You're not pulling that on me."

"Pulling what?"

"Getting offended because I kissed you to piss off a murderer." He lowered his head. "Because now I'm going to kiss you simply because I want to."

And then he kissed her.

The other kisses had been hot, but this…

It was a whole other level. The way his lips played with hers, the nips of his teeth, the deep sensuality of his tongue playing over hers…It was a kiss designed to shred all her defenses and make her his.

And it was working. Especially because she knew it was a kiss just for them.

His hands framed her hips, pulling her against him, making her viscerally aware of how hard he was for her. His touch burned through her jeans while his mouth continued its ruthless assault. Across her jaw, down the side of her neck, and then he was at her throat. Kissing along her collarbone as one hand slid up her back, locking her against him. His body was hard, ribbed, and he smelled so amazing. The sensation of being held, of being cradled so intimately, of the way his lips were working over her chest, as if she were a treasure, an erotic temptation.

Then his mouth was back on hers, the kiss wild and desperate, no longer in control. Everything inside her responded to the intensity, and she was kissing him back just as fiercely. Needing more. Wanting his hands on her skin. Touching her everywhere.

She slipped her hands beneath his shirt. Oh, God. His skin was so hot, so smooth, and it was hers to touch, to do whatever she wanted. To lose herself in—

There was a loud crash, and Cort jerked her behind him as a man ran into the bar, the door slamming open. "Cort! You better get out here!"

"What's going on?" Cort moved between Kaylie and the man at the door, one hand tight on her hip, keeping her anchored against his back.

"Your truck. You better get out here."

Cort took one look at Kaylie, and then grabbed her hand and charged out the door.

Cort was furious when he saw what had been done to his truck.

Every window was shattered.

Headlights destroyed.

The hood dented as if someone had taken a baseball bat to his truck and beaten the hell out of it. Again and again and again.

"Oh, wow." Kaylie came to a stop beside Cort, her voice trembling. "You think—?"

"I think that kiss worked." Anger boiled inside him, fury that someone thought he had the right to destroy Cort's truck, to scare Kaylie. Jesus. What if Kaylie had been out here when this guy had snapped?

Because that's exactly what had happened.

Someone had lost control. Completely. The assault on Cort's truck had clearly been the result of a blind, frenetic rage, and anyone who'd been around at the time would have been included in the attack.

Cort threw his arm around Kaylie and yanked her against him. "Stay with me." Adrenaline jacked, he looked slowly around, hoping for one sign, one signal, to tell him which of the bystanders had done it. Etsy was there. Titus. Richie. And about twenty others, still with their beers in their hands. Cort's hands bunched into fists, but he didn't move. Didn't react. Kept the same calm he did when shit was going south fast in the air. Went into overdrive with his focus and his concentration.

No one met his gaze.

Dusty, one of the ones mentioned by Annie as having been there earlier in the evening, wasn't there. Dusty, who'd been a guide for forty years and could easily have been in a position to meet a single female climber thirty years ago. Dusty, whom Sara had hired to fly Kaylie around in a move that made no sense.

Cort sensed Luke behind him, covering his back, but he didn't turn around.

Richie muscled his way through the crowd. "Anyone see who did this? Anyone hear anything?"

The crowd mumbled, but no one spoke up.

"Jesus, you must have pissed someone off," Luke said. "Kaylie have a jealous ex?"

Kaylie looked sharply at him. "It's not funny."

"Hell, no," Luke agreed. "I'm not kidding. That kind of assault…" He whistled softly. "That's personal, my friends."

Cort turned his gaze back to the truck, saw something glittering in the driver's headrest. "What the hell's that?" Keeping an eye on the crowd, he walked over to the truck to check it out. He brought Kaylie with him, unwilling to leave her behind even for an instant.

But when he got there and saw what it was, he wished he had.

# Chapter Fifteen

Kaylie recoiled when she saw what was wedged in the cushion. A huge knife with a black handle and a serrated blade was embedded in the driver's seat, right where Cort's throat would have been if he'd been sitting there.

As if someone had been pretending to slice Cort's neck.

Or promising to do it.

The memory of Jackson's gaping wound flashed into Kaylie's mind, and she covered her own neck, her mouth going dry.

Then she saw there was dried blood on the knife.

Jackson's?

Sara's?

Her mother's?

Blindly, she reached out. "Cort—"

He wrapped his arm around her shoulders, tucking her against him "I'm here, sweetheart. I've got you." He pressed his lips to her forehead, and she closed her eyes, trying to focus only on the strength of his body, letting his presence chase away the ugly thoughts trying to consume her. "You okay?" he asked.

She nodded once. "Yeah." But her voice was shaky, and she felt exposed. Vulnerable. What kind of monster was after them?

His brow was furrowed. "Want to get out of here?"

"No." She managed to shake her head. "This is what we wanted to happen. Let's see it through."

Cort smiled, and there was no mistaking the flash of re-spect in his eyes. "You change your mind, let me know."

She nodded, hooking her hand over the waistband of his jeans to keep him close. "I'm fine."

"You're more than fine." He squeezed her once, then looked past her to search the crowd. "Richie! Get your ass over here!"

Kaylie took a deep breath while Cort gestured to the trooper, forcing herself to look at the knife in his seat again.

Cort hadn't been there. He was fine. No one had been hurt. It was a message meant to scare them.

That was all.

She bit her lip and forced herself to look inside the rest of the truck.

The passenger seat had been sliced open as well. Not just on the headrest, like Cort's, but the whole seat.

"He marked the seat as if you were sitting there," Cort said grimly, and she realized it was true.

Long, furious slashes outlined the shape of her body, like a chalk outline on a murder scene. The fabric was stained, as if he'd cut himself and kept stabbing. She stared at the pink foam, saw Sara's bloodied body in her mind, and she started to shake. Dear God—

"Fuck." Cort's grip tightened on her. "Come on."

He pulled her away from the truck as Rich hurried up. Cort had a low conversation with him while Kaylie franti-cally scanned the crowd, barely reassured by Cort's secure grip on her.

Was the killer there now? Imagining stabbing her in per-son? Waiting for a chance to do it for real?

Kaylie tensed when she saw a man in the back of the crowd, a hat pulled low over his face shielding him from view. She couldn't see him well enough to know if he was one of the men she'd seen inside the bar, but the hunch of his shoulders…was familiar. She knew she'd seen him before. "Cort—"

"Just a sec." He was still talking to Rich, and they were arguing about whether to bring Trooper Mann back for this. The young state trooper was saying he couldn't go solo on it, and Cort was telling him to get on it.

The man in the hat blew her a kiss and held up an envelope, then set it on the hood of a red truck he was standing next to.

"Cort!"

He jerked his gaze at her, then swung around to face the crowd. "Where?"

The man was moving, sliding off into the darkness. "There! Black hat—"

Cort was already on the run, tearing through the crowd, yelling something at Luke.

He shoved his way through, then tore down the street after the man. Luke was by her side in an instant, Charity with him. "Come on, Kaylie. Back inside."

"No! I have to get the envelope." Kaylie followed Cort's path through the crowd, but no one was watching her. People were far too interested in the grisly state of the truck, and rumors were circulating fast, but it still took several minutes to work her way through the crowd.

Cort was just returning as she reached the red truck. "Lost him," he growled. "Did you see his face? Recognize him?"

"No, but he left something." Kaylie reached the truck, but there was no envelope. "Dammit! I saw him set it down." She described it, and soon they were all looking.

It was Charity who found it in the mud beside the tire. She held it up. "Is this it?"

"Looks like it." It was streaked with brown. Mud or blood?

Cort plucked it from Charity's fingers, saving Kaylie from having to touch the soiled paper. He ripped it open and scanned the contents. His face became hard, and he crumpled it up, sharing a hard look with Luke.

"What does it say?"

"Nothing of importance." He shoved it in his pocket. "Can I grab your truck, Luke? I want to drive around and see—"

"Dammit, Cort!" She marched over and grabbed his arm. "Stop trying to protect me. I deserve to know what it is! I can handle it."

He caught her wrist as she reached for his pocket. "No." His voice was unyielding. "Not this time. This note was about me."

She frowned. "You?"

"Yeah." He nodded at Luke, who held up his keys.

"I'm going with you," Luke said.

"Someone needs to stay with Kaylie," Cort snapped.

"Then bring her with us. The guy's too good with a knife. You're not going alone."

"You guys aren't leaving *me* behind," Charity said. "If he was in the bar, he knows I was with you two as well. No way am I going to be added to his list of ways to toy with you."

Kaylie frowned as the three of them battled over who was coming. Cort had gone three shades pale when he'd read that note, and he hadn't made eye contact with her since.

Whatever was on that note was big.

Luke and Charity finally ran off to get his truck, leaving Kaylie alone with Cort.

Kaylie folded her arms over her chest. "Show me the note, Cort. He wanted me to see it, and I want to know what it was."

Cort's jaw flexed, then finally he reached into his pocket and yanked out the note.

He handed it over, then turned his back on her, ostensibly to scan their surroundings, but she suspected it was because he didn't want to watch her read it.

She carefully smoothed out the crumpled paper. The words were scrawled in rough, angry, black letters.

MURDERER.

She frowned. "How do you know this is about you? It just says 'Murderer.'"

He didn't turn around. "Other side."

She flipped it over.

ASK CORT WHAT HAPPENED TO HIS WIFE AND SON.

Her stomach congealed, and she looked up at him. "You're married? And you have a son?"

He finally turned around. "No."

The answer didn't ease her sudden tension. "*Were* you married?"

His jaw worked, and he gave a curt nod.

"And your son?"

His eyes were hard as steel. "Dead."

She swallowed, her throat thick. "What happened?"

A muscle ticked in Cort's cheek. "Are you asking me if I'm a murderer? If I killed them? Just ask it. Get it over with."

His voice was so cold. Waiting for judgment. Expecting it.

And she thought of Charity's words, that most people judged Cort harshly. That she should give him a chance, trust him.

"Well?" Cort sounded angry now, challenging her to say the words.

But his eyes... There was pain in them. So much grief. Betrayal. Years of torment.

She knew, because those were the eyes she saw in the mirror every day. Eyes filled with self-hatred.

But more importantly, she saw the man in them. The man

who had cried for Jackson. Who had given up the chance to get his best friend's murderer to keep her safe. A man who had held her and carried her through her grief. An adrenaline junkie who was her only rock in this world that was sliding out of control.

Cort McClaine was a lot of things, but he wasn't a killer.

Though something *had* happened to his family. Something had happened to him. And suddenly, he made a lot more sense. "Did she wear diamonds?" she asked quietly. "Your wife?"

His mouth tightened, and he said nothing.

It was enough of an answer, and she finally understood so much more.

"Just ask," he growled. "Ask me if I'm a murderer. You know you want to. I'm already on the edge, right? Slowly cracking?" Cort grabbed Kaylie by the arms, hauled her close. "Just *ask*."

Lifting her chin defiantly, she crumpled up the paper and threw it in the mud. "No. I'm not going to ask."

His eyes narrowed. "Judging me without even giving me a chance to defend myself?"

"No." Kaylie set her hands on his chest and felt him tense beneath her touch. Felt his heart hammering in such contrast to the rigid control he appeared to be exercising. "When you're ready to tell me, I'll listen." She stood on her tiptoes and pressed a kiss to his chin, not quite able to reach his mouth. He didn't bend down for her, his eyes dark and inscrutable. "And just so you know, I will never believe you're a murderer, so don't bother trying to tell me you are. I'm not asking, because I don't need to."

He stared at her, searching her face for a lie, for a trick.

"He left that note to drive a wedge between us," Kaylie said. "It won't work. If our being together threatens him, then that's how we're staying."

This time, when she wrapped her arms around the back of his neck and tugged, he let her pull him down.

And for the first time, she was the one who initiated their kiss.

No kiss had ever tasted so unbelievable.

Cort was suddenly ravenous for Kaylie. For her kiss, for her body, for her touch. Kaylie knew about his past. She *knew*, and she didn't believe the lies. Didn't judge him. Didn't care.

The bastard had tried to turn her against him, twisting a truth he knew Cort wouldn't be able to deny, a truth the whole town had already condemned him for.

And it hadn't worked.

A thousand weights fell from Cort's shoulders, and he pressed Kaylie up against the side of the truck. The metal was cold and wet, but she didn't protest. Her arms went around his neck, holding him tighter.

He slid his hands beneath her jacket and cupped her breasts. She arched into him, and he flicked a thumb over her nipple. He grunted with satisfaction when she shuddered from the contact and her fingers tightened in his hair.

She had just learned the worst about him, and yet she was kissing him with the same passion as before. There was no flinching from his touch, no coldness in her kiss. Just hot passion.

Jesus, she drove him mad with need. His blood felt as if it was burning as it raced through his body. Cort didn't want to hold back. He wanted to lose himself in her. He palmed her belly, slid his hand over the zipper of her jeans—

"Cort!" Richie's voice cut into the haze.

Swearing, Cort jerked his head from Kaylie's, but he didn't lift his body off hers. It felt too damn good to have her under him. Besides, they'd already been seen. Why bother?

"What?"

Kaylie pushed at Cort's chest, but he didn't move. Just cupped the back of her neck and rested his forearm on her collarbone. Keeping her close. Right where he wanted her.

"Can we talk privately?" the trooper asked.

Kaylie leaned around him to look at Richie. "Why does everyone around here want to hide things from me?"

Richie glanced at Cort, and Cort saw a flicker of fear in the trooper's eyes for the first time. His face was pale, and he looked a hell of a lot younger than he actually was.

Cort eased off Kaylie. "What's wrong?"

Richie's gaze flicked toward Kaylie. "Shouldn't we—?"

"She can handle it. What's wrong?" No way was he leaving Kaylie alone so he could have a private chat with Richie.

Richie hesitated. "Did you…see the passenger seat?"

Anger surged through Cort again. "Hard to miss."

"Um, yeah…" The trooper glanced around. "See, here's the thing. I gotta say…" He hesitated.

Cort grew impatient. "Say *what?*"

"Yeah, listen, I just wanted to say." Richie looked at his shoes, then finally at Cort. "I blew it by not taking you seriously before. Whoever chopped up those seats…the guy's a sick bastard."

Kaylie's hand went to Cort's belt, her fingers digging into his side.

Cort set his hand on hers, giving it a light squeeze of reassurance. "So that means you're going after him now?"

"Oh, yeah." Richie hesitated again. "The thing is, Bill told me not to bother taking notes before, about Jackson and Sara's murder, so I wasn't really paying attention. I'll need you guys to go over all the details again."

Luke chose that moment to drive up, Charity in the passenger seat. "We don't have time for a recap of the cabin." Cort told Richie about the guy Kaylie had seen by the red truck, and her description of the man.

He left out the part about the note.

Richie looked even paler. "He's still around? Shit." He grabbed for his hip. "I was off duty, so I don't have my gun. I have to go back and get it. *Shit.*"

Luke rolled down the window. "You coming or what?"

Cort realized for the first time that Richie's attitude and his being a pain in the ass were nothing more than a cover for the fact he was incapable of handing anything. But now wasn't the time for Rich to try to come into his own. "Try to reach Bill again."

"See, I can't." Richie grimaced. "He took off for the weekend. Said he was going to Anchorage, but his cell phone's off, and I must have written the wrong number down for the hotel."

"Isn't there anyone else you can call?"

Richie shook his head. "Bill's pretty possessive about his cases. He'd ride my ass if he knew I brought someone else in." He ran the back of his hand across his brow and looked at Kaylie. "You need to get out of here. Go to the airport. Take a flight anywhere. I don't know what—"

"Hey!" Cort caught his shoulder. "Rich! Go get people off the truck, retrieve the knife for fingerprinting, and start talking to witnesses. Someone has to have heard the guy beating up my truck. Find out who heard what." He slammed his hand on Richie's shoulder. "You're the man tonight, Richie. Step up."

Richie stared at him. "Bill always takes charge. I'm not supposed to—"

"You are. Tonight you earn your badge. Screw Bill. It has to be you."

Rich nodded, pulled back his shoulders. "Yeah, okay. Yeah. I'm on it. I can do this." He turned his attention to Kaylie, a new determination in him that Cort hadn't seen before. A purpose. He could only hope it held up until Bill returned to take over.

"What are you doing to stay safe?" Rich asked Kaylie. "You want me to lock you up at the station?"

Cort couldn't suppress his smug satisfaction when she put her hand on his arm. "I'll stay with Cort."

"Yeah." Richie nodded. "Yeah, that's a good call. What's your mobile number, Cort?"

Cort rattled it off, and Richie put it into his phone. There was a new set to his shoulders, a new strength to his voice. "Yeah, okay. I'll keep in touch." He didn't wait for an answer. He just spun on his heel and marched back toward the truck, shouting at people to get back.

Taking charge.

About damned time.

"Are we going or what?" Luke leaned out the window.

"Let's do it." Cort took Kaylie's arm and began to guide her toward the truck. Something caught his attention and he paused, turning to survey the street. People were still clustered around his truck.

Then he heard the unmistakable click of a rifle being cocked.

"Get down!" Cort tackled Kaylie and rolled her beneath the truck, covering her with his body.

Dirt kicked up inches from their heads, and then there was nothing.

No more bullets.

Silence, except the beating of Kaylie's heart beneath him.

"Cort—"

"Shh." He put his hand over her mouth, straining to listen, but he heard nothing. No footsteps, no scrape of metal across the ground.

The passenger door opened above their heads. "Get in," Luke said quietly. "I can't tell where he is. We need to get the fuck out of here."

Cort wrapped his arm around Kaylie. "Stay close." Keeping her shielded by his body, he helped her up and shoved her onto the floor of Luke's truck. Charity was already on the floorboards in the back.

Cort jumped in, staying low as Luke peeled out. Kaylie's eyes were wide, and she was silent, staring at Cort.

A shotgun and a rifle were on the gun rack behind Charity. Cort helped himself to the shotgun. "What the fuck was that?"

"No idea. Could have been a drunk shooting rats." Luke was grim as he sped down the street. "But I'm not driving around a bunch of dark alleys waiting for him to pick us off. I search by plane, or I don't search at all."

"Amen to that." Cort fisted the shotgun, watching intently as the buildings rolled past.

"Where to?"

"Home. We're getting the hell out of here."

"Wait!" Charity's voice was muffled from the back. "I'm not going to your airfield. Drop me off at my place."

"And let him know where you live if he's on our tail?" Luke shook his head. "No way. You're staying with us."

"No." Kaylie crawled up on the seat beside Cort. "I don't want to involve Luke and Charity. I can't do another Jackson and Sara," she said. "I can't be responsible for them."

Charity sat up. "Jackson and Sara? Did something happen to them?"

No one answered, and Cort looked over at Luke. "You and Charity get out at her place. Cover her back until you know you guys aren't a target."

"No way," Luke scowled. "I'm staying with you."

"No." Cort knew Kaylie was right. "I'm not endangering you. You get out, or we do."

They looked at one another, and Luke took a hard right. "I'm doing this for Charity," he snapped. "But the minute I know she's safe, I'm coming after you guys."

"Deal."

Luke pulled back up to the bar, next to Charity's car. He hesitated. "Don't get killed."

Cort nodded, and Luke got out of the truck with Charity and the rifle. Charity reached through the open door and hugged Kaylie while Cort shifted over into the driver's seat. "I don't know all that's going on," she whispered. "But be safe."

Kaylie nodded. "I'll do my best. You too."

"Always." Charity stepped back with a worried frown, then yelped when Luke grabbed her and tossed her into her car with an order to stay low.

Kaylie sighed and leaned back in the passenger seat.

"Get down," Cort ordered, scanning the streets for a threat. But he saw nothing.

It didn't reassure him.

Because it meant he didn't know where the threat was coming from, making him nothing but a sitting duck. Powerless, with Kaylie's life in his hands.

He shifted the truck and floored the gas.

Screw that.

It was time to take back control.

# CHAPTER SIXTEEN

The streets were empty and wet as Cort sped through the town. The only sign of life was an occasional corner street-light.

It was after midnight in Twin Forks.

No one was going to be out there.

No one except a murderer.

Cort glanced at Kaylie, who had hunkered down in the seat at his command without protest. Some folks would have said Cort's being on the road meant there were two murderers stalking the streets tonight.

But not Kaylie.

Cort had already been determined to keep her safe, for Jackson.

Now?

Now it was for her.

Her diamonds caught the light, and he grimaced, realizing she was such a contradiction. He was getting sucked in by her, and it could only end badly. Again.

He needed to find a way to keep his distance. But, hell. He didn't want to.

For a few minutes, neither of them spoke, Cort watching for a tail, Kaylie slumped in the seat. "Where are we going?" she finally asked.

"My place to get my plane, then to Old Tom's. I want to be there when he lands. Find out what the hell is going on."

She nodded.

Said nothing else.

But he saw a tear slide out of her eye and down her cheek.

He tried to ignore it.

He really did.

But when a second one broke free, he cursed under his breath. Then he took her by the arm and pulled her across the bench seat toward him. Tucked her against his side and pressed his lips to her hair.

Because he couldn't stop himself.

Kaylie burrowed into his side, her body trembling. "If this man…If he's the one who called me and told me my mother is still alive, and if he has her…" Her voice broke.

Cort grimaced. "Kaylie," he said gently. "If your mom is still alive, we'll find her."

"Do you think she's dead? What about my dad? My brother? I don't even know what happened to them." She was clutching his arm, and he liked the feel of her hanging on to him. "What if he killed them all? Slaughtered my brother and dad, like he did Jackson? Hurt my mom, like he did Sara? Do you think he—?"

Cort squeezed her firmly. "One of the first lessons a bush pilot learns is to never imagine the worst-case scenario. It paralyzes you, and pretty much guarantees that's exactly what you'll get. Focus on surviving the next five minutes. Think about what you can do right now to change things. Don't think about the rest of it."

Kaylie was quiet for a minute, the tires whizzing over the damp pavement. "I can't do that. I can't stop thinking about the way the truck was cut up, about Sara and Jackson and—"

"You can." Cort cut her off. He could feel her tensing against him, and he knew she was on the verge of panic. "What do you have power over? What's within your control to do?"

She closed her eyes, letting her head fall back against his shoulder. "We're going to talk to Old Tom."

"Yep. What are you going to ask him?"

"Who was in the party. Where he left them. If anyone was hanging around or anything. Or came with them."

"If he flew your mom when she was here thirty years ago."

Kaylie turned her head. "You think he was the one from before?"

"You find a bush pilot you trust with your life, and that's who you call next time. It's how it works. I've been flying some of my clients since I was fifteen."

"You've been flying clients since you were *fifteen?* You shouldn't even have been driving a car, let alone a plane."

He grinned, pulling out on the highway. Empty and abandoned, it was pitch-black except for his headlights. No one following him that he could see. But he was still itchy. Still tense. Needed to get in the air and put some distance between the psychopath and Kaylie. "It's Alaska, sweetie. We have different rules."

"It's not Alaska. It's you. You live by different rules." She tried to move away from him, but he didn't let her go. "Cort—"

"I need to know something."

She stopped fighting and turned to look at him. "What?"

"You had no problem taking my word about my ex-wife and my—" He still choked on the word. "My son. But you still have a problem with me. I want to know what your deal is."

She didn't hesitate. "You live to risk death."

"No, I don't risk death. I do what I do. Death isn't an option." A bush pilot who thought about death might as well hang up his wings, because Death would be coming on the next train for him.

"Oh, come on, Cort." She punched him in the chest in frustration. "Do you seriously believe that? You risk death all the time. That's what makes your heart beat and your soul come alive. Just admit it!"

He opened his mouth to deny it, then shut it. Thinking of

how to explain it to someone who didn't understand. "I don't risk death," he said. "I just like to flip it off."

She frowned at him. "That sounds like the same thing."

"No. Russian roulette is risking death. You might die, you might not. It's luck." He gestured up at the sky. "I'm in complete control up there. It's a constant challenge, and it's hard as hell, but I'm never in danger of dying."

"Oh, come on! You can't tell me in all your hours in the air, you've never come close to dying."

"I've come close, sure. But that's not the same thing as risking death."

She groaned, folding her arms over her chest as she sat up, moving away from him. "I don't understand how it's not the same thing."

He let out his breath. How many times had he had this conversation with his ex-wife? And it had always been like this. Around and around, never coming to an understanding. He'd given up trying to explain himself to anyone who didn't get it. For some reason, though, he wanted Kaylie to understand. He *needed* her to understand. But he had no idea how to explain it. "What does your family say? They're climbers, right? So they must—"

She looked out the window. "I haven't seen my parents in over ten years. The only one I keep in contact with is my brother, but it's awkward because he's caught in the middle. My parents hate me, and he tries to keep the balance. He's the only one I really have, and I haven't even seen him in about five years." She stared out the window. "The phone call didn't mention him," she said quietly. "I don't now if that's bad or good."

"Why do your parents hate you?" He couldn't imagine that.

She sighed, hugging herself tighter, as if she was withdrawing into herself. "Because they hate the fact I'm not like them, and I hate that they forced hell on me for the first sixteen years of my life. And I resent that getting a high from some stupid mountain is more important than their own daughter."

His grip tightened on the wheel, tensing at the accusation he'd heard so often from his ex-wife. "That's crap. Just because they like to climb doesn't mean you aren't important."

"It is! Don't you get it?" Kaylie made a noise of frustration. "I'm not enough for them. I never was. They're like drug addicts, living from one high to the other, and anyone who gets in their way gets burned. They'll keep going after the next hit until it kills them." She leveled a gaze at him. "Just like you."

"I'm not a *drug addict*—"

"You are. It's just the name of the drug that changes." She turned her attention to the window again. "I couldn't watch them destroy themselves, so I left. And now"—she spread her hands—"here I am. Back in the world I hate, trying to find my family, who may have finally fulfilled their destiny in a way even more horrible than I thought. And the only way I can find them or save them or whatever is to go back into this world. They win. Even in death, they win. They make me come back."

"No one made you do anything. You chose to come back."

"Like I had a choice! They could be dying on the mountain somewhere!"

"Of course you had a choice. You made the courageous one." Now that he understood her a little bit more, he knew he spoke the truth. Despite the image she presented, Kaylie was strong. And her loyalty—there to the core, despite ten years of separation. He moved his hand, tapped her boot where her feet were curled up on the seat next to her, then thumbed the necklace hanging between her breasts. "Who are you really, Kaylie Fletcher? Are you diamonds, or are you hiking boots?"

She was quiet for a minute, and he didn't think she was going to answer. "I'm just trying to be me," she finally said.

"Which is what?"

"I don't know." She rubbed her forehead wearily. "I guess, between those two? Diamonds, maybe. I hope." Her voice was quiet. Exhausted.

He shot her a look, saw her eyes were closed. "You hope? What does that mean?"

"Could you ever like me, really like me, if I was exactly what you think I am? Someone who likes heated mattresses, high heels, and manicures?"

He narrowed his eyes. "I don't think that's who you really are." He thought of her out in the woods at the cabin, her family...No, there was more to Kaylie than what she put on. Yeah, she was diamonds. He got that. But his ex-wife was only diamonds, and Kaylie was so much more than Valerie had ever been. Was she different enough from Valerie for it to work between them?

Hell if he knew, but he couldn't risk going through another Valerie. Just wasn't going to go there again.

"My family says I'm more than high heels and manicures, but it's just because they want me to be someone else, not because they're privy to some inner secret even I don't know about." She rolled her head to the side, her eyes half-closed as she regarded him. "Your aversion to someone like me...It's because of her, isn't it? She was like me, and then she hurt you?"

"She?"

"Your ex-wife. What's her name?"

He ground his teeth. "Valerie."

"Valerie," she repeated with a yawn. "Well, Valerie tried to change you, didn't she?"

He nodded. "She did." His reply was curt.

"She failed."

He didn't answer. Yeah, he still flew, but he'd never been the same since his marriage to Valerie. She'd changed him, just not in the way she'd wanted.

"I've tried to change adrenaline junkies, too," Kaylie mumbled. "I always fail. Then they die." A tear leaked out of the corner of her eye again. "Everyone dies on me," she whispered. "I'm so tired of it."

Something tightened in his chest. "I'm not going to die."

"That's what they all say. They all lie." She opened her eyes and looked up at him. "Don't make promises you can't keep, Cort. That's all I ask."

He met her gaze. "I never break my promises."

"You said you weren't going to die."

"I'm not."

She snorted. "Everyone dies sometime. That's a promise you can't keep." She rolled onto her side, leaning against the seat as she studied him. "What happened with Valerie to make you hate me so much?"

"Trust me, everything would be a hell of a lot easier if I did hate you, but I don't." Cort ground his jaw, his hands tightening on the wheel. "And Valerie is a long story."

"So?"

"So, we're home." He pulled into the garage next to his house. "Let's pack and hit the road. We'll probably be sleeping out at Old Tom's."

Kaylie settled more deeply into the seat, a stubborn set to her jaw. "Tell me."

He draped his forearms over the steering wheel, staring out the windshield, while he thought about what had happened with Valerie. With their son. All the old feelings came back, and he shut them off. Ditched the trip down memory lane. Useless and a waste of energy. "Let's go. We don't have time for this."

"But—"

He got out of the truck and slammed the door.

\* \* \*

"Well, hot damn," a raspy male voice said. "I knew I'd been a good boy today. I just didn't realize how good."

Kaylie jerked awake. A older man with gray hair and wrinkled skin was leaning over her, a lascivious gleam in his bloodshot eyes. She scrambled back, fell off the edge of the couch, and leapt to her feet. "I—"

"Tom. Stop scaring my woman." Cort came around from the kitchen, a cup of coffee in his hand.

*My woman.* A tingle went through Kaylie on hearing Cort's words. She knew it was for show, but she couldn't stop her response.

"Cort, you old bastard. Who gave you the right to invade my house while I was gone?" Tom thumped Cort on the shoulder and helped himself to the coffee. "Hope you made the same strong brew you used to make."

"Sure did." Cort glanced over at Kaylie, and their eyes met. They'd barely spoken since they'd left the truck. She'd slept most of the flight here and had fallen asleep on the couch once they'd arrived and let themselves into Old Tom's cabin.

Granted, it was the middle of the night, but she'd slept mostly to avoid talking to Cort. The conversation in the truck had upset her. Yes, she'd known Cort was an adrenaline junkie, but for him to basically admit he didn't like her the way she was, to tell her she wasn't actually who she wanted to be…He was like her family. Like everyone else.

*Diamonds or hiking boots?* His question still burned in her mind.

Diamonds, right?

But sitting in that bar with Charity, a woman as natural and Alaskan as a woman could get, Kaylie had felt at home. She'd felt, for the first time in a long time, like she belonged. And Luke…Once he'd finished grilling her about her intentions toward Cort, he'd relaxed. Funny, charming, and clearly brilliant. They'd both made her feel welcome.

They hadn't cared if she was a flier or an adrenaline junkie. They'd just made her feel good.

And dancing with Cort...She looked over at him while he traded insults with Tom. There were shadows under his eyes, his whiskers thick and dark. His hair was tousled, and his face was grim.

Guilt tweaked her belly. She'd been so consumed with herself, so reliant upon Cort for strength, that she hadn't even thought of what he was facing. Jackson, a dead son, the anniversary of his parents' death...Cort hadn't so much as hinted that anything was on his mind, but as she studied him, she saw a great heaviness in his eyes. Weariness. A multitude of emotions he was keeping under tight control.

As if aware of her perusal, his gaze slid to hers. Surprise flickered across his face at whatever he saw in her expression, and his eyes softened before he returned his attention to Tom.

Kaylie sighed and looked up at the ceiling of Tom's living room. Raw wood beams. It reminded her of Cort's place, which had made her feel so drained that first night as a blatant reminder of Alaska.

But now it made her think of a night in Cort's arms, of Charity, of a feeling of belonging she'd had, however brief. Without flying, without climbing, would there be a place for her here?

Not that it mattered. With Cort, with this world, there was no way to be in Alaska without climbing and flying. She hadn't been able to tolerate parents who lived that life. What made her think she'd be able to survive a man who did?

But she wanted to, didn't she? Kaylie realized she wanted a chance to try. Oh, God. What was she thinking? The most horrible wave of vulnerability hit her, and she felt raw and exposed, as if she were stranded on a bitterly cold mountaintop without clothes, or—

"How's the knee?" Cort asked Tom, drawing her attention back into the room.

She took a deep breath, trying to regroup.

"Good as it ever is." Old Tom limped over to the couch and sat down where Kaylie had been sleeping. "You going to introduce me to your woman, or what? I could have sworn she was mine when I walked in and saw her all bundled up on my couch."

Cort grinned and held out his hand to Kaylie. One eyebrow went up, and he waited.

A challenge.

She looked down at that hand, callused and weathered. Strong. She knew she was crossing the line by thinking of him as a man, not just as an adrenaline junkie who would destroy her. By allowing herself to see the man beneath, she was digging her own grave.

She should put up barriers. Now. Big ones.

But instead of rejecting Cort's offer, Kaylie set her hand in his. His palm was warm as it closed around hers. She didn't resist as he wrapped an arm around her shoulders and hooked his arm around her neck. "This is Kaylie Fletcher."

She looked up at him, startled by the possessiveness in his tone. Was it for show, or for real? But Cort was looking at Tom, not at her, and she couldn't read his expression.

"Yours, eh?" Tom leaned forward, studying her intently. "Looks a mite fragile for breeding the kind of stock that'll survive out here. Nice lines though."

"She'll do," Cort agreed, squeezing her tightly, but she felt the sudden tension in his muscles, heard the edge to his voice.

Was it the reference to breeding? Thinking of his son? How did anyone ever get over that kind of loss? No matter how it happened, it would be awful.

Tentatively, she slid her arm around his waist, tucking her hand in waistband of his jeans.

He looked down at her, the same surprise on his face as before. Then his gaze went to her mouth, and her body heated up.

"I only got one bedroom and I'm using it," Tom announced. "If you two want to get horizontal, you'll have to do it outside."

Cort cleared his throat and sat on a lopsided armchair and tugged her down with him. She managed to avoid his lap and perched on the arm instead.

"We're looking for information," Cort said. "Kaylie's family has gone missing on Denali, and rumors say you're the one who flew them."

Tom narrowed his eyes at Kaylie. "You here to find a way to sue me for their tragedy?"

"No, no." She held out her hand, uncomfortable at Tom's instinct to distrust her as an outsider. Maybe she should give up the jewelry. Try to fit in. God, she didn't even know who to be anymore. "I just want to find them."

Tom ignored her. "You bringing shit to my plate, McClaine?"

"No. I'm not."

Something passed between the two men, and then Old Tom nodded and he leaned back on the couch, took a gulp of his coffee. "Give me the rundown. Who are you looking for?"

"My family was lost on McKinley a week or so ago, from what I can gather. I know my mom and dad and brother were in the party, but I don't know who else. My mom is Alice Fletcher. My dad's Kix Fletcher. And my brother is Mason. Did you fly them?"

Tom studied her, and his face grew pensive. He leaned forward, peering at her more closely. "Well, damn it to hell, I knew you looked familiar. You look exactly like her."

Kaylie sat up. "Like who? My mom? Did you fly her?"

"Fly her?" Tom leaned back with a grin. "Hell, yeah, I flew her. Took her right up to the heavens and back down, more'n once. Yeah, she's a keeper, that one."

Kaylie stared at Tom, cold dread settling in her chest as she absorbed the implication of his words. "You mean, you *slept* with her?"

# CHAPTER SEVENTEEN

"Hell, yeah, I slept with her," Old Tom said. "Alice is the kind of woman you never forget, no matter how long it's been." He gave Kaylie a thoughtful look. "You have that same sparkle in your eyes, missy."

"Kaylie's mine, old man. Keep your distance." Cort's voice was mild, but a warning in his tone had both her and Tom looking at him.

Kaylie moved closer to Cort. Was *Tom* the one they were looking for? She looked wildly around the room, half expecting to see a bloody knife hanging from the wall. Had there been a snowmobile out front?

Tom burst out laughing, a guttural, untamed sound. "Hot damn, McClaine. You're as whipped as I was. Take my advice. Don't let her leave Alaska. They don't come back."

Kaylie jerked her attention back to Tom. "You knew my mom *before*? When she was here thirty years ago?"

Tom raised his gray brows. "You think I slept with her when she was here with her husband? I'm a lot of things, missy, but I don't go playing in another man's backyard." He winked. "At least not when he's around to catch me."

Kaylie gripped Cort's shoulder. She didn't want Tom to be the killer. She didn't want to think that she was sitting in the living room of a murderer. Cort's rifle was still in the plane. They had nothing to defend themselves with. But if it was Tom, wouldn't he be hiding his relationship with Kaylie's mom?

"Was there anyone *else* my mom..." Kaylie stumbled over

the words, not used to thinking of her mother as a sexual being. "…slept with before? Someone who was around her this
time? Who knew she was back?"

"Anyone else?" Tom took another drink of coffee. "Hate
to break it to you, missy, but the line to your mom's room was
damn long back then."

Cort set his arm across Kaylie's legs, holding her in place,
his hand cupped around her calf. "Did anyone in particular
stand out?" he asked. "Someone who didn't seem too happy
to see her again? Or maybe was a little too interested in seeing her?"

Tom studied them, and she could see him thinking.
"Why?"

"Because you don't seem too upset that her party went
missing." Cort's voice was even. "Seeing as how you were
both the pilot and the ex-lover of one of the climbers, seems
odd you wouldn't care that they disappeared."

The amusement vanished from Tom's face, and the energy
of the room shifted instantly. "Don't judge me, McClaine.
You're in no place to cast your shit on anyone else. You and
me, we're the same. You forget that because you've got a
Lower 48 in your bed now and think you're too good? You
already forget what happened last time you went that
route?"

Kaylie grabbed Cort's arm as he went to stand up and go
after Tom. "Cort," she said quietly. "Let it go. Look at his
eyes."

She felt Cort hesitate, then saw him look at Tom's face.
The pain in his eyes was obvious. Centuries of loneliness.
Old Tom felt something. What it was, she didn't know, but
he felt something. Regret that he'd loved her mother and
lost her? Or something deeper and more sinister?

Cort eased down, but his hold on Kaylie was relentless.
"The truth, Tom. Tell us what the hell's going on. Now."

Tom's voice was expressionless. "I dropped her party off on

a glacier. Came back two days later, like we agreed, and they were gone. Found their base camp, but no sign of anyone. I flew searchers for twenty hours a day for the next three days, and we found nothing. Yeah, it pissed me off. It always pisses me off when I lose a client, and it's worse when it's personal—and Alice was personal." He pulled his shoulders back. "But you know as well as I do that you have to shake it off and forget it." His gaze went to Kaylie. "It's the only way to survive out here. People die. You shake it off. It's the way it works." His face softened. "Let them go, missy. They're gone."

"It's too late for that," Kaylie said. On so many levels. "I can't. Please, tell me everything you know. Was there anyone else there? Anyone from before who seemed interested in her return?"

Tom picked up an old cigar and began to chew on the end. "Yeah, yeah, there was actually." He studied them. "Billy Mann. That son of a bitch is always trying to fuck with me."

Cort paused. "Trooper Mann? The Statie?"

"Sure thing. Billy was the reason I had only a couple nights with the little lady thirty years ago. None of the rest of us had a chance with Alice once Billy showed up. She was interested in no one but him." He grinned. "Busted up our friendship, she did. Billy never forgave me for having her first. Every time he tries to arrest me for something, I get a kick out of the fact that it still pisses him off."

Kaylie looked at Cort, her heart racing. "It would explain a lot."

"Bill's place isn't too far from here," Cort said. "Let's do a flyby. See if he's really in Anchorage, like Rich said he was." He stood, held out his hand. "Thanks so much, Tom."

Old Tom clasped Cort's hand in a bear grip. "Always like a visit from friends. Place gets too damn lonely out here. Don't fly safe. Too boring."

"Will do." Cort nodded to him, then took Kaylie's hand and guided her out.

She looked over her shoulder as Old Tom came out to stand on the porch and watch them go. Cort looked tense. Did he think Old Tom was sending them off on a wild goose chase?

Cort herded her toward the plane. "Get in."

Old Tom watched her climb aboard. Cort was on board a split second after she was, and he had the plane taxiing in less than a minute. He was silent, and a muscle was ticking in his cheek.

"Cort? Do you think Tom's lying?"

"I think we're being toyed with. I'm just not sure by who. If it's Bill, I don't know how much I can trust Richie. And if it's Old Tom…" He shook his head.

"If it's Old Tom, *what*?"

He glanced over at her as the plane lifted off. "If it's Old Tom, we've got a problem."

"Why?"

"Because he's the only reason I'm not in jail for murder."

The footsteps outside made Mason jerk back to full consciousness.

He fisted the stake he'd found in the corner of the shed, hiding it beneath his hip as he waited.

His mouth was parched. He was too cold, and every joint in his body ached. Fever had hit, and that was bad.

Really bad.

He had to get the hell out, and fast.

The door opened, and Mason had to duck his head against the sudden light, the brightness from the outdoors blinding after such darkness.

Fingers closed around his hair and jerked his head back. He fisted the stake and swung hard, hitting flesh with a thud that made victory sing through his veins.

His assailant went down, and Mason lunged to his knees, adrenaline overriding all pain and physical limitations as it had so many times in the past. He slammed the weapon down toward his assailant, who rolled out of the way faster than Mason's depleted body could react.

His assailant lunged for the shackle, jerking it hard as he dove out of the way. The metal band dug into Mason's infected leg. He screamed and swung for his opponent's hands.

Then a kick landed in Mason's broken rib and he was down.

"Nice try." His captor climbed to his feet, holding his side as he walked over to Mason and stood over him. "I like spirit. You take after your mother."

Mason stared at him, gasping for breath, each breath sending spirals of agony through his body, trying to follow the conversation. "My mother? What the hell does she have to do with anything?"

The beard was gone, his eyes haunted, angry. Shit. Not just angry. Enraged.

His captor picked up the mallet. "Tell me, is your sister as much of a slut as your mother?"

Mason closed his eyes for a split second. *Kaylie*. She must have come.

"Don't close your eyes when I'm talking to you!"

Mason jerked his eyes open just in time to see the implement slam toward his busted shoulder. No time to brace himself, he doubled over from the agony, biting his tongue to keep from making a noise of protest.

The second time he wasn't able to suppress a grunt.

The third hit, on his leg, made him vomit from the pain.

When his captor finally pulled out a camera and began to take pictures, Mason was too gone to even care.

Or wonder what the son of a bitch was going to use them for.

# Chapter Eighteen

"You have to tell me what happened with your wife and son," Kaylie said on their way to Bill's property.

The muscle on the right side of Cort's neck twitched, and he felt it knotting up at Kaylie's urgent tone. The sun was already beginning to rise, but it was still too dark to see anything from the air. But Cort didn't care, and he was flying straight toward the land he knew was owned by Bill. Cort had never been there, and he had no idea where to land. But Bill had owned a few planes over the years, and Cort figured there had to be somewhere to set his plane down.

The wind had been picking up for the last half hour, and Cort's little plane was hopping, demanding most of his concentration. His gut was telling him the weather was bad, heading straight for hellish, but he hadn't checked in. Why bother? It wasn't as if he was going to turn around.

Had to find out what was going on. Who was fucking with him? Bill? Old Tom?

"Cort!" Kaylie interrupted his thoughts. "If Old Tom is the one after us and it relates to what happened with your wife, you need to tell me—"

"I know." Cort cut Kaylie off. Knew he had no choice but to spill. The stakes were too high right now for him not to tell her the full story. "I met Valerie in Anchorage." He couldn't keep the bitterness out of his voice. "She was there on some corporate retreat. I was taking her group on sightseeing tours."

Kaylie raised her brows. "Sightseeing tours? That doesn't sound like you."

"I was short on cash. It was before Luke came on board." The plane lurched again, and Cort had to focus for a moment before resuming. "Valerie was the daughter of some rich guy who'd bought her a job at the company. I was a dangerous hothead, and she wanted to rebel. Love at first sight."

"You loved her?"

Cort shot a glance at Kaylie. Her face was deceptively serene. The only thing revealing her tension was her tight grip on her seat belt. The weather, or the topic of discussion?

"Valerie reeled me in like a fish that couldn't resist the lure of fresh bait." He checked the gauges, made a couple adjustments, and then continued. "She was rich, she was beautiful, and she lit my fire. She was so far beyond what a guy like me ever thought he'd get. I took her back to my place and didn't ask questions about why she'd slummed with me. Didn't want to hear the answers, I guess." Cort thought back to that moment when he'd brought Valerie home to stay. She'd been the first person who'd lived with him since his parents had died nearly a decade before.

It had been such a rush, having someone a part of his life again. Cort had been desperate for her, spent more hours in bed than anywhere else for those first few months. Even cut down on his flying for a while.

"And then what?"

He cleared his throat. "Valerie's dad told her he was coming here to bring her home. So we got hitched." He ground his jaw. "I thought it was because she was too hooked on me to leave. I was too stupid to think it was because she wanted to thumb her nose at Daddy."

Kaylie was silent, but he could feel her watching him.

"So yeah, he came, he saw, and he cut her off." Cort gave a bitter smile, catching the plane as it suddenly dropped a couple hundred feet.

Kaylie caught her breath, and he looked over at her. "It's okay. I'm in control."

She nodded once. "I'm fine." But her voice was tense. "Keep talking. It's a good distraction from the fact the plane sounds like it's going to come apart any second."

At her words, Cort became aware of the sound of the wind whipping across the metal, of the creaks of the airplane—things he didn't even notice. But they could be disturbing as hell to a groundie. "She's just warming up," he said. "It's all good."

"I just..." Kaylie glanced out the window. "You wouldn't fly us into a dangerous situation, would you? Not with me on board."

Cort heard her undertone of fear, and it gnawed at him. He knew it was because of the comments others had made, that he was treading to close to the edge, and it bugged him that Kaylie wouldn't trust him at what he did best. "What do *you* think?"

She glanced at him, chewing on her lower lip, and didn't answer. Which made him even more annoyed. But what did he expect? It wasn't as if he'd done anything to make her trust his flying judgment, other than to get annoyed when she questioned it.

"So, what happened after you got married?" Kaylie's voice was tight, her hands fisting her harness. "Please, keep talking. It's distracting."

"Yeah, okay." He adjusted his altitude, trying to find quieter air to relieve her stress. "After Valerie got cut off and realized she was stuck with me, the glow faded fast. She didn't like the fact I was always in the air, and she hated all my friends. Hated Alaska. Hated it all."

Kaylie nodded. "Yeah, I can see that."

His mood got blacker at her comment. *Don't let her leave Alaska*, Old Tom had said. *She'll never come back.*

"When we first got together, Valerie used to fly with me, a

lot. But then she quit, saying she hated flying and had done it just to make me happy. That I'd forced her into that. I thought that if I could get her to fly again, she'd realize she loved it, too." Cort took a hard breath. "My parents flew together all the time, and that's what I wanted. I knew I couldn't be happy with a groundie, and I wanted her to be like my mom." His voice flattened. "Then Valerie got pregnant."

Kaylie turned sharply to look at him. "Your son?"

"Yeah." The old anger began to rise. "Valerie told me she was leaving me. She told me she would never allow her child to suffer the nightmare of having a bush pilot for a dad."

"Because…?"

Cort shot a look at her. "Because I'm a big kid who will never grow up. Because all I do is run around looking for my next high. I'm going to die young and leave my wife and kid broke and alone to pick up the pieces."

Kaylie's cheeks turned red. "That's what she said?"

"Oh, yeah. And more." He scowled. "I wouldn't let Valerie leave. Couldn't let go of the dream. Wife, a kid." Just like his parents. "We fought for months. It was…brutal." Yeah, *brutal* pretty much described it.

"And then what happened?"

The plane began to twist harder, and Cort realized the wind had really picked up. He thought he should check in with Max, see what was going on.

"What about the baby?"

Kaylie's quiet question jerked him back to the present. "Contractions came early. Weather was bad. Something was wrong." He thought back to that night, the sleet and snow pounding his cabin, the roads cut off. Valerie screaming with pain. "She wanted me to drive her into town, but I knew it would take too long. Knew we didn't have that kind of time. Told her I'd fly her instead."

"Did you? Fly her?"

"Yeah." God, how Valerie had cursed him when he'd carried her out to the plane. The wind had been blowing so hard he could barely make it to the hangar. It had been weather he had no right in God's name taking off in, but he'd done it anyway. No choice. "I had to. I called in to see if the roads were clear, and it was bad all the way to the nearest hospital. Couldn't have made it if I'd driven her. She was bleeding, and—"

Kaylie leaned toward him, and he felt her hand on his leg.

He fought back the fury, struggled to regain control. "Yeah, the weather was hell. Fucking hell. Valerie was screaming. Blood everywhere." He wiped the sweat off his head, barely aware of the way the plane was fighting him, the roar of the wind. "I couldn't make it. Couldn't fucking make it to the hospital. Had to bring the plane down near Tom's place, and he came out." Cort shook his head, trying to clear his vision. "Bad landing. Plane flipped. Valerie busted her head open."

Kaylie's fingers dug into his thigh.

"Tom helped me transfer her to his plane. He had a heavier one. He flew while I sat in back with Valerie." Cort's hands were shaking now. "The baby...He came early...on the plane...not breathing...couldn't save him...My hands... He was so small, and he wasn't breathing. I did CPR, was certified for it as part of the tour-guide thing. Tried, couldn't..."

Kaylie's hand was in his hair now, her touch soft. "I'm so sorry, Cort."

"We landed ten minutes later. Too late. Valerie...So much fucking blood..." The plane lurched, and his hands slipped on the controls. He grabbed for them, wiped his palms on his jeans.

"Did she die?" Kaylie's fingers were tangling in his hair, slow circles, comforting.

"No. No, she survived. But..." He had to stop, fight down the emotion. "She and her dad convinced the state to bring charges against me for the murder of my son and attempted murder of her."

Kaylie's fingers froze in his hair. "What? Why?"

"For flying. The crash…It was rough. Banged her up. Said that it caused the premature birth. Said that if I'd driven her, we would have made it. That the rough flight banged her around and…Yeah, she said that I kept her from getting medical care to spite her for wanting to leave. That I tried to withhold hospital care in the air to coerce her into giving me custody of the boy." He swallowed the anger, the betrayal. "So, yeah, Tom testified on my behalf. Said how I tried to save my family in that plane. How fucking hard I tried. How I used my rifle to force him to fly us. He explained that I couldn't have made it to his place as fast as I did in that weather if I hadn't been hauling ass for the hospital as fast as I could."

"Did you? Threaten Tom with your gun?"

"Yeah. I would've shot the bastard, too, if he hadn't agreed to help me." Cort felt that same anger, that same betrayal, as he'd sat in that courtroom and listened to one person after another testify that he pushed the edge in the air too much. People had claimed in court that the roads had been passable that night and he should have driven. "It was Tom's testimony that saved me. That he'd been in that air, that the weather hadn't been that bad. That I made the only choice a bush pilot could have made. He told them I was good enough to have a chance to make it through that storm, that it hadn't been irresponsible or murderous. It was his thirty years of experience and his flawless reputation that saved me. His word over an outsider's." But when Cort had walked out of that courtroom, people had never looked at him the same.

And his son was dead.

His fist bunched, and he wanted to punch the dash. Slam his hands into it until they bled. "Valerie sat in that courtroom and looked right at me. I saw in her eyes that she knew the truth, that I'd done everything I could have, and she didn't give a fuck. She was hanging me out to dry so she could get back to the world she belonged in with her reputation intact."

"Cort."

He didn't look at Kaylie. Couldn't. He was angry all over again, his heart bleeding for that child, that tiny boy who'd died in the belly of a plane. The bitch who'd made his son's death into a spectacle and a lie. "She took my son's body back with her. I don't even know where he's buried."

Kaylie touched his arm. "I'm so sorry."

He caught a softness in her voice, and he jerked his gaze over at her. Kaylie didn't look away, and her face was sympathetic, not condemning. "Valerie wronged you."

Cort narrowed his eyes. Her words were honest, her concern genuine. But there was something else. "You get her, don't you?"

She frowned. "What?"

"You get why she had to leave. You get why she didn't want her child raised by me, don't you?"

Kaylie's cheeks flushed. "She was horrible to you! You don't deserve that! I know you did everything you could to save them!"

"But you know why she had to leave, don't you? You *get* her." He was beyond pissed now. "Don't lie to me."

"Fine, yes!" Tears were in her eyes, but Cort didn't care. "I understand her initial fears. Of course I do. But that doesn't mean I think what she did was right on any level at all! She betrayed you so horribly, and—"

The plane lurched, plummeting a hundred feet before he regained control. Shit. The weather was from hell, the rain and sleet pounding at his windshield, the wind railing at them. He'd been so caught up in the damn story, he'd lost track of the weather. Goddamn, how did he still give Valerie, and women like her, the power to mess with him?

"Cort—"

"Not now." He cut Kaylie off, not wanting to hear more lies from someone who would betray him. Instead of dealing with her, he checked in with Max. "Tell me what's going. I'm feeling a lot of wind." He gave his coordinates and his destination.

"Bring it home," Max said. "It's a no-go for the next twelve hours in that area."

Cort listened grimly as Max filled him in with talk about a front that had formed off the coast and was closing fast. Snow mixed with ice, gusts of wind too high for his plane to take. Seventy miles south and moving quickly, gearing up for a head-on collision with the place they were going.

But they were only about ten minutes away from Bill's property. No point in turning back now. Cort needed answers. He needed to get this damn mess figured out and get the hell away from Kaylie and the way she reminded him of Valerie. Away from all this shit. Get back to his life and just focus on flying.

"You know anywhere to land on Mann's property?"

"Are you crazy?" Max asked. "You've got to turn around."

"Do you know a place?" Cort ignored Kaylie watching him. The wind was tossing the Cessna around now, howling with a ferocity he didn't like. His skin began to itch, a sure sign the danger level was getting beyond what he could manage.

"Dammit, Cort," Max yelled, his voice barely audible over the wind screaming around them. "Don't be a damn fool. Get the hell out of there."

Cort didn't back down. He wasn't going back. "Tell me where I can land, or I'm just going to put her down and hope I remembered to pay my dues to the Grim Reaper this month."

"Jesus, man." There was silence for a minute as Max pulled

up the charts. "Yeah, okay. On the north side, there's a clearing. It's small, but if you come in just right and the weather's perfect with good visibility, there's a slight chance you could land without crashing."

"That's all I need. Thanks." He got the coordinates and then signed off.

Kaylie was clenching her harness. "Turn around. Now. I know you're pissed about Valerie and me, but that's not a reason to get us both killed."

He didn't answer. His brain was hammering at him to go back. This was more than he had a right to do. It pushed his boundaries. He was smarter than this. *Abort.*

But Cort didn't turn the plane. Kept on going. Right into the storm. He could handle it. A few more minutes. That was it.

"Cort! Dammit! What is wrong with you?"

He hunched over the controls, felt the little plane buck harder. She was straining, fighting him hard.

"Cort!"

Valerie. His son. Murder. Old Tom.

*If you let her leave Alaska, she won't come back.*

Jackson. His parents. Kaylie's truck seat. His son. Murder. His wife.

*Murder.*

"Cort!" Kaylie hit him hard in the shoulder, and he jerked back to the present. The nose of the plane was too low, gravity taking over.

"Shit!" He fought the controls, swearing as he tried to sweet-talk his plane into coming back to him. Something dark flew by the window, and he realized it was a tree. Below tree level already. "Come on!"

He brought her up hard, the plane twisting and lurching as the dark shadows of trees skimmed just below his wing lights. Too much. He had to bring her down. Now.

Kaylie was silent beside him, and he looked ahead, saw a break in the darkness below. The clearing that Max had mentioned?

It better be.

"Hang tight."

He brought the plane down hard and fast, the wind buffeting her ruthlessly. The wheels hit, bounced, the right wing came up.

Just like before.

With Valerie.

Kaylie grabbed the dash and sucked in her breath, and the sound brought his focus reeling back. He jammed the controls and pulled the plane back. The left wing caught the dirt, jerking the plane, and then it stopped.

They were down.

# CHAPTER NINETEEN

The silence was overwhelming.

After the screaming winds, the roar of the rain, the shriek of the plane as it fought the storm, the silence was shocking.

Kaylie closed her eyes and leaned her head back against the seat. "Dear God," she whispered. She tried to peel her hands off her harness, but her fingers wouldn't release it. She gradually became aware of other sounds. Of the rain pounding against the plane, of branches screeching across the metal, of the creak of the plane as it shifted under the buffeting wind.

Of Cort breathing hard, utterly still beside her.

"How close...?" Kaylie swallowed, her mouth too dry to speak. "How close to dying did we just come?"

He didn't answer.

Slowly, she peeled her eyes open and peeked at him. His hands were still on the controls, and he was still staring out the windshield. His hair was slick with sweat, his face pale in the dashboard light.

Okay, so it had been close.

Or, given who he was, it was probably the conversation, and not the flight, that had him looking like that.

"Cort?"

He still didn't look at her.

Kaylie pried her hands off the belt, and attempted to unbuckle herself. It took three tries, because her hands were shaking so badly, but she was finally free. She crawled across the seat and touched Cort's shoulder. "Hey."

He turned his head, his face haggard, eyes dead. "Simon."

Not the flight, then. God, were his nerves made of steel or what? "Simon?"

"Simon Wilson McClaine. Named after Valerie's dad. It was supposed to be Simon Huff McClaine, after both of our dads, but when she was in the hospital, she filled out the birth certificate without me and changed it."

Kaylie gently brushed the sweaty hair off his forehead. "I'm so sorry," she whispered. "I truly am."

"Valerie wore diamond earrings. All the time. No matter what. Her way of reminding me and all my friends that she was better than we were. That she didn't belong. That her daddy could buy us all up in an hour and destroy us with the snap of his fingers."

Kaylie touched her earlobe, understanding now. "I'm not her," she said evenly.

His hand went to the back of her head, fisting in her hair. "Why do you wear them? All the time, like she did."

Kaylie winced at the tug in her hair, but she didn't pull his hand away. "I wear them because my mother always thought it was a waste of money and completely impractical."

He scowled, and his grip on her hair tightened. "You did it to piss off your mother?"

Kaylie recalled how he said Valerie had hooked up with him just to annoy her dad, and winced. "No, I just…I don't want to be a climber. I don't want to be like my family, and I was forced into it for so many years. When I finally couldn't take it anymore, my goal was to become someone as different as possible from who they were. To wipe out all influences they had ever had on me and become the person I wanted to be."

His gaze went to her mouth, and there was something hungry in his eyes, something that had her belly tightening. "And did you succeed?" He pulled her closer until his mouth was a mere breath from hers. "Did those diamonds make you into the person you want to be?"

"Yes," she whispered, even though she wasn't sure it was the truth anymore.

He stiffened. The he dropped his hand. Turned away.

"Wait!" Kaylie grabbed him. "I'm not Valerie! For God's sake, Cort, I would never betray you like that! If I married you, if I gave you my word, I would never betray you! I've been completely honest with how I feel about everything. I never lied to you!" Tears started to form, and she blinked them back as he reached into the back for his coat, ignoring her. "Damn you, Cort! Damn you for making me care about you, and your son and—"

He grabbed her and pulled her against him, slamming his mouth down over hers.

She froze for an instant, too startled to react.

Then she started to fight him.

He broke the kiss immediately, but didn't let go. Instead, he stared down at her with the darkest of eyes. He said nothing, but his grip tightened on her, the intensity of his gaze holding her immobile. There was such pain in his expression. Heartache and grief and loneliness. Things she knew... all too well.

She laid her hands on either side of his face. "It's because of my grandpa," she whispered.

He didn't answer, but his eyebrows raised slightly.

"When I was sixteen, he took me climbing for my birthday. My parents had gone off on another climb that was too rigorous for me, so it was only my grandpa. We were up on the mountain by ourselves, and I was so miserable. I wanted a sweet-sixteen party with boys and dancing and a ruby ring, and instead I was freezing cold with my grandpa on a mountain. For my birthday, my parents gave me a backpack, a carton of oxygen tanks, and a five-day excursion on a barren mountainside in Nepal."

His hand went to hers, thumbing over her bare fingers. No ruby ring for him to find.

"Two days in, there was an avalanche." She closed her eyes, remembering. "We were falling, getting tossed around. There was all this snow and branches and rocks, and I couldn't breathe."

Cort squeezed her hand, and Kaylie opened her eyes, focusing on his face, the intensity of his gaze, to keep the memories from consuming her.

"I was so scared. I thought I was going to die, to suffocate to death on that mountain. When the avalanche stopped, I was buried. I freaked out—I mean, completely freaked out. But by unbelievable luck, I was barely covered, and I got out. But when I saw where I was…" She started to shake, remembering that feeling. "There was just an endless expanse of snow. My grandpa was gone; all our equipment was gone. It was just me, up on this mountainside, with a broken ankle. It was so much worse than when I'd been left behind when I was eleven, because that time I knew my parents would be coming for me. This time, there was no one."

Cort's fingers glided over the back of her neck, rubbing the tension out while he studied her. Listening. Not interrupting. His expression was inscrutable, and she dropped her gaze, reaching out to fiddle with the pocket on his shirt.

"I crawled around for hours, searching for my grandpa. I found him right as the sun was setting. His right hand was sticking out of the snow. I was so excited, I started crying, started to dig him out. His fingers…They were stiff…cold… frozen." She could still feel that desperation, that hope. "But I kept telling myself it was just frostbite, that he was still alive under all that snow. I dug and dug; my hands were freezing. It took all night, and when I finally got him out…"

Cort's hand tightened around the back of her neck and she looked up at him.

"I'll never forget that moment," she whispered. "Holding my dead grandpa on that mountain, I was so sure I was going to die. I was so alone, and I was so scared, and I was so angry, so mad that I was going to die at age sixteen doing something I didn't even want to do. Such a stupid way to die. Such a stupid way to live. I promised myself at that moment that if I got off, if I survived, I would never set foot on a mountain again. That I would live the way I wanted, and no one would ever force me to risk my life again." She closed her eyes. "That I would never let myself love anyone who would die for a high like that. And I would never trust anyone like my parents again."

Cort's lips feathered over her forehead, and she lifted her face to his, still not opening her eyes. Just embracing the comforting warmth of his lips brushing over her skin.

"My grandpa left me," she whispered. "He died, leaving me alone. My parents were off climbing, out of calling range. No one knew what had happened. No one to check in. They all just left me there."

Cort's arms went around her, and he pressed his lips to her left eyebrow, and then her right. She leaned into him, let the strength of his body wrap around her. "I was dragging my grandpa's body down the mountain behind me, and I couldn't walk anymore. I knew I would die if I stopped. I couldn't feel my hands, and then I couldn't even crawl anymore. I just stopped, lay there in the snow, so unbelievably mad that this was the way I was going to die, so angry that the people who were supposed to be taking care of me weren't there."

Cort's hands tunneled through Kaylie's hair. His touch grounded her, and he kept the nightmare from consuming her as it always did. Cort kept it distant enough for her not to fall apart, though the fear, the loneliness, the pain were all still present. Kaylie could feel the anguish as if were happening now.

"Then I heard this voice. A man. I thought it was God. Or an angel. But someone picked me up and I opened my eyes, and this man, this most beautiful man ever, was looking down at me. He smiled this amazing smile, and he said, 'I'm

going to take care of you, little one.' And he did. He carried
me the whole way down to his camp. Never let go of me. Not
even for a minute. Not until the helicopter came."

She opened her eyes, saw Cort's face. Real. Alive. Unlike
the man who'd saved her, Cort was real. Not a memory, a fig-
ment of her imagination. She touched his cheek and ran her
finger over his cheekbone, across the ragged growth of a
beard. "The man who saved me is the face I see in my dreams.
The person who was there for me. Who held me when no
one else did." She touched Cort's earlobe. "He had a diamond earring in his left ear. A diamond. On a mountain. So
impractical."

Cort cupped Kaylie's chin and lifted her face, and then
he kissed her. A gentle kiss, with soft, warm lips. "I never
went on a mountain again," she whispered against his mouth.
"I've never been in a real snowstorm since. Not until I got
here. Not until we got out of your plane at Sara and Jackson's
cabin."

Cort trailed his lips along her jawline, to her earlobe.

And then he kissed her diamond earring.

Tears filled her eyes at the gesture, and he pulled back. His
eyes were hooded, still haunted. His strong hands spanned
her face, and he turned her head slightly, kissed along the
right side of her jaw and pressed his lips against her other earring. "Do you remember?" His voice was a whisper against
her ear, his breath warm as it teased across her skin.

"Remember what?" She shivered, her belly tightening as
he caught her around the waist, pulling her closer.

"Do you remember when I said"—he kissed her earlobe
again, then worked his way down the side of her neck—"that
the next time we made love, it would be without those earrings?"

Her belly tightened up, and her breath caught. "I remember."

"You can keep the earrings on." Then he caught her face between his hands and kissed her.

Cort felt Kaylie's hesitation as he kissed her. Her body was stiff, her hands still on his shoulders. But she wasn't pulling away. Not yet.

Cort hooked his arm behind her back. He hauled her close and took control of the kiss. Deeper. Harder. God, she tasted good. Like spring, like flowers, like *life*.

She was so wrong for him. But when he'd heard her story, something in his chest had broken for that sixteen-year-old girl.

Because that had been him at fourteen, alone at the wreck of his parents, all the blood and—

He swore and broke the kiss, released her, and leaned back against the seat. "Shit."

Kaylie was still perched on the edge of her seat, staring at him. "Why—why did you stop?"

He turned his head, saw the fullness of her lips, the flush of her cheeks. "God, you look good." He knew he should get of the plane. Go to Bill's. End this shit.

But Bill wasn't going anywhere in this weather, and he couldn't stop thinking of what Kaylie had been through. So, instead of opening the door of his plane, he caught a lock of Kaylie's hair and tugged gently.

She allowed him to pull her closer, her eyes uncertain.

"You and me…" He twirled her hair around his finger. "We couldn't be a worse match. You have a legit beef with my lifestyle. I don't blame you for hating what I do, for how I live."

A small frown puckered between her eyebrows. "I don't hate you," she said quietly. "I wish I did. It would be so much easier."

He lifted his hand to touch her face, then dropped it. "I

can't change. I'm always going to fly. In bad weather. In high-risk situations. A lot."

She shook her head. "I can't handle that. I can't stay here. I have to leave." She hesitated. "Like Valerie did."

"I know. I understand that now." He hesitated at the guilty look on her face. "You—you're not like Valerie. I get that."

"Thank God." Kaylie smiled, a brilliant smile that made something inside his heart ache.

God, that smile. Despite all Kaylie had been through, she still carried a fire Cort hadn't seen in so long. One he hadn't felt inside since…shit, too long. "How can you be so alive?"

Her smile faded. "What are you talking about?"

"You." He turned sideways in his seat, setting his knees on either side of hers, boxing her between his thighs. "You're a groundie. You're indoors. You hide from life. But somehow you've got more spark than anyone I've ever met."

She shook her head. "Don't make me into something I'm not. I'm so tired of everyone wanting me to be what I'm not. Can't you just accept what I am? Just ordinary. I'm not this font of life, of energy. I just want to curl up on the couch with a book and a blanket. I want to be at peace and—"

"No." He lifted her legs, set them across his thighs, on either side of his hips.

Her eyes widened, and her cheeks flushed. "No, what?"

"You're not ordinary." He grabbed her butt and hauled her onto his lap, crushing her pelvis against his erection. "I can't sit back and let you undercut yourself. Yeah, maybe you like to curl up with a book and read. That's cool. But that doesn't make you ordinary or weak." He palmed her back, sliding his hand under her jacket. The wind howled past the plane, and he didn't give a shit.

Didn't care where they were.

He was taking her. Now. "You like your sex in bed with candlelight, don't you?"

Her cheeks burned brighter, her hands bracing against his

chest, unsure whether to push him away or pull him closer. "Cort. We can't go down this road. We *can't*. I have to leave, you're going to fly, and someone's stalking me and my family, and—"

"And we have right now. We have this moment." He dropped his head and kissed the hollow of her throat.

"But what about—?"

He lifted his head. "You never know what tomorrow will bring. You get a chance to live now, you take it."

"That's exactly the attitude that destroyed my family."

"Did it?" He grabbed her hair again, holding her head captive as he leaned closer. "Or did it give them joy every day? Would you rather exist in a shell for a long time, or truly live for a short one? Feel the wind in your hair, run through life with laughter in your heart? Wouldn't you love to allow your spirit to soar free and then follow it, without fear, without hesitation?"

"When my family talks like that, I hate them. I feel inadequate, and I don't understand." Kaylie stared at him. "But you make it sound…amazing. Like the one thing I've been searching for my whole life, but never found."

"Maybe it is."

And this time, when he kissed her, she kissed him back.

# CHAPTER TWENTY

A little voice in the back of Kaylie's mind shouted at her to stop.

To push Cort away.

To think about the ramifications.

About the morning.

About the moment she would have to walk away.

About the terrifying flight they'd just had and the fact that it hadn't bothered Cort in the least.

About the fact that Cort was so much more than she'd thought. That crossing this line with him a second time would trap her emotionally.

*He is so wrong for you!*

She kissed him anyway.

Gave him everything she had.

Cort's mouth was hot and demanding. His hands were caressing her back, and his erection was hard between her thighs. His kisses were so intense, as if he couldn't survive another moment without her. A most incredible sensation. To be needed. To be wanted. To be taken against all common sense, simply because he didn't have the willpower to resist her.

Not breaking the kiss, Cort anchored his hands around Kaylie's butt and stood. He squeezed them both between the seats, and then they were down in the cramped back, on blankets, on duffel bags. He grunted, shifted, and her bag went sailing through the air, hitting the windshield before it dropped with a thud somewhere up front.

And then Cort was on her, the weight of his body pinning her to the floor as he kissed her again. His hips were between her legs, his hand was beneath her shirt, moving across her ribs, cupping her breast. His tongue was demanding, and Kaylie welcomed it, holding him close, closer, fighting against the voice in her head trying to stop her. Trying to keep her from falling.

Cort broke the kiss and looked at Kaylie. His hair was tousled, and his gaze was intense in the dark shadows of the interior. "I'll give you one chance to say no, and then there's no turning back."

An opening.

A chance. To walk away.

To do the right thing.

To be the responsible, safe adult she'd worked so hard to be for so long. To protect herself.

One shake of her head, and he'd roll off her. Climb back into the front of the plane. She saw it in the hard set of his jaw and knew he would walk away.

An icy coldness made her shiver, and she knew she couldn't do it.

Couldn't let him leave.

Couldn't give up this moment.

This wasn't for her parents.

It wasn't to prove herself to be something she was or wasn't.

It was because she simply wanted him. So much. Right now. With the wind howling, the little plane shaking, and the rain pounding on the metal, Kaylie knew what she wanted. She looked up at him, at the strength of his body as he braced himself over her, and repeated his words back to him. "You get a chance to live now, you take it," she whispered.

The smile that creased Cort's face shattered the final protections around Kaylie's heart, and she knew there was no going back.

Cort lowered himself onto her ever so slowly, his gaze heated and intense, as if he knew he had all the time in the world. And then he kissed her, the most erotic, seductive, intense kiss she'd ever experienced. It was slow and tantalizing, his tongue licking around the corners of her mouth, sliding between her lips and back out, interspersed with the deepest, most deliciously tantalizing kisses. Hot. Wet. Like liquid heat sliding down her nerve endings, igniting her body cell by cell. A slow building of fire and passion, until her whole body was trembling, every fiber tingling, damp heat building between her thighs.

Cort was heat. He was fire. He was utterly without inhibition, and she could feel him coaxing her to drop her own inhibitions. To stop thinking. To simply feel. To embrace. To turn off her mind and lose herself in the sensation of his body pinning her down, in the strength of his shoulders beneath her hands, in the roughness of his whiskers as he kissed her.

Cort was daring and adrenaline, and he was without apology or hesitation. He made her so aware of how little she was living. He made her realize how tightly she held herself, and she felt the first thread of that control begin to unravel as he continued his seduction.

His fingers brushed over her throat as his mouth continued its magic, and she heard her jacket zipper being lowered, inch by tantalizing inch. His mouth left hers, following the path of the zipper. Kiss by kiss, he worked his way down her body, the heat of his mouth burning through her sweater as the jacket bit the dust.

His mouth was on her belly, hands spanning her hips. And then Cort was working his way back up, but this time, he kissed her bare flesh as he shoved her shirt out of his way. Her stomach trembled as his tongue circled her belly button. Liquid heat pooled low and hot, building as he kissed along her

ribs and between her breasts, his wrist resting on her nipple,
drawing hot nerve endings to life.

A quick movement and her bra was undone, and his
mouth...

"Oh, God." Kaylie couldn't stop herself from arching up as
he sucked on her. She was barely aware of the shirt and bra
coming off, her entire body overwhelmed by the sensations
rippling through her. Her self-control was slipping with each
kiss. Moment by moment, he was stripping away her defenses, and Kaylie knew he would consume her completely if
she didn't fight it. If she didn't hold on.

"But I don't want to fight it," she whispered.

"Then don't." Cort's voice was gravelly and rough, as if he
was on the edge of control himself. The realization made another surge of heat pool between her legs, and suddenly Kaylie had to touch him. She needed to feel the hard strength
beneath his skin, his muscles rippling as he touched her with
such gentle passion.

She tugged his shirt out of his jeans, and within a fraction
of a second, he had it off. Boots hit the side walls of the plane,
his and hers, following by jeans and underwear, and then
there was nothing between them. Nothing but skin. Hot and
warm, he sank onto her, his kisses deeper and more intense,
no longer slow and teasing. The need was building, hers and
his, and she kissed him back just as fiercely.

His shoulders were taut, his muscles flexed. She ran her
hands down his arms, over the ripples of his biceps. Raw
strength, hard steel beneath his skin. She ran her hands
down his back to a hard ridge.

The scar.

Kaylie tensed, remembering the brutality of the injury and
how it wrapped around his back and his side. An accident
that should have killed him.

Cort didn't seem to notice her hesitation, shifting to the
side to wrap his hand around the back of her leg, bringing her

knee up as he kissed her. He slid his hand along her thigh and licked his way down her body, his teeth grazing over her breast as his fingers slipped inside her.

Her body responded instantly, and she threw her head back, gasping at the invasion, at the rightness of him inside her. He thrust again, her body clenching, spiraling. She clutched his shoulders, and she froze at what she felt beneath her hands: His upper back was rough, a mass of scars. His burns. Marking him forever as a risk taker and a dangerous man.

She realized he'd stopped kissing her, that his fingers had stilled inside her. He hadn't lifted his head, but he paused, waiting for her reaction to his scars, to the irrefutable evidence of who he was.

She propped herself on her elbows and spread her palm across his scarred back.

Then she pressed her lips to the scars.

He instantly tossed her onto her back as he kissed her so fiercely, she felt like he was going to strip her soul right out of her, and she embraced it. Completely and fully. His scars, his life, his past, his body, his passion.

Kaylie took it all in and let it fill her completely. She felt a part of her shift, then simply dissolve. And she became someone she didn't know. Someone of raw emotion, heated desire, and uncontained need.

For the first time in her life, she was truly alive. She was no longer thinking, but simply being who she was and following her spirit....And finally, after a lifetime of searching, she finally understood what it felt like to be at peace with who she was.

Cort whispered her name and moved between her thighs. Kaylie didn't hesitate, kissing him fiercely, her hands clutching at him. He broke the kiss and pulled back. "Look at me," he said. "Know you are with me."

The instant she opened her eyes and met his intense gaze,

he thrust deep. One move and he was sheathed inside her. They were forever bonded.

He didn't move for a minute, and they locked gazes, her body trembling at the feel of him so deep inside her. Last time had been desperate and needy, tainted by grief and loneliness. Two strangers brought together by trauma. This time...This time it was them.

Cort.

Her.

Because they both wanted it.

Kaylie's throat tightened, and emotions filled her, emotions she couldn't and didn't want to identify, but they filled her until she felt as though her skin was stretching, barely able to contain them.

A smile flicked across Cort's face, and he bent his head and took her mouth in a seductive kiss as he slowly withdrew, sliding out like a carnal tease. Then he thrust again, harder this time, and she forgot everything but him. The feel of his body, the taste of him, the strength...his fire, his passion. The kiss grew more intense, he sank deeper each time, again and again, until her mind and body was screaming for him, for only him, consumed by the magnitude of his presence and how he made her lose herself. She was no longer herself, she was him, she was passion, she was raw, elemental need and fire, her body and her soul one need, one being, one existence, tied inextricably to the life force that was Cort.

He thrust one more time, and her body exploded. All she could do was cling to him as he hammered her, went rigid, shouted her name, and filled her with all he was.

As he collapsed on top of her and pulled her into his body, all she could think of was that she'd lost everything that had kept her safe for so long. Raw and exposed, she knew she was going to pay for what she had just done.

But as he cradled her against him, his leg wrapped around hers, his lips feathering her temple, she decided not to care.

Not yet.

There would be time for that. The future would come, no matter what.

But right now, in this moment…she was happy.

Kaylie was going to leave him.

Cort knew it in the marrow of his bones.

The minute this situation with her family and Sara was over, if they survived, Kaylie was going to leave.

And it was wrong.

She belonged here. In the wilds. Not in a concrete prison built of fear and bad memories.

Cort pressed his face to Kaylie's hair and inhaled, breathing deep the scent of flowers she carried with her everywhere she went. It wasn't roses, carefully cultivated in a greenhouse. It was wildflowers in a meadow, the air heavy with the moisture of a spring rain. Of new life. Fresh buds.

Keeping his eyes closed, Cort ran his hand down her arm, over her bare hip, a smug satisfaction rising when he felt her shiver and realized she couldn't resist his touch.

If he could keep her naked and in his arms, she would never leave.

He grinned. Worse ways to go.

"Cort?"

"Mmm." He nibbled her neck, the tiny hairs at the base of her skull tickling his lips.

"I wish—" She wrapped her fingers around his wrist, where he had his arm around her belly. "I wish I were someone different."

He stopped kissing her, his mouth hovering over the nape of her neck. "Why?"

"I wish I were the person you just made love to."

Scowling, he rolled her over so he could look at her, something tight beginning to form in his chest. "What are you talking about?"

Her face was still flushed, her eyes at half-mast, like a sated lover. She trailed a fingertip across his forehead and down his jaw. "You're so beautiful."

He resisted the urge to bring that finger into his mouth. "Don't change the subject. What did you mean?"

She blinked, and some of the haze faded from her eyes. "Why are you mad?"

He took a breath to calm himself. "I'm not mad," he said evenly. "But that was you I was just inside. It was you who was writhing for me, who gave herself over to the moment, to me." His voice grew harder. "Don't try to tell me that I seduced you, or that you were too scared to think straight, or that I somehow manipulated you—"

"No." Kaylie put her hand on his lips. "I'm not saying that. I just—" She sighed. "I wish I could be like that all the time. That I really was that person."

"You are—"

"No. I can't live like that." She laid her hand over his chest, over his heart. "You make me want to be you."

He set his hand over hers, holding it in place. "I don't want you to be me."

"Yes, you do." She looked up at him. "You want me to have sex in the back of airplanes while a storm is raging. You want me to fly with you. You want me to live on adrenaline and nerve, right by your side."

He scowled. "You underestimate yourself."

"How would you feel if I asked you to be home for dinner at five every night? To sit with me by the fire and read? To fly only on nice, sunny days and land only on paved runways?"

He ground his jaw. "You don't really want that."

"Dammit! Don't tell me what I want."

He flipped her over, pinned her beneath him, furious. "Listen to me, sweetheart. I've had enough of you selling yourself short. You're not some fragile flower who needs to hide behind four walls and a fancy pair of shoes."

"Get off me!"

He let more of his weight settle on her. "You're scared. You deserve to be afraid. But by God, I'm not going to let you rob yourself of truly living because of something that happened when you were sixteen."

"You're not going to *let* me?" She hit his shoulder, but he didn't even flinch. "I have news for you, McClaine. I stopped allowing anyone else to mold me when I almost died on that mountain. Neither you nor my family is going to make me into—"

"I'm not going to make you into anything. It's already there. You just need to let it out." He bent his head, let his breath mix with hers, felt her go still beneath him. "I've touched the very core of who you are, and I know a fire burns deep within you. Maybe it's not about flying or taking crazy risks. But it's more than the life you've been letting yourself live. I know that for sure."

That very fire he was talking about flared in her eyes, and then she slammed her heel into the back of his calf. He swore as his muscle knotted up, and he knew then the truth.

He was keeping her.

Something in the back of his mind reminded him that that was the exact thought he'd had about Valerie. That he could force her to stay.

No.

This time was different.

This time, Kaylie needed to stay.

If she didn't, her soul would die.

"Damn you, Cort McClaine." Her voice was low, furious. "Don't you dare try to manipulate me, to turn me into the woman you think I should be."

Something outside caught his attention, and he slammed his hand over her mouth. "Shh!"

Her eyes widened, and she stared at him.

He waited.
And then he heard it again.
A thump against the side of the plane.
Not a branch or a rock.
A person.

# CHAPTER TWENTY-ONE

"Get dressed!" Cort commanded as he grabbed for his clothes.

Kaylie lunged for her pants, not bothering with her underwear. "What is it?" *A bear. God, please let it be a bear.*

"Someone's outside." Cort was already dressed, his boots on, as he grabbed his rifle from a rack on the side of the plane.

"Someone—" Kaylie shot a glance at the front of the plane. "Do the doors lock?"

"Technically, but it's designed to keep the doors from flying open in flight. Not for keeping out anyone who wants to get in." Cort checked the gun, then grabbed a huge knife from another pocket on the side of the plane. A knife much like the one that had been in her seat.

She stared at it. "Where did you get that?"

He strapped it to his hip. "Standard issue for the bush." Cort turned toward her as she yanked her jacket on over her bare upper body. "I'm going out there. You stay put, and don't leave for any reason."

"But—"

The door on the driver's side flew open with a crash and they both whirled toward it, Cort's rifle up and ready.

Waiting.

The wind smacked the door against the side of the plane and then back again, making Kaylie jump.

But still no one.

"Could it be the wind?" she whispered, not taking her gaze off the entrance.

"No chance." Cort still hadn't moved, still ready.

Rain was slanting sideways into the cockpit, soaking the seat. The door continued to rattle off its hinges.

The passenger door flew open with a crash, and they both spun toward that.

No one appeared.

Just the wind howling through the plane, blowing the rain back into their faces. Cold, bitter, wet, going right through her jeans. She still didn't have her shoes on, just jeans and a coat.

Both doors were banging loudly, rattling against the plane, metal crashing against metal.

Cort swore, swinging the gun toward the pilot side, then back toward the passenger side. "Get your boots on." His voice was low, menacing.

She scrambled for her shoes, found them in the corner. She yanked them on and stood up. Rainy mist was filling the plane with a damp chill. "What now?"

Slowly, keeping his gun ready, Cort eased toward her, crooking one finger at her.

She quickly moved over to him, and he bent his head, speaking quietly into her ear. "We're sitting ducks in here, so we need to get out. We're going to jump out the pilot door. The minute you land, start running and don't look back. Just haul ass until I find you." His hand clamped around her arm, his grip like a vice. "Whatever you do, don't stop. Do you understand? Just. Keep. Running."

She nodded, the vision of Sara's bloodied body all too vivid in her mind. "What are you doing?"

"Covering you." He slapped a small knife in her hand. "Just in case I fail."

She stared at him, dread tightening in her chest. "But you don't believe you can fail."

He gave her a grim smile and tugged her toward the door. "Make up your mind. You want someone who thumbs his nose at death, or someone who will admit he can die?"

She jumped as the passenger door banged again. "Right now, I go for option one."

Cort took her arm. "Women. So fickle. Drives me nuts." He leaned up against the side of the plane and pulled her against him. Slowly, he began to slide them along the wall toward the pilot door. "If you jump out and go straight, you should eventually reach Bill's cabin, where there should be a phone or a radio. Don't go inside until you've given up on me catching up to you, though."

Kaylie swallowed. "Have I mentioned that it pisses me off when people in my life die?"

Cort grinned. "Yeah, you might've." He pulled close, kissed her once, too brief and too short, then readied himself. "On three."

The passenger door slammed again, and she didn't have to look at Cort to know it hadn't been the wind. It had been too precise and too hard.

It had been a direct challenge.

"One." Cort edged up next to the door.

"Two." He braced himself.

"Three."

He shoved her out in front of him and they jumped.

Kaylie stumbled when she landed, but Cort yanked her to her feet, and then she began to run. Rain slashed at her face. The muddy ground sucked at her boots, like a quagmire trying to drown her. The wind howled so loudly she could hear nothing but the roar of nature crushing her.

A branch raked across her cheek. She ducked her head and slogged onward. She tried to run, but her pace was torturously slow, dragged down by the woods and the mud.

No sound behind her.

No footsteps.

Just the storm.

Where was Cort?

Kaylie heard the loud crack of a rifle, and she whirled around, heart racing. Then she heard the crash of heavy footsteps coming toward her. "Cort?"

The footsteps stopped.

Silence.

Waiting for her to call again so he could pinpoint her location.

If it had been Cort, he would have answered.

Dear God, what had happened back there?

Panic hammering at her, Kaylie began to move again, trying to be silent. But twigs snapped and mud sloshed. It sounded so loud…but was it really audible over the howl of the storm?

She could hear nothing behind her.

Not a sound.

Not a—

She tripped over something and hit the ground. Hard. Her hands on something that felt too much like the cold body of her dead grandpa.

"Oh, God."

She scrambled backward, but not before she saw the shadowed face of her mother.

Dead.

"Mom!" Kaylie fell to her knees, a crushing pain slicing through her heart.

Then she saw the rest of the bodies. Not just her mom. Her dad. Other bodies. So many. Numbly, she stared in disbelief at the pile, became aware of the rank odor of death mixing with the driving rain. Death, decay, the loss of life…

A hand was sticking out of the pile, as if entreating her to come closer.

There was a carved gold band on the right index finger.

Sara's ring. Sara's body.

Kaylie whirled around, doubling over as she retched, as all

the grief and fear and horrors caught up to her. She went down to her knees as the tears burst free—the anguish, the loss, the guilt. She was too late, too late....

Gradually, she became aware of a hand stroking her hair, of a low murmur of a male voice comforting her.

She went rigid.

Because it wasn't Cort who was touching her.

Kaylie lurched to her feet and whirled around.

Old Tom was still crouched on the ground behind her.

She blinked. "Tom?"

He slowly stood, not with the stiffness of an old body, but with the easy grace of a predator trying not to scare his prey. "It's okay, Kaylie."

His hair was matted to his head, rain streaming down his face.

"Where—where's Cort?"

Tom shook his head. "No, it's not about Cort. It's about you. Come here. Let me get you warm."

"Me?" She inched backward. "What did you do to Cort?"

"What did *I* do to *Cort*?" He snorted. "That list is too long to go into while we're standing out here freezing our asses off."

The backs of her legs hit the pile of bodies, and she froze.

Tom's gaze flicked behind her, and then his eyes widened. "Holy fuck. What the hell's that?"

She didn't move. "You—?"

"Shit!" Tom suddenly moved past her, pushing her aside as he examined the pile. "Mother *fucker*."

Kaylie whirled around and raced away from him. She'd gotten only a few yards when he tackled her, throwing her face-first into the wet ground.

She screamed, fighting him, but he pinned her easily, his wiry body not heavy like Cort's, but just as strong.

Old Tom slammed his hand over her mouth, anchored an

arm around her throat, and pinned her face to the mud. "Shut the hell up," he snarled. "Or I drown you. Right here. Right now."

She froze, her face already half-submerged.

Tom bent down, his mouth next to her ear. "I'll say this only once."

She nodded. The water she was lying in was icy cold. She was already shaking. Had to get up. Had to get away.

"I didn't kill those people." Old Tom's voice was low. Hard. "Which means you and I need to get the fuck out of here before whoever did comes back, pissed off that we found his stash. He's not going to let us live long enough to tell anyone about it. Got it?"

She scrunched her eyes shut.

"I'm going to let you up, and you're going to stand silently and follow me back to my plane. Understand?"

She didn't answer, frantically trying to think of what to do. What if he was lying, and she went willingly with him? But what if he was telling the truth, and someone else was coming after them? Shit!

"Kaylie." His voice was a growl. "I'm not getting my ass killed because you're going to freak and reveal our location to the bastard. You agree to shut up, and I'll bring you with me. Otherwise, I'm knocking you out and leaving you here for him to find." He scowled. "And where the hell is Cort?"

*Cort.*

If Old Tom hadn't taken him down, then someone else had. Or he'd have been here by now.

Someone had gotten to him.

She fought back the sudden swell of tears, of panic. She had to keep it together. She had to make a decision now. She thought of Cort's story about how Tom had stood in Cort's defense.

Decision made. She would trust Old Tom. It was the only choice that made sense.

"Where is Cort?" Old Tom asked again.

"He's at the plane," she whispered, praying she wasn't making a mistake. "Someone came after us. He'd be here by now if he was okay."

Tom didn't move. Didn't react. Then he swore. "Stupid bastard always needs me to bail him out. Let's go get him." He was off her and on his feet in an instant. Grabbed her hand and hauled her up.

A dark shadow leapt out of the woods right behind Tom. She shouted a warning, too late. The glint of a blade. Tom's face contorting in pain as his hands went to his slashed throat. Then he was facedown in the mud.

Not moving.

His face shadowed in the early-morning dawn, Tom's assailant turned to face her.

Bill.

And then it was her turn.

Despite the freezing rain, Bill was wearing only a T-shirt and jeans. His drenched shirt clung to his body, showing the physique of a man who had spent his life doing hard labor. Not an ounce of fat, not a wasted muscle. A ragged growth of beard on his face, mud caked to his chest and arms, eyes wide and agitated.

A wild man.

"It's about time you got here," he said.

Simple words, but there was such hatred, such lust, such… intensity in those words, Kaylie couldn't stop the shiver, couldn't keep herself from taking a step back.

A mistake, she realized instantly, when his face contorted into a twisted rage. "Bitch!"

His fist came in a wet blur, smashing into the side of her head. She stumbled, went down, fighting against the blackness swirling at the edge of her vision. Her hands went out to brace herself, accidentally landing on Old Tom's leg.

She stared in horror at his face, at the blood everywhere, at his glazed eyes.

"On your knees. Exactly how it should be." Bill caught the back of her hair and yanked her head back, shoving her face into the front of his pants, into the erection straining at the front of his jeans. "You owe me. For thirty years I waited, and now it's time to show me it was worth it."

She fought to get free, to breathe, but he pressed harder. Frantic, she clasped her hands and slammed them upward into his crotch. He gasped and doubled over, releasing her.

She was on her feet and running before she even had time to think, nearly tripping over Old Tom's body—

Kaylie sensed rather than saw the knife hurtling through the air and ducked…too late. Pain exploded in the back of her thigh. Her leg collapsed. She crashed to the sodden dirt.

Bill was standing over her in an instant, and he ripped the knife out of her leg. Kaylie screamed, grabbing for her thigh, but he shoved her hand aside.

"Stupid bitch, making me hurt you." He crouched beside her, and she couldn't move, holding herself rigid against the pain. Fighting for breath. He stripped off his drenched T-shirt and lifted her leg.

She tensed, preparing for another blow, but his hands were gentle and skilled as they wrapped her leg. "Don't you understand? It hurts me to hurt you. Why don't they understand that? They never understand that." His words were a distracted monologue, creepy and unsettling, as he bandaged her leg.

Kaylie let her head sink back into the mud, too exhausted to fight, as he finished tending her wound. Was Cort dead? Like her family? Dear God. They were all dead. Total loss. Ten years since she'd seen them. She'd been waiting for them to admit she was right. To ask her to come back. To say they accepted her the way she was.

Ten years, and for what? For death in the Alaska woods at the hands of a madman?

It was as stupid as dying on a mountain when she was sixteen would have been.

"Up we go." Bill slid his arms beneath her, and she shuddered as his forearm crushed her breasts. "I'll try to be gentle, my love. Don't struggle, or it'll make it worse." He lifted her in a fireman's carry. "We need to get you cleaned up, or infection will set in." His hands dug into her wound, and she gasped at the pain. "You'll piss me off if you allow your injury to get infected. Stupid of you to get hurt in the first place, but I forgive you. I always do."

Kaylie braced herself against his bare back as he began to walk, fighting not to jar her leg. Her head was still ringing from the blow, and her injury was killing her. Going numb. "Where's Cort?"

"Shut up!" His thumb jammed into her injury, and she screamed. "I tried to get Cort away from you. Tried to save him from your temptation, but you sucked him in anyway. His dad saved my life once and died before I could repay him. So I owe Cort, instead. Because of Huff, I owe Cort his life. But you won't leave Cort alone. You involved him in your mess, and you've forced me to hurt him for having his hands on your body, for kissing you. I've tried to spare him, and you're fucking with my plans. You ever say his name again, and I swear I'll cut your heart right out of your body."

Kaylie closed her eyes, her throat tightening at the hatred, at the violence in her captor's voice. There was no way he'd allowed Cort to live. Oh, God, what had she done? She'd blamed him for being the risk taker, yet she was the one who had brought death to his doorstep.

And to Sara and Jackson.

Why did Bill want her? What had she done to bring him after her? What had happened thirty years ago?

Her mother. Her mother had come thirty years ago. This

wasn't about Kaylie. It was about her mother. "I'm not her," she said. "My name is Kaylie, not Alice—"

"Shut up!" Bill jabbed something into the wound again, and she gasped, fighting not to scream.

They passed a wooden shed, the door half-ajar, darkness within. She thought she saw the faint outline of a person's body, and then they were past.

Bill's boots were loud as he stomped up stairs, each movement making her leg throb. Nausea churned in her belly, and she closed her eyes, fighting a wave of dizziness.

Then they were inside.

The barren cabin smelled of rotten meat and mold. A mound of animal skins dominated the middle of the floor, a dark circle of wetness bleeding out from the base of it. A small fridge in the corner, filthy and rusted. A sink.

Bill carried her across the room, kicked open another door, and set her gently on the floor of a very small bathroom with an old porcelain tub. Dark rust stains coated the cracked surface, and thick mildew coated the floors.

Bill rubbed her shoulders, and Kaylie pulled back…then realized she'd made a mistake when she saw his expression go dark. "You will learn to love me," he snarled. "I'm your world now. No one but me. You're lucky I chose to give you this chance instead of killing you for being a slut." He grabbed her shoulders and he shook her. "Apologize!"

"I'm sorry." The words spilled out of her, even as she searched the small room for a window. An escape.

But there was nothing.

Just solid walls.

As if she could run. Her leg was useless, screaming with agony every time she moved.

Bill stared at her, then nodded. "You're forgiven. Again. But my patience runs thin." He yanked a pink towel out from under the sink. It was faded and worn…and it had Kaylie's mother's initials on it.

"I saved this for you, all this time." He pressed his face to it and inhaled deeply. "It'll be like before. Together. Like before..." His eyes narrowed, his gaze on her neck.

Kaylie touched her throat a split second before Bill threw the towel aside and slammed her up against the wall. He yanked at the zipper, and too late, she remembered she had nothing on beneath the jacket.

She tried to cover herself, and he pinned her hands above on the wall, slammed a knee into her stomach to pin her there. He had the jacket off and on the floor, then gazed down at her body.

The air was cold on her breasts, and she was utterly defenseless as he ruthlessly inspected her.

She was temped to close her eyes. To hide from it. To pretend it wasn't happening.

And then she thought of her parents.

Of Cort, who'd been willing twice to go out and risk himself to go after this very man.

They all deserved more.

She couldn't hide. She needed to fight. For them.

She forced her gaze to his, couldn't help shuddering at the violence on his face, at the intense fury.

"You let him mark you."

She lifted her chin. "I love him. Not you. I'm not Alice. I'm not her. You don't know me. Just let me go."

"Shut up!" He crushed his forearm into her throat, cutting off her air. "I gave you a chance! I waited for you, and you let him violate you while you were *in my backyard!*" He threw her down and her head cracked against the toilet.

Pain shot through her, and then he was dragging her out of the bathroom, across the floor. Knife in his hand, still covered in Old Tom's blood.

He grabbed and tossed her onto something soft.

A mattress.

Metal chains attached to the headboard.

She lunged for the chain and swung it, just as he leaned over to grab it. The chain hit him in the temple, and he pitched forward. He swung with his knife, slicing across her wrist. She swung the chain again, got him in the back of the head with a sickening thud, and then he was down.

Rolling off the bed, she tried to run for the door, and her leg gave out. She hit the ground, crawling as she heard him rolling around behind her. Panicked, she grabbed the door and yanked it open as he fisted her hair, yanked her back—

A rifle shot exploded through the night, and she ducked as Bill fell on top of her.

Then Cort stepped out of the shadows.

Bloody, a black eye, and a limp.

But alive.

# CHAPTER TWENTY-TWO

Cort felt like his soul had been ripped right out of his body when he saw her on the ground beneath Bill, both of them saturated in blood, Kaylie half-naked. "Kaylie!" He lunged forward, ripped Bill off her, and dropped to his knees beside her, pulling her into his arms.

"He got my wrist." Her face was pale, too pale, her hand wrapped around her wrist.

The blood was cascading from a gash in her arm, and Cort swore. "Jesus, Kaylie." He ripped off his shirt and tied it around her wrist, while she leaned weakly against him. "It'll be okay. Don't worry." Shit. It had to be okay.

Tourniquet in place, he scooped her up and ran farther into the cabin, where there were lights.

He took one look at the bed, with the chains and the blood, and he sat her on the floor on the other side of the room. Picked up her wrist and swore when he saw her shirt was already drenched with blood. "I think he clipped an artery."

Kaylie slumped against him, her head resting against his shoulder. "I was so scared that he'd hurt you. I can't believe you're here."

"I'm fine." But he'd gotten here too late. Too damn late! Cort looked frantically around the small cabin for the something else to use on her wrist. Saw Kaylie's jacket on the floor of the bathroom and a towel. "Stay here." He propped her carefully against the wall, then sprinted across the cabin. Grabbed the towel, then checked under the sink.

Medical kit. Just like the one Cort had stashed in his plane.

His dad has always claimed that sometimes it was the only thing between life and death. For Kaylie, Cort had a bad feeling it was. He grabbed the kit and her jacket and raced back to her. Her eyes were closed, and her head was resting against the wall, her breasts bare and exposed.

*Son of a bitch.* Something in his chest tightened, a sharp pain digging in, and he fell to his knees beside her. "Did he rape you?" The question felt thick on his tongue, but he had to ask it. Had to know.

She opened her eyes slightly, then reached up and laid her hand on his cheek. "No. I'm fine."

Tears suddenly burned at the back of his eyes, and he grabbed her hand and pressed his lips to her palm. "Jesus, I'm so sorry I took so long."

"No. You did just fine." Her fingers brushed weakly over his cheek. "Thanks for coming."

He blinked a couple times to clear his vision, then tucked her into her coat, zipping it up to her chin as her eyes closed again. "You with me?"

She nodded once, not opening her eyes. "Don't leave me."

"Wouldn't think of it." A noise sounded from the porch, and Cort shot a sharp glance at the still-open door. He could still see Bill's foot as he lay there. Not moving. Dead? If not, damned close.

Cort had hit a dead shot from close range.

He returned his attention to Kaylie, working efficiently as he properly bandaged her wrist, using gauze and tape to seal the wound as best he could. It was still bleeding heavily, and she was even paler by the time he was finished.

"My leg," she whispered.

Cort had noticed the shirt wrapped around her leg earlier, but he hadn't had time to think about it. Frowning, he tried the knot, couldn't get it.

He pulled out his knife, then stopped when Kaylie sucked in her breath, her eyes going wide with panic.

Slowly, Cort reached for her. He cupped the back of her neck with his hand. "It's okay, sweetheart. I'm just going to cut his shirt off your leg, okay?"

She met his gaze, and something in his chest broke at the pain in her eyes. Then she nodded. "I'm okay. Just panicked for a sec." She squeezed his arm lightly with her uninjured hand. "I'm good."

"You sure?"

She nodded, her gaze fixed on his. "Yeah. Just do it."

"Tell me if you want me to stop." Holding the knife loosely, he worked it beneath the shirt, gritting his teeth at her wince. But the razor-sharp blade cut through the shirt easily.

"My jeans. Help me get them off." Kaylie struggled to her feet, and he caught her around the waist. She was trembling now, and he was getting worried.

"Just lean on me."

She did as he said as he unbuttoned her jeans and pulled them down, revealing a deep gash in the back of her leg. A knife wound, for sure. Anger festered inside Cort, but he kept his demeanor calm. Kaylie needed him right now, and that's what he had to focus on. "Let me look at it." He helped her lie down on her belly and began to clean the blood off and disinfect the wound. "We need to get you to a hospital."

"Well, do you know anyone with a plane who can get me there fast?"

He couldn't help smiling at her impatient tone. "Yeah, I think I know someone." He hesitated, thinking of how crappy the weather was, and he forced himself to make the offer. "Want me to drive? I'm sure Bill's got a truck around here."

"No. Fly. I want to get away." Her head was buried in her arms, her voice muffled. "My mom. My dad. They're dead."

"Yeah, I figured. I'm sorry." He'd seen the stash of bodies on his way and had assumed as much. He'd caught a glimpse of Jackson's face, but hadn't stopped to look more closely.

Had been able to think only about getting to Kaylie.

He finished wrapping her thigh, helped her get back into her jeans, then pulled her onto his lap. He needed to hold her, feel her body against his. Alive. Warm. Jesus, he'd been so scared when he'd come to and found her gone. "I saw Old Tom, too."

"We were coming to save you," she whispered, into his chest. "And Bill just came out of nowhere and killed Tom, and—"

He kissed her lightly, cutting her off. Not wanting her to force herself to relive that moment right now.

Her mouth was soft and welcoming, her hand clutching at his shoulder as she kissed him back. But her lips were cold—too cold—and he broke the kiss. "We need to get you out of here." Reluctantly, he began to lift her off his lap.

"No." She looped her arms around his neck, buried her face in his neck. "Not yet. Just hold me, please. Just for a minute."

Cort was unable to resist her plea. He desperately needed to feel her against him, to know she was alive in his arms. He tucked her trembling body against his chest and wrapped his arms around her. He kissed her forehead, her cheek, her eyelashes.

"Cort."

"Yeah?" He lifted her chin and kissed her mouth. Forced himself to be gentle.

"Your scars."

He paused. "What about them?"

"What are they from?"

He pulled back to study her. Her eyes were still closed, her head resting on his chest. "You want to know this now?"

"Yes."

"Why?"

She shook her head. "Just tell me."

He let out his breath and hugged her closer, unable to deny her anything. Hell, she could ask him to burn his entire fleet of planes right now, and he probably would. Sure, he'd regret it in the morning, but right now, with her blood all over the floor, he wouldn't deny her a damn thing. "When I was fourteen, my parents and I were flying in bad weather, on our way to Devil's Canyon for a weekend campout."

She snuggled deeper against him. "Where Old Tom was yesterday?"

Cort nodded, tunneling his fingers through her hair. It was matted and muddy, so much less than she deserved. "Devil's Pass is tough enough in good conditions, but almost no pilots will risk it during even slightly bad weather. My dad flew it all the time."

Kaylie set her hand on his chest, her fingers drumming weakly on his ribs. He placed his hand over hers, entwining their fingers while he relived the day he tried never to think about. "A gust of wind came up, and my dad caught a wing coming out of the pass. The plane hit hard, caught on fire." Cort rubbed his thumb over the back of her hand, thinking that the story didn't feel nearly as bad with Kaylie in his lap. "My dad was killed instantly. My mom took a little longer."

Her eyes opened, and she lifted her head. "Oh, Cort…"

He smoothed her hair off her face, thumbed some dirt off her forehead. "She was tangled in the metal and I couldn't get her free. Then my clothes caught fire and I had to leave her to beat them out." He shrugged. "I'd been cut almost in half. I was bleeding so bad that by the time I got the flames out, I was so weak I could barely move. My mom was unconscious or dead. I didn't know which, but between the intense flames and my own condition, I couldn't get to her. I watched her burn up, not able to do anything to save her."

Kaylie framed his face with her hands, and he held them to his cheeks. "I'm so sorry," she whispered. "It wasn't your fault."

"I know." But he saw in her eyes that she truly meant it, and for the first time in his life, he understood what it meant to have someone else believe in him. He'd always told himself it hadn't been his fault, but he'd been ashamed to believe it. Until now. He bent his head and kissed her. "Thank you."

She smiled. "You don't fly there anymore?"

"No."

"Why?"

He leaned his head back against the wall. "Because it killed my dad."

Kaylie made a noise of understanding, drawing his attention.

"What?"

She looked up at him, those brown eyes full of wisdom. "Devil's Pass makes you realize that you could die." She tapped his heart. "It makes you human."

"No, that's not—" Then he stopped himself as her words sank in. Was that it? Was that why he'd never been able to fly that pass, despite numerous attempts? No. "They died there, Kaylie. That's all. Nothing more than that."

She sighed and leaned her head against his chest again. "Thank you for telling me. I needed to know."

He glanced at her to ask again why she'd needed to know, then frowned when he saw her skin had become even paler. Circles beneath her eyes.

"Time to go. Let's get you to the hospital." Keeping her secured in his arms, he stood, taking a quick survey of the cabin to see if there was a phone he could use to call the police.

No phone, but he saw a stack of photos on the kitchen sink. "I think we found the pictures of you."

She turned her head sharply, her gaze falling on the counter. "I want them burned."

"I'll take care of it." He carried her across the room to the photos, not liking how limp she was in his arms. He doubted she was the type to let anyone carry her, and the fact she wasn't struggling to be released told him exactly how badly she was injured.

They reached the counter, and as he'd thought, there were dozens of pictures of Kaylie. In all of them, she looked bright and put together. Perfectly made up, nice jewelry. Nothing like the matted, bloody heap he held in his arms. The real, living, breathing, heart-stopping woman who was hanging onto him.

He picked up a picture of her standing on a dock. The wind was blowing her hair, and her cheeks were flushed. She was smiling, but her eyes were empty. Guarded. Unlike the woman he knew, whose eyes were full of passion and life and energy…and fear…and pain.

Which was better? An empty life without fear, or living every moment with passion and being chased by a stalker? Somewhere in the middle.

Did she think she was going back to Seattle now that Bill was dead?

Because she wasn't.

He couldn't allow her to go back there and let her soul die.

"Cort!" She pointed to a stack of pictures at the back of the counter. "Will you grab those for me? What are they of?"

Cort leaned forward and picked one up. It was a photo of a man who'd seen better days. His face was bruised, his shoulder twisted. The poor bastard's leg was in a shackle, and his calf was swollen and discolored. Rotting, crushed, and—

"That's my brother, Mason!" Kaylie grabbed the photo from him. "Dear God, look at him." Tears filled her eyes, and he felt the last vestiges of her control snap. "I didn't see him with my parents. His body wasn't there. Bill must have him somewhere," she whispered, clutching the photo to her chest. "We have to find him."

Cort grabbed the rest of the photos and quickly sorted through them. The fourth photo was of Mason on his back, half out of a shed, eyes closed as if he'd given up. That shed—

He looked at Kaylie and knew she'd seen it too.

Out front.

Cort was out the front door and down the steps before either of them said a word. Grimly, he shoved open the door to the shed and stepped inside, expecting the scent of rotting flesh.

Of more dead bodies.

But an empty shackle lay on the ground.

Open.

The cuffs were crusted with something black. Blood? Mud? Rotted flesh.

"He's not here." Kaylie slid down him, her voice thick with tears. "We're too late. He must be with the others."

Cort heard the roar of a plane, and he sprinted back to the door of the shed.

That's when he realized Bill's body wasn't on the porch anymore. He'd been so caught up in Kaylie that he'd walked right across the porch without noticing the bastard had somehow gotten up and fucking *left*. Hell, he hadn't even checked to make sure Bill had been dead when he'd rushed to the cabin to get to Kaylie. And now the bastard was getting away. "Son of a bitch!"

The plane flew overhead, the engine so loud he knew exactly what it was. Old Tom's plane.

Bill was gone, along with Kaylie's brother.

Kaylie hobbled up behind him. "Please tell me that's Luke, searching for us."

Cort put his arm around her to help take some of the pressure off her injured leg. "It was Old Tom's plane."

The plane circled overhead again.

"Does Bill know how to fly?"

"Pretty much everyone out here can." Cort stared up into the dark clouds, the hair on his arms standing up as the plane circled again. It was the same thing Bill had done with the snowmobile at Jackson and Sara's cabin.

Kaylie followed his gaze. "He's taunting us," she whispered.

"He's telling us it's not over. Only this time, it's going to be on his terms. Because he's got your brother."

# CHAPTER TWENTY-THREE

Cort sat next to Kaylie's hospital bed, his knee bouncing in agitation as the nurse worked on her leg. The nurse had tried to throw him out, but he'd refused to leave, and Kaylie had supported him.

He was staying.

Her wrist had been fixed, and now they were cleaning the wound on the back of her thigh. Nothing life threatening. But Kaylie hadn't let go of his hand since they'd gotten there.

He was still so worked up, he couldn't sit still. Couldn't stop thinking about all those bodies. About Kaylie at Bill's mercy.

Shit.

"What do we do next?" Kaylie asked suddenly.

He almost grinned at her question. Here he was, obsessing over her injuries, and she was thinking about next steps. A fighter, for sure. How could she possibly classify herself as someone who hid behind storm windows and heavy blankets? As it turned out, it appeared he was the one incapable of handling the stress of Kaylie being in danger.

"Cort?"

He forced himself to follow Kaylie's lead and focus on the situation. "I don't think Bill's going to hop on a plane to the Lower 48 and disappear. He's got an unfinished agenda, and he's not going to walk away."

She nodded, her gaze flicking toward the door. "If I go

home, he'll be able to find me. Now that he knows my name, it wouldn't be difficult."

His grip tightened. "You're not going home," he growled.

Kaylie's attention snapped toward him. "Ever?"

There was a challenge in her eyes, and Cort didn't dare push it. So he simply shrugged. "Not while Bill's out there."

The nurse began to wrap Kaylie's leg, and a light knock sounded at the door. It was a state trooper Cort didn't know, wanting an interview with Kaylie. Rich was at Bill's right now. Cort was pretty sure Richie had nearly wet himself when Cort had delivered the news, but the young state trooper had stepped up and called in all the right people. The place was probably swarming with law enforcement and spotlights now. One of their own going bad was a huge deal. Cort and Kaylie had already been interviewed, but the uniforms had been hovering, wanting more information.

As if that would help them find a lifelong Alaskan who wanted to hide in the bush. No one would find Bill until he decided he wanted to be found.

"No interviews yet." The nurse shut the door in the trooper's face. She eyed Cort as she returned to the bed. "I'm fixing you up next, so don't think about going anywhere."

"I'm fine." He was worried about Kaylie. She was still too pale.

Kaylie frowned at him. "What did happen to you at the plane?"

He shrugged. "I lost." Because he'd been thinking about her instead of the fight. The sight of Bill taking off after her had snapped something inside Cort, and he'd gone crazy, attacking Bill without a plan or a weapon. He was lucky he hadn't gotten himself killed, he'd been so insane with fear for her.

The nurse finished and snapped her fingers at him. "Shirt off."

He glanced at Kaylie, then pulled his shirt over his head, well aware of the how the gash on his side would look.

Kaylie gasped. "You were *stabbed?*"

He managed not to flinch as the nurse probed the wound. "He didn't hit anything vital. I'm okay." Though, he had to admit, for a brief moment, he hadn't been so sure. And looking at it now, he saw the wound was a good seven inches long, skin flapped open. Thank God for adrenaline. He hadn't felt a thing once he'd charged after Kaylie. But now…

Shit.

"This is filthy." The nurse made a *tsk* noise as she peered at his side.

He shrugged. "First aid wasn't my top concern at the time."

He ground his jaw as the nurse scrubbed it, doing his best not to wince. Damn, it felt like she was taking her own knife to his side.

"Be more gentle," Kaylie ordered. "You're hurting him."

The nurse glanced up at him, then softened her touch.

Kaylie leaned closer to watch as the nurse continued to work, periodically telling her to soften up.

Cort rested his hand on Kaylie's hair. When was the last time anyone had worried about him getting hurt? Worried about him in general? He didn't need it.

Really, he didn't.

But as he thumbed Kaylie's matted tresses, he couldn't deny that it felt damn good.

His phone rang, and he flipped it open, ignoring the nurse's barked warning that no phones were allowed in the hospital. "Richie. What's going on?"

"There's no sign of Bill," Rich reported. "He's definitely gone. We found evidence that someone's been living in that shed really recently, so I think the odds that the brother is still alive are high."

Kaylie closed her eyes, and Cort knew she'd heard what Richie said. "You guys tracking him?" he asked.

"Got no idea where to look. He could land anywhere with that plane. He's not going to show up at an airport, but we've alerted them anyway."

As Cort had expected, Bill had disappeared.

Kaylie tugged on his arm, and he bent over so she could press her ear up next to the phone.

"My suggestion is to take that girl and hide out until Bill turns up." Rich's voice got a little shaky. "You should have seen the state of some of those bodies. He sliced them up pretty bad, especially the one who looks like an older version of Kaylie. I've never seen anything like it. The wounds are all postmortem though. Kaylie's damn lucky you showed up when you did."

The nurse applied something to Cort's side that had him hissing with pain.

Or maybe that was Kaylie's sharp intake of breath. Cort wrapped his arm around her and pulled her up against his good side, kissed her forehead. She leaned against him, her hands cold on his bare torso. In fact, her whole body was cold. He rubbed his hand down her arm, trying to warm her up.

"We found a stash of pictures from a long time ago," Richie continued. "Photos of him and a woman who looks like Kaylie. Hundreds of letters he wrote to a woman named Alice, but never mailed. Pretty fucked-up stuff. Some letters are about how much he worships her. The others..." He hesitated. "Bad shit, Cort. Don't let him near Kaylie."

Cort looked down at the woman by his side. "I won't."

She leaned her forehead against his chest.

"Hang on a sec," Richie said. "I'll be right back."

The nurse pulled out a massive syringe. "You need stitches." She jammed the needle in his side, making him swear. "A few more times, and then I'll be back to see how the numbness is going."

"We don't have time for that." Cort caught the nurse's wrist as she went for his side with the syringe again. He had no idea when Bill was going to show up, but he needed to be prepared, not sitting on his ass with a needle in his side. For all he knew, Bill would waltz into the hospital in full uniform, and no one would stop him. Cort needed to get Kaylie out of there and into a situation he controlled. "Just stitch it up."

The nurse shot him a disgusted look. "Don't be an idiot. It'll only take five minutes for the numbing to set in."

"Cort, please. I can't deal with watching her stitch you without novocaine," Kaylie said. "Just let her do it."

Damned if he could resist the plea in Kaylie's eyes. He saw she was at the end of her rope and if seeing him stitched was going to put her over the edge…"Fine," he grumbled to the nurse. "You have five minutes to let that set, and then you're finishing."

Kaylie shot him a grateful smile. The nurse hit him up a few more times, making him wonder whether the shots were worse than the stitches would have been without them. Better to think about that, than how it made him feel knowing that Kaylie couldn't deal with seeing him hurt.

Valerie, even at the start, had never given a shit when he knocked himself around. She just told him it served him right for the lifestyle he'd chosen and his reckless attitude.

But Kaylie…The pinched look to her face as she watched the nurse work was genuine.

Again, he found his hand in her hair, and his chest tightened when she gave him a tired smile.

Richie returned to the call. "I'm back. Sorry. Listen, I have to go. It's crazy here."

"Yeah, thanks for the update."

•

"We'll find him, though," Richie said. "Just hang tight."

Cort closed his phone. "You catch all that?"

Kaylie nodded. "My poor mother."

Cort set the phone on the table and leaned forward, taking Kaylie's hands in his as the nurse quietly let herself out of the room. Cort ignored the blood seeping down his side. "Listen to me, Kaylie. Right now, we need to focus on survival. Keeping you out of Bill's hands."

She nodded, biting her lower lip. "We can't hide. He has my brother. We have to find him. He's all I have left, and—"

"No. You have me."

Tears filled her eyes. "I almost got you killed."

"Bullshit. I'm here, aren't I? Not dead. I'm fine."

She stared at him. "You're insane."

"No, just indestructible." He held her hand tighter, pressed his lips to her knuckles. "I've got a place. Family place. Well protected."

"Won't Bill know about it? Won't he come there?"

Cort nodded. "I'm hoping. But it's my turf and I have the advantage. It's the only place I can think of."

"And if he doesn't come? What about my brother?"

He ground his jaw against the one outcome he didn't want. "If he doesn't come, I suspect we're going to get an engraved invitation to meet him somewhere on his terms. He'll hold your brother out as leverage. I suspect that's what the photos were for. Now that he has you this close, he's going to want to close the deal."

Kaylie searched his gaze. "So, you think he'll keep Mason alive as long as he doesn't have me?"

"Yeah." Cort decided not to mention how bad that leg had looked in the photos. He knew they were short on time for her brother. They weren't going to go to Cort's place to hide. They were going to his place to lay a trap. Cort was going to publicize the hell out of the fact they were there.

"If he comes...what do we do?" she asked. "He's knocked you out twice."

Cort narrowed his eyes. "First time, I wasn't expecting him. Second time, I was worried about you." He winked. "Third time's a charm." Then he sobered. "This is risky, and you don't need to come. I can send out the word that we're both there, even though you're not—"

"No." She was already shaking her head. "I'm in. I'm doing it."

It was the answer Cort had been hoping for, because he didn't like the idea of Kaylie being where he couldn't protect her. But it still made his skin crawl to think of using her as bait. Yeah, he'd be there to keep her safe, but it just felt wrong.

But not as wrong as walking away and leaving her in someone else's hands. "It's way the hell out in the middle of nowhere," he warned. "On a mountain."

She hesitated. "Do we have to climb to get there?"

"No. I can land right next to the house. But there are mountains on three sides. You'll feel like you're at base camp, I'm sure."

She managed a grim smile. "My family would never forgive me if I stayed out of this because I was scared."

"Your family?" He took her shoulders and forced her to face him. "This is too dangerous to do it so you can prove to your family that you're good enough. This has to be for you, because you want it." His grip tightened. "For once, for one time, look inside at yourself and do what's right for you."

She raised her chin. "I'll do it for any reason I want."

He scowled at her. "Bush pilots whose hearts aren't in it die, and I won't stand by and let you go down this road if you're not committed. It's the fastest way to get killed." His fingers dug into her shoulders. "I won't let you get yourself killed."

"I'm not a bush pilot! Stop making me into one! Just because I don't get off on the high of risking my life doesn't mean there's anything wrong with me. I can step up if I have to, and that's just going to have to be enough for you!" She shoved him off her. "For once, for just *once* in my life, I want to be enough for someone just the way I am."

"That's what I'm trying to tell you. It's not what I think, or what your family thinks." He tapped her heart, ignoring her when she tried to shove his hand away. "It has to be enough for you."

"What makes you a philosopher?"

"See enough of your friends die, and it changes your view on life."

Her face stilled, then softened. "I have to agree with that one." She tilted her head. "Your parents...Did they love to fly? Really love it?"

He pushed off the bed and strode to the window, looking out over the town lit by the dawn. "My parents have nothing to do with this." One more day until the anniversary of his parents' death.

"No?" Kaylie moved off the bed and came to stand behind him, her hands sliding over his back. "You're pushing me so hard to be someone I'm not. Why? Because you don't want to slow down enough to feel anything, to make room for me? Instead of becoming someone who actually has two feet on the ground, you want to drag me along in your world, thinking that'll make you happy?"

"And now you're the philosopher?"

"I've had a lot of time to think about why my family takes so many risks. I have theories."

He snorted. "Were any of them simply that they loved what they did?"

"No."

"Then you're wrong."

"If you're so happy, why is everyone concerned that you're on the verge of cracking? Of going over the edge?"

He didn't turn. Didn't respond. The denial rose to his lips, as it always did, but he couldn't voice it this time.

Because he knew it was true.

He'd been riding that edge for a long time. Nothing felt right anymore. And since Kaylie had arrived, everything was even more screwed up. Made him almost wish he could be some washed-up accountant who had never felt the power of a plane beneath him, never knew the freedom only the sky could give him. Never knew what he'd be missing if he gave it up.

But he did.

And he couldn't.

He would die without the air.

"Maybe you're the one who needs to change," she said quietly. "Maybe you're the one being haunted by demons."

He turned to face her, caught her face in his hands. "I can't," he said. "Not even for you. Not even to keep you."

"Not for me." She repeated his words back to him. "For you." She smiled at the expression he had on his face. "See how crazy that sounds when you're on the receiving end? I am who I am, Cort. And you are who you are. We simply don't match up—"

"No." He bent his head and kissed her, cutting her off. Didn't want hear any more about how they didn't match. Her grip on his arms was delicate, as if she was afraid to hold too tight as she kissed him back.

The door opened and they both jumped as Luke walked in, followed by Charity. "Need some help?"

Cort grinned. "Now we're talking."


"You love him yet?"

Kaylie glanced at Charity as she changed into the clothes Charity had brought for her. She'd taken a quick shower and dried her hair. It had felt so good to cleanse herself of all the blood and mud that had caked her. Cort and Luke were out in the hall, talking to the state trooper who had tried to come in earlier. "Why?"

"Because that was just like the sweetest kiss I've ever seen, when Luke and I came in. Made my heart stutter and melt. If Luke weren't like my own brother, I would have jumped him just to get a piece of that action myself."

Kaylie bit her lip, not sure what to say. To her, it had felt like a good-bye kiss. A kiss that said, *Yeah, it's been great, but I'll see you around.* An amazing good-bye kiss that had made her insides tremble and her throat tighten.

Charity held up some lingerie. Black lace. "Since the two of you are going to be shacking up until the bad guy shows up, I figured you might want to entertain."

Kaylie's cheeks heated up and she took the bra, quickly putting it on. It fit pretty well. Risqué enough that she knew Cort would like it. If she showed him. "Can I ask you something?"

"Sure." Charity plopped down on the bed and crossed her ankles. "What's up?"

Kaylie hesitated, then sat across from Charity, pulling on a tight long-sleeved shirt. Charity had certainly brought clothes designed not to let Cort forget she was a woman. "Did you love flying? When you were doing it?"

Charity's smile faded. "I don't really like to talk about it."

Kaylie sighed. "I respect that. I had no right to ask. I just—"

Charity cocked her head. "You just what?"

"You're the only person I know who lived that kind of lifestyle and walked away. How does that happen? Are you happy? Or did it break you? Did you never really love it, and that's why you could leave?"

Understanding softened Charity's face. "You're asking about Cort. Could he be happy being the man you want him to be?"

Kaylie thought about that. "I guess, yeah."

"The bigger question is whether you would still love him if he weren't the man he is, or do you love him precisely because of the man he is?"

"I don't—" Kaylie bit her lip, remembering her words to Bill. *I love Cort.* Did she? She knew she admired him and respected him. He was so strong and determined. So alive… But he'd called *her* alive. She wasn't anything like him. He was…

She looked at Charity, an ugly realization dawning on her. If he were a conservative suit wearer, would he still make her insides melt? Or was it the fact that he was so free that appealed to her? She stared at Charity, a sinking feeling in her chest. "I'm masochistic, aren't I?"

Charity grinned. "You do love him. I knew it! That's too cool!"

"Stop!" Kaylie grabbed Charity's hands. "Shh! It's not a good thing. It's stupid!"

"Okay, okay." Charity leaned forward, her eyes glowing. "Have you told him?"

"No! It's not…I don't…" Kaylie sighed. "I have to find out how to stop this." Look what her mother's rush for a hot relationship had gotten her. Dangerous men made sense only in fantasies and movies.

One delicate eyebrow arched high. "Are you sure you want to stop?"

"Of course I am! I don't belong here, Charity. I can't—"

"What do you mean? Of course you do." Charity leaned forward. "Don't use his flying as an excuse. It's just one part of who he is. The man, his heart, that's what matters. If you love him, it can work. If you don't, it won't. It's that simple."

"It's not that simple."

"No, not if you don't let it be." Charity squeezed her hands and lowered her voice. "I know what it's like to be afraid, Kaylie. It's killing me. Don't let it kill you, too."

Kaylie heard the truth in Charity's voice, and she felt her

heart tighten for this woman who had reached out to her. A woman she knew could be a true friend. "You're scared to fly?"

"Oh, God, I wish that's all it was." Charity mustered a smile. "But I'll tell you one thing."

"What's that?"

"I never loved to fly the way Cort does. I had fun, but it wasn't necessary for me to live. Taking flying away from Cort would be like cutting out his heart. He would die. You have to accept that and let it go. See if there's another way."

Kaylie bit her lip at the confirmation of the truth she'd known in her heart all along. "He wants someone to live that life with him. To have sex in airplanes and never be on the ground. I can't be that person."

Charity's brows shot up. "You had sex in his airplane? While it was in the *air*?"

"Charity! That's not the point! The point is that he wants someone like *him*."

She folded her arms over her chest and gave Kaylie a long look. "And how do you know *that*?"

"Because—"

"I think you're using it as an excuse because you're afraid." Charity paused. "Cort's a good man, and if he loves you, he's going to be every bit the man you want him to be."

"But you just said he'll always fly."

"And he will." Charity raised her brows. "But is that really a problem in itself? Truly?"

Kaylie frowned. "Of course it is, but—"

The door swung open, and Cort stepped inside. He'd apparently been stitched up out in the hall, because he had a large bandage on his side. He pulled a T-shirt over his head, his body ripped and muscled, despite the injury. He spared a nod for Charity. Then his gaze fastened on Kaylie, making her body heat up. "You ladies ready?"

Kaylie nodded, and he went over by the bed to help her to

her feet. "How do you feel?" he asked. "You sure you're up for this?"

Charity squeezed her hand, giving her a knowing look, then hopped off the bed to make room for Cort.

Kaylie's gaze jumped to his as he helped her to her feet. He was watching her intently, his face deadly serious. She swallowed, her heart suddenly pounding, and reminded herself that the woman he wanted wasn't the woman she wanted to be. She would have to deny her true self to make him happy.

But as he set his hand on her lower back to guide her out the door, a part of her wondered if maybe, just maybe, she should.

And at the same time, she knew she couldn't.

And then she thought of Charity's words, and wondered if maybe, just maybe, there was another way.

# Chapter Twenty-four

Cort flexed his hands when he caught sight of the cabin that had been in his family for four generations. The one his great-grandpa had gotten by trading a pile of furs and an ax.

A building Cort hadn't been to since his parents had died.

It was smaller than he remembered, a tough little log cabin with thick walls and a three-quarter porch for kicking back and drinking beer while watching the sun set over the mountains. He could almost see his parents out there, talking about their latest flight, feet up on the railing while Cort took apart the airplane they'd flown in on.

Something in Cort's chest tightened, something he didn't like. Something that made him miss his family. A feeling he hadn't had in a long time.

He'd been just fine being alone.

Hadn't been lonely for even a day.

Until now.

He tensed his jaw as he banked for the landing, no longer certain it was the right thing to do. To come here. To bring Kaylie.

Too late.

Luke and Charity were already spreading the word, and Luke would be there by midnight, ready to set up shop in the trees with a shotgun. The snares had been set, and it was too late to back out.

Kaylie leaned forward, peering out the windshield. "Is that it?"

"Yeah, that's it." Cort landed smoothly, taxiing the little

Cessna around so she was banked at a forty-five-degree angle down the slope, ready for a quick take off. The sun was bright for the first time in days, the temperature almost balmy.

Kaylie opened her door and stepped out, putting on the same high-fashion sunglasses she'd been wearing that first day Cort had met her. He paused to watch her as she walked across the damp grass. She shaded her eyes to look across the valley below them, then peered up at the sheer cliffs that stretched above them on the other three sides.

Kaylie was wearing a pair of dark blue jeans, which fit her body as if they were meant for her, and a light blue jacket. Her hair was soft and blowing in the light wind. It was less perfect than when she'd first set foot on the tarmac in Alaska, but it was a hell of a lot more tempting.

She still looked as beautiful as she had the first time he'd seen her, just as sensual and female. But the difference was that now, she also looked vibrant and alive.

She looked human. Fragile and strong, a woman letting life touch her and enrich her. No longer a woman with a shield around her, keeping out the world.

Now Kaylie looked like she fit right into his life, despite the diamonds and the expensive clothes. The diamonds and the clothes...He didn't have a problem with them anymore. They were part of who she was, and he liked the whole package. And that thought made some of the loneliness in his chest ease. It felt right having her here, sharing in what had been his family's retreat.

But he'd been wrong about Valerie.

Hellaciously wrong.

Scowling, Cort grabbed their bags out of the back of the plane and climbed out, pausing to grab two guns and a knife. Set the throttle lock so no one would be flying it except him, then headed toward the cabin, resisting the urge to walk up to Kaylie and sink his face into that lush hair.

She didn't turn as he passed her, but he caught a whiff of her scent, making blood rush to his groin.

The door was still bolted shut with a log across the door, and it took both hands and some serious leverage to get it to move. But it finally slid free with a creaking groan, and he opened the door.

He froze at what he saw inside.

Dishes set out to dry on the sink.

A pile of clothes on the couch, ready to be folded.

A paperback book of his mom's, facedown on the coffee table to hold the place.

His dad's pipe, sitting out, ready to be smoked.

A small knife and a half-whittled piece of wood sitting on the coffee table next to his mom's book.

There was a faint scent of mold, but the dust wasn't as thick as it should have been after so many years. The place actually looked in good repair. Then Cort saw a faded green ball cap on the back of the chair. Jackson's hat. Cort realized his friend had been checking up on the cabin all this time, keeping it ready for the day Cort was finally ready to come back.

Shit.

He dropped the bags and walked over to the table. Picked up the knife and brushed the dust off it. Folded it over in his hands, recalling the feel of it. A dark green pearlized handle. Blade still sharp. It was small, so much smaller than he remembered. Too little for his hands now, but for a fourteen-year-old, it had been the best present he'd ever gotten.

He picked up the partially carved piece of wood, grinned when he saw it was a woman, naked as a jaybird.

What parents let their fourteen-year-old sit around whittling naked women out of pieces of wood? He'd have thought he'd been whittling planes back then, not women.

A shadow fell across the room.

Turning, he found Kaylie in the doorway, backlit by the sun. Like a damn angel.

"Is it weird to be back here?"

He shrugged, tossed the knife and the woman back on the table. "It's fine."

Kaylie stepped inside, and he saw her notice the clothes, the pipe, the book. "It's as if they're about to come back."

"Yeah, I know." He picked up the bags again and carried them over to the bed. A one-room cabin—he'd been the one who slept on the couch. Or out on the porch, when his parents had wanted privacy.

He grinned, remembering it had taken him a few years before he'd figured out what they wanted the privacy for.

Kaylie slowly walked inside, trailing her fingers over the paperback. Her movement was slow, and he felt a weight emanating from her.

He folded his arms over his chest, watching her as she moved around. Waiting for her to talk.

Eventually, she turned to face him. "You were fourteen when they died?"

"Yeah."

"Who took care of you?"

He shrugged. "I took care of myself. No big deal."

"No big deal," she repeated softly. She eased herself to the couch, hugged her knees up to her chest. "We're the same, now."

He raised his brows. "How so?"

"Both our parents are dead." She rested her chin on her knees. "Did you feel alone afterward? Scared? What did you do?"

He ground his jaw for a minute, not wanting to go there.

He never went there.

"I don't know who I am," she whispered. "I spent my life fighting my family, and now they're gone. I feel like…I feel like I did it wrong. That I missed out. That I made the wrong choice." She was staring out the door, at the afternoon sun. "But I don't know what I could have done differently. And now Mason is all that's left. And he might die anyway. And if he doesn't, what then? Do I start climbing again so I can be close to him?" She turned her gaze to him. "Is that why you fly? To be near your family?"

Cort dropped the bags on the bed and walked over, took a seat on the edge of the coffee table, facing her. He leaned forward, forearms resting on his thighs. "You really want to know why I fly?"

She nodded, still hugging herself.

"I fly because it's the only time I feel alive."

She cocked her head, studying him, and for a moment, he felt as if she was seeing inside him in a way he didn't even see himself. "The only time? Really? There's nothing else?"

He ground his jaw against the word struggling to emerge. *You.*

She looked so sad. "I wanted my parents to feel alive with me, but they never did. It was only the mountain. I simply wasn't enough for them."

"I'm sorry about your parents, Kaylie. I really am." And he was. He knew the loss of having them ripped out from under you with no warning. No time to say good-bye.

Knowing they suffered.

Kaylie hadn't been witness to it the way he had, but seeing the aftermath...he suspected it didn't make a difference. She knew.

"But you need to understand that just because they climbed and couldn't share that with you, that didn't mean they didn't care or that you weren't enough." He set his hands on her knees, not quite ready to speak the rest of his thoughts—that he was beginning to think it wouldn't matter if Kaylie never flew with him. Simply having her be a part of his life, to share moments like this…She would be more than enough just being herself.

As Valerie had been, until Cort had learned the truth about her.

But Kaylie wasn't like Valerie. Kaylie might still be hiding from her true self, but behind her walls, she was courageous and alive and passionate. Nothing like Valerie, and more than enough to make him happy.

Kaylie managed a smile. "It's weird because I'm sad, but at the same time, I haven't seen them in a decade. So how can I miss them? But I do. So much. And what he did to my mom…" Her voice broke, and he slid his hands up the outside of her thighs, framing her hips.

She took a breath, her gaze flickering toward him, then slithered away. "This is awful to say, but on some level, I feel relieved that I don't have to deal with the conflict anymore. Relieved that I no longer have to worry that they're going to die on me. They died." She looked at him, tears filling her eyes. "They're *dead*. After all this time, they finally *died*."

He knew the moment the realization finally hit her, and he slid onto the couch next to her, pulling her onto his lap as the grief exploded. She sobbed against his chest, her body shaking, clinging to him as if he were the only solid thing left in her world.

And he knew he was.

She'd been robbed of everything. Of her family, of the safe little world she had built around herself, of her own sense of independence. She had been forced back into the environment that had stolen her childhood, her family, and her right to believe the world was a good place, a safe place, a place where she could be who she wanted to be.

He held her close, rocking her and whispering soothing words to her as she cried.

And he realized something.

Realized he was exactly like her parents, just as she'd claimed. Would he *really* allow her to be herself? Or would he keep trying to force her to become the vibrant woman he knew she was hiding? Thinking he knew better than she did about who she was and how she should live her life. Trying to force her outside her shell.

But holding her in his arms, watching her crumble...He brushed his lips over her hair, finally understanding the truth. That she was fragile. Human. Breakable.

She knew that about herself, and no one in her life understood it.

He couldn't truly comprehend it, because his entire way of life depended on his belief that he was unstoppable. By trying to make Kaylie stronger, he was weakening her.

Yeah, she had courage and strength, and Cort admired the hell out of her, but her courage was quiet, not flashy or aggressive. A foundation, not a high wire flapping around in the wind.

Kaylie didn't need Cort. She needed someone who would keep her safe and give her the world she wanted. Not someone who would put her through this agony again.

Kaylie needed security. And he couldn't give that to her.

He closed his eyes and pressed his face to her hair, finally understanding the truth.

He couldn't keep her.


It felt like forever before the tears finally stopped, leaving Kaylie drained and exhausted.

Her head hurt.

Her muscles ached.

Cort brushed his lips over her hair, his hand rubbing circles on her back. She was still on his lap with his arms wrapped around her. She could feel his erection underneath her, but he hadn't made a move on her.

He'd simply held her.

Comforted her.

The man who never slowed down had parked himself on the couch and hadn't moved for as long as she'd needed him. Despite the preparations that needed to be done for Bill's arrival. Despite his own issues with being back in the cabin.

Maybe Charity was right. Maybe his flying didn't matter. Maybe simply the man he was would be enough. She thought of the black lingerie Charity had given her, and suddenly she knew she wanted this moment with Cort.

Whatever happened in the future, this man, this amazing man…She wanted this moment with him, the bush pilot, the adrenaline junkie, the tender lover who held her until her tears were no more.

She wanted him. The ache in her heart began to fade, replaced with a growing awareness of the hardness of his body, the utterly male scent, the roughness of his whiskers as he rubbed his chin in her hair.

She hooked her index finger over one of the buttons on his shirt. "How long do we have until Bill arrives?"

"Luke and Charity are spreading the word starting at eight o'clock tonight at the bar. If he heard right away, it would take him a couple hours to organize, even if he was ready to go. So we have at least until ten tonight, probably later."

She looked at her watch. It was only five. "How much do you need to do outside?"

"Not much. It'll take me a couple hours at most." He was still rubbing her back, his hand slipping beneath her shirt periodically to brush over her bare skin.

She closed her eyes, absorbing his warmth, his energy, his solid strength. Her mom and dad had always been on edge, never sitting still, getting testy if they spent too long indoors.

But Cort…She could feel a peacefulness in him.

A core strength.

A solidity. Almost as if he brought a sense of stability with him, wherever he went.

*You love him yet?*

Charity's question popped into her mind, and Kaylie knew the answer in her heart, without even asking herself.

Yes.

For all that it might cost her, she did.

And she loved him for what he was. For his embrace of life, for his passion, for the way he made her feel beautiful and sexy and courageous. For the way he believed in her courage. Her parents had belittled her fears, scoffed at her choices. Cort praised her courage, believed she had strength. A difference. A core difference.

Did that mean Kaylie could stay? That she could live with watching him get into that plane every day, knowing he was going to push the edge? That she could handle being in love with a man who loved flying more than he loved her?

No.

But she could take a piece of him with her. To hold in her heart forever.

Slowly, she lifted her head and raised her face to his. Found him studying her, his eyes dark and hooded. Unreadable. Her courage faltered for a split second, but she knew what she wanted.

She didn't want him in the back of a plane or in the throes of grief. She wanted him tender and loving, in the present. For tonight. "Kiss me," she whispered. "Make love to me."

His eyes became darker, and his thumb brushed over her lower lip.

Anticipation swirled through her when he bent toward her, his hand cupping her chin.

He stopped when his mouth was a mere breath from hers, then swore and pulled back. "I can't."

Kaylie blinked. "What?"

Gently, he lifted her off him, settling her on the couch. "I need to go set up outside. Stay inside the cabin and bolt the door when I leave. There should be no surprises, but I don't want to take any chances."

"But—"

He paused, his fingers trailing through her hair, a look of such craving on his face that she knew he wouldn't be able to walk away. Not yet.

But he dropped his hand, grabbed a gun, and walked out the door, slamming it shut behind him.

# CHAPTER TWENTY-FIVE

Cort strode through the woods, his feet making too much noise, but he didn't care.

All he could think about was Kaylie back at the cabin.

*Make love to me.*

Shit.

He ran his hand through his hair, too agitated to focus.

He wasn't the kind of guy to let go of something he wanted. He took what he needed and didn't look back. Since when did he become some moral Boy Scout, willing to walk away from what he wanted?

Since he'd met Kaylie.

Since he'd seen into her heart and realized she was so much more than he ever would be and that he would destroy her if he kept her.

But if he made love to her again, he would never let her go.

So he had to let her go now. This minute.

Lucky for him, he had a distraction: there was a murderer on the way, and Cort had to be ready to cap his ass.

He reached the only other clearing large enough for a plane and surveyed it. No one had landed here. The grass was untouched; branches littered the ground.

If Bill tried to land here, Cort would hear him long before he landed. Bill would know that. So there had to be another way he was going to come in.

But Cort and Luke had discussed it, and there were no

other options. Flying was the only way in. Flying, or by car to the nearest access point, and then a long hike.

Cort paced the clearing, trying to think like Bill.

Something felt off about their plan.

Bill was a part of this state's terrain the way Cort was part of the sky. He would guess the plan. He would come up with an alternate approach.

Cort crouched in the middle of the clearing, gun across his lap, and found himself closing his eyes.

Listening to the earth.

To the sounds of nature.

To the wind teasing the trees.

Opening himself to his gut instincts, the ones his dad had taught him to rely on.

It had been so long since he'd slowed down like this. Hadn't thought of it in years. But sitting on that couch with Kaylie…he'd been at peace. He'd felt his spirit slow, embracing the moment. It hadn't taken sex to ground him this time.

Holding her had been enough, and he tapped into that sensation again, opening his mind to nature and the woods, to the spirit of the earth that he'd grown up with—and forgotten.

He closed his eyes and could almost hear his dad's voice guiding him, forcing him to reach within himself and find the spirit that would lead him to safety.

Cort became aware of the strength of the earth.

Of the weight of the air, light, with a hint of rain approaching. Heavy rain, hours away.

He concentrated on the feel of the wind on his skin, the whispers as it tickled the trees, heard the story of a strong wind on its way. His mind quieted, and he realized he hadn't felt like this in years. Completely and utterly at peace. In the moment.

He'd tried after his father had died. Had gone out in the clearing behind his house. Never heard the earth's messages again.

Not until now.

Not until he came back to the place where it had begun. Not until Kaylie had come into his life. Not until she had soothed his spirit.

And for the first time in years, the earth spoke to him, telling him of the one weakness of their hideout.

The cliffs.

Bill would be coming down the cliffs.

And Cort would be waiting for him.

Slowly, Cort opened his eyes and looked around, half expecting his dad to be leaning against a tree, watching him with a twinkle in his eye. To see Kaylie standing beside his dad, his mom next to her.

His parents would have liked Kaylie. They would have liked her soul.

His gaze stopped on a bent pine. That was the tree his dad had always propped himself against when they'd been out here.

Cort could almost see his dad, the utter relaxation of his body, the calm ease of his expression.

Cort sat back on his heels at the image, realizing that his dad had been at absolute peace with himself.

That he'd loved flying, because it was peace for him.

Not a way to outrun the restlessness in his soul.

Cort had never felt peace in his life. Not in the air. Not on the ground.

Not like his dad.

Not like *this*.

Not until Kaylie.

He turned and looked back in the direction of the cabin, thought of Kaylie back there. For the first time he could remember, his first thought wasn't how soon he could be back in the air.

He was thinking about her.

The woman he couldn't keep.

"Stupid jerk." Kaylie slammed her bag onto the dusty bed, covering her face as clouds of dust flew up. Of course, the minute she realized she loved him, Cort chose *that* minute to walk out on her.

Bastard.

She sighed as she sat down on the bed, knowing he wasn't a bastard.

He was smart. He had enough discipline not to destroy them both. Smarter than she was, apparently.

A light tap on the door caught her attention, and she whirled around. "Cort?"

A rustling from beneath the door caught her attention, and as she watched, a dirty white envelope slid into sight.

She hesitated, then walked across and picked it up.

Opened it.

A photo of Mason, wearing only a pair of boxers. Of his leg. Swollen, discolored. An open gash across his stomach. Infected, and oozing.

He was dying.

"Oh, God."

The light tap sounded on the door again. "Open the door now, or your brother's dead."

She recoiled at the sound of Bill's voice. Too early! He was too early!

He must have been there all along. Waiting for them. Dear God. Where was Cort?

She glanced over at the shotgun Cort has left behind, but she had no idea how to use it. And if she killed him...God knew where her brother was. He'd die. But if she went with him—

The picture window behind her shattered.

She whirled around as Bill stepped over the frame, a small handgun pointed at her. He was wearing a climbing harness and crampons, and she realized he'd come down the cliff. God, she should have thought of that! Those cliffs were nothing for someone like her parents. Like Bill.

"Let's go."

Her throat dry, she sprinted for the door. "Cort! Bill's here!"

She yanked it open, and Bill tackled her, driving her to the ground, hand over her mouth, knife at her throat.

The woods were silent.

No Cort.

And she knew she had lost.


As Cort stood in the meadow, a sense of wrongness began to trickle down his spine.

Of threat.

He turned his head, scanning the woods around him, but nothing was out of place.

Then he heard it.

The chink of metal on rock.

And again.

At the cabin.

At the cliffs.

*The bastard's early. Son of a bitch!*

Cort took off at a dead sprint, sheer terror for Kaylie driving him to run harder than he ever thought he could.

He reached the cabin, charged through the open door. "Kaylie!"

Empty.

Swearing, he ran outside, shading his eyes as he looked up.

Saw them at the top of the south cliff, two shadowed figures disappearing over the rim.

"Kaylie!"

Knowing he'd never make it up the cliff in time, he sprinted for his plane, jerked the door open, and hurled himself in. Whipped off the throttle lock and sped straight down the knoll. Caught air and banked sharply, heading straight up to the top of the cliff.

Got to the top, saw Kaylie fighting as Bill tossed her into Old Tom's plane.

Bill looked up at Cort, then stopped, watching the plane.

The old bastard didn't try to stop Kaylie when she squirmed free and started running toward the edge of the cliff.

He just stood there.

Watching.

As if waiting—

"Shit!" A sense of foreboding hit Cort a split second before the engine began to seize. Swearing, he looked down.

No oil.

Son of a bitch had drained it, and like some stupid rookie pilot, Cort hadn't noticed.

Smoke began to rise, and then the engine quit. Plane began a headfirst dive straight toward the ground

He shot a glance at Kaylie, saw her staring at the plane, willed her to turn away. Not to watch. Then he had no choice but to turn his attention to the plane, fighting to control the landing, to ease the damage.

And then he hit.

Kaylie stared in numb horror as she watched the smoke spew from the engine of Cort's plane.

It banked sharply, then plummeted straight down toward the ground. "No!" she shouted and ran to the edge of the cliff, falling to her hands and knees as she watched the plane crash.

The sound of metal tearing screamed through the air. The plane flipped, pieces flew off the body like shrapnel. The left wing tore off with an earsplitting shriek and the tail catapulted into the side of the cliff. "Cort!"

The plane hit the side of a rock and crumpled, as if it had been made of tinfoil.

And then it was still.

Smoke rose from the battered heap. A smoldering lump of metal, unrecognizable as a plane.

"My God. *Cort.*" Flames began to lick at the back, galvanizing her into action. She leapt to her feet and ran for the edge of the cliff. She had to get him out. If he was still alive—*he had to be alive*—he would be trapped in there. The flames were coming. She had to get down there—

Bill caught her arm and yanked her back from the edge.

"No!" she screamed, fighting him desperately. "I have to get down there! Cort!"

Frantic, she clawed at Bill's face, drawing blood, and he didn't let go. He just dragged her mercilessly back toward the plane, away from the cliff. Away from Cort. "No!" Tears streaming down her face, she struggled. "Cort!"

Bill threw her into the plane, then slammed a fist into the side of her head.

She went down hard, pain ringing through her brain, gasping at the agony.

"The bastard's dead," Bill snarled. "Let him go. It's you and me now. No one else. And I will never forgive you for making me kill him."

Her head throbbing, Kaylie fought to get back to her knees, only to be tossed back down as the plane bounced over a root. It lifted off, and she made it to the window, looking out as Bill flew over the crash.

She caught sight of the plane, and her heart froze. It was engulfed in flames. No body visible near it. No sign that Cort had somehow managed a miracle and escaped.

He was dead.

Grief hit her hard, and she began to shake. A violent, vicious rattling that shook her to the core. Dear God, *Cort*. She couldn't breathe, couldn't swallow, she was shaking so badly.

"Shit, woman. Don't die on me."

Bill tossed a blanket at her, and she ignored it as it hit her in the side of the head, silent tears streaming, pain so intense she couldn't make a sound, couldn't speak, couldn't even cry.

"Fuck!" A second item hit her. "Look at that. You die, so does he. Get it together!"

She caught sight of the photo of her brother, and her heart felt like a thousand knives had been stabbed through it. *I can't do it*. She couldn't fight anymore. Couldn't survive anymore.

Her legs gave out, and she fell to the floor of the plane. She curled into a ball, still shaking. *Cort*. Seeing her parents dead had been nothing like this. The agony…The grief…Like a part of her soul had been ripped out of her body and shredded.

The plane bumped slightly, and the photo of her brother slid off the seat, landing next to her. Blindly, she stared at it. At Mason's bruised face. His battered leg. The filthy gash across his stomach.

Mason's eyes were slitted open, barely staring at the camera. Empty. Hopeless.

Just like she felt.

She closed her eyes, unable to look at him anymore. Unable to take the pain. The suffering.

The death.

Groaning, she pulled herself into a tighter ball, rocking back and forth, just as she'd done the night they'd found Sara and Jackson. The night Cort had come to her. Held her. Made love to her.

Made her whole.

If Cort could see her now, he would take back all his words about her courage and her spirit.

The thought stuck in her mind, repeating itself over and over, until finally, she opened her eyes. Looked at the picture of her brother again.

She was the only thing standing between Mason and death.

She and Mason were the only ones left.

How many people had Cort seen die in plane crashes? His parents, and how many others over the years? And yet he was still flying. Still going. Because it was what made him alive, and he wasn't going to let anything take it away from him.

And he admired *her*?

She rolled onto her back, staring at the ceiling of the plane. What if Cort was right that she was strong? What if he saw in her a truth that she was scared to face?

She'd lost it all. Everything. Her family. Her world. The man she loved.

Tears filled her eyes and she blinked them back.

Everything she'd spent her life fearing had actually happened.

She'd run, she'd hidden, she'd cut herself off. Done everything possible to hide from the pain, from the loss, and all her nightmares had still come true.

What had she sacrificed herself for all these years? So she could let herself die in the belly of a plane with a madman?

Which was stupider? Dying on a mountainside when she was sixteen, or dying now because she'd let fear strip her of the ability to live, to fight, to survive?

At least when she was sixteen, she'd had hopes and dreams. She'd wanted to live because she'd had things she wanted to do.

Now…God, what did she have to live for? Jeweled shoes and an apartment with a good heating system?

After spending the last few days with Cort, after immersing herself in a land where people lived hard and lived with passion, Kaylie realized she'd been more alive than she had been in the last ten years.

Because of Cort.

Because he'd brought her to life again.

A few days was all she'd had with him. Only two times had they made love. It could have been so much more. So intense. But she'd pushed him away, too scared of what might happen. And now she had no chance for it again.

It was the same mistake she'd made with her family. She'd turned around and done the same thing again with Cort. Not learning her lesson.

Refusing to live for fear of death.

And still she'd ended up losing it all.

Kaylie thought of Cort's words, that bush pilots who expect to die do just that. Had she instilled in him an expectation of death with all her talk? Had she cracked that tough veneer and made him human enough that he finally lost his impenetrability? She'd worked so hard to bring him down to her level, to make him admit he wasn't as tough as he believed he was.

She got what she'd asked for, in spades.

And now…

The plane bumped again, and she heard pellets of rain hitting the windshield. The wind was beginning to pick up.

What did she want?

To hide?

Kaylie rolled onto her side and looked at the picture of her brother again.

No.

No more hiding.

No more fear.

She felt the protective shield around her begin to crack, exposing her. The air felt colder, clearer, expanding her lungs as she took in a deep breath that brought the fresh air through her entire body. She smiled, imagined Cort looking at her and nodding, his face crinkled with approval as she stepped out of the skin she'd worn for the last twelve years.

As she became herself.

Rolling to her side, she sat up, picked up the photo of her brother. "I'm coming for you, Mason," she whispered. "Today, I'm taking control."

The plane bucked again, and she pressed the photo over her heart.

She closed her eyes and thought of Cort.

Of the man he'd been.

This time, she didn't stop the tears.

She cried for him, for what she'd lost, for the light the world had lost when his plane had crashed. She cried for the years she'd thrown away, for the family she'd shut out, for the fear that had ruled her for long. She just let it all go, let it wash through her and over her. Then she embraced it and let it settle in her heart.

The fear…She finally released it.

And by the time the plane landed, her eyes were dry, her breathing was steady, and she was ready.

Ready to die if she had to, but she was going to go down fighting.

For her brother.

For her family.

For the man she loved.

# CHAPTER TWENTY-SIX

The scent of burning metal jerked Cort back to consciousness.

His eyes snapped open, and all he could see were flames consuming the plane. He could hear his mother's screams as she was burned alive. He could see his dad's mindless stare of death. He could feel the agony as the flames melted his jacket, his skin. For a split second, he was paralyzed by the memory, and then Kaylie's face flashed in his mind.

Kaylie!

Cort yanked the harness off, fighting to free his legs from the wreckage as the flames grew hotter. He twisted to the side, swearing as the plane seemed to close in on him, the twisted metal like a vise around his left boot.

He grabbed his knife, sliced through the leather, then yanked his foot free. Smoke was burning his nose. His flesh was on fire. His eyes stung as he crawled across the seat to the tiny hole that used to be the windshield. Shit. Too small.

The flames were hotter, and his seat caught fire. Swirling black smoke.

Cort shoved his shoulders though the gap, then his chest, braced himself with his arms, and hauled himself through. He landed with a jarring thud on the blackened earth. His pants caught fire. He beat the flames out with his fists, pounding frantically. And then it wasn't his own legs. It was his mother. Her body. On fire.

Screaming. Trapped. He couldn't help. Couldn't get her free. On fire. Leaving her behind. To die.

So he could save himself.

"No!" His shout of denial broke through his haze, and he was suddenly back in the present. Beating at his own legs. No more flames. Just singed pants.

Slowly, he sat up, blinking as the rain beat down at him, battling the flames for victory.

Trying to catch his breath.

The plane...It was the same as before.

No. Not the same.

He forced himself to look at the plane. To see there was no one there. Not his mom. Not his dad. Not a fourteen-year-old screaming and crying while his back burned up.

Instead, Cort looked up at the cliff. At the last place he'd seen Kaylie.

And now she was gone.

Because he'd fucked up. He hadn't checked the oil. Meticulous to a fault for the last seventeen years. One mistake, and it would cost Kaylie her life.

His body went cold, and a vise clamped down around his chest. *No.*

"No!" A scream ripped out of his throat and he broke into a dead run. He hauled ass toward the hill that led back up to his cabin. His body was screaming with pain, and he didn't care. Didn't take time to figure out what he'd broken or how badly he was burned.

Just had to get up there.

Call Luke.

Get a ride.

Find Bill before the fucker disappeared into the bush forever with the woman Cort loved.

By the time Bill landed the plane, the wind was brutal, rain battering the small plane.

Kaylie had buckled herself into one of the rear seats, despite threats by Bill that she'd better come up front with him.

Fighting the plane made it impossible for him to come after her, so she'd taken the space for herself. She knew from his rising fury that she would pay for it, but she didn't care. She was taking control now.

The plane touched down, tilting sideways, and then there was the screech of metal and the tail of the plane went up. She braced herself, and the plane flipped over, tail over nose, landing with a shattering crush.

It skidded a few more feet, twisting metal screaming, and then it was still.

There were grinding protests from the plane, and rain gushed through the shattered windshield.

Kaylie unsnapped her belt and fell on her shoulders while Bill tried to untangle himself. She climbed past him, diving for the passenger door.

He caught her ankle, and she kicked him, shoving her heel into his face. Blood poured out of his nose, and his grip loosened enough for her to yank her leg free. She scrambled out the side door and ran.

It was pitch-black, raining hard. Rocks everywhere. Trees. Somewhere out here was Mason. She had to find him before Bill caught her.

Kaylie heard Bill's roar of rage and the sound of his feet hitting the ground as he ran after her.

Scrambling over the wet rocks, she pushed harder, visibility nearly zero with the storm. Her injured leg was screaming, and she fell as she hit another rock. She could hear Bill close behind her. She'd never outrun him.

A small outcropping caught her attention, and she squeezed between two rocks. She made it through, then realized she was trapped. Rocks stretched high on all sides.

She quickly hunkered down, sliding into the shadows at the base of the rocks.

Bill pounded past, then stopped.

Silence.

Listening for her.

She covered her mouth, fighting not to pant from the exertion, but her breath sounded so loud.

"I can outwait you," Bill called, his voice singsong. "I've been waiting for thirty years. A little longer is nothing."

She closed her eyes against the onslaught of rain. Dear God, how long would he wait? The longer she sat there, the closer her brother came to death. If she continued to sit there and hide, Mason would die.

And so would she.

The only chance either of them had was for Kaylie to face the situation.

No more hiding.

That wasn't her anymore. She took a breath, then stood. She allowed the rocks to shift under her feet. They rattled along the ground, giving away her location.

Footsteps raced toward her, and she fisted her hands, forcing herself not to run.

A rock slid, and then another, and then a light shone down on her. A creepy chuckle drifted down to her. "There aren't that many places to hide out here, love. You knew I'd find you, didn't you? Teasing me like you used to do?"

She shaded her eyes against the light, but she couldn't see Bill. He was blinding her with the light. "Where's my brother? I need to see him."

"Oh, he's here. Don't worry. You'll see him. I think it would be good for you to see what you've forced me to do to him by toying with me. All his suffering is your fault. If you hadn't tried to hide from me, I wouldn't have had to use him against you."

Trying not to shudder, she took advantage of the light to look around. To see what weapons she could use. She picked up a rock, tucked it into her jeans. "Where are we?"

"Devil's Pass, of course."

Devil's Pass. The place where Cort's parents had died. The place where their plane had crashed.

No wonder Bill had chosen this spot.

Even if his plan to crash Cort's plan hadn't worked, Bill would have known Cort wouldn't come in here after them.

There was no chance anyone was coming for her.

There was a light thud, and a rope fell down beside Kaylie. "You know I have to punish you for being with another man, don't you? It will hurt me more than it hurts you, but once it's done, you will be cleansed, and we can be together."

She swallowed, staring at the rope.

Climbing mountains used to scare her.

Now she was going to climb right into the arms of a mad-man?

"*Now*, bitch." His voice had suddenly become dark, lethal, furious.

She thought of her brother somewhere out there in the darkness.

And she grabbed hold of the rope and started to climb.

Cort was halfway up the climb back to his cabin when he heard the distant roar of a plane.

He paused, listening. His muscles were aching, and he cocked his right leg to rest it. Something was wrong with his right hip, but he refused to acknowledge it. And his legs were still burning from where they'd been assaulted by the fire.

But he hadn't bothered to inspect them.

The plane grew closer, and he recognized it as a Cessna 206. The plane Bill had taken off in—and the plane that Luke was flying tonight.

Tensing, Cort began to haul ass up the hill, not wanting to be caught exposed if it was Bill. Needing to be there to meet Luke if it was him.

The plane landed right outside the cabin, and Cort fell to the side behind a rock as he heard footsteps racing to the edge.

"Cort!"

Luke's voice rang out over the side of the cliff, and Cort stood. "Where the hell have you been?"

Luke whirled toward him. "Son of a bitch. You're not dead. I saw that plane—"

"He got Kaylie." Cort started to climb again. "Took off in Old Tom's plane."

"Shit. Seriously?"

"Yeah." Cort made it to the top and swung himself over the edge, ignoring Luke's outstretched hand. "I have to find him."

"You know where he went?" Luke followed as Cort limped back into the cabin.

A photo stared at Cort from the ground, and he picked it up. It was Kaylie's brother again. More cut up than before.

On the ground this time, and—

Cort swore as he looked more closely at the photo. Behind Mason was the burned-out husk of a plane. Weeds had grown up around it, but other than that, it was exactly the same as it had been seventeen years ago, as if time had stood still. He went cold, stunned at the sight of the thing that had been haunting·him for seventeen years. "Son of a bitch."

Luke looked over his shoulder. "What's that?"

Cort crumpled the photo in his hand. "My parents' plane. The one that went down." He threw the photo down. "Bill took Kaylie to the crash site."

Luke picked up the photo. "You sure that's it?"

"Oh, yeah." Cort would never forget the triple outcropping of rocks right behind the downed plane. The rocks they'd peeled Cort's dad off of.

Cort went to the broken window and leaned on the windowsill, fighting back memories of that day as he stared out at the cliff. "Bill took Kaylie to Devil's Canyon."

"I'll go," Luke said.

Cort fisted his hands and turned. "Fuck that. This is my battle."

Luke raised his eyebrows. "You don't have to do this."

Cort didn't answer. He just picked up his guns and walked out.

By the time he made it to Luke's plane, his partner was right behind him. Cort climbed into the pilot's seat and strapped in. Luke glanced over at him as he sat in the passenger seat. "I can fly—"

"No." Cort's hands were cold, sweat trickling down his temples, but it was the god-awful pain in his gut that had him starting the plane.

Because that pain wasn't about finally facing the crash that had stripped him of his belief that he could beat all odds.

That agony in his stomach came at the thought of what was happening to Kaylie right then, and for every second of the one-hour flight it would take to get there.

Kaylie got to the top of the rope, and Bill grabbed her under the arms and hauled her the rest of the way to her feet.

He pulled her close, and she recoiled, jerking back as he tried to kiss her.

He swore and backhanded her, nearly sending her back down into the hole. "Don't fuck with me," he snarled.

Staggering to keep her balance, Kaylie tasted blood as he

dragged her down the side of the rock. There was a blood-stain on the front of his shoulder—from when Cort had shot him? But Bill was so crazed, he clearly didn't even feel the pain. He just slogged onward, dragging her along with him. For what felt like hours, he hauled her through the raging wind and rain, then threw her to her knees. "That's what you've done to him."

She gasped at the sight of her brother.

Mason's face was bruised and battered, his chest…cut up…bleeding…so infected.…And his leg…"Mason!"

His body jerked and his eyes opened. He took one look at Kaylie and swore. "Goddamn, Kaylie. You weren't supposed to get caught."

"I had to come for you." She crouched next to him, but he caught her hand and shoved her back.

"Fuck! You're supposed to stay alive!" He swore again and sat up, his face paling at the effort. "Get the hell out of here. I'm done. My leg's so damn infected, I'm toast." He pulled her close, his bloodshot eyes glazed. "You have to survive," he whispered. "Someone has to."

"Enough!" Bill yanked her back from him. "Every time you resist me, he suffers more. And it's your fault."

"No!" Mason shoved himself to his feet and charged.

Kaylie dove out of the way as Bill braced himself for Mason's assault. He caught Mason's head with his gut and the two men went down. "Run, Kaylie!" Mason's bellow echoed across the rocks.

But she saw a small tent—Bill's campsite. She raced toward it, dove through the opening. She saw a small bag and ripped it open. Inside was a knife much like the one she'd found in her seat. She grabbed it and raced outside to help her brother.

A heavy weight smacked her in the face, and she flew backward, crashing into the tent pole. She tried to roll to the side, and then there was a heavy weight on her.

A strong, wiry body, pinning her down.

She fought against Bill, but she had no chance as he dragged her out of the small tent. He threw her down, using his body to pin her to the ground.

It took less than a minute, but by the time he was done, he'd staked her out on the dirt.

She stared at him, felt the blood cascading down her forehead, the ache in her side from where he'd kneed her in the ribs.

He stood over her, his face snarled with anger. He wiped blood off his upper lip. "You're really pissing me off." He picked his knife off the ground where she'd dropped it. "I was going to take you to the river to cleanse you, but you'll try to run again, won't you? Stupid female." He crouched beside her and slid the knife under the collar of her shirt. "Option number two is a sponge bath." He smiled, leaning closer as he trailed the back of his other hand across her collarbone. "You will learn to love me, bitch." He stood, his eyes raking over her. "I'll be back with the water."

And then he was gone.

Quickly, she lifted her head. Saw Mason sprawled facedown on the rock nearby, blood oozing from a wound on his head. "Mason!"

He didn't move.

She turned her head to look at the ropes binding her wrists. Thick, the stakes anchored in the rocks.

She realized then that he'd set it up like this. For her.

There was a groan from Mason, and she lifted her head to look at him again. "Mason!"

His eyelids flickered, but he didn't open them.

Frantically, she looked around, trying to see if there was anything she could use to get free.

And then her blood went cold.

Carefully folded up on a rock beside her was a dingy white lace teddy, yellowed with age. As if it was thirty years old. As if he'd been hanging on to it all that time. Dark stains dotted it, as if he'd dripped blood on it and let it dry.

And next to it was a large knife, like the one they'd found in Cort's truck.

# CHAPTER TWENTY-SEVEN

The wind was battering the small plane. Rain was hammering at the windshield.

Just as it had seventeen years ago.

Cort's grip on the control stick tightened as he approached the entrance to Devil's Pass.

"You okay?" Luke's voice was quiet.

"Yeah." Cort banked the plane and came in low, aiming for the narrow passage between the two cliffs protecting the entrance. For a split second, he let off the throttle, staring at the mouth of hell.

So many times he'd tried to fly through there when he was alone.

Testing his resolve.

And every time, he'd pulled away at the last second.

Unable to face the grim memories. The raw statement that he could be broken. Die. Crash. Things a bush pilot had no business thinking.

The plane bucked against him, and Cort gripped the controls more tightly, his palms getting sweaty. This pass, this place, this was where mortality had hit him. The only place he'd fully comprehended the fragile nature of life. It was back. That feeling. That awareness that one mistake could doom them all.

The entrance was approaching fast. Another minute and he'd have to pull out or commit himself. He watched those high cliffs stretching up, a crevasse barely wide enough for the plane to pass through.

But as he neared it, thoughts of his mortality, of the death of his parents…all faded away until there was only one thing in his mind.

Kaylie.

Up ahead, somewhere, needing him. They'd called the state troopers, but those planes were about an hour behind them. It was up to Cort and Luke. A sense of calmness settled on him.

Death wasn't an option.

Not now.

Not here.

He leaned on the throttle and the plane leapt forward, dashing between the rock towers guarding the entrance. The sheer stone pillars whipped by, and then they were inside. Only a few feet of clearance on either side of the wingtips. The wind was raging, but Cort kept the plane steady. A faint memory of how his dad had slipped up, let the wingtip brush against the wall, passed through Cort's mind, and he released the thought from his mind.

Instead, he focused on the present. On his assault plan. "Bill's going to hear us come in," Cort said with a calmness he didn't feel. "He'll know we're here, so we have to go fast when I land."

Luke reached into the back and pulled a couple guns onto his lap. "How close can you land to the crash site?"

Cort thought back to that day, to catapulting through the air, rigid silence in the plane while his dad fought for control. He shut out the feelings of dread, of horror, and instead concentrated on the landscape whipping past beneath him. "The canyon widens out about two hundred yards before the crash site. There's a clearing about a hundred yards south where they'll be."

Luke shook his head. "Too far. It'll take us too long to hike to the crash site after we land. Bill will have too much lead time, and he'll have time to—"

"I know." Cort cut him off, all too aware of what Bill had done to that seat, to Mason, to Jackson and Sara. He replayed the terrain in his mind, but there was nowhere closer to land. He looked over at Luke. "I'm going to jump."

Luke shot him a sharp glance. "Changing pilots in the air in the middle of a storm in Devil's Pass is suicide."

Cort shrugged. "Yeah, the odds of surviving it aren't high."

"I knew you were a crazy bastard. Christ, Cort, is this the only way for you to live?"

Cort looked out the windshield at the rain battering the plane. "No, not crazy. Not anymore. Just focused. Got a lot at stake here. I'm not going down." It was tough enough flying straight up in these conditions. Doing a pilot switch? It was beyond even what he would attempt. He thought of Kaylie and knew he had no choice. "She needs me."

"And you need her."

"Yeah."

They looked at each other, and something passed between them.

Then Luke began unbuckling his harness. "For seventeen years you won't fly this pass, and now you're going to pull this shit? You're insane."

Cort jerked his harness off. "I know. But my insanity's going to come in handy this time."

Luke freed himself and set the guns on the dash. Met Cort's gaze. "All I can say is that it's a damn good thing you trained me to fly."

Cort smiled this time, knowing that there was only one pilot in Alaska he would trust with this move. "Learn from the best and the craziest, and it rubs off."

Luke shook his head. "Try not to sneeze or breathe or do anything else that's going to make us crash."

Cort nodded, settling his attention on the bucking plane as Luke eased across the seat. Poised beside him.

The two men went still, the energy tense in the cockpit. The wing lights were so close to the canyon walls that they were reflecting off the wet rock. It looked like inches, but it was probably a couple feet. At least.

"On three."

Luke nodded. "One."

"Two."

"Three!"

Bill rubbed his palm over her wet stomach, his hair slicked back from the rain, water beading off his jacket. "Doesn't that feel better, my love?"

Kaylie clenched her jaw, her body shaking uncontrollably. She was so cold, so wet. He'd dumped bucket after bucket over her until she was so cold and frozen she couldn't stop trembling. Her muscles were aching from the cold, and her teeth were chattering.

Bill hadn't touched her sexually, but the way he'd looked at her while he'd been cleaning her…

Dear God, she had to get away before he could get her clothes off.

She'd tried everything she could think of to get him to let her go, and nothing had worked. He'd been in his own world, not even hearing her. Calling her by her mother's name, replaying scenarios that he'd either imagined or recalled from his time with her mom thirty years ago.

And the whole time, Mason hadn't moved.

Just lying there.

Dead…or unconscious?

Bill picked up the old, yellowed lace and held it up by the straps. "You looked so lovely in this."

Mason shifted slightly behind Bill, as if he was starting to come around, and she jerked her eyes back to Bill. "I can't put it on if I'm tied up. I promise I'll put it on."

Bill scowled, looking at the teddy, then back at her. Finally, he walked over to her and untied her ankles. Kaylie forced herself not to pull her legs up to prepare to run. She had to keep Bill calm until he untied her arms. Her heart was thundering when he walked over to her head and reached for her left hand to release it.

*Yes, please. Let me go.* One chance, one time. That's all she wanted.

Mason shifted again and groaned.

Bill glanced over at her brother, then looked at Kaylie. "You try anything and he gets hurt."

She nodded, her mouth dry. "Yeah, okay. I get it."

He narrowed his eyes, then picked up the knife, the one that had been paired with the yellowed lingerie. Slowly brought it over her and traced the flat of it across her belly.

Kaylie froze, her muscles trembling. "Please…I promise I'll get dressed for you."

"Put it on." And then he released her hands.

Kaylie staggered to her feet, sneaking glances at the knife. She saw Mason's eyes slit open. Their gazes met, and then he looked at the knife as well.

She took a breath and snatched the teddy from Bill. The material was fragile with age, and she froze when she heard a tearing sound as she unfolded it. She shot a frantic look at Bill. He looked shocked, and then his face morphed into diabolical fury. He screamed with outrage.

And then he attacked.

She lunged for the knife, and Mason did the same. Mason was closer, and his fingers closed over it—

Horrible pain exploded in her lower body. She looked down, saw another knife embedded in her side.

"Get the hell away from her!" Mason lunged for Bill, and the two men fell in a fight she knew her brother wouldn't survive.

She grabbed the hilt and yanked the knife out of her side, doubling over at the agony. Staggering as she tried to regain her composure, she fisted the weapon and turned, just as Bill threw Mason on his back and drew back the knife Mason had stolen to rake it across his throat.

"No!" She slammed the knife into Bill's shoulder. He backhanded her, and she tumbled backward, smacking hard into a rock.

Stunned, she tried to crawl away as Bill leapt to his feet and came after her. He grabbed her, slammed her against the rock, and ripped at the fly of her jeans.

Suddenly a plane roared overhead. They both looked up, saw lights bearing down on them out of the night. She slammed her knee into Bill's stomach and tried to slip past him.

He caught her ankle, dragged her back toward him.

The plane swooped down, only feet off the ground, and she realized it was too low. It was headed right for the rock outcropping behind her. "No!" She threw her arms over her head, watching in horror as the plane came right for her.

Bill didn't wait. He grabbed her and threw her over his shoulder, sprinting effortlessly across the rocks.

He hadn't made it ten feet when something hit them hard from behind, and they both went flying.

# CHAPTER TWENTY-EIGHT

Cort hit the ground with an impact that knocked the air from his lungs. He skidded across the rock, his skin flayed, as he fought to stop himself and leap to his feet. His heart wrenched when he saw Kaylie sprawled on the rocks, and he quickly moved between her and Bill.

Bill jumped to his feet, blood pouring down his face. "How the fuck are you still alive?" He reared back to throw a knife at Cort, and Cort jerked the rifle up and fired.

Bill froze, his face twisted into surprise, and then he went down, a red stain spreading across his chest, right over his heart.

He wouldn't be getting up from that one.

Cort slung the rifle over his shoulder and ran for Kaylie as the plane circled around and landed. "Kaylie!"

She lifted her head, saw him, and her jaw went slack. "Cort?"

"Yeah, it's me." He crouched beside her, pulled off his jacket, and laid it over her. The sight of her battered body... Anger swelled inside him and he glanced over at Bill. Almost hoping he'd move. "I'm here." He helped her roll over, and his gaze went to the bruises all over her. She was shaking so hard, it felt like her bones were going to shatter. "Jesus, Kaylie—"

Her hands were on his face, her face shadowed and disbelieving. "I saw you die. How are you here?"

He caught her hands and kissed her fingertips. "I told you.

I'm always in control." A lie. A total lie. His self-control was about to snap. "Where are you hurt?"

She was already shaking her head. "No, no, he didn't." She held up her arms and he scooped her up, clutching her against his chest. For a moment, he couldn't speak, just buried his face in her hair. Holding her.

She pressed herself into his body, her small frame shaking violently. "I thought you were dead," she whispered. "I saw the plane and I thought…" Her voice broke. "I've never felt so awful in my life. I thought…I felt—"

"Shh, sweetheart. It's okay. I'm fine. I'm here." He lifted her face and kissed her gently. And again. Her lips…cold but alive. He leaned his forehead against hers, trying to catch his breath. "How bad did he hurt you?" Shit, he could barely ask the question, but he had to know.

"Not much. I just…" She looked up at him. "If you'd told me you were going to fake your death, and I'd known you were on your way, I might not have been quite so terrified, though."

He gave a strangled laugh, astounded by her spirit. "Jesus, I'm so sorry I fucked up." He cupped her face, his emotions too intense for him to cope with. "But I'll warn you, you didn't need to get yourself abducted by a psycho to get me to realize I love you. If you ever do that again, I'm locking you up for at least a month."

Despite her gray pallor and the weariness of her eyes, a slow smile lit up her face. "You love me?"

"I flew into Devil's Pass for you." He bent his head and kissed her, a slow, savoring taste of sweetness and honey. "I don't do that for just anyone," he whispered against her mouth. He couldn't pull himself away. He couldn't stop touching her.

"I love you, too," she whispered back. "But I swear to God, I thought my heart had stopped when I saw you crash. I can't live through that again."

He stiffened at her words and pulled back, searching her face for the meaning. Did she mean it had made her realize she couldn't live with his lifestyle? His fingers tightened in her hair. He knew he had no right to ask, but he couldn't stop himself. Not after almost losing her. He didn't care what was best for her. He simply couldn't live without her.

"Stay," he whispered. "Stay with me."

She frowned at him. "What do you mean?"

They were interrupted by Luke's shout about a survivor, and Kaylie paled. "Mason!" He saw the horror on her face that she'd forgotten about her brother in the midst of her concern about Cort.

Cort caught her as she tried to slide out of his arms. "No way. I'm carrying you."

He didn't give her time to argue. Just scooped her up, holding her against his chest. She was still trembling, but she didn't seem to notice him anymore. She pointed back toward the plane. "He's back there. Hurry!"

Holding her tightly against him, Cort carried Kaylie swiftly her across the rocks to where Luke was kneeling beside a prone body.

"Mason!" Kaylie struggled to get free, and Cort allowed her to slide down his body, catching her around the waist when she stumbled.

"Go check on Bill." Cort jerked his head back toward where he'd left the bastard. "Make sure he's dead this time."

"I'm on it." Luke loped off into the darkness as Kaylie reached Mason.

"Dear God, *Mason*." Kaylie fell to her knees beside her brother, leaning over him. "It's over," she whispered. "I love you so much. We're safe now." Tears were streaming down her cheeks. "Don't you dare die on me! I'll be so mad at you!"

Mason didn't move, and Cort set his hand on Kaylie's back. She was still shaking, worse than before. "We have to get you out of here."

"No! I'm not leaving him!" She tried to pull away, and Cort wrapped his arm around her, pulling her into the warmth of his body.

"I meant both of you." He reached around her, set his fingers on Mason's neck.

Waited.

Kaylie stiffened, her fingers digging into Cort's arm. "Is he—?"

Then he felt a faint beat. "Got a pulse. He's still alive."

"Thank God." Kaylie was on her knees, her legs bare on the wet ground, apparently oblivious to how badly she was shaking, how much she was hurt, focusing only on her brother. "You're all I have left," she whispered. "You have to live. Don't you dare die on me!"

Cort ground his jaw at her comment. All she had left was Mason. The words spoke volumes. After seeing him almost die, she had put Cort out of her life.

Luke jogged up. "Bill's toast." He crouched down beside Mason. "Shit. This poor bastard's in tough shape."

"Back to the plane with them both." Cort stood, picking Kaylie up despite her protests. "Hush," he ordered her. "We're taking you both back to the plane."

Luke picked Mason up, and Kaylie stopped fighting. Sagged against Cort, her head resting on his chest. "Thank you for coming to get us," she said. "I'll owe you forever."

He scowled. "I didn't do it so you'd owe me."

She lifted her head to look at him. "That's not what I meant. I just—" Mason groaned, stealing Kaylie's attention away from Cort. "Mason!"

Luke was already hiking toward the plane, staggering slightly under the larger man's weight, and Kaylie urged Cort to hurry.

He did as directed, a dark mood settling around him.

He didn't have to ask.

He knew the answer.

She was leaving.

There was a time he would have thought it was the right call. A relief.

Not today.

Today, the idea of her leaving was devastating.


Hours later, Kaylie found Cort in the hospital cafeteria eating with Luke and Charity.

She paused in the doorway, her heart aching as she looked at him. He was still in his wet clothes, his face haggard and drawn. Mud spattered his face. He was wearing a clean pair of jeans and boots that Charity had brought for him, as his other ones had nearly burned off.

He'd refused to let Kaylie in the room while the doctor had examined him, and he'd been completely uncommunicative on the extent of his injuries.

But Cort hadn't left Kaylie's side while the doctor had checked her and cleaned her up. He'd hovered, he'd fussed, and he'd challenged the doctor's treatment so many times he'd finally been ordered out of her room.

Not that he'd gone.

But despite all that, there was a wall between them. One Cort had erected, and Kaylie knew why.

She'd forced it by her comments about seeing Cort crash, by her remark that Mason was all she had.

Kaylie sighed, remembering Cort's expression when he'd dropped her off at Mason's room. He'd checked with the nurse, demanded information about her brother, and bullied them into letting Kaylie sit with Mason even though he was in critical condition.

And then Cort left, his face hollow and empty, as if he'd seen death so many times he could no longer rise above it.

He had left to get something to eat. Two hours later, he still hadn't returned.

Hugging herself, Kaylie leaned against the doorframe. She

rested her head against the rust-colored wood. Even in the hospital cafeteria, dwarfing a small plastic chair, an exhausted slump to his body, Cort was energy. He was life. He was strength.

And she loved him.

He looked up suddenly, his eyes narrowing when he saw her standing there.

Her heart tightened, and tears filled her eyes at what she knew she had to do.

Charity turned and waved, gesturing Kaylie to come over. Charity had been at the hospital all night supporting Kaylie and Cort. She could become a true friend, if Kaylie stayed. "Come eat," Charity called.

Kaylie shook her head. "Cort. Can I talk to you?"

He looked at Luke and Charity, then shoved his chair back and walked over to Kaylie. "How are you feeling?" His voice was cool, detached, and she knew it was her fault.

"I'm okay." God, his presence was overwhelming. She wanted to sink into the heat of his body, let him kiss her and touch her and wipe away the memories of Bill. Of the awful night. Tears suddenly sprung, unexpected.

Cort sighed and reached out, folding her into his body.

She buried her face against his chest. She took solace in his musky scent, allowing his strength to wrap around her.

"How's your brother?" he asked.

"He's probably going to live, but they don't know the extent of permanent damage. They're not sure if they can save the leg. They're flying him to Seattle tomorrow for a specialist to operate on him." She didn't lift her face from Cort's shirt. "It will break him if he loses the leg. If he can't ever climb again. I have to go with him. He has no one else."

Cort said nothing, but a muscle ticked in his chest.

"I also have to take my parents' bodies back with me. I need to arrange the funeral."

He made a guttural sound of pain, and he stroked his hand over her hair. "I'm so sorry about them."

She lifted her face, found him looking down at her, dark shadows in his eyes. "Since they're flying Mason out tomorrow morning, I can't stay for Sara and Jackson's funeral. Will you say good-bye for me?"

"Yeah." Cort tucked her hair behind her ear, his touch gentle. "Sara knows, though. I don't need to say anything."

Kaylie pressed her face into his palm, into the tenderness of his touch. God, she needed him. So much. "Can I stay at your place tonight? Before I go?"

He didn't answer.

"I know I'm leaving, and I have no right to ask you. But I—" She swallowed. "I need you to touch me tonight. To give me new memories after Bill."

Understanding hardened the lines of Cort's face, and Kaylie saw raw pain in his eyes. Anguish for what had been done to her, for what she had suffered—because he cared that much.

No one had ever cared that she was hurt before.

They had only cared that she was afraid of being hurt.

Cort tangled his fingers in her hair and bent his head. A gentle kiss, full of promise. A sensual oath to give her a night of tender loving that would wipe away all bad memories, replacing them with only him.

But there was reserve in that kiss, and she knew he was holding a part of himself back. She realized what she was asking of him was unfair. Not just unfair. Horrible, after what Valerie had to done to him. After what he'd sacrificed to save her. After…

She pulled back, breaking the kiss. "I'm sorry. I shouldn't have asked. It's not right."

He turned away, and she closed her eyes at his silent rejection. It was for the best. Spending the night with him, knowing she had to walk away for her brother's sake, would be too hard. It was selfish of her to ask—

"I need your truck," Cort said. "Kaylie and I are heading back to my place."

Her eyes snapped open as Luke tossed his car keys to Cort. He snagged them out of the air, then took Kaylie's hand. "Let's go."

Kaylie caught a glimpse of Charity's wide grin, and then Cort pulled her out the door.

Cort shut the door to his bedroom. He leaned back against it as Kaylie turned to face him. Her face was bruised, her hair still matted with mud, and her skin was pale.

"God, you're beautiful." He reached out, trailed his finger down the side of her face, then cupped her chin and lowered his mouth to hers.

Her response was instant and fierce, sinking right into his core.

"I love you, too," she whispered to him.

His hands snaked out and he pulled her against him, fighting the urge to take her, to consume her. He needed to be gentle, patient, loving. Tender. For her sake. Give her a chance to take a shower. Clean up.

But the thought of how close he'd come to losing her, the idea she was leaving in the morning…

A deep, carnal need to take her roared over him. He needed to make her his, to brand her as his forever, so she knew she belonged to him no matter how far away she went, no matter how much distance she put between them.

He fought to control himself. Struggled against the need. For her. This night was for her.

"Don't hold back." Kaylie pulled back, her eyes full of need. Of passion. Of desperation. "I need this."

The last shreds of his discipline broke, and he had her up against the door in a split second. He crushed his body against hers. His kiss was so deep and so penetrating, but still not enough. He needed more, and he opened himself to her. Consumed her. Inhaled her life force. Drank of her essence. Sucked all she was into his being. He basked in the feel of her body, the heat of her skin, the lingering expanse of her flesh as he peeled her clothes off, never breaking contact with her, never lifting his mouth from hers.

Her hands were as insistent as his. She yanked at his shirt, palmed his chest, his shoulders, his back, everywhere she could reach.

Clothes shed, he lifted her against him. Her legs went around his hips, and she sank onto him, taking him so deeply they both groaned. It was perfection, rapture, bliss, all of those poetic notions that had never made sense to him before.

Before now.

Bracing them both against the door, he withdrew, then drove again, deeper and harder. Fiercer.

"Yes. Like that." Her fingers dug into his shoulders, her head back against the wood, her gaze locked on his. "I love you."

The words struck at the core of his being, ripping apart his defenses. The orgasm came fast and hard, and he held on to her as she came in his arms, as they clung to each other as if nothing could tear them apart.

But he knew better.

Muscles shaking, he leaned his forehead against hers, the aftershocks still rippling through his body.

She looped her hands around his neck.

"I could come with you," he said finally.

She lifted her head, surprise on her face. "To Seattle?"

He nodded. Feeling uncertain for the first time in his life. "If you need me."

"But what about your business? All the clients?"

He shrugged. "There are other pilots. I'd shift them off."

She stared at him, her eyes glistening. "You would die in the city, Cort. You know you would."

He ran his hands down her spine, knowing she spoke the truth. Knowing also that he couldn't just let her go. Old Tom's words rang in his mind like the wail of a siren. *Don't let her leave Alaska. They don't come back.*

She searched his face. "I need to do this by myself. I need to help my brother. I need to do this."

He ground his jaw. Said none of the things he wanted to say. "I understand."

And he did.

Because there was something else he needed to do for himself. There was one more flight he had to make.

But first he had to ask the question. "Are you coming back?"

She didn't avert her gaze from his. "I love you."

He waited.

"I'll come back."

But he heard the hesitation in her voice, a reluctance that was so deep in her soul that she might not even have known she'd voiced it.

But he'd heard it, and he knew what it meant.

When Kaylie left, when she got back into her safe little world, promises meant nothing.

Tonight was all they had.

Cort was going to make tonight last forever.

# CHAPTER TWENTY-NINE

The night hadn't lasted forever, and Kaylie had left Alaska with the bodies of her parents and a brother on the edge.

Cort had offered again to go, and again she'd declined.

So he'd let her leave, alone, to face that hell by herself.

A month since she'd left, and she'd called once to say the surgery had gone well and it was looking good for her brother's leg. She hadn't called since and hadn't returned his calls.

He'd stopped calling two weeks ago.

Instead, he'd buried himself in his work to try to forget about her. He'd tried to distract himself from the aching loss in his soul, the hole that had formed when she'd boarded that plane and left. He'd done six search and rescues, which had been successful. He'd been flying about twenty hours a day with clients.

And it hadn't been enough.

Two days ago, Cort had been flying six inches above a black river, searching for missing boaters, knowing he was one gust of wind from getting sucked into the water, and the near-death moment hadn't been enough to fill the gaping hole in his chest.

Not anymore.

Flying simply wasn't enough anymore, no matter how many risks he took.

So he had finally given up and taken the day off. Handed his clients off to another pilot so he could make the trip he'd been needing to make for seventeen years.

The twin towers blocking the end of Devil's Pass appeared, bright sunlight making the rocks sparkle.

Cort almost smiled, and he didn't hesitate as he flew right past them. No more fear. No more hesitation. Just a place he needed to be.

The plane was smooth in the perfect weather. The blue sky such a contrast to the last two times he'd flown in here.

Cort landed easily in the clearing and then hiked the distance to the crash site.

He'd barely noticed it when he'd been here with Kaylie, but now...

He paused when he saw it.

The shiny metal corpse was glistening as if it were brand new. Seventeen years of Alaska weather had stripped the carbon from the frame, leaving it pristine and untouched.

Slowly, he walked over to it and laid his hands on the corpse.

He closed his eyes and let the memories in.

But this time, he didn't see the crash.

This time, he heard his mother's lighthearted laughter and his dad's infamous chuckle. Cort saw himself sitting in the back of the plane, grinning at his parents' happiness. He felt their joy. Breathed in their love. And he knew that they'd been happy, truly happy. That they'd flown for the sheer joy of it, not to run away from demons.

A sense of peace descended over him, and he raised his face to the sunshine, breathing in the scent of fresh air, of spring vegetation, of new life, and he knew his parents were at peace.

Seventeen years of tension slipped away, and he felt his muscles unknot.

And then he opened his eyes and knew what he had to do.

* * *

"God, I'm going to miss you." Kaylie hugged Mason fiercely, unable to stop the tears.

He squeezed her tightly, then released her, wiping his finger across her cheek. "I've got some stuff to figure out."

She nodded, clenching her hands by her sides to keep from holding onto him. "I know. But I'm still going to miss you."

The last four weeks had been amazing. He'd stayed at her place so she could take care of him, giving her more time with him than she'd had in the last fourteen years. She'd grilled Mason on her family and had learned more about her parents and him than she had in a decade. The stories had made her laugh, made her cry, and most importantly, turned her family from strangers to friends. After all this time, she had found them again. Bittersweet, because her parents were gone, but at least she had Mason back.

They'd talked for many hours about Bill and what had happened in Alaska. Based on comments Bill had made, Mason had figured out that their mother had died in the climbing accident that Bill had caused. Her death had snapped what remaining sanity Bill had. He'd fixated on Kaylie, and he'd used Mason to get to her. Sara had died because she had figured out that Bill had caused the accident, and he'd needed to silence her before she could warn Kaylie. Jackson had just been an aside because Bill knew the Alaskan would have hunted him down for killing his wife.

So many deaths, for no reason. And now Mason was leaving. "I just got used to having a brother again."

Mason gave her a smile that didn't reach his eyes. "Yeah, well, this time don't cut me off when I leave."

"I promise. I'll call and e-mail. Often." She hugged herself, watching as he slung a heavy backpack over his shoulders, deftly maneuvering the crutches. The large backpack was the only luggage he was taking, for a duration unknown and a location undisclosed. Kaylie had argued until her throat hurt, trying to get him to stay until his rehab was finished, but the minute it was deemed safe for him to leave, he'd started packing. "You really don't know where you're going?"

"Nope. I just need to go." He gave her a look. "No lectures on my leg. I'll take care of it."

But she didn't believe him. Despite the hours of talking they'd done in the last four weeks, she knew he was holding back. Something heavy was weighing on him, and she had no idea if it was what had happened in Alaska, or if the issue predated that experience.

She had a feeling he wanted to get away from Kaylie so he could just stop fighting, and that worried her.

So much.

"Kaylie. Stop. I'll be fine."

She managed a smile and told herself to stop worrying. She'd learned her lesson. The fear, the worrying—they wouldn't change anything. And she understood Mason in a way she never had before Alaska. Before Cort. "Do what you have to do. I respect that."

Mason's eyebrows went up. "I believe you actually mean that."

She brushed a piece of lint off his heavy waterproof jacket. "I do."

He cocked his head, studying her. "You've changed."

"I know."

"I like it."

Kaylie couldn't stop the grin. "That's just because I'm not riding your butt anymore about being safe."

"No." He smiled slightly, and this time, there was the faintest hint of life in his eyes. "It's because you're finally happy." He touched her cheek. "I would never have wished that psychopath on you, but if that experience helped you finally find a way to be happy, I'd almost say it was worth it."

Ah, her family. Still the same. Believing that a little suffering was good for the soul.

Except this time, she agreed. "I wouldn't change a thing."

Mason cleared his throat and dropped his hand. "Gotta go. Don't be safe."

Her throat tightened. "Back at you."

She watched him all the way to the elevator, and he never looked back.

When the doors shut behind him, she had a sudden feeling she would never see him again. "Be safe, Mason. Please."

Then she forced herself to turn away and go back into her apartment.

And what she saw made her smile.

The melancholy lifted, and she walked into her apartment tracing her fingers over a cardboard box.

The time had finally come.

Oh, wow.

Then, just as quickly, her excitement faded, replaced with a trepidation that made her heart start to hammer. What if she was making a mistake? What if—?

"Going somewhere?"

She whirled around at the sound of a familiar voice, her heart lifting when she saw Cort standing in her doorway. "Cort!" She started toward him, then stopped when she saw the grim look on his face. She paused, suddenly unsure. "What are you doing here?"

"Where are you going?" His voice was hard. Not friendly. He was wearing jeans and a lightweight black coat. Well-worn boots. His eyes were the same beautiful eyes she remembered, and he was clean-shaven for the first time. He looked amazing and beautiful, and her heart ached for him.

"Trying to slide out of town without leaving a forwarding address?"

She looked around at the stacks of moving boxes, regret hammering at her. It wasn't supposed to have been like this. With him angry. "I'm sorry I haven't called you back, but I had some things to sort out."

Cort walked into the apartment, his bulk and raw masculinity filling up the small living area. He looked so out of place next to the inlaid wood floor and pale yellow walls. "I have one thing to say, and then I'm gone," Cort said. "I'll let you go wherever you were planning to go."

"I was going—"

"I love you."

Kaylie stopped, her heart starting to pound.

"You were sort of right. When you said I was running from something." He rubbed at his jaw as if not used to being clean-shaven. "I wasn't running from it. I was trying to run *to* it, but I didn't know what it was." His eyes were dark, hooded, and so intense. "I was trying to find something to light a fire in my heart. I thought it was flirting with death I needed." He looked right at her. "Turns out, it was you."

Her throat tightened. "Cort—"

He held up his hand. "I still love to fly. I'm still going to do it. I'm still going to do search and rescue. But I don't…" He made a small noise of irony. "I'm just going to have fun with it and not try to kill myself."

She couldn't help but laugh. "Well, that's good, at least."

He went still at her comment. At her laughter. Then slowly, he went down on one knee and pulled a ring box out of his pocket. "I am what I am, and if you can live with that, I promise I'll cherish you and love you every day of my life. You never have to fly. You never have to climb. You never have to do a damn thing but love me. I'll buy a place in town, fix it up nice for you, whatever you want." He hesitated. "Damn it, Kaylie, I'd move here for you if I could—"

"No." She stopped fighting the need to go to him, rushing across the room and throwing her arms around him.

His arms snapped around her waist, and he pressed his face into her belly. Holding her so tightly she could barely breathe. "Shit, Kaylie, I'm lost without you. Come back, please." He pulled back, his hand closing around the blue velvet box. "You don't have to marry me. Just hang out. See how you like—"

She held out her hand.

He faltered in his speech, then wordlessly, he set the ring box in her palm. "It's not a diamond," he said gruffly.

All her excitement faded. After all that, he still couldn't accept her? No diamonds even for this moment? Tears blinking at her eyes, she opened the box…then saw it was a ruby ring.

Like the one she'd wanted for her sixteenth birthday and never gotten.

She stared at him, her hand starting to shake. "You remembered."

"I remember everything you've said." He looked as uncertain as she'd ever seen him, his hands clenched on her hips. "Shit, Kaylie. Don't leave me hanging."

She took the ring out of the box, dropped the box on the floor, and then handed the ring back to him.

His face darkened, and a shield closed over his expression. "I get it."

"No." She caught his arm as he started to stand up, her heart racing. "I want it."

He hesitated, confusion evident on his face. "Then what—?"

"If you still want me to have it after I tell you something, then I'll take it."

His eyes narrowed, and he waited.

Nervously, she twisted her fingers. "I faced the worst with you, watching you die, as you know. It made me realize how much I loved you, but it also really scared me."

He said nothing.

"I wasn't sure I was strong enough to deal with that, and I used my brother as an excuse to get away and get some space." She gestured around the apartment. "But being here isn't the same anymore. It feels closed in, and tight. I missed Alaska. I missed you." She met his gaze. "I already knew I loved you, but I realized that it was more than that. You're a part of my soul, and I need you."

A faint edge of tension eased off his face. "Okay."

"But then…" She licked her lips. "I remembered Valerie. How the final straw was when she became pregnant and was forced to think about what kind of a father she wanted for her son."

His face went hard. "And?"

"I made myself evaluate that decision, to make sure how I knew how I felt about it. What it would be like to have my child have a daddy who's a bush pilot. Could I live with it?" Kaylie managed a smile. "I decided I could. That's when I started packing. To move to Alaska, if you'll have me."

His jaw was tense. "If you had to debate about whether you could deal with me as a father, then you can't. It'll be a thousand times more intense when you have a baby. When you've got someone to protect from me." He stood. "I won't go down that road again."

She caught his arm, drew him back to face her. "I already know how I'll feel when I face that situation, Cort. I'm pregnant, and—"

"What?" His hands dug into her arms, a look of such intense pain and joy on his face, her eyes immediately teared. "You're *pregnant*?"

She nodded and gestured to all the boxes. "I was packing to move to Alaska. To you. I know it was awful with Valerie, and I'm still going to wear my jewelry and demand you're home for dinner as often as possible, and if this is too much for you to handle, I understand."

*"Kaylie."* He was kissing her before she could finish, and she smiled when she felt him slide the ring onto her finger.

And she knew she'd been wrong.

She hadn't died in Alaska.

She'd finally come alive.

# ELISABETH NAUGHTON

Antiquities dealer Peter Kauffman walked a fine line between clean and corrupt for years. And then he met the woman who changed his life—Egyptologist Katherine Meyer. Their love affair burned white-hot in Egypt, until the day Pete's lies and half-truths caught up with him. After that, their relationship imploded, Kat walked out, and before Pete could find her to make things right, he heard she'd died in a car bomb.

Six years later, the woman Pete thought he'd lost for good is suddenly back. The lies this time aren't just his, though. The only way he and Kat will find the truth and evade a killer out for revenge is to work together—as long as they don't find themselves burned by the heat each thought was stolen long ago . . .

# STOLEN HEAT

ISBN 13: 978-0-505-52794-3

# MELANIE JACKSON

## Author of *Night Visitor* and *The Selkie*

A ghostly hound stalks Noltland Castle. For years, such appearances have signaled doom for the clan Balfour, and there is little reason to believe this time will be any different. Wasn't their laird cut down while defending the Scottish king, leaving a boy to take a man's place?

Frances Balfour has done all she can, using guts and guile to keep her cousin safe in his new lairdship, but enemies encroach from all sides, and now the secluded isle of Orkney is beset from within. A stranger has arrived, and his green gaze promises to strip every secret bare. The newcomer is a swordsman, a seducer and a sometimes spy for the English king, but for all that, he seems a friend. And Colin Mortlock can see into the Night Side, that spectral world between life and death. He shall be the destruction of all Frances loves—or her salvation.

# *The Night Side*

ISBN 13: 978-0-505-52804-9

# COLLEEN THOMPSON

"[Thompson] more than holds her own in territory blazed by Tami Hoag and Tess Gerritsen."

—*Publishers Weekly*

### *In Deep Water*

Ruby Monroe knows she's way out of her depth the minute she lays eyes on Sam McCoy. She's been warned to steer clear of this neighbor, the sexy bad boy with a criminal past. But with her four-year-old daughter missing, her home incinerated and her own life threatened by a tattooed gunman, where else can she turn? Drowning in the flood of emotion unleashed by their mind-blowing encounters, Ruby is horrified to learn an unidentified body has been dredged up, the local sheriff is somehow involved, and Sam hasn't told her all he knows. Has she put her trust in the wrong man and jeopardized her very survival by uncovering the secrets...

# BENEATH BONE LAKE

ISBN 13: 978-0-8439-6243-7

# ☐ YES!

Sign me up for the Love Spell Book Club and send my FREE BOOKS! If I choose to stay in the club, I will pay only $8.50* each month, a savings of $6.48!

NAME: _____

ADDRESS: _____

TELEPHONE: _____

EMAIL: _____

☐ I want to pay by credit card.

☐ **VISA**        ☐ **MasterCard**        ☐ **DISCOVER**

ACCOUNT #: _____

EXPIRATION DATE: _____

SIGNATURE: _____

Mail this page along with $2.00 shipping and handling to:
**Love Spell Book Club**
**PO Box 6640**
**Wayne, PA 19087**
Or fax (must include credit card information) to:
**610-995-9274**
You can also sign up online at **www.dorchesterpub.com**.

*Plus $2.00 for shipping. Offer open to residents of the U.S. and Canada only. Canadian residents please call 1-800-481-9191 for pricing information. under 18, a parent or guardian must sign. Terms, prices and conditions subject to change. Subscription subject to acceptance. Dorchester Publishing reserves the right to reject any order or cancel any subscription.